THE MARKED PRINCE

MARK OF VALLIATH
BOOK TWO

M. H. WOODSCOURT

Edited by Sarah B. & E. L. McNicholas

Cover design by MiblArt

Published by True North Press

www.mhwoodscourt.com

Paperback ISBN: 978-1-959619-04-8

Hardback ISBN: 978-1-959619-05-5

For those battling to find your purpose.

Fight on.

CONTENTS

NAKANIA
Neminar
KryTeer
Tivalt
Vylam
Clanslands
Keep Lunorr
Amantier
Bahadronn
Kavacos
Shing
Lily River
Kyon Taro
Tindo River
Snowblinds
Tild
Frostfire Canton
Kilitheer
Keep Falcon
Snow Wastes
Drifting Sands

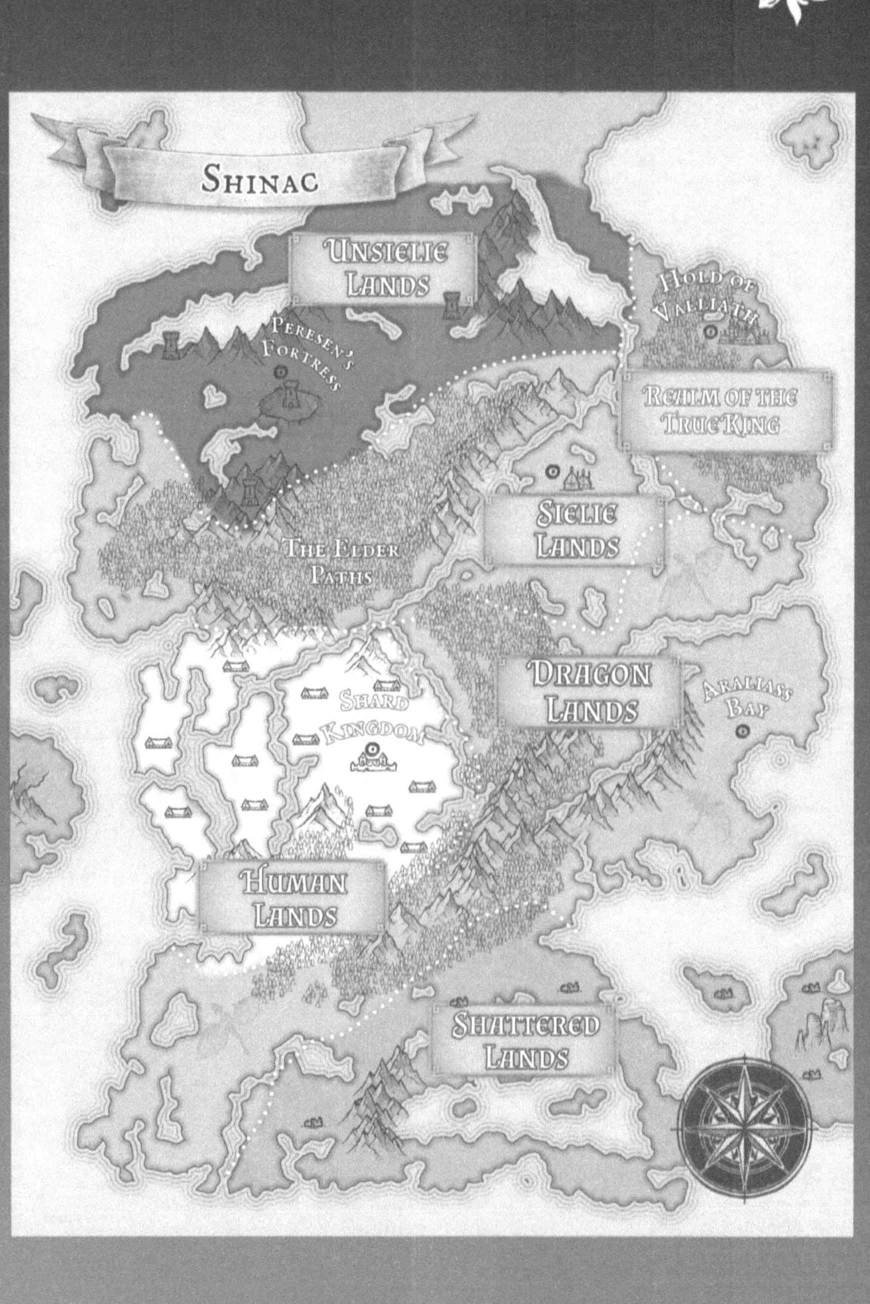
Shinac
Unsielie Lands
Peresen's Fortress
Hold of Valliath
Realm of the True King
Sielie Lands
The Elder Paths
Dragon Lands
Araliass Bay
Shard Kingdom
Human Lands
Shattered Lands

CONTENT WARNING

This book contains fantasy violence, brief gore, and death, as well as trauma caused by past manipulation and abuse. Proceed at your own discretion.

—M. H. W.

CHAPTER I
TOUGH DECISIONS

Light cradled the ancient city of Kyon Taro in Shing, nudging Prince Jetekesh of Amantier from a restless slumber.

The first whispers of dawn glittered on raindrops dotting the red roofs, while wisps of cloud crawled over the sky, mere tendrils remaining from last night's storm. Throwing a silk robe over his nightshirt, Jetekesh tiptoed onto the balcony. His bare toes flinched over the cool stones. He leaned against the balustrade and drew a long breath of clean air, letting it fill his lungs, banishing the chokehold of his nightmares.

A figure slipped up next to him: Sir Lafe, clutching his sword as though an enemy might appear on the second-story balcony of the Lotus Palace.

The garden below the balcony tinkled with fountains, serene in the stillness of the hour. Yet, something was wrong. Jetekesh's dreams had been more unsettled than usual.

Closing his eyes, he stretched his senses. Since he'd purged *Erisyrdrel* from the Lotus Palace one week ago, he'd been able to feel something distinct yet far away. It might be Navolleth, the stranger in Norva that Kajsa had warned him about. The young woman—thin and bedraggled—had traveled over the mountains, betraying her own people, to prevent war. Her bravery astounded Jetekesh. He'd seldom seen its kind before.

It's something Jinji would do.

That distinct presence hovered on the dawn-rimmed horizon, south, past the snowy mountain ridge where Kajsa had lived. The Snow Wastes. Jetekesh knew so little about them.

People live there, enduring frostbite and worse.

He'd read a life of hardship in Kajsa's eyes when she'd stood before the Lotus throne and pled for peace. Jetekesh wasn't certain that an armistice was possible—not against a foe who so carefully gathered forces to march against the fertile northern lands. Not if Navolleth was the same person who had wounded the dragon, Kethalas, at the Jade Arch. Not if he had been the one who unleashed the demon, *Erisyrdrel,* from Prince Sharo's magic.

Howls rose from beyond the imperial city walls. Jetekesh tensed.

The sun slipped from its slumber in the east, spilling molten gold over the rice fields that stretched wide across the ancient countryside.

More howls rose to pierce the retreating storm clouds. The *vashalan* had circled Kyon Taro every night since Jetekesh and his company had entered the city, but none had attacked even a stray lamb by all reports. Nor had they molested the Shingese army stationed outside Kyon Taro's walls, despite several sightings of the horrible creatures.

Why do they linger? What are they waiting for?

He scrubbed his face with a hand, then dragged his fingers down the back of his neck, trying to ease his tension. His damaged ear throbbed.

We can't stay here any longer.

The question of the company's next step had come up during

a state dinner the night before. Lord Emerin had led the verbal charge in favor of continuing to the Clanslands. He'd insisted that they prioritize the search for another Arch, and Dakarai had jumped in to agree. Jetekesh ached to follow that course at once, but the nearness of the *vashalan* and the tidings of war Kajsa had brought stayed his hand. He hung in an agony of indecision, unwilling to step wrong.

What should I do?

He longed to speak with Lord Father, or Jinji, or even King Aredel of KryTeer. They would know better than him.

Prince Liu was adamant that everyone should remain and fortify Shing against the coming conflict from the Snow Wastes. He desired the aid of the dragon, Kethalas, most of all. But if Navolleth was the intruder from Shinac, as Jetekesh suspected, then no mortal army could long stand against him. And if history held up under scrutiny, Kajsa's Norvian people were the fiercest warriors Nakania had ever known, kept sharp by a hard life.

We need aid from Shinac. We need more dragons.

Exhaling, Jetekesh leaned an elbow on the balcony and eyed his protector. "What say you, Sir Lafe? You didn't express your feelings last night at table."

Lines appeared around the knight's deep-set eyes. "You truly wish for my opinion?"

"One more voice might open the right path."

Lafe sucked in a breath, eyes skimming the city. The first noises of carts clattered near the palace walls. Somewhere, a cock crowed. "We originally set out to find Shinac, Your Highness."

"Yes, but that was before we defeated the water demon and heard of war brewing in the Snow Wastes."

"Yes, Your Highness." Lafe shrugged. "But from what the lass has said of this Navolleth, he won't strike fast. His work is meticulous; he's grooming each Norvian canton one by one. And the warm season is short over those mountains. He'll bide his time rather than condemn his army to death of cold. I think we have a year or longer before he moves."

Jetekesh weighed the knight's words. "That *is* meticulous." He shifted to lean both arms on the balustrade. "What if the cantons fall into accord more quickly than that?"

Lafe shook his head. "Even if all came to heel before the lass left her village—which is unlikely, considering human nature—even then, they'd still not march this year. They'll need to forge armor, weapons, and conveyance to move equipment. If the Norvians haven't waged war since they fled over the southern passes, they'll not have what they need. Skirmishes aren't enough to keep war preparations in order. Any seasoned general would recognize this."

Jetekesh rubbed a knuckle against his mouth. "You're right, and from what Kajsa has described, Navolleth is no fool. He uses charisma, not force, to achieve his ends." He let his shoulders slump as relief bled through him like a draught of wine. "Then we have time."

"Lord Emerin thinks so, too," Lafe said.

"Does he?"

The knight nodded. "We spoke after the meal."

"Well, if two such seasoned warriors agree..." Jetekesh straightened. "Let's head for the Clanslands as soon as possible. We may have time, but we should make every moment count."

"Yes, Your Highness. By your leave, I'll speak with Lord Emerin right now."

"Please do." A breeze raked through Jetekesh's tresses, and he tugged his robe tighter. "I'd like to have everything well in hand long before Navolleth crosses those mountains—including an army of dragons at my back." He allowed himself a full smile.

Sir Lafe answered with a wolfish grin, bowed, then slipped inside to find the master of the Keep of the Falls.

We'll likely leave tomorrow. Jetekesh turned back to the view of

Kyon Taro. He stared out at the southern climes glowing a fiery orange as the sun slipped higher in the pinkish heavens. War brewed over there. Yet his destination lay northward.

The Clanslands. Dakarai and Anenyasha's home. Jetekesh knew little of that strange place; only legends, probably inaccurate from what he'd observed of the cheerful clansman and his quiet but loyal companion.

Had Jinji ever gone there in his travels before he died? Had he shared his stories with the clans of the northeast? Jetekesh might never know; not unless the True King returned and brought Shinac back into the same sphere as Nakania during Jetekesh's lifetime.

"Don't focus on that, Kesh. One task at a time. First, the Clanslands; then war—if we can't prevent it." He curled his hands into fists and dragged in a long breath.

Finding the Arch would mean finding a way into Shinac. A thrill shivered up his arms, and he turned from the ancient city to step inside. He must dress and find his way to Lord Emerin. If the keep lord agreed to leave tomorrow, a lot must be accomplished beforehand, including the decision of who remained and who left Kyon Taro with the company.

Liu won't be happy about any of this.

But then, the churlish Shingese prince seldom seemed happy about much.

At breakfast, Jetekesh studied the faces of each companion who had traveled to Shing with him: Lord Emerin, Sir Lafe, Kethalas, Dakarai, Anenyasha, Song, Yin, Prince Liu, and Harn.

Also seated at the low table, kneeling upon plush cushions, were several Shingese ministers, as well as Liu's father—Prince Jung Tep—and Kajsa of Norva. The young woman sat with her shoulders hunched, platinum hair hanging like a curtain to hide her face from the large group of imposing figures.

Dakarai had positioned himself beside her and spoke to her from time to time, which only made her lean into herself more. But the clansman was undaunted as he passed steaming Shingese dishes her way. Despite her shyness, she took each dish and ate with relish.

"We're leaving for the Clanslands tomorrow," Lord Emerin announced into the silence of the dining crowd.

Jetekesh lifted his eyes from Kajsa and Dakarai to pin them on the keep lord. *You really don't beat around the bush, do you?* He spoke above the start of Liu's protest: "We'll understand if anyone wishes to remain here or even return to Amantier. Certainly, circumstances have changed since we set out—but our goal remains steadfast."

Liu turned his black eyes on Jetekesh, venom glittering in their depths. "You would abandon Shing *now,* while we're still swabbing up the mess you caused?"

"No, Your Highness," Jetekesh answered, pressing down the memories of Liu's cruel words in the rolling hills of Amantier. *Think on his accusations later.* "We're leaving to gather reinforcements. We already knew we had an enemy. Only two things have changed since we set out for Dakarai's country. First, *Erisyrdrel* is no longer a threat. Second, we have an idea of *where* the threat from Shinac is, and that he is mustering an army. We still have no idea *why* he's attacking Nakania, nor how to defeat him with our scant resources."

"Scant?" Liu slammed a fist against the table, rattling the dishes. "The forces of Shing are mighty."

Emerin spoke up. "Then you can't expect that any aid from our quarter would make much difference as we now stand, Prince Liu. Better for us to seek Shinac and bring back reinforcements impressive enough to stall our enemy's advancement."

Liu scowled. "You can make no guarantee of such success."

"No," Kethalas spoke up. "But there is a strong chance that Prince Sharo would answer."

That name silenced the room. Every eye settled on the Shinacian dragon in human form seated at the table, a spoon perched in his hand. His silver eyes gleamed in the ample light streaming in through the wide, arching windows, and his silvery-blue hair stood out in contrast with the muted earth tones of everyone else.

Well, all but the chalk dye that Dakarai and Anenyasha had used to color several of their black braids.

"Will Prince Sharo answer?" asked Prince Jung Tep. His slicked-back hair shone in the morning light. His narrow eyes settled, not on Kethalas, but on Jetekesh.

Shifting his legs on the cushion, Jetekesh allowed himself a moment to consider his reply while the aroma of chicken and fish teased his senses. "If he can, he certainly will. But Shinac has its own perils, and he fights for the glory of the True King of Shinac. His calling may lie elsewhere. We can only ask."

Emerin waved a hand across the air, snaring the room's focus. "As His Highness says, we can only do what's possible—and what's smart. Kethalas is still recovering from his wounds, and we can't expect him to fight alongside our armies until he's better. Even if Sharo himself can't join us against Navolleth, why would we waste the chance to ask his kin to join our cause?"

"They would come," Kethalas said. "If we can find the Arch, they will answer my cry."

Jetekesh studied the man-dragon's profile, trying to weigh the truth in his words. Kethalas had admitted that he was exiled from his clan after a witch had controlled him and forced him to attack his liege lord, the great dragon elder, Taregan. Would the dragons really answer his plight?

If not, they're fools. Navolleth is a real and potent threat. He's brought magic back to Nakania.

Exiled Kethalas may be, perhaps dishonored in the eyes of his kin, yet the dragon couldn't defeat what had destroyed the Jade Arch. He'd been badly wounded trying. Surely they wouldn't let him fight alone.

Liu sulked while Emerin discussed the logistics of travel with Dakarai, Jung Tep, and Song. Throughout the discussion, Jetekesh's eyes weaved among the faces until his gaze struck Kajsa. She watched him through threads of pale hair, her ice-blue eyes keen despite her hunched shoulders.

She's shy but not stupid. Jetekesh offered her a smile. She returned it with a feeble lift of her lips, then turned back to her food.

What will she do? She can't return to Norva after betraying her own people. He sipped a spoonful of soup. *Poor thing must be scared spitless. If only Rille were here to keep her company.* But then, Rille would likely refuse to remain in Shing. She'd demand to go along to the Clanslands.

Instead, the young seer was in KryTeer, answering the threat she'd foreseen surrounding King Aredel.

I hope they're well and safe. Erisyrdrel was here in Shing, so what troubles met them there?

Jetekesh could do nothing for them, whatever they faced. He could only do his part.

He stared out the northward windows. *Off to the Clanslands, and whatever dangers await me there.*

CHAPTER 2
THE TASK

King Aredel of KryTeer stood within a wooded swamp, frogs singing in his ears. A black lake stretched out before him, and a dense fog hung over the water, hiding anything beyond the depths. Twilight painted the world a dusky blue. Yellow lights danced before him like fireflies, but he suspected they weren't that.

He turned to scan the shoreline and found Rille and Anadin seated on the bank, both still enchanted by the *Unsielie* song that had brought them to Shinac. They were smiling at the world around them like small children admiring the first snow of winter in Amantier. Rille's long, wavy, platinum hair twined down her shoulders, while Anadin's long, sleek, black tresses netted over his head in a tangle. He didn't notice.

Something moved in Aredel's periphery, and he turned back to the lake. One of the dark fae creatures floated across the water; tall, ethereal, gloriously dark with wings like lace. It halted a few feet before him. The yellow lights shied away and ducked into the reeds along the shoreline. Frog song faded away. The *Unsielie* considered Aredel for a moment.

"Welcome, Blood King," said the fae in rich, singsong tones.

Aredel clutched his sword hilt. "Where is Artassa?"

"In the Hold of Tarradarryn." The fae gestured, and the fog parted to reveal a towering fortress made of black stone on the far side of the lake. "Thy wife shall remain there until thou hast accomplished the task set before thee."

"What task?"

The *Unsielie*'s wings fluttered. "Thou shalt slay Prince Sharo of the Blood of the Wood."

Aredel arched his brow. "You wish me to assassinate your enemy? *This* is why you've brought me here?" He glanced at his brother and Lady Rille. "What of them? Why were they taken?"

"To aid thee. The seer shall guide thy course, and thy brother shall be a second incentive." The *Unsielie* stretched out a hand and curled a finger inward, as though beckoning.

Anadin climbed to his feet, still smiling an absent smile. He eyed the yellow lights winking in the twilight sky far away from the *Unsielie*.

"Until thou dost return to Nakania, his mind will belong to *us*. We shall free his conscious thoughts, but if thou shouldst betray thy quest, we shall shatter his will forever."

Aredel narrowed his eyes and thumbed his hilt. "But why go to such trouble to end Sharo? Aren't there wizards or fae powerful enough to end his life? I cannot be more able than them, surely."

"Thou hast Prince Sharo's trust. Few others could come close enough to slay him."

"Ah." Aredel nodded. "And if I fail?"

"Then none who have come with thee into Shinac shall live, save thy brother alone. And he shall be made mad."

Aredel glanced at Rille, then turned back to the *Unsielie*, shoving down a coiling serpent of anger. He would do nothing to risk his brother's mind. "Can you give me a general location?"

“Prince Sharo musters an army west and north of this land to march upon the Shard Kingdom.”

He plans to defeat his own father, does he?

“Very well.” Aredel whirled and strode to Anadin’s side. “Wake their minds.”

A song floated across the black lake, soft, sad. Anadin blinked and shook his head, and Rille rubbed her eyes.

“*Shaqin?*” whispered Anadin. “What happened?”

“We’ve entered Shinac.” Aredel rested a hand on Anadin’s shoulder. “We must accomplish a task before we will be allowed to return home.” His mind tripped over a memory, and he angled to eye the *Unsielie*. “According to Jinji Wanderlust, once a human crosses into your magical realm, he cannot return to Nakania—unless he had been invited here by the proper authority. Have you trapped us in Shinac forever?”

The fae’s wings fluttered. “Thou hast been invited by our lord and master.”

Aredel considered the unreadable alien face. “I don’t suppose you’ll tell me who that is?”

The *Unsielie* didn’t stir. “Such is not required to complete thy task.”

“True.”

“What task?” asked Anadin.

Rille slipped up beside the KryTeeran prince. “This creature is made of darkness, Blood King. We shouldn’t do what it asks.”

Aredel allowed himself a dry smile. “Yet hostages compel me to, nonetheless.”

Rille’s eyes roved the swamp. “Queen Artassa. And who else?”

“Both of you.” Aredel studied the woods. “We should start off. Talk can be had along our journey.”

“Succeed, Blood King,” said the *Unsielie*. “Do not test our resolve.”

"I understand." Aredel started west. "Be careful. The ground is unstable."

Anadin and Rille caught up with him, and they traveled into the dense woods, leaving behind the bank, the dark fae, and the dancing yellow lights.

Progress was halting as Aredel picked out a path along the spongy earth. He said nothing, though Rille and Anadin aimed questions at him. What task lay before them? How could they rescue Artassa and keep from accomplishing whatever dark deed? Was he listening? Why wouldn't he speak?

Hours stretched on, and the dusky light never changed. It was impossible to determine the time of day.

Anadin cried out. Aredel whirled to find his brother knee-deep in a mud hole.

The prince chuckled. "My toes feel funny."

Aredel stifled a smile and offered his hand to his brother, who took it in slimy fingers. Aredel hauled Anadin from the shallow pit as the mud protested with a series of sucking noises. As Anadin stumbled into his arms, the Blood King grimaced. "Be careful, *shaqel.* Follow my trail exactly, or you might be swallowed up."

Anadin bobbed a nod. "I thought I *was* being exact, but I'll be more vigilant." His dark eyes skimmed the ground. "I smell terrible now. And I'm starving."

"Best we cover more ground before we stop," said Aredel. "I'd like to escape this swamp as soon as possible."

Rille slipped a hand into a pocket in her skirts. "Here, Anadin." She drew out a few nuts. "These should tide you over for a little while."

Anadin accepted them with a smile. "Thank you, Sahala. Let's share."

They carried on walking. The contented smacking of Anadin and the quieter chewing of Rille filled the air, mingling with the frog song and whirring of insects. Yellow lights floated near to dance at Aredel's ankles. So close, he glimpsed the details of the fingernail-sized winged creatures. Smaller than Lady Ashea, Prince Sharo's companion fairy. Likely a different type of fairy altogether.

Rille gasped. "Fairies?"

A tiny voice replied. "Pixies, fair lady. Not fairies."

"Oh." When a yellow light settled on her shoulder, Rille beamed.

Aredel frowned. "Talk with them if you must, but maintain your pace, Lady Rille."

She quickened her steps. "Are you swamp pixies?"

The light offered up an airy laugh. "We are Dusk Pixies."

"What a pretty name."

Aredel glanced back to be sure the girl hadn't slowed and found Rille looking more child-like than she ever had before. Anadin trod beside her, a halo of the yellow lights crowning his head. His dark eyes reflected their glow.

With a sigh, the Blood King halted and turned to face his companions. "Anadin, did I not say to follow in my steps exactly?"

The prince grinned. "Sorry. I forgot." He turned toward the halo, wonder in his eyes.

Aredel settled his attention on the floating lights. "Do you reveal yourselves to us for a reason, Dusk Pixies?"

"You are Nakanians," the voice said. "We have never seen Nakanians before."

"This one doesn't smell Nakanian," piped up another tiny voice. "She smells of scrying."

"I am Nakanian," said Rille. "I'm from Amantier. But I've been blessed with Sight since my birth. My mother had the gift as well."

A chorus of voices sang out.

"Does magic stir in Nakania?"

"Does it, truly?"

"How wondrous."

"It cannot be so. Once Cavalin fell, once the humans turned greedy, the blessing was taken."

"Taken."

"Taken."

All the voices joined together. "Taken."

"Why?" asked Anadin, folding his arms. "Not everyone was greedy, were they?"

"Some were good," sang the chorus.

"Many were bad."

A tiny light landed on Anadin's nose, making him cross his eyes.

"Your distant ancestor was greediest of all."

"Greediest of all.

"Of all."

"Greedy."

"Cruel."

"Evil."

Anadin shrugged. "Tallat's gone. Dead. Long dead. And magic is coming back."

The voices rose in a sound too chaotic to understand.

The lights converged and twined together above their heads. "We must speak with the Elders. We must tell them. Magic is back in Nakania. Magic is back."

They rose in a column and vanished above the trees.

Anadin canted his head. "Elders?"

"The firstborn of each fae race in Shinac if I understand rightly," said Aredel. "Shall we continue?" He turned and picked his way around a puddle of brackish water.

"Your Majesty," said Rille, raising her voice. "Tell us why we're here. We've a right to know."

Aredel sighed. "Keep walking."

The girl let out an exasperated cry. "*Aredel.*"

He halted. Turned. Glared at her. "Yes, little girl?"

Rille stomped closer, hands on her hips. "Do *not* condescend to me—and do *not* try to spare me. I can guess already that no dark fae creature would summon us to any good purpose. I'm prepared to hear the worst. I already recognize that you'll do anything to protect your brother and your wife. Tell me."

He exhaled through his nose and stared past the young seer, past Anadin, to study the strange, chain-like plants draping from the oaks and cypress trees of the swamp. "I must kill Prince Sharo."

Rille drew a sharp breath. "But—but you can't."

Aredel lowered his gaze to meet the girl's amber eyes. "Yet I must."

She shook her head. "There must be some way to rescue Queen Artassa and return to Nakania without fulfilling their demands."

Aredel tipped his head to one side and arched his eyebrows. "I'm open to any feasible ideas. Until then, we head northwest toward Prince Sharo's war camp."

Rille opened her mouth, but Aredel raised a hand.

"Not now, Lady Rille. No arguments. No debates. We must leave this swamp before it swallows one or more of us." His gaze darted to Anadin. "The dangers here are plenty without the heat of dispute. Follow my steps. Keep silent. Let us hurry to drier ground. At that point, we might better discuss our options."

She nodded. "You're right. Best keep walking."

"I appreciate your good sense, Lady Rille." He turned and moved on. The sounds of his companions' footfalls pounded in his ears like drums.

THE SWAMP DIDN'T END. It kept going on, on, endlessly on. At last, even Aredel's strength flagged, and he halted at the first patch of dry earth he could find wide enough for the three to sleep upon.

"I rather like this place," said Anadin, eyeing the stooping trees filled with frog song. "It's eerie yet cozy."

Rille scratched at her hand. "You only say that because the insects like my blood better."

Anadin chuckled, but his smile faded fast. "What will Kyella do when we don't return to Bahadronn?"

Rille sighed. "And what happened to Sir Yeshton, I wonder. Is he being held with Queen Artassa?"

Aredel scanned the ground for any kindling he might use. "Your knight remains in Amantier, along with Shevek and Ledonn. They'll leave Mahadri and inform the others of our fate. I've ordered them to find Prince Jetekesh and locate another Arch. Perhaps together they'll find a way in and a means for us to leave."

Rille tucked her soiled skirts around her ankles. "That's good news, at least."

Anadin nodded. "I'm glad Kyella won't be abandoned. She's a strong woman, but she hates to be alone."

Aredel stood, gathered the few sticks and wood chips he could find, and dumped them into the center of the dry patch. "Shevek and Ledonn won't let any harm befall your beloved."

"Neither will Sir Yeshton," added Rille. She glanced around. "Is anything edible in this swamp?"

Aredel dug flint and steel from a small pouch on his hip. "I will go hunting if you and Anadin will finish building a fire."

They agreed, and Aredel left them to stalk the animals of this unsavory land. He'd had a few dealings with terrains of this kind, most recently in the Clanslands. Gripping the sword on his belt, he ached to slay something. Anything to unleash his pent-up fury.

He was a man of great control—but current circumstances were testing that resolve. He set his teeth and plunged into the darkness, ears stretching for any hint of prey.

Anything at all.

CHAPTER 3
A NEW DESTINATION

Once Sir Yeshton, Ledonn, and Shevek left the Mahadri riverhead where the Arch into Shinac hid, they broke base camp and rode hard for Bahadronn. Travel took days—days Yeshton hated to waste.

Upon reaching the scarred Royal Capital, he threw himself to his knees before Kyella at the inn where Aredel had set up headquarters after the palace had been destroyed. The knight's heart twisted in his throat.

"Forgive me, Kyella," he whispered. "I've failed my mistress and your beloved."

Kyella collapsed before him and caught his shoulders. "They're dead?"

"No." He took a breath. "They were pulled into Shinac by dark forces."

Kyella's fingers tightened against the sand-crusted fabric of his shirt. "But not you..."

He shook his head, unwilling to meet her eyes. "We were attacked. Several dark fae *things* fought against us while a song spell lured Rille, Prince Anadin, and King Aredel toward the hidden Arch. Queen Artassa was taken first. I believe that's why King Aredel allowed himself to be entranced. Before he vanished, the Blood King ordered me to find Prince Jetekesh. I must leave at once. He's our best hope of bringing them all home."

Her fingers dropped from his shoulders. "Then go, Yesh. Bring Anadin and Rille home. Bring them all back."

He climbed to his feet and brushed back his length of light brown hair. Weariness pressed against his spine and limbs, but he squared his shoulders and met Kyella's pale eyes. "I'll do all I can." He wouldn't stop, not for anything—not until he'd recovered Rille. He wouldn't fail his charge again.

Kyella offered him a gentle smile. "I know, Yesh. You always do. Be safe."

He inclined his head, pivoted on his boots, and strode from the inn to where Ledonn waited. Shevek had gone ahead to the harbor to charter a ship across the channel to Amantier. No matter how hard they pushed, they'd not reach Kavacos for a fortnight.

Upon reaching the outskirts of Kavacos in Rose Province, Yeshton allowed himself to ease his hard pace long enough to stop at the riverbank and clean up. Shevek and Ledonn agreed, both eager to appear presentable before King Jetekesh the Fourth of Amantier.

As he scrubbed the weeks-long travel dust from his body, Yeshton reflected on his failure with deepening frustration. He'd sworn to protect Rille with his life; instead, she'd been forced to enter Shinac without him. Instead, she was with the Blood King, Queen Artassa, and Anadin, none of whom Yeshton was confident would care for Rille properly. Yes, Anadin would try, but the KryTeeran prince was a child himself in many ways.

"Will Prince Jetekesh have returned from the Clanslands by

now?" asked Shevek from the shore. He stood in fresh clothes, tackling the tangles in his long black hair.

"I doubt it," Yeshton replied. "That's a long journey, and there's no certainty of finding an Arch there. He's likely still seeking it."

Ledonn caught up a spare blanket from the shore. He slipped from the rushing water to dry himself. "We found one."

"The Clanslands are harder to navigate," Yeshton said.

"True." Shevek tied a jeweled ornament into his hair, then flipped the tresses over his shoulder. "We once traversed those lands with our Blood King. He had been weighing whether to conquer the jungles or not. Ultimately, he chose to wait. Anything else would have been logistical madness. Jungle wars require different strategies—especially since the clans aren't united. There's no one king to surrender."

Yeshton nodded, then plunged under the water to wash away the last specks of sand and dirt. Breaking free of the frigid water, he sucked in a breath or two, then waded toward shore. Shevek passed him another blanket. He wrapped himself in it and splashed from the current onto dry ground.

"Jungle or not," Yeshton said, "Prince Jetekesh travels with clansfolk. If there's anything to find, they'll find it." He dried himself thoroughly.

"Yet you think he's not returned?" Ledonn finished tugging on his curl-tipped shoes, then straightened up, his dark eyes pinned on Yeshton.

The Amantieran knight slipped into his last set of clean clothes. "If Prince Jetekesh finds the Arch, now or a week from now, he'll enter Shinac rather than return to Amantier." He pulled on his boots, straightened his tunic, and dug out a leather cord to tie back his waves of wet hair.

"Ah." Shevek hoisted the saddle onto his borrowed horse.

"That makes a great deal of sense. Smart, too. The boy's come far from where he was last year."

Ledonn snorted. "The boy learned hard lessons; he had no choice."

That was definitely true; Jetekesh had grown a lot since his first adventure far from home, thanks in large to the storyteller Jinji Wanderlust. A pang throbbed through Yeshton's chest. He missed Jinji, despite all the troubles the Shingese man had caused Rille and the rest of the company. He missed Sir Palan and the quiet, unobtrusive Tifen as well. All sacrifices who should've lived. All the clearest reasons for Prince Jetekesh's change.

Yeshton understood well how loss could alter a person. He'd faced such heartbreak himself: first his own family; then comrades-in-arms; and then Duke Lunorr, Rille's father; and Sir Palan.

With a heavy sigh, he saddled his horse. Then he mounted up and caught up his reins. The two KryTeeran Blood Knights mirrored his actions, and without another word, the three rode on to Kavacos, the Royal City of Amantier.

King Jetekesh met them at the front doors of the palace, his expression harried, blue eyes bright with concern. "Where's Rille?" His long mane of brown curls twined down his shoulders, free of its binding, and his fine clothes were rumpled like he hadn't changed since the previous day.

"Your Majesty." Yeshton dropped to one knee. "She was taken into Shinac by dark creatures."

The king's face paled a shade. "Come inside." He glanced at the Blood Knights of KryTeer. "Come, please. Be welcome."

As they followed King Jetekesh to his royal study, Yeshton

explained the fae attack and subsequent disappearances at Mahadri in KryTeer.

Upon entering the study, Yeshton skimmed the shelves bursting with leather tomes, the broad window letting in the light of midmorning, the velvet curtains framing glass panes, and the polished desk behind which the king sank into a wingback chair. The scent of white roses wafted from a vase on the wooden surface.

"Shing declared war," King Jetekesh said. "Fortunately, my son detoured and put a stop to Emperor Majinglee's machinations." He plucked up a loose scroll. "Word reached me early this morning of all that's transpired in the east." He dropped the scroll, then locked his fingers together and perched them on the desk. "Majinglee is dead. At his request, the legendary Lady Song killed him to free him from *Erisyrdrel*'s possession. Luckily, witnesses observed the exchange, and the armies marching on Amantier were called back."

He massaged the bridge of his nose. "Now, Shing prepares for a conflict coming over the southern mountains in the Snow Wastes. Evidently, a man named Navolleth—who Jetekesh suspects hailed from Shinac—is raising an army among people called Norvians. Kesh believes *they* are descended from Prince Norvik, Cavalin's second son. Are you familiar with that history?"

Yeshton shook his head. "No, Your Majesty."

"Ah." The king lowered his hand. "Once Cavalin died, his two sons disagreed on which should become the next ruler of Amantier. When Prince Norvik didn't receive the crown, he took his closest kin and faithful faction south into the mountains and vanished. No more of them appear in any scholarly texts."

King Jetekesh took up the scroll to roll it tight. "Interestingly, Kesh's report mentions that a young Norvian woman braved the high passes to bring word of Navolleth's schemes. My son is still determined to head for the Clanslands as soon as he can, but he requests Amantier's support to set Shing's concerns to rest. Our silence could inflame the tension my son's managed to avert."

Yeshton lifted his eyes from his king to study the green world beyond the study window. Gardeners strode along the lawn, rakes and buckets in hand, ignorant of the politics within the walls they kept up.

"What would you have me do, Your Majesty?" Yeshton asked.

"Travel to Kyon Taro. Take a contingent of my soldiers with you." The king's expression gentled. "I realize I'm asking you to delay your duty to Rille—but I need to make certain Shing knows we're allied with them against this new foe—and I want your read on the situation there. Once you've done what you can to alleviate Shing's concerns, you can proceed to the Clanslands if you still feel it's the smartest course."

Yeshton inclined his head despite how rigid his spine had gone, despite the lump lodged in his throat. "Yes, Your Majesty. As you command."

The king considered the Blood Knights flanking Yeshton. "What will you do?"

The Blood Knights exchanged looks, then Shevek shrugged. "By Sir Yeshton's leave, we'll go by way of Shing alongside him, then head for the Clanslands to find your son. Better than traveling over Bard Pass with all that snow."

Ledonn shifted his weight. "Yes, I think we must. The Blood King would be wroth with us if we didn't glean all possible information about this threat from the Snow Wastes. If the girl who traveled over the southern mountains is still there, we have questions for her."

"Very well." King Jetekesh stood. "Sir Yeshton, provision your advance contingent with anything needful. And bring extra coin. Here's my seal and orders to bring you safely past the border of our country."

"Thank you, sire." Yeshton accepted the Crowned Rose seal,

then bowed. Usually, he would be glad to have a company of Amantieran knights at his back, but this time all he could think about was finding a way to get back to Rille. The contingent would slow him down considerably, but it couldn't be helped.

Dark fae, his charge captured, and now impending war against an unseen threat.

He turned and strode for the study door, mind roiling like waterfalls cascading into a dark pool.

Are you so confident that the two incidents aren't related, Yesh? Didn't King Jetekesh state that this enemy from over the mountains may have come from Shinac? Isn't it likely all these events are intertwined?

No comfort came with that thought. Yet he *could* state he was helping Rille, even slowed down as he was. She'd want him to ride for Kyon Taro to support his king if he could consult her. Steeling himself, he led the Blood Knights toward the royal treasury.

Soon, they'd be off for Shing. Off on a new adventure, fighting with former enemies. That seemed to be a recurring theme in Yeshton's life, come to think of it.

He smiled wryly, his pace never faltering. He was a knight now, as he'd always wanted to be. He must obey his liege's will—to save Nakania yet again.

CHAPTER 4
TO THE CLANSLANDS

"Your Highness?"

Jetekesh whirled, heart beating loud enough that he swore it echoed off the walls around him. He stood in a palace corridor with Lafe at his side. They were on their way to the courtyard where Lord Emerin and the rest of the company had gathered to leave.

He hadn't heard Kajsa come up behind him, and judging by his protector's half-drawn sword, neither had Lafe. She stood with one hand clutched to her fur-lined cloak while the other carried a satchel and bedroll, all bearing unfamiliar embroidered designs.

"What is it?" Jetekesh asked, aware that silence had hung suspended several seconds too long.

Kajsa drew a breath. "Please let me come with you, Your Highness."

He blinked. "Whatever for?"

She dropped her gaze, fingers fidgeting with the hem of her cloak. "The wisewoman who sent me... She wished me to remain with—with you." She lifted her head, fear bright in her pale blue irises. "May I?"

Jetekesh shifted his weight to buy himself a moment to consider. He fluted out a low breath. "My lady, I don't think coming with me is wise. We're traveling into a wild and dangerous region, largely unknown to all but our guides. You've suffered quite enough to bring your news. Better to stay here and rest in the safety of Kyon Taro."

She shook her head. "I...I am determined to go with you."

He searched her face and read the fear, the uncertainty, and the determination poking through her timidity. "Why?"

"Ingrid told me to stay with you. You are the Marked Prince. Where you go, I must."

He shook his head. "I'm sorry. I don't wish to disrespect your wisewoman, nor you. But the Clanslands are deadly, and we may never return. My conscience won't let me grant you the path to death."

Her face fell, and she bowed her head. "I understand."

"I'm sorry." He offered her a farewell bow and turned to continue down the corridor. Sir Lafe kept pace with him.

"Do you think I was wrong to deny her?" Jetekesh whispered when they'd turned down a brightly lit corridor wafting with the scent of blossoms. Windows adorned the west walls, wide and open, revealing the lush green outside.

"No, Your Highness," Lafe said. "She's a frail lass, unlikely to last long on such a venture."

Jetekesh's brows knitting together. "To her credit, she lived in the Snow Wastes and survived the pass, even with *vashalan* on her trail."

"Which is more than enough for anyone to accomplish," Lafe said.

"True." They neared the doors leading out into the western courtyard, where Harn, a new wagon, and all their horses were gathered. A breeze stirred, carrying the perfume of cherry blossoms. Song, Yin, and Liu stood near Jung Tep and several other officials, including the deceased emperor's grandson, Hyeun, soon to be named the new emperor of Shing. Commander Hon and several guards stood sentinel around the officials.

As Jetekesh approached the group seeing them off, he glimpsed Lord Emerin already atop his horse and ready to go. Dragging his eyes back to the Shingese officials, Jetekesh halted, clicked his heels together, and bowed at the waist.

"Thank you for your hospitality, especially in these strange times, Prince Hyeun."

"Thank you, Your Highness," Hyeun said, "for destroying an evil that would have tainted Shing forevermore."

Jetekesh stifled his wince before he rose to meet the incumbent emperor's black eyes. "I'm truly sorry about the venerable emperor's end."

Hyeun shook his head. "He was an old man, ready to die. And he commanded the Songbird to end his life with honor. There is no better finish."

Jetekesh swallowed a lump. *It was certainly a better end than my mother's.* He inclined his head. "As you say." His eyes flicked to Song, Yin, and Liu. "We'll miss you on our journey."

Song smiled. "May the good earth protect your paths, and all good spirits attend you. I would come if I could, but Shing needs her children here to prepare for war."

"I understand." Jetekesh met Yin's gaze. "I'll miss your sharp eyes most of all."

Yin grinned at him. "Try to stay alive, Your Highness."

Jetekesh chuckled, but his mirth faded as he eyed Liu. "Farewell, Prince of Shing."

Liu inclined his head in a rigid motion. "Safe paths to you, Prince Jetekesh."

The Shingese noble had never apologized to Jetekesh for his

cruel words, and Jetekesh suspected he never would. Perhaps that was justice. How many terrible things had Jetekesh said and done over the years, thinking himself superior, safe from consequences, inconvenienced by friendship?

Swinging into his saddle, Jetekesh stroked Hickory's neck and murmured gentle words to the buckskin stallion. Then he smiled at Emerin among the company. "Ready when you are, my lord."

Emerin clicked his tongue and flicked his reins. The company trotted out of the imperial courtyard, Harn driving the new wagon. Lord Emerin led out, and Jetekesh and Lafe rode right behind him. Flanking the wagon, Dakarai and Anenyasha rode, and Kethalas presumably sat under the covered wagon—built with an arced wooden roof, peculiar but practical—while his horse followed, tethered to the wagon rail.

There had been some debate about bringing Kethalas, but not much. The man-dragon must come along or entering Shinac would be foolhardy at best. Besides, he stood a better chance of healing on magic soil than in Nakania's barren realms.

Traveling due north through Kyon Taro's wide tidy streets, Jetekesh barely heard the call of hawkers, the clatter of carts, the laughter of passersby dressed in strange tunics and calf-length pants or colorful robes tied with large bows at their waists. His thoughts were pinned on far-off places he'd never seen. The company soon left the city by way of arching red gates. Men in plate armor saluted them as they started along the highway between the sprawling rice fields surrounding the city walls.

They journeyed in companionable silence for the better part of the day, pausing at the outskirts of a thriving trade village on the shores of Shing's great Purple River. There, Emerin spoke with the bridge guards and presented a paper granting the company passage wherever it wished to go. Moments later, the company crossed the sturdy bridge that arched over the rushing water.

A bamboo forest rose around them, where the strange song of

birds brought Jetekesh's attention to the thin trees. This had been Jinji's homeland, the roots of his wondrous soul. So close to Amantier, yet so foreign, like Jinji himself.

Dakarai took up a song in his peculiar, clicking tongue, and like before, Jetekesh glimpsed the flicker of fairies harmonizing among the bamboos. This time, Jetekesh suspected they were real.

Shinac isn't as separate or as distant as it seems.

Before Cavalin the Third fell against *Erisyrdrel* and Tallat, Shinac had stood in what was now called the Drifting Sands. If that fairy country returned, would it still fit within that desert, or had it expanded well past its previous boundaries?

As the land swelled into gentle slopes, the road turned rutty. Hickory quickened his trot. The wagon rattled along the deep grooves. A gasp sounded inside, and Jetekesh twisted to eye the conveyance.

"All right, Kethalas?" he called.

"It's just a little bumpy," the man-dragon called. "I'm well enough."

They pressed on until the sun sank behind the thin trees, casting finger-like shadows across the road. At Jetekesh's command, Lord Emerin called a halt and ordered the camp to be set up on the highway. It was a sparsely traveled route, and the Shingese officials had asked them to spare the sacred forest as much as possible.

Jetekesh swung from Hickory's saddle. He patted the stallion before he traipsed to the back of the wagon to help carry the canvas tent. He pulled aside the flaps, and his gaze collided with Kajsa's. She sat beside Kethalas, staring at him like a frightened deer.

Jetekesh's absent smile died.

"Don't be angry at the lass, good prince," Kethalas said,

holding up a clawed hand. "I'm the culprit who sneaked her aboard."

Jetekesh slammed his fist on the side of the wagon. "Whatever for? She can't join us—she'll come to harm."

Kajsa ducked her head, though he knew she couldn't understand the trade language.

"What's the trouble?" asked Emerin, coming up alongside the wagon. He peeked inside to track Jetekesh's glower, and his body tensed. "Hello there, Lady Kajsa. What are you doing here?" He spoke in the Old Tongue.

Quivering, Kajsa hefted her gaze until it met the lord's frown. With a slow breath, she sought words. They came out small. "I couldn't stay there. Please. Let me come."

"I already told her no," Jetekesh growled, still using the trade tongue. "The Clanslands aren't any sort of place for non-fighters."

"They're barely a place for anyone else," Dakarai said from Jetekesh's other side, startling the prince. Jetekesh tossed the clansman a glare, which Dakarai ignored as he offered Kajsa a kind smile. "You must desire to stretch your legs after that jostling journey. Come on out, Kajsa." He, too, spoke the Old Tongue.

She offered the clansman a tiny smile, then glanced at Kethalas for reassurance. The Shinacian proffered an encouraging nod.

Jetekesh threw his hands up. "I'm not responsible if she dies."

Emerin caught his shoulder. "This is your expedition, my prince. If she comes, you're as responsible for her life as you are the rest of ours. Your command is law."

Jetekesh dragged a hand down his face. "We're a day out from Kyon Taro. Backtracking now is a delay we can't afford. What am I supposed to do, send her back alone?" His eyes swept over the forest. Despite the tranquil chatter of evening wildlife, the *vashalan* were likely near. "We can't send anyone with her. That will reduce our number too much."

"Then, should she come?" Emerin spoke in low, neutral tones.

Sighing, Jetekesh nodded. "No choice now."

The lord of the keep turned toward Kajsa, who had inched her way to the back of the wagon and peeked out at them, her brows pinched together. In the Old Tongue, Emerin said, "You're coming, my lady. I recommend you stay very close. We've not got the force of arms to protect you if you wander."

She bobbed a hasty nod. "Thank you." Her eyes caught on Jetekesh's. "Thank you, Marked Prince."

"Prince Jetekesh," he said. "Please." He exhaled through his nose. "If you don't mind, my lady, we need to set up camp and..." He tried to gentle his tones. "You're, well, rather in the way."

She blushed and stumbled from the wagon bed. "Apologies." She backed off to one side of the wagon, cheeks brightening more. Ducking her head, she twisted her heavy skirts in her hands.

Jetekesh and Emerin tugged the new canvas tent from the interior, and Dakarai joined them to haul it to the chosen campsite. As he unfolded the canvas, Jetekesh mulled over the girl's decision to join the company. She was so timid, yet bold enough to sneak inside the wagon and swear Kethalas to silence. The dragon's actions were less surprising. Kethalas was obviously a free spirit like Jetekesh could only long to be.

Dakarai slipped off, then returned with the tent poles, and soon the three men had erected the shelter. Jetekesh turned to fetch the bedrolls and faltered as Lafe and Kajsa drew close, carrying several between them.

Jetekesh lifted an eyebrow at Lafe, who managed a one-shouldered shrug, then shifted his grip on the bedrolls. Slipping out of the way, Jetekesh allowed them to step inside the tent.

Well, she's not lazy.

She'd already proven as much, climbing the high pass into Shing, but watching a girl step forward to help still surprised him. It shouldn't, not with Song and Rille as examples of feminine strength, but Mother's constant unwillingness to ruin a nail or snag her silk gown had pervaded his earliest memories.

Song was Shingese, and Rille was a child. Somehow, he'd seen them as exceptions. Kajsa, on the other hand, was dainty, nearly frail, with pale hair and delicate fingers, so much like Queen Bareene.

He grimaced. *I must grow past my misconceptions.*

When he'd faced *Erisyrdrel* in the Lotus Palace and banished the water demon to King Ehrikai's faraway court, Jetekesh had seen Mother's ghost. Her voice, which had plagued him for the past several months, had been more than his imagination—but she was gone now, expelled by Jinji. Jetekesh was left alone with his thoughts at last. He shouldn't let doubts crowd into the spaces where ghosts once dwelt.

Dragging a hand over his golden tresses, Jetekesh entered the roomy tent and knelt to untie each bedroll while Kajsa and Lafe left to grab the rest. Fumbling with the knot, Jetekesh shook hair from his face and chewed at the inside of his cheek. Despite Kajsa's actions, he shouldn't have lost his temper. He'd grown better than that, hadn't he?

Apologize. Prince Sharo would.

The knot came undone, and the roll loosened. Crawling forward, he pushed the bedroll flat and flopped down, exhaustion crushing his will to aid with the camp's setup. Fluttering out a breath, he resisted the pull of sleep and dragged himself back to his feet. Turning, he found Kajsa in the doorway. She and Lafe entered with the last of the bedrolls.

Now or never. As they set the bundles down, he approached.

"Give us a moment, please, Sir Lafe."

The knight bowed, then slipped outside.

Dodging Kajsa's wary look, Jetekesh stared at her fur-lined boots. "I lost my temper earlier. I'm...sorry."

Silence. Then a faint breath. "You had every reason to be

angry, Mar—um, Prince Jetekesh." Her tongue staggered over the name, punctuating her accent. "I disobeyed your orders."

He lifted his eyes and blinked. Her gentle gaze infused him with warmth. Her shy smile bloomed like a summer rose, full of understanding and compassion.

She dipped her head, breaking off that warmth. "Forgive my insubordination. I meant no disrespect."

Fire scored his cheeks. "That's...entirely unnecessary. I'm not even your prince. We're strangers. You honestly didn't need to ask permission of me to come, now that I think about it. I just...don't want more people to die on my watch."

She hoisted her head. "Yet this is your trek, isn't it?"

Jetekesh hesitated. "Yes, that's true."

"Thank you for allowing me to stay." She dipped her head again, then backed out of the tent without ever glancing back, gone like a rabbit frightened back into its hole.

Jetekesh stared after her, bewildered. *She's more apparition than my mother was.*

Shrugging off the Norvian girl's peculiarities, he left the tent to help Kethalas move to the makeshift pit where Emerin had begun building a fire. As he neared the wagon, he kept his gaze averted when Kajsa and Lafe passed him again, each carrying satchels.

Inside the conveyance, Kethalas had propped himself against a barrel. His eyes were closed, his lips pressed tight.

"Are you in great pain?" asked Jetekesh with a spasm of sympathy.

Kethalas cracked one silver eye open, and he tried a weary smile. "Those jostles did me no favors."

Jetekesh reflected on his earlier outburst and caught his lip between his teeth. "Uh, Lord Kethalas?"

"So formal, Prince?"

"This is important." He set his teeth, mustering the strength to apologize again. Despite all his efforts to alter himself from the prince he'd been before, hot prickles lanced his cheeks as he faced an admission of guilt.

Swallow your pride and do it anyway, Kesh. Sharo would.

He met Kethalas's eyes. "Forgive me...for earlier. I—I lost my temper, and I shouldn't have."

Kethalas blinked twice, then he canted his head. "No need of that, good prince."

"Yes," Jetekesh said. "There *is* a need."

"Very well. I accept your apology."

Exhaling, Jetekesh lifted his head. "Thank you." He held out his hand. "Want support getting to the fire?"

Kethalas offered a fanged grin. "Please." He eased himself into a crouch and half crawled the length of the sturdy wagon bed, then he slipped his legs out and let Jetekesh take his weight while he lowered himself to the packed dirt road.

Sir Lafe appeared and walked beside the two as they hobbled to the fire. Jetekesh deposited Kethalas on the man's saddle near the flames. It seemed Dakarai and Anenyasha had been tending to the horses.

"Food will take a little longer." Emerin rubbed his hands on a handkerchief. "Fortunately, we're well stocked on meat, so it won't be rice alone." He tossed peat moss onto the open flame, then rose and surveyed the camp. "Anyone feel like sparring? I need a good stretch."

"I will, my lord." Jetekesh squared his shoulders.

Emerin eyed him, perhaps surprised, then he grinned. "All right. Broadswords?"

"Please." Jetekesh tied back his hair with a spare cord he kept in a pocket with his handkerchief. Then he slid his blade from its scabbard with an electrifying thrill. He wouldn't win against Lord Emerin—few could—but he would learn, and that was just as good. The legendary Sir Palan had taught him briefly, and Master

Ivam was no slouch, but here was a chance to learn from another legend. Jetekesh would be a fool to forgo the opportunity.

The keep lord moved his neck from side to side until something popped. "Shall we cover our blades, Your Highness, or do you prefer stop-short?"

Usually, Jetekesh spent his training periods with a heavy wooden sword, but he welcomed these moments to practice with the real thing. "Let's cover our blades."

He wanted the freedom to hone his instincts.

"Excellent." Emerin slid his sword free, emerald-studded hilt flashing in the firelight. His eyes likewise danced with flames, and the memory of the keep lord wielding fire to scare off the *vashalan* sparked in Jetekesh's mind.

Lafe fetched durable cloth they'd procured in Kyon Taro, and both swordsmen wrapped their blades before moving away from the fire.

Setting his feet, Jetekesh waited for Emerin to strike. How the man proceeded would say a lot about his fighting style.

Emerin charged on powerful legs, muscles corded as he stabbed at Jetekesh straight on. The prince sidestepped, bringing his blade up to knock Emerin's aim off course—but the lord pivoted as though he'd seen Jetekesh's counter ahead of time.

Swinging high, Emerin's sword met Jetekesh's with a thud. Emerin's grin broadened. His green eyes gleamed with an almost feral light.

Jetekesh disengaged with a wide backward step, then swung low, but Emerin met him again with a resounding clash. Each time Jetekesh withdrew, then attacked, Emerin was there, catching his blade like he could see three steps ahead. Jetekesh's limbs ached as the heavy sword dragged him down, one engagement at a time.

Emerin took the offensive again, driving Jetekesh back and back, toward the bamboo trees. His sword hacked at Jetekesh's.

The prince's bones rattled under the barrage he barely blocked, over, over, and over again. His teeth ground together as he calculated how to break the lord's rhythmic strikes—power, step, and motion in flawless alignment.

Jetekesh's heel caught on a half-buried rock, and he careened backward until the ground struck him with menacing force. Spots spangled in his vision. Blackness filled his lungs—then he hacked out a fit of coughs, gasping for oxygen.

Sir Lafe reached his side mere seconds after Emerin knelt close by.

"Your Highness, are you injured?" asked the lord of the keep. The feral glint in his eyes had vanished, replaced by a reasoning human being.

As Lafe helped him sit up, Jetekesh nodded, drinking in more air, unwilling to waste any on words. His lungs burned and his lower back spasmed where a second jutting stone had punctured flesh even through his thick tunic.

"Forgive me," Emerin said in low tones. "I lost myself in the fight."

Still gulping down breaths, Jetekesh batted his apology away. "N-no need to apologize. It was a fair duel." He craned his arm to brush his fingers over the gouge through his tunic and cringed. "Lafe, can you help me up?"

The knight hooked his hands under Jetekesh's arms and hoisted him like he weighed nothing. Through a mounting headache, Jetekesh thanked Lafe, then gingerly trod to his saddle at the fire. He eased himself onto the leather seat and tugged up his tunic to glimpse the wound. He frowned, unable to tell how deep the gouge was.

Lafe knelt behind him and pressed his gloved fingers around the stinging wound. "Not too serious, Your Highness, but it needs to be cleaned."

Jetekesh nodded, then slumped forward while the knight trotted off to the wagon.

Emerin crouched before Jetekesh, the billowing steam from the pot on the trivet curling around him. "Forgive me. I've wounded you."

"Barely, my lord," Jetekesh said. "It's a scratch. And Master Ivam beats me half-senseless every day. He'd thank you for an invigorating lesson." He grinned. "I'll be sore, but that's part of training, isn't it?"

Emerin grinned in answer. "You're more like your father every day." He rose, then stooped before the pot to stir the roiling stew. The aromas of carrots, spices, and savory meat met Jetekesh's nose, and his mouth watered.

Lafe returned, carrying clean water and a salve. He knelt to patch Jetekesh's injury, but Kajsa plucked the salve from his hand.

"I'm a healer," she whispered. With deft fingers, she tended the wound while Lafe hovered close to keep an eye on her every motion. Jetekesh held still, surprised by the gentle brush of her fingers and how little he felt the sting of her treatment. After the girl tugged Jetekesh's tunic back down, Emerin pronounced supper ready.

Kajsa started to move away.

"Thank you," Jetekesh said.

She glanced at him with that same shy smile, then hid her face.

As Jetekesh settled back with a bowl of steaming stew over rice, a glimmering shape snagged his eye, and he glanced at the sky just as a fairy winked out of sight. A smile caught his lips. Soon, saints willing, he and his companions would find a way into Shinac. Soon, he might meet Prince Sharo again.

And dragons.

CHAPTER 5
TRIALS

The dreary swamplands gave way to pastoral views so reminiscent of Shing's hills near Jinji's home that Aredel faltered. Sheep grazed on a hillside where a stand of deciduous trees trembled in a soft, warm breeze.

Behind him, Anadin gasped with relief and flopped down where he stood. Rille padded up beside Aredel and gazed out at the open space, green grass, brilliant sky of cloudless blue, and a wide stream cutting between rolling hills.

"I thought we'd never escape that awful place," Rille said, then drank in a long breath.

Aredel allowed himself several fresh breaths as well. Nothing had attacked them or harassed them beyond the horrible stench of stagnant water and the insects that infested the dreary realm—but the last three days had been arduous. Food was scant; Aredel's efforts to hunt had produced a meager mouthful of rabbit and little else. A single stream of clean water on their second day had been all they'd dared drink from. Fortunately, the stream ahead of them now looked like it ran toward the wetlands, not away.

"Keep moving," Aredel said, glancing at his brother.

The KryTeeran prince pushed a smile to his lips, then swayed to his feet. "If we must."

Aredel pointed to the stream. "Are you thirsty?"

"What a question!" Anadin broke into a run. He stayed ahead of Aredel as they raced toward the water, Rille taking up the rear on her much shorter legs. She protested, but neither brother heeded the little girl. Anadin plunged into the flowing water with a whooping shout. Aredel arrived seconds later, sank to his knees along the muddy bank, and dipped his hand into the icy water for a drink. Cold needled his fingertips.

A bellowing cry rent the air. Aredel clambered upright and drew his sword. A winged beast raced over the sky toward them. It looked like a cross between a great lion and a giant eagle; its head was arrayed with feathers and a golden beak, with talons for front legs. Magnificent wings beat the wind. Its back end was the body of a cat, with razor claws and a lashing tail.

A gryphon, Aredel realized, recalling Jinji's many tales of Shinac and depictions found on ancient landmarks across Nakania.

The creature landed on the stream's far bank and transformed. The woman who stood in the gryphon's place had bronze skin, tawny hair falling in a thick mane, and eyes like flames burning bright and fierce. She was draped in a long flowing gown glittering with crushed pearls and diamonds. Large hands tipped with talon-like claws hung at her sides, flexing as she eyed Aredel across the rushing water. Wings still protruded from her back, feathered, glossy, and golden in the sunlight.

"You have both touched the sacred waters of Alasiilay." The gryphon's voice rang out, powerful as a trumpet.

Aredel shifted his grip on his blade. "We did so in ignorance, mighty one. Forgive us." He glanced toward Anadin. The prince backed out of the water, which poured off his baggy pants.

The gryphon's wings beat the air once, throwing wind at them. "You must pay the cost nonetheless, strangers from another land."

"What is the cost?" asked Aredel, hefting his chin.

The gryphon's blazing eyes flicked to Rille as the girl reached the stream, gasping for breath, then the gryphon returned her stare to Aredel. "You must face the Trial of Bitter Flames."

The name sent a thrill through Aredel's frame. "And can I face this trial on behalf of my brother and myself?"

The gryphon hissed out a breath. "All who trespass must face the trial alone. None may intercede."

Rille marched forward, her mouth open, but Aredel held out a hand to stop her. "And the girl?" he asked. "She did not touch your sacred stream."

"'Tis not my stream," said the gryphon. "It belongs to the Fae of Valliath. These are the sacred waters of the True King. I, Terinvala, am but its guardian." Her wings beat the air as though to punctuate her point. "The girl is innocent. She shall not face the trial."

Rille stomped her foot. "This is ridiculous. If the waters can't be touched, best put up some sort of sign, or everyone will have to face the trial."

"Hush, my lady," Aredel said. "We have broken a sacred law. We must pay the cost."

With a growl, Rille dodged Aredel and halted on the very edge of the water as Anadin let out a squeak. "What does this trial entail, Lady Gryphon?"

"Only the accused may know," Terinvala said. "You must stand aside."

Rille turned to Anadin, then back to the gryphon. "It's not fair. They didn't know it was sacred."

The gryphon fluttered her wings. "None may defile the True

King's waters. Only he or his heirs may dismiss the heinous charges laid against the accused."

Rille's head snapped up. "Oh? Then let us speak with one of his heirs. We seek Prince Sharo. Surely, he would dismiss the charges. After all, Aredel aided him in the fight against Lord Peresen."

Aredel fought down a wince. Didn't the girl remember he had been tasked with killing Sharo once they were reunited? "Stand down, Lady Rille." He reached for her shoulder, but she dodged sideways.

"The trial cannot wait," said the gryphon. "Justice demands that it begin now."

"Then let's get on with this," Anadin said, glancing toward Aredel and Rille. "The sooner we face the trial, the sooner we can find Prince Sharo."

Had he too forgotten Aredel's fell purpose in Shinac? The Blood King rubbed a hand across his brow, then nodded. "Let us commence this trial, whatever comes of it." As Rille started to protest again, he spoke over her. "This is a country of magic, Rille. We must abide by their laws, no matter how we perceive them."

Her mouth snapped shut like a turtle, and her shoulders slumped a little. Exhaling, she nodded. "Please be careful, Anadin." Her amber eyes met Aredel's gaze. "I already know *you'll* be fine."

His lips rose in a humorless smile. "You assume this trial is combative. It may be something else."

She shrugged. "You still have my utter confidence in your superior abilities, Blood King."

He inclined his head, then cut his gaze to the gryphon. "How shall we proceed, mighty one?"

"Enter the stream and walk toward the ring of flame." One wing lifted to point upstream.

"*Now* we can touch the water?" Anadin flashed a grin at

Aredel, then plunged his feet into the water before the Blood King moved. "I will go first," the prince said.

Aredel tensed, then loosened his grip on his blade. "Very well, *shaqel.*" The familial term of endearment gripped his heart like a vise, but he blew out a breath and held himself steady. Despite Anadin's innocent demeanor, a devil lurked beneath. The prince of KryTeer was no slouch, nor was he stupid.

As Anadin trudged upstream, Aredel turned back to the gryphon. "What happens if we should fail this trial?"

"You will be dead," Terinvala answered.

Nodding, Aredel returned his gaze to Anadin—just as the prince vanished into the air. "So, the trial begins," Aredel whispered.

Terinvala stood like a statue, unmoving, perhaps viewing the trial in her mind's eye. Meanwhile, Aredel and Rille paced and sat in turns, both too agitated to hold still for long. An hour or longer passed before the gryphon stirred on her side of the stream. She unfolded her wings and stretched them.

Aredel rose from the shore, steeling himself. "Has my turn come?"

"Yes." The gryphon motioned to the stream. "Follow the current and enter the ring of fire."

"And my brother? Did he succeed?" Aredel scanned his surroundings like Anadin might reappear.

"I cannot tell you his fate. Discover for yourself."

Aredel held his ground. "Does that mean that Rille will remain here alone?"

"I shall see her safely brought to Prince Sharo."

"No," Rille said, throwing her hands to her hips. "I'll journey with Anadin and Aredel, or I'll stay here."

"Don't be stubborn," Aredel said. "If you reach Sharo first, all the better for us."

She blinked, then sighed. "Very well." A heartbeat passed. "Good luck to you."

He inclined his head. "I accept your wishes." Turning back to the glistening water, he stepped into the stream, fingers itching to draw his blade. He prayed the trial was combative, for he could then make short work of it. Whatever the case, the Blood King held no fear of losing.

As he slogged up the stream, a faint orange glow sparked before him, then stretched into a wreath of flames spinning fast and hot.

Setting his teeth, Aredel caught his sword hilt, then stepped through the spitting ring of fire and into a wide dim cave. The portal of flames vanished behind him, plunging him into darkness. Frigid air climbed his limbs, lifting the fine hairs on his neck and arms. Water dripped nearby. The odor of mildew curled around Aredel's nose, urging him to sneeze. He resisted.

As his vision adjusted, he skimmed the shadows, seeking any sign of Anadin or a threat. Rock shelves rose above him, and stalactites hung from a high black ceiling. He stepped deeper into the cave. A faint rumble welled up from the darkest shadows before him. Wind rose to toss his long hair and billow his clothes. Aredel stood straight against the blasting gale, then heard the *shuff* of something large and heavy slithering over the stone floor.

Stories Jinji had told him years before flooded Aredel's mind with images of foul monsters. Instinct whispered what this one might be. He slid loose his sword and turned his back on the creature that approached him.

Light flickered into being, brilliant amber, glowing far above Aredel's head. A hissing noise confirmed the Blood King's suspicion: a giant basilisk.

Aredel slipped his feet into a defensive stance. A wild grin caught his lips. *This* was something he could fight. He just couldn't make eye contact.

Hot breath fell on him, stinking of rot and iron blood. Aredel's grin weakened. Had Anadin met this monster? Had he survived? Did he know not to meet its deadly gaze?

Another hiss fluttered the Blood King's hair. Aredel risked a glance around the dark cave. His skin prickled. He wrenched his sword upward as the light dove toward him, presumably its eyes, blazing like torches.

He swung his blade, slicing air—until it struck something hard and bounced off, rattling his bones.

As the searing breath buffeted his back, Aredel stumbled, then lunged sideways.

Jaws snapped shut near his ankles. He scudded over the rough wet ground.

He scampered back to his feet. Clutched his sword tighter. Squeezed his eyes shut.

Wheeled and swung again.

The sword struck the same hard something.

Aredel backed up, his arm throbbing. His heart kicked his ribs. Adrenaline flooded his body.

The hissing grew, and the air rippled as the basilisk slithered closer. Its eyes bored into his back. He kept his own eyes sealed shut, unwilling to peek, even to seek Anadin.

Survive first, then find him.

Jinji had cataloged so many monsters in his stories, from ogres to harpies to goblins—and yes, basilisks.

Pebbles clattered. The creature's breath ruffled Aredel's hair again. His foot hunted for solid purchase, then he adjusted his grip, and whipped around—eyes still shut—to stab at the basilisk. The sword struck a surface stronger than stone. The impact reverberated up Aredel's arm and he retreated toward the shelves of rock, risking a glance at his feet as he splashed through a puddle—then he pressed his eyelids shut. Meeting the monster's eyes in a reflection could be his end.

No. Hadn't Jinji said that if the basilisk saw its own reflection, it would die?

That and a gryphon's tears could kill it.

Should have throttled a few drops out of Terinvala while I was there.

In the darkness of the cave, how could Aredel hope to use the puddles effectively? He couldn't see them well enough to form a solid strategy. Gritting his teeth, he sprinted through the darkness. He'd have to act by feel and scent. The odor of mildew grew stronger as he raced over the uneven terrain, and he veered toward it. A resounding splash met his toes and he plunged into water reaching his ankles.

He moved through it at a slogging pace, gauging its width. The slithering basilisk neared. Its hiss was loud in his ears. Its breath wrapped around his body, rank and hot. The imaginary vision of its long fangs, so near his flesh, lifted the hairs on his neck.

There. The far side of the puddle reflected the amber glow of the monster's eyes.

Light. Of course.

His grin stretched wider. He backtracked to the center of the shallow pool. He knew that the basilisk thought he was cornered. He was counting on its slow slither. It approached like a hunter savoring the kill.

Aredel knelt in the water, ignoring the cool liquid seeping beneath his baggy pants and the bite of pebbles under his feet. He bowed his head, hiding his grin, keeping his eyes shut. His fingers flexed against his sword hilt, while his free hand settled on the cool stone floor beneath the pool. Waiting. Counting. Drawing on his newfound power. He hadn't wielded it since Bahadronn, but it seemed to answer him in his need.

The air shifted. The rancid breath closed in, swift, silent.

Aredel lurched sideways, dragging his sword across the ground, slicing through water until the pool gave way. As the basilisk lunged toward the spot where the Blood King had been mere seconds before, the sword sparked with white lightning.

The basilisk met its gaze in the rippling pool.

It roared.

A cracking noise climbed like a pillar toward the stalactites. The snake-like creature hardened into a colossal stone statue.

Aredel straightened up and turned to eye the looming black shape against the gloom.

Squaring his shoulders, the Blood King slid his blade back into its curved sheath.

"I presume that's the end of my trial." His voice rang across the cavern, but all that answered was the steady drip of water.

A presence shifted behind him. Drawing his sword, Aredel spun to face his new assailant.

CHAPTER 6
VOICE IN THE STORM

The cry of wolves jolted Jetekesh from sleep. His heart thudded in his ears. He lay within the large Shingese style tent. The soft breaths of his companions surrounded him, quieting his nerves as the howls fell away.

He sat upright. His muscles protested, sore after three days of endless riding and evenings spent training with Emerin and Lafe in turns. Neither man was prone to fits of mercy in their swordplay. Still, Jetekesh didn't mind the pain. It meant he was getting stronger.

Moonlight soaked into the canvas walls, illuminating the interior enough for him to make out the forms around him. One patch of canvas glowed orange, suggesting that someone still sat at the fire, keeping watch.

Casting a glance around the bedrolls, he guessed Dakarai was the man outside. Jetekesh shifted in his blankets, weighing whether he'd woken too much to fall back to sleep.

The howls rose again. Prickles scored Jetekesh's arms, and he sighed, then shoved aside his coverlet. Tossing on the silk robe gifted to him in Shing, he tiptoed around the sleeping bodies and slipped out of the tent.

Chill wind wrapped around him, slithering under his collar. The bamboo trees flanked the forest road, tall, slender, and ominous, glowing a strange blue beneath the influence of the full moon.

He tugged his robe closer and followed the wagon ruts to the campfire. Sure enough, Dakarai sat near the open flames, sharpening his jagged spear tip. Orange light painted his dark skin. He shifted to eye Jetekesh with kind brown eyes.

"Restless?" asked the clansman.

Jetekesh nodded, trudged to his saddle, and flopped down. "The wolves... If they *are* wolves."

Dakarai lifted his head toward the sky. "They're not close, whatever they be." He smiled at the prince. "I suspect they are Nakania's variety rather than Shinac's, or the chill in your blood would be deeper, Your Highness. Beyond that, Lord Emerin would already be awake, I think."

The prince pinched his hands between his knees and stared into the flames. "I hope we're doing the right thing."

"You doubt your decision?"

"Often," Jetekesh whispered. "Jinji always seemed to know what he was doing, where he was headed. I don't think I inherited that with my...mark."

"Do you not know where you're going?" Dakarai asked.

"I...well, yes. To the Clanslands, obviously." Jetekesh grimaced and tried to peel the impatience from his words. "I just mean—"

"I understand. Leaving Shing after learning an army is amassing over the southern mountains unsettles me as well. But as you yourself argued, we need help that no Nakanian force can provide. And Kethalas needs to return home. His wounds may be unable to heal properly in our magicless lands."

"I still think my decision was right. I just wish I knew for certain." Jetekesh plucked up a handful of dried peat moss from the pile near the fire.

"I do not think your storyteller was always as certain as you believe him to be. I think he followed his instinct, as well as his code of morality, and prayed for the best."

Jetekesh tossed the moss into the fire and watched the flames devour the fresh fuel. "Let's hope that's enough. It's all I'm doing now."

Dakarai smiled. "We do what we can, and the gods—the spirits—your One God—whatever the powers that light this world—will meet us where we must stop." He rubbed an oil cloth across his spearhead. "I believe good deeds are rewarded; light always wins out. Do not fear your part in it."

"I fear my weakness." The words tumbled loose before Jetekesh realized he'd spoken. He blinked, then let his shoulders droop. "There, I've admitted it. I'm weak. I want to be strong, to protect what I love, but I keep failing."

"You defeated *Erisyrdrel*, did you not?"

"With *help*." The bitterness in his voice burned Jetekesh's ears.

"No one could do otherwise. Your Highness, no one—not any of us—can survive this life without others. It is not possible. We all need help. I cannot do most of what I attempt without Anenyasha's aid."

Jetekesh's eyes flicked to the tent where the clanswoman slept. Dakarai's betrothed. His beloved. Until recently, Jetekesh hadn't believed romantic love was real—but Dakarai had assured him it was, and his relationship with Anenyasha seemed to prove his claim that people could wed, not for monetary or political gain, but for mutual adoration and respect toward each other. Prince Sharo of Shinac had made a similar statement once.

The prince sighed and rubbed a stiff muscle in his shoulder.

"I'm not really disputing that help is necessary sometimes. But I always feel helpless. I'm tired of it. Sick of it. I want to become someone whom others can always rely on."

"That is a weighty wish. *Always* is, perhaps, too much to heap upon yourself. After all, you deserve to rely on others from time to time."

"I've already done too much of that. People died for it."

The fire popped, then Dakarai blew out a breath. "To desire strength is not bad. To desire the skill to defend others is also good. But to refuse the kindness of others—their own eagerness to do their part—is a disservice. An army is made up of many. Even the strongest captain must rely on his men to help him obtain victory. You are a prince, and so, you must allow others to serve you in their turns. Not for your sake alone, Your Highness, but for those who rely upon you to make the best calls, in war and in peace.

"Your father is a good man. He is strong and reliable. But he also relies on others." Dakarai snared Jetekesh's gaze. "If you wish to become as he is, emulate his actions. Think to those moments where he stands aside to let men with different strengths take the lead rather than himself. True strength is in the heart, not in the sword. Knowing when to act, and when *not* to act, will serve you better than the greatest blade skill."

A lump formed in Jetekesh's throat. *Am I upset or grateful?* He couldn't weigh the brimming feelings swelling within him; perhaps they were a combination of both. Until recently, he'd sneered at criticisms and lectures from those beneath his station, yet Jinji had taught him that even the humblest shepherd had life lessons to offer.

Listen to Dakarai, Kesh. Even if it stings.

Why the clansman's words stung, he didn't know. Dakarai's tones had been gentle, even compassionate. There'd been no malice, or even any judgment, in those words.

Is that what stings? His kindness? Do I feel so undeserving of it?

Perhaps he did. Hadn't he goaded Jinji into the last stand against the emperor of KryTeer, which had resulted in the story-teller's death? Hadn't Jetekesh's temper caused Tifen and Palan to be killed in their efforts to protect their prince?

Will I ever learn not to spew out my feelings like a poison?

He sighed and dragged a hand down his face. His eyes burned in the fire smoke, his lids growing heavy from the day's long ride.

I should sleep.

Jetekesh shoved off the saddle and stood straight. "Thank you for listening to me. I don't mean to sound unreasonable..."

"You do not," Dakarai said. "You sound sorrowful." The tall man stood, smiled down at Jetekesh, and set a hand on the prince's shoulder. "You *are* becoming strong, Prince of Amantier. You must simply come to recognize your type of strength, and then it will be easier to harness. Fretting will not help you. Let your guilt rest."

Mist filled Jetekesh's eyes, and he swallowed hard. "I—I don't know how."

"See outside your own eyes. How would Jinji view your past actions? With accusations or with mercy?"

Jetekesh exhaled a shuddering breath. "With mercy."

"And so, heed his voice rather than your own, until yours echoes what he says. His was always a high path. It can be frightening to walk such a narrow height, but far more courageous and worthwhile than the low roads of self-doubt and regret. Tread slow and soft, and heed kindness." He squeezed Jetekesh's shoulder, then released him and sat down again.

Jetekesh glanced away to swipe at a loose tear, then turned back to the fire. "Thank you, Dakarai. You...you're a true friend."

"I do try to be," the man replied. "Goodnight, Prince Jetekesh."

"Goodnight." Jetekesh padded toward the tent, his step lighter than it had been in days. Perhaps even months. Dakarai hadn't shed his burdens; the prince knew that well enough. But for the moment, his doubts slumbered, and he suspected sleep would come readily.

Thunder drummed in the sky. Jetekesh halted and lifted his eyes to the clouds rolling across the starry heavens, racing toward the moon. His instincts bristled. The storm looked normal, yet something whispered a warning.

Lightning speared the clouds, turning them silver. Chills pattered up his back like frozen fingers. He whirled to face the growing shadows just as clouds snuffed out the moon's glow.

For a split second, he imagined a cloaked man staring back at him up the road, eyes of liquid gold piercing him to his core. Thunder boomed again, and the image died like wafting smoke on a breeze.

Jetekesh's heart rammed against his ribs. His mouth went dry. The view of the road narrowed, and a soft, sad voice tickled his ear. "*I have found you, Marked Prince.*"

Dakarai caught his arm and wheeled him around. "Your Highness?"

Jetekesh stared, trying to register the clansman's words. His vision wavered. *I'm not breathing.* He shook himself and drew in a hasty breath, then another, until his mind settled. With a thread of panic coiling through him, he risked another glance up the road. No cloaked figure. Just the rutted path, the looming trees, the churning storm above.

Lightning flashed again. Thunder answered almost at once, shaking the earth. The prince's damaged ear throbbed.

"What did you see?" asked Dakarai.

Jetekesh frowned, rubbing his ear. "Our enemy, I think. He knows who I am. It seems he's been seeking me." The words came out calm, level, though his mind reeled at the implications. First, Kajsa had sought and discovered him. Now, the man who had likely unchained *Erisyrdrel* from the ocean depths had done the same.

To what end?

He didn't want to know the answer, but he didn't doubt he'd learn it just the same.

"Come," said Dakarai, taking his arm. "We should inform Lord Emerin."

CHAPTER 7

HERALD OF TRUTH

Emerin wasn't pleased by Jetekesh's story. The keep lord barely waited until dawn breached the world under a gloomy sky before he ordered the company to break camp.

Jetekesh munched on an apple for breakfast while he rode Hickory, muscles protesting the prospect of another full day of travel after a sleepless night. He did his best to bite back a tirade of curses and complaints—and managed it until noon.

As the midday sun peeked over a plume of storm clouds, he reined in his buckskin stallion. "Blast it, Emerin. We need a respite. I'll not budge without some proper food in my belly and a moment's rest, ghost enemy or not."

Emerin craned his head and slowed his horse's pace. Heaving a sigh, he wheeled his stallion around. "As you command, Your Highness. But I request that we not dawdle too long."

"Agreed." Jetekesh swung from his saddle and landed in a muddy puddle. He leaned close to Hickory's ear and murmured soothing compliments, stroking the horse's coarse hair. Hickory nickered at him.

Nearby, Kajsa swung down from behind Anenyasha's mount and shook her dress straight. The heavy fur-lined fabric looked stiff and worn—probably one of the girl's only outfits, battered from crossing the mountain pass.

With a frown, Jetekesh limped to Emerin's side, his muscles refusing to loosen. He wrestled an urge to rub his posterior as he reached the keep lord. "Any villages ahead before we leave civilized Shing for the wilderness?"

"A few." Emerin patted his horse's flank, then turned to face Jetekesh. "One of a decent size. Need something?"

Jetekesh nodded toward Kajsa. "She'll need a better wardrobe for traversing the Clanslands' jungles."

Emerin's vibrant eyes cut to Kajsa, and he looked her up and down. "I should have taken note. We've plenty of coin. I'll see to it."

"Thank you, my lord." Jetekesh dipped his head, then hobbled to the wagon and circled to peek inside through the back door. Kethalas was sound asleep, settled between two sacks of rice. The man-dragon's metallic blue hair gleamed in the gloom, and his breath sounded steady.

Jetekesh heaved himself into the wagon bed and rummaged around for a wedge of cheese and manchet bread. He was resigned to the fact Emerin wouldn't let anyone cook until supper.

He located the cheesecloth-wrapped goods and climbed from the wagon, careful not to drop his spoils. Bringing them around the wagon, he lifted his bundles. "Anyone hungry?"

The company congregated around him. He divvied up the food, then cradled a thick slab of cheese and a fluffy handful of bread as he sought a place to sit. Unable to find a patch of grass, he settled for a flat surface to one side of the road, and munched on his fare with relish. Growing up, he'd taken fine food for granted and wasted it often—but out here, along the byroads of a foreign land, he'd worked up a proper appetite. Just like when he'd traveled with Jinji, Rille, Yeshton, and the rest of that ragtag company.

A smile tugged at his lips. He ate in silence, content to observe his present companions' routines. Dakarai watered the horses from a bucket they'd filled the night before, while Anenyasha rubbed the beasts down. Harn checked his hitches, then inspected the wagon for any damage from the ruts. Emerin and Lafe conversed quietly between mouthfuls of bread, gesturing northeasterly, probably reviewing their ultimate objective: finding the Arch into Shinac.

Kajsa flitted from horse to horse, shy, but determined to win them over, then she went around the far side of the wagon, likely to check on Kethalas.

Perhaps she fancies him. Jetekesh found the thought amusing. He supposed Kethalas was a comely man in his strange Shinacian way—slender yet well-built, with high cheekbones. Mother would've been taken with him.

Jetekesh's grin died. *Yes, she would've tried to seduce him, too.*

But the prince doubted Mother would succeed with that one; he was a dragon, after all.

Should I warn poor Kajsa that he's not human?

He shrugged off the thought. Supplying the Norvian girl for the trek to the Clanslands was appropriate. Interfering in her personal affairs was something else entirely.

He bit hard into his cheese and chewed with fervor. *You've meddled with enough lives already.*

His attention settled on Lord Emerin instead. The strange lord of the Keep of the Falls, who'd vanished for years, then returned one day in time to claim his title upon his father's passing. Emerin could command fire. He'd used it against the *vashalan* in Bard Pass.

But he won't talk about it. I wonder why.

There Jetekesh went again, digging into the private matters of other people. He tore off a bit of bread with his teeth and skimmed the cloudy sky for any hint of the storm moving on. Despite approaching summer, the rain had conjured up a chill. A fire would be nice.

Sighing, he shoved the last bite of cheese in his mouth and stood.

Then he froze, his hands still on his thigh. The hair on his neck rose, and a sudden instinct barked at him to run. He bolted away from the forest edge, his boots slipping in the mud. "Emerin! Lafe!"

The keep lord whirled. He paled and raced toward Jetekesh, sliding his sword loose. Flecks of mud painted the lord's face as he rushed the unseen assailant. Lafe was three strides behind.

As the prince neared the wagon and spun, Dakarai reached him. The clansman flung himself in front of Jetekesh, spear held before him.

Beyond Dakarai, a lone *vashalan* leapt at Emerin. The lord's blade sank deep between the bony creature's ribs. The beast snarled, then it slumped to the ground, red eyes flattening.

"They are growing bolder," Dakarai murmured.

"They were already bold on Bard Pass." Lafe kicked the canine monster. "Why only one?"

"A scout, perhaps." Emerin scanned the forest.

Lafe grunted. "Better double the watch."

"Yes, and not take breaks midday." Emerin cast Jetekesh a glance. "If that's acceptable."

Scowling, Jetekesh nodded. "Agreed. But that means we *need* a proper breakfast before heading out."

"As you wish." Emerin gestured to the horses. "We should ride on."

The company moved out within a few minutes.

Coaxing Hickory into a fast walk, Jetekesh's mind returned to the moment the *vashalan* had targeted him.

I somehow knew it was there. Paranoia, warrior's instinct, or my newfound gift?

The lattermost seemed the likeliest reason, and yet the gift still scared him. Jinji's sight had been his death. Would Jetekesh also fade into a skeleton and die? He didn't think Jinji would select him for this if that were the only outcome.

If so, how do I prevent death?

Or would he not face it like Jinji had?

So many questions, and no one to ask concerning them. He wrung his reins and nudged Hickory into a swifter pace.

A drizzle plagued the company for over an hour in the midafternoon, then the clouds rolled back, and sunshine dried them out. Near sunset, Emerin called a halt.

Dakarai hauled peat moss from the wagon for the fire, while Lafe and Anenyasha trudged into the bamboo trees for a supply of water. Lafe had assured Jetekesh that a stream followed them close to the road until the northern bay. Unfortunately, Emerin wouldn't let Jetekesh approach the woods—especially after the morning's attack. Not even to bathe.

If Jetekesh wanted to stay clean, he would be forced to scrub himself using one of the water buckets Lafe hauled into camp. After last night's storm, however, Jetekesh decided to skip his wash. The glimmer of sunlight hadn't been enough to warm his bones. Instead, he wrapped himself in his black cloak—the strange one Emerin had gifted him—and huddled near the fire.

Emerin cooked supper. The scent of stew and almond pesto teased Jetekesh until his mouth salivated. A chunk of cheese, some bread, and an apple weren't enough to survive on—not for a growing boy pitting himself against adults every evening.

Tonight, Lafe rose to take his turn pounding Jetekesh into pulp while supper simmered. "Ready?" asked the knight.

"As I can be." Jetekesh threw aside his cloak. At least he'd soon be warmed up.

The company looked on, exchanging grins. Kethalas sat among them. The Shinacian dragon had felt up to joining them on his own—a sight that Jetekesh would usually rejoice in, but not just in time to witness his nightly defeat.

When Lafe knocked him off his feet for a fourth time, Jetekesh remained sprawled out and flung his blade aside. "Enough. I yield."

A coin flashed in the firelight, and Jetekesh tracked its descent into Kethalas's outstretched hand. The dragon pocketed the gold coin with a wink of one silver eye. "You lasted longer than Emerin thought you would."

"True, that." The lord tucked away his leather purse with his free hand while he stirred the stew. "I'd wagered three solid hits."

Jetekesh heaved himself to his knees, then accepted Lafe's hand to stand. He fetched his sword, limped to his saddle, and flopped down to unwrap the weapon. "Am I improving?" He slid his sword into its sheath with a satisfying click.

"Aye," Lafe said. "At an acceptable rate. Footwork needs help though."

"You and I will focus on that tomorrow, Your Highness," Emerin said. "Food's ready." He dished up a bowl and handed it to Jetekesh.

Clasping the bowl in both hands, Jetekesh let the steam curl around his face before he started chasing carrots around with his spoon. The evening was growing colder, and the warm food helped fend off the worst of the biting spring gusts. Kajsa alone seemed unaffected by the chill, but that made sense. She'd come from higher elevations, where winter lasted more than six months by her own report.

How can anyone survive such a harsh climate?

He studied the girl's face; her nose, reddened in the chill; her pale blue eyes; her faint, shy smile. Again, the marvel of her surviving to bring her message over the southern climes swelled in his chest.

We'd never have known about the Norvian army until it was far too late.

Careful not to spill his stew, he twisted toward her and spoke in the Old Tongue. "Lady Kajsa?"

She stiffened, eyes widening, then she dipped her head. "Yes, Your Highness?"

"This man who's building an army in Norva—what does he look like?"

Kajsa's tension bled away. Her thumb rubbed against the rim of her bowl and she stared into the campfire. "His complexion and hair are pale like all Norvians—but his eyes are different. Golden. Piercing. And very sad." She dipped her spoon into the stew and stirred the contents. "He is tall and very lean."

Dakarai clicked in quiet tones to Anenyasha, likely translating Kajsa's descriptions.

Jetekesh took a bite of stew, dredging up the memory of the man in last night's storm. Gold eyes had peered out at the prince from under a dark cloak.

'I have found you, Marked Prince.'

Jetekesh shuddered. That voice, a mere whisper, heartbreakingly sad, filled Jetekesh with despair even now. It was so much like the cry on the wind that had silenced the *vashalan* one night, not so long ago, on Bard Pass.

He glanced at Kajsa again. "What did you say his name is?"

She swallowed a mouthful of stew and lowered her spoon. "Navolleth."

A glimmering image flitted across his mind, like the remnants of a dream. Someone weeping. Nothing more. Jetekesh pressed his palms tighter around his bowl.

No matter what sorrow you've faced, it's never cause for warfare.

He finished off his food, then rose. Lafe followed him to his feet.

"Sit, Sir Knight. I'm just stretching my muscles. I'll only circle the fire."

Lafe sat back down, eyes trailed Jetekesh as the prince paced around the cluster of bodies, his mind churning over the few facts he knew. Kethalas had been the guardian of the Jade Arch, which had connected Shinac and Nakania within the Drifting Sands. The dragon had been attacked by a dark creature, wounded in the fray, and sent through the Arch by accident before the portal had shattered.

The dark creature had come to Nakania as well, and shortly thereafter, unleashed the demon *Erisyrdrel* from her underwater prison. Judging by the plethora of *vashalan*, the dark creature might have the ability to create the unholy monsters. That, or another Arch somewhere in Nakania had weakened enough to let them through.

Perhaps all the Arches have weakened.

Navolleth was stirring up the faraway Norvian people, after centuries of quiet, to march against their northern neighbors. It wasn't a leap to presume Navolleth was the creature who'd escaped through the Jade Arch. And now, war was at the north's threshold, a mere year away at most.

Jetekesh ran his fingers along his cloak's hem, vaguely aware his companions were watching him. They must reach the Clans-lands and hope against hope that another Arch existed there. Somehow, they must contact Sharo in Shinac. Against a supernatural power, no mortal army would last long.

If nothing else, Jetekesh must ascertain whether the Arches had been weakened or otherwise damaged and shore them up. And Kethalas needed to return home.

One year. Once, that had felt like an eternity away—but not now. Not setting out on a quest with little chance of success. The jungles of the Clanslands were enormous, wild, dark, and unknown. Thank the saints for Dakarai and Anenyasha, sent by their watchwoman to aid Jetekesh on the heels of half their clan's destruction.

The prince's heart throbbed. *It seems I was destined for this. Saints guard me. God guide me.*

He halted under the weight of intense eyes. Turning, he met Emerin's gaze.

"How long until we reach the border of the Clanslands?" asked Jetekesh.

"From here," Emerin said, "six days to the harbor, then a few hours more to the southernmost beach of the Clanslands, at our present pace."

"From there, we'll be greatly slowed, yes?" Jetekesh rubbed his hem again.

"Yes, Your Highness," Dakarai said. "The jungles are treacherous at best. Better to go slowly and live, than to race and die."

Jetekesh swallowed. "And what are our chances of survival there?"

The clansman fell still. "The parts of my country which I know well will not be troublesome for us. But if we must press deeper into the heart of Zindwéa, we will be at the mercy of the gods alone."

"Zindwéa." Jetekesh curled his tongue over the word. "Is that the true name of the Clanslands?"

"'Tis," the clansman said. "At least, most clans would call it so. Some—those who dwell in the deep jungles—may call it by other names. We have never spoken." Dakarai shrugged. "That realm is where our greatest danger lies."

A shiver raced up Jetekesh's arms. "Are those clans hostile?"

"Some have been, yes. Others merely keep to themselves."

"Do you think the Arch will be in the deep jungles?"

"Likely, Your Highness," Dakarai said. "Otherwise, we would have heard stories from other clans."

"Not necessarily." Emerin's voice was a soft rumble. "The Arch only shows itself under certain conditions."

Jetekesh raised an eyebrow. "How do you know that, my lord?"

Emerin's eyes held an almost feral light. He tipped his head to one side, blond hair slipping into his face. "The storyteller true visited my hearth more than once, Your Highness."

He's dodging.

Jetekesh straightened his shoulders and marched up to Emerin still seated on his saddle at the fire. "My lord, I don't mean to pry into your private life. Heaven knows, I'd like to keep a few secrets of my own. But there's one matter we must discuss."

Emerin's eyes narrowed, but he nodded. "Go on, my prince."

"Have you or haven't you visited Shinac before?"

Memories of Emerin wielding that blazing torch, and his hungry desire to restore something he'd lost—something he needed the Arch in order to recover—flitted over Jetekesh's mind.

The prince inhaled. "I realize I'm treading on your pain, but if you've seen or used a Shinacian Arch, we've a right to know. Not the details. Just the facts: Where, when, and why you can't return to it directly." He lowered his voice. "Please."

Emerin's gaze dropped to the ground and his shoulders hunched forward. "The Arch I've seen no longer exists, Prince Jetekesh. Isn't that enough?" A hollow tone pealed through his voice, deep, sorrowful.

Jetekesh cleared his throat. "Yes. I suppose that's enough."

"Where?" asked Dakarai. "Where was the Arch, Lord Emerin? That would be helpful to know."

Emerin grimaced, staring at his hands. "Amantier."

Jetekesh released a breath. "So then, if there *is* an Arch in each nation, the one in the Clanslands may still exist."

"May, yes," Emerin murmured. "But my efforts to find it were fruitless. Dakarai is right—if one exists there, it's deep within the jungles, farther than my guide would take me."

A pang caught in Jetekesh's chest. The feral lord stooped before him, wounded, broken in some deep way, and Jetekesh had caused the resurgence of his pain.

But I needed to know.

Did he? Or had Jetekesh let curiosity guide his demands?

Running a hand through his hair, Jetekesh knelt before Emerin and rested a hand on the man's forearm. The lord lifted his eyes, vivid with pain, and pierced the prince to his soul. Hadn't he explained to Jetekesh that trauma created a kind of reaction; an emotional scar that changed a person?

He admitted he knew that pain firsthand.

"We'll find the Arch," Jetekesh found himself saying. "I swear an oath to you, Lord Emerin, we'll reach Shinac."

The keep lord searched Jetekesh's eyes until his own softened, and pain drew deeper lines into his face. "So declares the Marked Prince, herald of truth. I believe you, Your Highness. And I thank you, too."

CHAPTER 8
FAIR FOLK

"Don't kill me, *shaqin*!"

Aredel froze, his blade mere inches from Anadin's throat. The steel glinted in a dull glow emanating from beyond his brother. The Blood King scowled, stepped back, and sheathed his sword with a curt snap. "You know better than to approach me from the rear, *shaqel*."

Anadin scratched his neck. "I was too anxious to wait. When the barrier fell, I raced in at once. They told me your trial was a different kind from mine."

"I'm glad of that." Aredel stepped forward to draw his brother into a brief embrace, something in his chest loosening. He clapped a hand to the prince's back, then retreated a step. "Explain yourself. What barrier, who are *they*, and what was your trial?"

Anadin cast a glance into the gloom behind Aredel. "I think it would be better to show you. Come." He gestured toward the dim glow. "The exit's this way."

Following on Anadin's heels down a cavern corridor, Aredel winced in the growing light. They slipped between two close-standing rocks and came out into a twilight forest. The fragrance of moss, dew, and loam permeated Aredel's senses, driving out the tang of minerals and blood.

The brothers stood in a small clearing surrounded by tall, lean, silver-haired fae. Arrows were nocked and pointed at Aredel's chest. He searched the fair faces until he spotted the one wearing a circlet on her brow.

Aredel inclined his head. "I am Blood King Aredel elvar Gilioth d'ara KessRa of KryTeer."

"We know," the woman said, keeping her arrow on target. "What is the fate of the basilisk?"

"Dead," chirped Anadin. "As I told you it would be. He turned it to stone."

Several of the tall fae exchanged glances.

The woman took a step forward and lowered her weapon. "As skilled as the stories say, then." She tapped a fist to her collarbone, and the sapphire jewel in her circlet flashed. "I am Thrissa, Watcher of the HaSharril Wood, Shield of the True King of Shinac."

Anadin's voice rose in a loud whisper. "Isn't she pretty?"

The prince had always been a master of blunt statements.

Aredel examined the fae woman with her high cheekbones, long silvery tresses, and lithe, slim form. Her eyes were a greenish-silver hue in the forest gloom. She was clad in material like silk but somehow softer; it changed shades under the towering aspen trees, adopting the dancing shadows as the leaves clacked overhead in a faint breeze. Likely, she could meld into any background without trouble.

"What happens now?" asked Aredel.

Thrissa answered. "You and your brother will be taken to Prince Sharo's camp. There your fates will be decided. That is your right, having passed the gryphon's trial."

"We have another companion."

"I told them that, too," Anadin whispered in the same loud tone.

"According to your brother," Thrissa said, "your young companion did not disturb the sacred waters. She will have been taken to our prince directly, as Terinvala promised. Gryphons do not lie."

"Most inconvenient for them." Aredel tipped his head forward. "Lead on. I wished to speak with Prince Sharo, and so I'll not fight your will."

"How fortunate that our goals align." Thrissa spoke in level tones, her emotions hidden in her proper speech. She motioned into the trees. "This way."

As Aredel and Anadin strode after the fae woman, the flock of other fae closed in to flank the two KryTeerans. The company moved at a fast pace.

"Tell me of your trial, *shaqel*," Aredel said, matching the gait of the fae escort with no trouble.

"It was a riddle. I solved it." Anadin flashed him a proud grin. "I didn't see who gave it to me—they lurked in the gloom—but I suspect it wasn't your basilisk. Once I answered the riddle, the wall opened, and I stepped out of the cave to find" —he gestured at the company— "our new friends."

"Then the trials were tailored for us." Aredel knew his brother could win a difficult fight, but Anadin required a lot of pushing before he switched into a killer's mindset. "What was the riddle?"

"Ah, it was a good one. It took almost the entire length of time allotted to me before I guessed it right." Anadin chuckled. "Had I not, I'd have lost my right hand." He rotated his wrist. "It was caught under a blade, you see."

Just like Anadin to tuck that little detail into his narration so late.

"The riddle?" Aredel pressed.

"Right." Anadin rubbed his hands together. "You get three guesses, then you lose."

"What do I lose?"

"Nothing. You just lose."

Low stakes, but Aredel agreed to play.

Anadin proudly shared the riddle, careful to enunciate each word:

> "Truly, no one is outstanding without me, nor
>   fortunate.
> I embrace all those whose hearts ask for me.
> He who goes without me goes about in the
>   company of death;
> and he who bears me will remain lucky forever.
> But I stand lower than earth and higher than
>   heaven."

As he turned the riddle over in his mind, weighing each word, an image of Jinji crossed Aredel's mind. "Humility. That is the answer."

Air exploded from Anadin's mouth. "How dare you guess it so fast! It took me an entire hour."

The Blood King chuckled. "You were under considerably more pressure, facing much greater risk—and besides, once you truly know someone who fits such an answer perfectly, you'll see it at once."

Anadin scowled. "I did know Jinji, lest you forget."

"Yes." Aredel's heart panged. "But not as well as you ought to have. There wasn't time. He was too ill..."

A faint grunt was Anadin's reply. They didn't speak again for a long time, each lost in his own thoughts.

THE FAE of the HaSharril Wood traveled through the night, stopping to rest twice and only briefly. They kept the brothers hydrated from a stream whose course they followed. The water was cool and sweet running down Aredel's throat.

Dawn flooded the world with golden light, filtering between the tall aspens, burnishing the mossy earth. Birds trilled a greeting. Anadin trilled back, his pitches nearly flawless. He kept practicing until the birds answered.

Still, the company marched on. Aredel was used to the grueling travel of war, but he kept one eye on Anadin in case the prince wearied. That seemed unlikely. Anadin had more vitality than he used to, now that he was freed from Father's oppressive reign.

And in love.

Aredel knew true love existed. He'd seen it often among peasants and artisans. He'd seen the heartbreak of losing it. Most prominent in his memory was Jinji's solitary pain, hidden except in the quiet hours of middle night, or in a moment he'd thought he was unobserved.

I want none of that pain.

As the Holy Prince of KryTeer, he'd faced ample trials. As Blood King, even more. Why add the weight of love to his bulging pack of responsibilities?

Yet Anadin is happier than he's been ever before in his life.

The prince offered up another high whistle to his feathered audience, then he tripped over a jutting root with a grunt. He struck the ground, laughing, before Aredel reached him. Anadin batted his brother off. "I'm all right. Just not watching my feet." The KryTeeran prince hefted himself upright and brushed off the twigs and dead leaves from his baggy pants. "What a beautiful wood this is. So alive."

It did seem to breathe a magic, like spices, between the boughs and trunks. While the woodland sounds were familiar, an ancient hush acted as a soothing counterpoint. An almost hallowed feeling permeated every speck of life.

If Aredel didn't hold his many burdens close, he might lose sight of them and wander off, content to let the HaSharril Wood heal his hidden wounds.

Fortunately, he was too disciplined to act on impulse.

They pressed on until the heightened rush of water quickened Anadin's step. Aredel followed, and the company of fae sped up to maintain their guard over their prisoners. Soon, the brothers reached a bridge arcing over the wide stream. Sunlight played on the water, and the stones beneath flashed and sparkled like gems.

"Oh," breathed Anadin. He pointed down. "Look."

Aredel blinked. The stones beneath the roaring stream *were* gems; many familiar, others not.

Thrissa stepped lightly onto the bridge, then turned toward them, a brightness in her silver-green eyes. "Come, KryTeerans. Sharo's camp lies yonder."

So close. Aredel's stomach clenched. Soon, he must accomplish his dark mission.

"Ah, good." Anadin trotted onto the bridge. "Rille will be worried for us. Come, *shaqin*."

Aredel glanced once more at the precious gems winking beneath the water, so close, yet undisturbed by the fae. Perhaps they didn't use them for money. He couldn't remember any details of fae monetary systems in Jinji's stories. But then, Jinji had put little stock in wealth.

Aredel stepped onto the bridge. It was a sturdy structure of pale wood polished until it gleamed. He'd never seen workmanship to match. Each plank was so closely hewn, he couldn't spot the seams as he thudded across the bridge.

On the other side, the world shimmered, then shifted from a view of the aspen forest. Instead, an open field of tents spread before him, its borders lined with trees. Palisades surrounded the encampment, while smoke rose from cookfires to the west of the large central tent. The odor of smelting metal wafted across the air, while the clang of hammers drifted up from the armorer nestled somewhere within the orderly rows of tents. Horses raced within the confines of a large corral, and pale blue pennants snapped high above the thriving camp, bearing the symbol of a golden crown broken in half.

Prince Sharo was preparing for battle against his kin. Not for his sake, but in the name of the True King of Shinac.

Standing before the force of arms, Aredel felt more at home than he had in nearly a year. He'd done all he could to repair the damage of his campaigns under Bloody Gyath's hand—and he knew Jinji would be pleased with his efforts. Yet he missed the thrill of battle. The scent of the ironworks. The camaraderie of the soldiers under his command.

What a creature I am to miss warfare.

He should feel shame, but he didn't. Merely resignation. He had been bred for battles. He must leave peace to others more suited.

A tinkling laugh pealed near his ear. Wrenching his eyes from the camp, he sought out the familiar sound. There. The handspan-sized fairy, Ashea, sparkled under the sun's rays. Her long lavender hair flowed behind her, and delicate gossamer wings beat the air at a rapid pace. She looked the same as the last time they'd met, when Aredel had entered Shinac with Prince Jetekesh nearly one year ago.

Her warm golden eyes crinkled with a smile before she dipped her head. "Welcome back to Shinac, Blood Prince."

"A fairy." Anadin's voice was breathless.

"*Shaqel*, this is Lady Ashea," said Aredel. He gestured to Anadin. "My lady, this is Prince Anadin of KryTeer, my brother."

"The resemblance is there." The little fairy lighted on Aredel's outstretched palm and curtsied to Anadin. "It is an honor, Prince of KryTeer." Her wings fluttered lazily like a butterfly upon a flower.

"How is Prince Sharo?" asked the Blood King.

"Busy," said Ashea, twisting to face him after a last lingering study of the younger KryTeeran man. "His father, King Darint, lusts after the fae lands—likely to burn them. Sharo has no choice but to defend his mother's folk. This army grows daily. Sharo is not here just now, but he is expected back soon."

Aredel lifted a brow. "He leaves his army at such a crucial time?"

"His captains are able, and his gift of persuasion may bring many more to our cause." Her wings batted the air in two quick beats. "And with you here, Blood Prince, he has another able hand or two."

"King," Anadin said. "My brother has taken the crown of KryTeer."

"Ah." Ashea searched Aredel's face. "King, only? Not emperor?"

"Things are changing in Nakania," Aredel said, skimming the palisades again.

Ashea flew into his view to hover at eye level, her wings humming faintly. "Dear Aredel," she said. "You are a startlingly humble man for one so mighty. Your words carry great weight, and with them, I feel hope. Perhaps the day when Shinac and Nakania unite once more is not so far off as I'd believed."

He answered with a grim smile. Perhaps, or perhaps not. He'd never reached for faith or hope; such delicate, fragile things would break in his iron grasp. He would leave those feelings for kinder folk—the ones like Jinji and Anadin. Like Kyella, Palan, Rille, and Sharo. Perhaps even like Jetekesh, who was growing into someone kind.

That thought gave Aredel pause. He shifted his eyes back to the war encampment. "Is Rille here?" he asked aloud. But his heart asked a different question.

"Yes, she arrived yestereve," the fairy said.

Aredel hardly heard her. Could a hardened person, such as a spoiled prince, change into something soft and sweet? Was there hope for Aredel of KryTeer?

He let the question hang.

Who could even answer?

Jinji was already dead.

CHAPTER 9
GINGERBREAD

On the fifth day of travel, Kajsa didn't wake up sore. Finally. Riding horses wasn't natural; not if the jostling was any indication. Yet the others endured it well enough.

She refused to complain. Words were difficult to utter anyway, so she didn't have to fight to hold her tongue. Her riding companion—the dark-skinned woman named Anenyasha—seemed content to keep quiet as well. The silence was comfortable during the long days of riding, and Kajsa fell into a routine that settled her nerves.

Until they entered a large village.

Crowds milled around the market square. Shouts and stringed instruments filled the air. Children raced around the edges of the market, pushing, shoving, and bullying each other.

Kajsa hunched against Anenyasha's back, avoiding eye contact with passersby.

Somewhere close, a dog barked. Kajsa's heart clenched at the memory of Raum. The wolf had been her dear friend and had given his life to save her. How she would someday tell Axel—her dearest human friend—that his pet wolf was dead, she didn't know. Dizziness washed over her. Dread cinched her throat.

No, don't panic. Think of something else.

Kajsa ducked her head and drew several breaths. Her mind moved to Prince Jetekesh, the young man she'd crossed the pass of the Snowblinds to warn. A light cocooned him, so brilliant it dazzled her to meet his eyes. Whenever he spoke, she expected lightning to strike under his power, but his voice was light and warm like a blazing campfire.

Kajsa's lips tugged up in a smile. She was frightened of nearly everyone, especially the Marked Prince. But this fear wasn't one of panic. Nor was it sinister. This was awe.

He's a real prince.

She'd heard stories clear back to Cavalin the Great and his three heirs. Wise kings, knights of valor, princes and princesses full of merriment and kindness. She often stole glances at Jetekesh riding ahead of her in the company.

But she didn't risk it now, in a village bustling with Shingese merchants and tradespeople. She clung to Anenyasha and prayed to the mountain gods that they would soon reach the edge of the village.

To her horror, Lord Emerin called a halt near the brimming village green. Kajsa jerked her head upright and stared at the market stuffed with colorful awnings and bleating voices in a language she didn't understand.

A hand brushed her arm. She jumped, then pried her eyes from the stalls to stare down into brilliant turquoise eyes. The Marked Prince smiled up at her from under his black cloak and spoke in her tongue. "We need supplies. Please come with me, Kajsa."

She swallowed, then uncurled her fingers from Anenyasha's

waist and dismounted with some difficulty. Riding with a dress was impractical.

Think of this as Tild. You're just making a quick trip into the market, then home again.

Except she was leagues away from a home she might never see again, and even if she did, it wouldn't be the same. Ingrid was dead. Axel had joined an army intent on plowing through the lush fields and towns of Shing to conquer all of Nakania. Raum was gone. And Kajsa had betrayed her own people. Her throat closed and her chest tightened.

As she allowed Prince Jetekesh to lead her toward the stalls, she swallowed hard. Aromas of fish, baking bread, and pungent incense slammed into her senses, making her eyes water. She watched the tips of her boots peep out from her heavy embroidered skirts as she walked.

The prince halted and rattled off words in the trade tongue. Kajsa couldn't understand most of the words; it had steered too far away from what Jetekesh now called the Old Tongue, the first language of Nakania. The language she knew.

A second voice answered the prince, probably a merchant.

Kajsa hoisted her head and tensed. She'd expected food or weapons or maybe tack for the horses—not ladies' dresses, cloaks, shoes. Rich bolts of silk were stacked in rows on either side of the stall. Kajsa's fingers itched to touch the cool blue damask cloth sandwiched at eye level between pale yellow and crimson floral bolts.

Jetekesh and the female merchant haggled for several minutes, Lord Emerin interjecting once or twice, then coins passed hands.

The prince turned a proud smile on Kajsa. "She'll outfit you for the Clanslands. Your clothes will be too heavy and warm as we travel farther north."

Kajsa froze, startled by his consideration. At the Shingese palace in Kyon Taro, the imperial tailors had gifted her several new dresses, but none had been suitable for accompanying the Marked Prince to the Clanslands, so she'd left the beautiful things behind.

The merchant woman came around the stall. She flung words at Kajsa while she pinched and prodded her for measurements, then the woman stooped behind the stall and came out with several plain dresses, as well as tunics and pants. Kajsa stared at the foreign styles, and her training as a seamstress flooded her blood. She plucked up a tunic to admire the cut and fabric before the merchant wrenched it from her hands and barked more words at her.

Kajsa glanced toward Jetekesh, but he'd wandered to the next stall to admire the leatherwork on display. Sir Lafe stuck to his side. Lord Emerin remained near Kajsa, but his eyes scanned the green, likely to give her as much privacy as possible in such a busy square.

The merchant's torture continued. She shoved Kajsa behind a wall of curtains, then joined her in the cramped space to fit and tuck and pin.

At last, Kajsa exited the curtained space wearing a tailored Shingese-style tunic and calf-length pants, strange stockings and slippers. She clutched a bundle of other clothes: Two dresses and another tunic set, a heavy cloak, a lighter cloak, boots, and gloves rather than her mittens. Several undergarments—so much lighter than she was used to—were tucked carefully within the bundle to hide them from observers.

The merchant plucked up Kajsa's old things and tucked them behind her stall counter. Kajsa stared, horror dancing through her.

"I forgot to mention," Jetekesh said, approaching. "Part of our bargain included her keeping your old clothes. I hope you don't mind. She was very insistent. She's really taken with the embroidery."

Kajsa's ears burned. "Y-yes, that's fine. I can embroider these easily enough." She shifted the bundle of clothes.

Jetekesh eyed them, then blinked. "Let me carry them."

Kajsa stiffened. Was it proper to let a prince take her burden? On a generous day, Axel might have offered, but she suspected princes didn't stoop to such menial tasks.

"It's fine," she said, several heartbeats late.

Lord Emerin and Sir Lafe flanked the two youths as they moved back toward the wagon at the edge of the green.

"We should buy some food before we leave." Emerin glanced at the high sun. "It'll save time on the road—and frankly, I'd enjoy anyone else's cooking right now other than my own."

The prince chuckled. "No offense, my lord, but so would I."

Kajsa was touched that they carried on speaking the Old Tongue; it could only be for her sake that they did. She listened in polite silence, still trying to level her thoughts after dealing with the merchant and the crowds. And the gifts. The clothes in her arms were double the amount she'd ever owned at one time—with the brief exception of the gifts in Kyon Taro. But she doubted she'd ever see those again.

They reached the wagon, and Kajsa piled the clothes inside, then climbed in after them to attempt fitting them into her small satchel. A quick examination proved that would be impossible.

Kethalas watched her from his perch against the fore of the wagon bed. "You can put a few things in my satchel. There's room."

Jetekesh poked his head between the canvas flaps. "Problems?"

Kajsa shook her head, but Kethalas spoke over her silence. "She needs a bigger pack."

The prince's eyes settled on Kajsa. "Emerin and I are going to bring food back. I'll see about a proper satchel for you."

"Thank you. But I can make do—"

"I'm certain you could," Jetekesh said, "but it's unnecessary." He slipped his head out, and the flap settled into place.

Kajsa sat still and breathed. She wasn't used to so much attention, so much noise, so much—everything.

Kethalas chuckled. "Don't feel bad. It's good for him."

"Who?"

"The prince. I understand his mother coddled him. Very nearly ruined him. He's making so many strides now—and looking out for others offers the most growth. So let him help you." The man's silver eyes were bright in the sunlight bleeding in through the canvas. "It might be very good for you too."

Kajsa played with the hem of her extra tunic folded on her lap. "He...seems kind."

"He is." Kethalas shifted, wincing. He settled into a new position, one knee propped up, with his arm resting on it. "His father is a good man—perhaps one of the most generous and genuine people to come out of the Royal House of Amantier in decades. But his marriage was political, and the queen was an unpleasant woman." His smile crooked. "That may be an extreme understatement."

Kajsa fumbled with the sleeve of one new dress, examining the close stitching. "Was? Is the queen dead?"

"Yes. I understand she was killed nearly a year ago."

Sympathy gutted Kajsa. She knew too well the loss of a loved one. "He must be suffering."

"I imagine so." Kethalas rested his head against the wooden wall and shut his eyes. "I'd best sleep before we start moving again. Rest is hard to find when you're being jostled about."

She nodded, fetched her needlework kit and a small hoop, then scampered out of the wagon bed to let him slumber in peace.

Moving toward the wagon seat, she clasped her hands and watched Harn brush down the horses as he whispered to them in soothing tones.

Kajsa hadn't interacted with Harn much. He couldn't speak the Old Tongue. But he smiled at her often, and he'd let her feed the horses several times. Everyone in the company was either pleasant, quiet, or considerate—or all three at once. She'd spent most of her life avoiding interactions, but in such a small circle, with people aiming for the same goal as herself, she'd become at least a little comfortable among them.

Where Dakarai and Anenyasha had vanished, she didn't know. Rather than seek anyone else out in the bustling rows across the wide green space, Kajsa found a patch of shade under a tall oak tree, and she set to work embroidering a design into the thigh-length hem of her tunic front. Embroidery always calmed her nerves, and Kajsa could use some calming. The methodical pull, tuck, pull of her needle set her mind into a meditative state, muting the shouts and clamor of the field.

She'd just finished her third yellow flower when a voice broke the silence.

"You're very skilled at that."

Kajsa jumped halfway out of her skin, pricking her finger in the process. Stifling a yelp, she jerked her head up, stuck her finger between her lips, and sucked at the bead of blood. Copper teased her tastebuds.

"Sorry." Prince Jetekesh crouched before her, holding out a small piping hot pie. "Hungry?"

Kajsa's mouth watered, and she accepted the meat pie with murmured thanks. The prince set aside a large satchel, then flopped down beside her, and accepted a second pie from Sir Lafe who stood nearby. The knight munched on his own pasty while he surveyed the distant crowds.

A quick glance told Kajsa that Emerin, Dakarai, and

Anenyasha had returned and were sharing their sustenance with Harn and—presumably—Kethalas.

Nibbling at her meal, Kajsa found herself smiling. She rarely had the opportunity to enjoy something so delicate and flaky. She could cook pies, but wheat was hard to come by in Norva.

"I indulged in a treat," Jetekesh said, his eyes lazily tracking a bee as it hummed past them.

Was this not treat enough? She sank her teeth into another melting bite.

He didn't seem to mind her silence. Lifting a cloth, he unwrapped it to show her several small, round, dark brown confections.

She blinked. "What are those?"

"Something called gingerbread. Usually, I only find it in Amantier during the Holy Nocturne, but it appears to be a summer treat in Shing." His eyes shone with excitement. "Finish your food, and I'll share it with everyone."

She obeyed, consuming her food faster than she'd wanted to—but she'd never tried gingerbread before, and judging by his enthusiasm, it sounded sumptuous. Using the grass to wipe the remnants of her pie from her fingers, she shifted to face the Marked Prince.

He'd divided the gingerbread rounds into equal sections and proffered one to her. "It has a strong flavor," he said. "Best savor it."

Licking the gooey candy, the sharp taste exploded across her tongue. She almost shuddered. Yes, it was certainly ginger, but strangely sweet. Honeyed, perhaps? She licked it again, then took a small nibble. Strange, but delicious. Kajsa savored each tiny bite. The sweet confection warmed her soul.

Jetekesh seemed to relish his bites just as much. The others examined their portions, then plopped them in their mouths. All but Harn, who tucked his away in a handkerchief, probably for later.

Dakarai approached. “That is a very tasty dessert, Your Highness.”

Jetekesh grinned. “A favorite of mine. My mother was obsessed with gingerbread a few years ago.” His smile weakened, but he pressed on. “My Lord Father indulged her. It was just before he took sick.” He halted, then sighed. “Before she *poisoned* him.” He seemed to state it for his own sake—to bring himself to believe it.

Kajsa’s stomach knotted. Poisoned by his own wife? Who could do such a dreadful thing to their spouse? Kethalas had called their marriage a political alliance. She’d heard of such things in the higher echelons of the Norvian Cantons. The Archon of Frostfire was even now seeking an appropriate match for his daughter which had nothing to do with love or affection, only political advantage.

What kind of advantage is it when a wife tries to kill her husband?

Luckily, Kajsa wasn’t anyone significant. If she did marry, it would be because she chose it. Her mind flitted to Axel, then skirted away. The knots in her stomach tightened. He sought war and ruin over resolution and peace.

Kajsa realized she was wringing her hands.

Don’t think about him just now. He’s far, far away.

“Oh.” Emerin pulled something from a pouch at his hip. “I got these for you, Kajsa.” He stooped toward her and turned his palm to reveal three colorful spools of thread. “Figured you might want more options. You’ll find no better threads than in Shing.”

She stared, heart stuttering. The vibrant purple, deep red, and rare blue hues were breathtaking. “Th-thank you. So very much.” Taking the spools with care, a mist filled her vision.

“Well,” Lord Emerin said, stretching as he straightened. “Shall we be underway, my prince?”

"Yes." Jetekesh brushed crumbs from his lap, then sprang to his feet with the grace of a swordsman. He turned and offered his hand to Kajsa. "We need to keep ahead of the *vashalan*." His eyes darkened as he spat out the last word.

A shadow crossed Kajsa's heart. The *vashalan* had been tailing them since Kyon Taro. What kept them from attacking, she couldn't say. But they wouldn't hold back forever.

Not those monsters.

CHAPTER 10
What Can Be Seen

Jetekesh landed hard in the dirt, teeth clenched to avoid biting his tongue. His sword thudded nearby on the road.

"Better." Emerin tapped the hard-packed earth with the covered tip of his broadsword. "But you're still favoring your left side. Distribute the weight more evenly."

"I'm trying." Jetekesh's teeth were still clenched, and his words came out in a low growl. He twisted to his knees, grimacing as his tailbone throbbed, then he eased himself to his feet with an exaggerated effort. Maybe Emerin would take pity on him.

"Again," the lord of the keep said in glacial tones.

Jetekesh liked Emerin. He did not like this side of the man.

"I think I'm done for the night." Jetekesh stooped to claim his sword from the ground.

"You don't get to rest in the middle of a battle, Highness." Emerin's eyes were narrow slits, his stance ready for a lunge.

Groaning, Jetekesh hefted his blade. His muscles protested. *But this is what you want, Kesh,* he told himself. *You need to become strong enough to protect others.*

“Engage,” Emerin said.

Jetekesh charged, swinging his blade from the right. He caught Emerin’s sword, digging his weight into his right foot—then he dropped to one knee and hefted his sword higher. Cut off contact. Rolled under the opposing sword. Straightened behind the enemy, and aimed for Emerin’s spine.

The keep lord spun and caught the weapon with his own. Covered metal vibrated. Emerin’s grin was feral now; the icy exterior had melted. “Good. Excellent.” He shoved Jetekesh back with his sword, then kicked out. His boot smashed into the prince’s shoulder.

Jetekesh rolled and fell spread-eagle against the dirt. Stars laughed at him in the velvet sky.

“But you become vulnerable if you fail the killing stroke.”

Jetekesh sat up, dragging his sword with him. At least he hadn’t lost his weapon this time. He staggered to his feet, tailbone aching more. He lifted his blade. “Again.”

Emerin knocked him down thrice more, but Jetekesh got closer to slitting the man’s throat each time. Well, he imagined he did, at least. He certainly wanted to.

“That’s enough for tonight,” Emerin announced while Jetekesh lay sprawled across the ground, trying to pick out which bones weren’t bruised.

Sir Lafe came forward and offered Jetekesh a hand. The knight lifted him with little effort. Spitting out dirt, Jetekesh tried to smooth his hair from his face. He must look like a beggar. Still, bathing could wait until after supper. He was too famished to care about his appearance.

Jetekesh limped to the campfire and eased onto his saddle between Dakarai and Kajsa. Before they’d left the village the previous day, he’d offered to buy a horse and saddle for the young Norvian woman, but Kajsa didn’t seem enthused about learning to ride. Instead, he’d purchased a clever fold-out chair. She used it to sit at the fire with the rest of the company, her head several inches above everyone else's when she didn't duck down—which she usually did.

Tonight, she was wrapped in a thin blanket to fend off a spring breeze, though Jetekesh welcomed the cool fingers of wind through his hair and down his collar. His cheeks burned from exertion, and his heart rate was still rapid.

Kajsa offered him a shy smile, which he returned with a pained grin.

"Food's going to take a minute longer," Emerin said, stooping over the trivet where Anenyasha's rice roiled. "The peat moss is damp. It's not burning hot."

"Why aren't we burning bamboo?" Jetekesh asked, staring longingly at the pot.

Dakarai chuckled. "You would not enjoy the sound of *that* wood burning, Your Highness. All and sundry would know our precise location in seconds."

Emerin grunted. "Truth. It's not unlike Shingese firecrackers."

Jetekesh tried to remain patient while his stomach conjured up bellowing noises loud enough to wake the dead saints. He hunched forward to mute the sounds.

"Your Highness?" Kajsa's small voice wafted toward him like a stray breeze.

He glanced at her without straightening up. "Yes?"

She stared at him, wide-eyed, like she hadn't initiated conversation, then she dropped her head. "Forgive me. I shouldn't pry."

Jetekesh eased himself upright. "Did you have a question?"

"I... well, um... Kethalas said your mother is—is gone."

Jetekesh's lungs hitched, and he turned to study the sputtering fire. "That's right."

"Did...she... How did...?" The girl's voice faded into silence.

The fire popped and glowing embers climbed above the boiling pot before fluttering back down. He tracked one until it lost its spark. "She was stabbed through by one of the Blood King's men. She'd been trying to kill Jinji Wanderlust."

Kajsa tipped her head to one side. "An enemy? Or a friend?"

He pulled his eyes from the fire. "You mean Jinji?"

She nodded.

"Her enemy. My friend. Jinji was a storyteller true."

Kajsa's eyes widened. "Like Cavalin's taleweaver?"

Jetekesh jolted. "Cavalin's... Did he have a taleweaver?"

"According to legend, yes," she said, then tensed. "You said... was. Is your friend also—"

"Yes," Jetekesh whispered. "He was sick. Very sick." Panic shot through him, but he choked it back. He wouldn't focus on the implications for himself just now. He couldn't.

"I'm so sorry." She twisted her blanket around her thumb. "Grief is the deepest kind of pain, I think."

"You've lost people, too, I take it."

The faintest nod was her answer.

Stupid question, he thought. *Who would travel alone over the mountains and leave their family behind?* She was likely an orphan.

"I'm sorry," he said. "It *is* the deepest kind of pain."

Words always sounded so hollow, so utterly useless, against such sorrow. Jetekesh tipped his head back to eye the stars winking into life against the purple sky. His damaged ear throbbed, and he rubbed it until the ache subsided.

"Food's ready."

Jetekesh rose with the rest to accept his bowl of chicken, carrots, and rice. The fare of Shing was peculiar, but he could appreciate the warmth of his evening meals. And the rice was starting to grow on him.

Settling again on his saddle, his sore muscles protested. As bruised as he was, did he even resemble himself these days?

Mother would faint straight away to see me in this condition.

He expected guilt to pulse through him with the thought—he

half-expected her voice to chide him—but only his stomach rumbled for more food. He stuffed his mouth and basked in the silence.

Until howls filled the air. Close. Deadly.

Emerin rose from his crouch beside the fire. His hand fell to his sword.

Jetekesh clutched his spoon in mid-air, straining his good ear for any rustling sounds in the trees. Few wagons or peddlers had been seen on the road since the last village, and Jetekesh had assumed that was because little compelled them so far north—but what if less savory reasons kept them from traveling?

Setting his bowl aside, Jetekesh stood along with the rest of the company.

"Harn, please grab the holy water from the wagon," the keep lord said.

The wagoner obeyed without a word, then returned, clutching a glass flask. He tossed it to Emerin, who snatched it from the air.

Dakarai flexed his fingers around his jagged spear, beads and feathers clacking. "It is nice of the beasts to inform us of their nearness." He clicked a few words at Anenyasha. She replied in her usual clipped manner as she ran a thumb along her spear tip to test it.

Howls sang out again, closer. Jetekesh's blood ran more chill.

He glanced at Kethalas, still seated among the standing company. The man-dragon studied the treeline intently, then blinked, and turned his face to meet Jetekesh's gaze. Kethalas flashed him a fanged grin.

"Do you need help getting back into the wagon?" asked Jetekesh.

Kethalas shook his head. "No need. I can fight if I'm careful."

Jetekesh grimaced, then glanced at Kajsa. "And you?"

The young woman took a steadying breath. “I will take my chances out here. I don’t wish to be pinned inside the wagon.”

That made sense. Jetekesh nodded, then drew a spare dagger from his belt sheath. “It’s not much. Have you ever used any weapon?”

She tipped one shoulder up in a half-shrug. “Axel was teaching me archery before he grew too busy with his hunts.”

“Then, how is this for a deal? We make it out of this fight alive, and I’ll teach you what I know. A long-range weapon would be helpful right now.” Losing Yin’s precise aim was an unwelcome consequence of Song’s decision to remain in her homeland to prepare for war, but it couldn’t be helped.

Jetekesh was fair with a bow, but rusty. Mother had detested the idea of him callusing his fingers in practice. Perhaps teaching Kajsa would improve his own aim.

Eyeing the wagon, Jetekesh weighed which to use now—his sword or the bow and arrows hanging inside the conveyance.

On impulse, he darted around Kajsa and circled to the back of the wagon. Sir Lafe’s heavy footfalls followed close. Jetekesh climbed inside the wooden contraption, snatched up the single bow and accompanying arrows, then scrambled back outside just as the howls rose again. They were so close. Jetekesh suspected he’d soon spot the gleam of their red eyes among the trees’ shadows. He clutched his bow tighter.

Lafe met the prince’s eyes, nodded his approval, then gestured to the top of the wagon. “Better aim up there.”

“You’re right.” Jetekesh hoisted himself up the side of the wagon, careful to keep his footing as the contraption rocked and swayed. He reached the rounded wooden roof, positioned himself squarely in the center of the dome, and pulled a wrist guard over his hand.

There. The flash of glowing eyes winked at him near the forested edge of the road. He set his sights toward the rustle.

"Sir Lafe," he called.

"Yes, Your Highness?"

"Send Kajsa up here." He pulled the guard strings tight.

"Yes, Your Highness."

Jetekesh risked a glance toward the company below. Emerin's broadsword gleamed in the firelight. Would the man wield fire again? Could he? Close by, Dakarai and Anenyasha sported smiles, like this was no different than a fox hunt. Kajsa raced toward the wagon, her borrowed dagger glinting. Harn held the horses steady, his whip gripped in white knuckles. Kethalas's back was turned toward Jetekesh, so the prince couldn't read his face, but he could imagine the dragon's inhuman grin.

I'm in the company of lunatics again. Jetekesh realized he was grinning, too. Adrenaline rushed through his veins. *How far I've fallen, eh, Mother?*

Canine eyes met Jetekesh's gaze in the dark. The odor of rot and sulfur coiled over the air. Jetekesh nocked his arrow. Took aim. Drew his string.

Fired.

The arrow struck the *vashalan*'s skull with a thunk. The beast thrashed in the undergrowth. One down. Jetekesh nocked a second arrow. Skimmed the treeline. Squinted into the gloom.

A shadow flitted past. He took aim but held his bowstring taut.

The wagon jostled. He swayed, trying to keep his balance. A second later, Kajsa climbed up onto the arced roof. She fell to her knees near where he stood, clutching the dagger, a faint look of panic bright in her pale eyes.

Jetekesh offered a tight smile, then turned back to the trees. A flash of glowing eyes skirted by. He adjusted his hold on the bowstring, licked his lips, and searched the gloom. Perspiration beaded his brow. His tender fingers ached under the string's bite.

The night had fallen silent. The scent of rot clung to the air like an unseen vapor, digging under Jetekesh's eyeballs as he tried not to blink. His nose wrinkled to fend off the odor, and he breathed through his mouth.

Foliage rustled.

Vashalan exploded from the trees and surrounded the company. Dozens of them. More. Jetekesh unleashed an arrow, striking one creature, then he reached for another arrow to take down another.

Snarls and growls filled the air. Below the wagon, Emerin barked commands. Someone wielded a torch, and Jetekesh resisted an impulse to follow the trail of sparks with his eyes as it swung toward a single *vashalan*.

His third arrow missed its mark. Jetekesh swore under his breath and nocked another, mentally counting the arrows he had left.

The wagon rocked. Jetekesh staggered forward, swinging his arms for balance, while desperately clutching his bow to avoid dropping it. A *vashalan* caught his eye. He corrected his stance and aimed. Behind him, Kajsa shrieked. Startled by the sound, Jetekesh's fourth arrow missed its mark and struck the ground near the front wagon wheel.

Spinning, Jetekesh found the hideous snout of one beast jutting up as it dragged itself onto the wagon dome. Bones gaped through its matted, oily fur, and its red eyes bored into Jetekesh as though the flames of the two hells burned within its soul.

Fingers slick with sweat, Jetekesh groped for another arrow, but Kajsa swiped at the *vashalan* with her dagger before he could aim.

The beast snapped its jaws at the girl. Kajsa flinched back, then swiped again. Fangs slammed over the blade, shattering the metal. Kajsa dropped the dagger hilt, then lurched backward to avoid the monster's teeth. As she moved, the wagon jostled again, and Jetekesh struggled to keep from tumbling off. The *vashalan* nearly lost its hold on the edge of the sloped roof.

An idea struck him.

"Kajsa," Jetekesh said.

When the girl met his gaze, the fear fled from her eyes. She scrambled to the front corner of the wagon, caught the edge, and started to rock, back, forth, back. Jetekesh dropped to his knees to snatch the other edge.

The beast slipped and dug its claws into the rooftop. Slivers of wood broke loose.

Still kneeling, Jetekesh nocked an arrow and unleashed it on the *vashalan*.

Thunk.

The beast lurched back, then tumbled from the wagon top.

Kajsa stopped rocking, and Jetekesh sprang to his feet to survey the battle below. More and more of the nightmarish canines poured in from the woods. Shivers tracked up Jetekesh's spine as he tried to count the numbers.

Dakarai and Anenyasha stood back-to-back, spears slashing and gutting every *vashalan* who charged them. Emerin wielded his broadsword and a torch, fending off all comers. The glass flask lay near a heap of beasts, empty of holy water.

A whip cracked—then a scream sounded on the wagon's far side.

Jetekesh darted across the bowed roof. Below, Kethalas ripped a vashalan in half with his clawed hands, then darted toward the source of the sound. Too late. Jetekesh's heart throttled his throat. Harn lay across the ground, entrails ripped from his midsection.

Bile burned in Jetekesh's mouth and he twisted away, swallowing hard.

Kajsa caught his wrist. "Lafe."

Jetekesh tracked her pointing finger. The knight was

surrounded by a horde of the hellish beasts, sword stained with gore.

Unthinking, Jetekesh dropped his bow, unsheathed his sword, pounded over the wagon roof, and flung himself off the edge. He sailed over the air for a breathless moment, then landed with a crunch on the back of one *vashalan*. The creature buckled, howling. Jetekesh drove his sword tip through its skull.

Dragging himself off the corpse, he plowed through another beast, then another. Adrenaline surged through his mind, clearing it of every distraction. He cut down another *vashalan* and reached Lafe's side.

The knight stared at him, lips parted, then he wheeled to stab at another creature.

It's not ending. Jetekesh probed the ground. Too many of the fell beasts had climbed back to their feet, wounded but not dead.

Jetekesh ground his teeth. Unless they found an answer soon, the company would be massacred.

His chest throbbed. Harn was already dead.

The prince found Emerin. The man slashed and hacked at a cluster of *vashalan*.

Why won't you summon flames again?

Sir Lafe cut down another creature, then wrenched his blade free.

An arrow pierced another beast's neck. Jetekesh whirled to find Kajsa standing atop the wagon, another arrow ready to fly from the bow she'd claimed. He rammed his sword through the chest of a lunging *vashalan*.

But the beasts kept coming.

We're losing. We'll die.

Moonlight filtered through a thin veil of clouds, painting the ground silver. Blood spattered the road, and Jetekesh's fingers were slick with it.

A howl stabbed the night sky. The beasts faltered, then fell back.

Something glimmered in Jetekesh's periphery. He spun toward it, and his heart stammered to a halt. The cloaked figure stood amid the carnage, golden eyes peering out at Jetekesh, spearing his soul.

"*You can end this, Marked Prince,*" whispered a sorrowful voice in his head. "*Surrender yourself to me, and I will call off my pets.*"

Jetekesh grimaced. "Surrender, how?"

Lafe's hand fell to his shoulder. "What do you see?"

"Our enemy," growled Jetekesh. "He wants me to surrender to him."

"*Slit your throat. End your life. Do this, and your companions will be free to do as they wish.*"

Jetekesh scoffed. "You're insane. For a hundred reasons, I won't do as you ask. What drives you to hunt me like a fox? Do I frighten you?"

Silence fell, then the cloaked figure stirred. "*Yes.*"

Jetekesh didn't know how to reply. He hadn't expected honesty. Drawing his shoulders back, he hefted his chin, tapping into his training as a prince. "I cannot comply with your demands. We'll take our chances."

"*Very well then. Die together.*" The image of the man rippled, then faded away.

Jetekesh whirled toward Emerin. "He plans to end us now!"

The song of the *vashalan* raced to the sky. The keep lord thrust his torch above his head and called out strange words.

Lightning answered, striking the blazing torch.

Emerin strained under the bolt as flames rose—climbing the streak of lightning—then broke free to lift in a wrathful column of fire.

The *vashalan* faltered, hackles lifted, teeth bared in rolling growls.

Emerin gritted his teeth and swung his torch like a sword. The flames rode the sky, hot enough to brush Jetekesh's cheeks. The *vashalan* fell back under the tirade.

At the same moment, Kethalas took to the air, still in human form except for leathery wings protruding from his back. He conjured ice in his palms and blasted spear-length icicles at the *vashalan* sneaking up on Emerin's back. Jetekesh nearly called Kethalas back, afraid the dragon would reopen his wounds—but the prince understood the dragon's desperation to act.

Yips and howls answered the frigid assault. Several beasts slipped across a streak of ice glazing the rutted road.

It isn't enough. They'll keep coming.

Skimming the sky, Jetekesh noted the pallor of Kethalas's skin. The dragon couldn't stay aloft for long. Dropping his eyes, the prince sought Emerin's face. It was taut, a sheen of sweat bright on his brow, eyes such a vivid green they might be glowing.

What can I do?

Jinji's voice entered his mind like a faint song. "*Look for truth, Jetekesh, and you will find it.*"

Truth. What truth was here beyond approaching death?

If I don't look, I won't know.

He scanned the road, the *vashalan*, his battling friends—and then, he fell still. He looked again.

Only a dozen *vashalan* corralled the company—the rest were phantoms. Jetekesh's arrows jutted out from tree trunks, and the road itself, where he thought he'd aimed true.

So, Navolleth deals in lies, does he?

Jetekesh gripped his sword tight and bolted toward the congestion of creatures surrounding Dakarai and Anenyasha. Those Emerin fought were illusions.

"Lord Emerin, direct your flames here!" Jetekesh called, ramming his blade through the spine of one very real beast.

Emerin didn't question his prince. He wheeled away from his

battle, aiming the torch at the threat Jetekesh indicated. Flames curled over the *vashalan*, and one let out a roaring scream as its matted fur curled.

Jetekesh swung hard at its throat. His sword bit deep into bone and flesh. He wrenched his weapon loose and the creature fell at his feet. The prince moved on, not glancing back as the whoosh of flames followed on his heels, scorching his prey.

He swiped at another *vashalan* while Dakarai speared yet another.

"Not that one," Jetekesh called out as Anenyasha started toward a phantom creature. "There." He jabbed a finger at a real *vashalan* near her.

Reading his tones, Anenyasha veered to attack the proper enemy. From the top of the wagon, Kajsa shot her last arrow to strike one *vashalan* creeping up on Jetekesh. He whirled in time to watch it fall.

Chasing down the last of the pack took moments longer. As Kethalas encased the last true *vashalan* in ice, Dakarai speared its heart. Immediately, the phantom images vanished.

Panting, Jetekesh surveyed the field of victory, seeking any stray creatures.

Emerin's torch sputtered. The lord sank to his knees, trembling, then he tossed the smoking torch. His blond hair stuck out in a sweaty tangle, and he gasped for air, then collapsed.

Kethalas landed beside him and knelt. "That taxed him a great deal." The dragon looked up to meet Jetekesh's gaze. "He'll likely need to stay in the wagon several days if last time was any way to judge."

"Agreed." Jetekesh dug out a cloth to wipe his sword clean. "Lafe, please help Kethalas to get him there. Dakarai, will you and Anenyasha help me heap up the remaining corpses? We'd best burn them." His gaze cut to Harn lying across the ground near the wagon, and a pang ripped through him.

Rubbing his sweaty palms against his hosen, Jetekesh turned away. *See to the refuse first. Then we can give Harn a proper burial.*

He snatched a *vashalan*'s leg and dragged it toward the concentration of canine bodies. Its bulk was even heavier than he'd expected, as though the ground tried to claim the other-worldly creature. His grip slipped twice on oily fur.

"How did you know?" Dakarai heaved a *vashalan* corpse atop another.

Jetekesh's brow furrowed before his mind caught up. "Oh, do you mean about their actual number?"

"Yes."

He dragged the corpse next to Dakarai's. "Jinji said to look for truth. I found it."

The clansman's white teeth flashed in a grim smile. "Marked, indeed. No doubt the man of the mountain will not be pleased when he learns that you saw through his trick."

"No doubt." Jetekesh walked toward a corpse, fingers itching at the prospect of touching another filthy hide.

I wonder what other tricks he'll attempt—or will he adjust his methods, once he discovers my Sight?

Certainly, Navolleth wouldn't give up after one defeat. Not when he wanted Jetekesh dead.

CHAPTER II
SPARROW

Rille sat munching on a fluffy roll, watching Aredel and Anadin approach her across the wide war camp. She perked up and stood from the chair outside the mess tent, smoothed her skirts with one hand, and swallowed her bite of bread.

"Anadin!" she called.

The KryTeeran prince picked up his pace, trotting around cookfires and waving his hand over the air. "Sahala!" *His sparrow.* He always called her that.

Rille let herself smile, too excited to stifle the emotions brimming on the surface. Anadin was safe. Aredel, too. And they were all together in Shinac, the fae country considered a myth in Nakania. She'd been so jealous of Cousin Jetekesh when he'd come here nearly a year ago. Now, she could swap stories with him...if she ever got back home.

Reality sank back in. She wasn't in Shinac by choice. Aredel must assassinate Prince Sharo, or the *Unsielie*'s hostages would die—including herself.

Anadin reached Rille and scooped her up into his arms. A startled laugh exploded from her mouth, and warmth spread through her. The prince's innocence was a boon to her soul; Anadin always did the unpredictable. On the heels of Rille's father's death, Anadin's exuberant affection and Yeshton's quiet devotion were what kept her treading the waters of grief.

Rille wrapped her arms around Anadin's head and laid her cheek against his scalp. He twirled her around twice, a slow, gentle turn; squeezed her tight; then lowered her to the ground. King Aredel looked on, smiling faintly.

She handed Anadin the remaining half of her roll. "Shinacian food is excellent."

Anadin grinned. "I'm pleased to hear it." He took an exaggerated bite while his dark eyes roved the ordered rows of tents and the high log palisades. "I understand Prince Sharo isn't here."

"Not just now." Rille shifted her gaze to Aredel. "Which is lucky."

"Yet short-lived," Aredel replied. "Lady Ashea said he is likely to return in a matter of days."

Rille lowered her voice. "Have you said anything?"

"Of course not." His eyes narrowed. "You?"

"No. I wouldn't risk Artassa and Anadin." She would only have warned Sharo directly, had she been given the chance. Rille turned a sharp look on the younger KryTeeran royal. "And *you* had better keep quiet as well. At least until we think up a good plan."

"Keep quiet about what?" asked Anadin, after swallowing the last bite of roll. "Oh, Sahala. Did you know I solved a riddle? It seems I'm actually clever from time to time."

Rille's face softened. "I've no doubt you are."

He chuckled, then sniffed at the air. "That might be lamb. I'm famished. Let's eat." He trotted toward the mess tent, and Rille tripped after him, leaving Aredel behind. She glanced back when she reached the tent flap and found the Blood King standing still, his deep brown eyes lifted heavenward. His eyebrows were pinched together, his hands clenched at his sides.

What will you do, Aredel, faced with such a choice?

She slipped inside the tent and followed Anadin to the line of knights waiting for their morning meal.

CHAPTER 12
UPROOTED PAST

Aredel spent the day sparring, first with Anadin, then with any knight willing to try. He defeated all of them, one by one, and the frustration boiling within him died down to a simmer.

But in the silence of camp after night fell, his emotions spilled over again.

In the dark, Aredel sat outside the palisades, facing north and the flickering lights of a sky bursting with stars above a range of mountains. Pale fairy lights darted around the trees surrounding the wide field where Sharo's encampment spent its days training and crafting weapons.

The Blood King had intentionally left his curved sword and daggers inside the tent Thrissa had provided for Aredel, Anadin, and Rille. He didn't want to take his wrath out on some unsuspecting sentry if they came too near.

What was he supposed to do? He'd reached Sharo's camp well before he'd thought he would. Only a few days separated him from the horrific task set upon him. Visions of Artassa within the cold confines of the *Unsielie* fortress beset his thoughts.

Should he explain himself to Sharo once the prince returned to his army? Or should Aredel merely run the elven prince through? Surely, the *Unsielie* would know the moment his task was accomplished. But would they keep their word in the end?

"Troubled thoughts?"

Aredel was on his feet before he registered he'd moved. He narrowed a look on the fae woman, Thrissa, standing nearby, wrapped in a cloak of deep green velvet. Her silver-green eyes pierced him with a look that peeled back layers of his soul.

"Often," he answered in a quiet rumble.

Thrissa tipped her head, then turned her gaze outward to the gray and blue hues of night. "You smell of blood."

"So I've often heard."

"Is it true you bathe in the blood of your victims?"

"Only the strong ones."

She studied him from the corner of one eye, and a faint smile cracked her lips. "And are you as fearless as the stories say?"

"No." He pinned his sights on a bright star. "I am always afraid."

"Of what?"

Aredel lifted his shoulders in a shrug. "Of losing the few things that live within my heart."

"I didn't expect such honesty."

He turned toward her. "Do the stories call me a liar?"

"No." Thrissa folded her arms beneath her cloak. "Forgive my assumption."

He inclined his head, then sought out the bright star again. Jinji could probably have offered a tale surrounding its birth. On impulse, Aredel pointed. "What is that one called? The brightest."

Thrissa tracked his finger. "Ah, that. The Light of Valliath. 'Tis the birth star of the True King. It appeared when he issued the first cry of life."

Somehow, Aredel had sensed as much. "Have you seen the Hold of Valliath?"

"Oh, yes," said Thrissa. "Many ages ago, before the Shard Kingdom was formed. Before a blight seized these lands. When the True King was but a youth."

"You're rather old, then."

Thrissa gave a soft laugh. "So I am."

"I've heard tales of Valliath." Aredel let his gaze skim the shadowed forest. Fairies danced in a circle near its border. "Jinji of Shing weaved many stories of Shinac. He told me of the light and the darkness."

"Jinji wields a rare gift. None since Cavalin's taleteller have been so blessed. He is favored by the True King, 'tis said."

Aredel spun to face her. "You speak of Jinji in the present. Does he live here, transcending his death in Nakania?"

The elf's smooth face tightened, then she frowned. "Of that, I have no knowledge. Apologies if I have offered up false hope. I did not know he had died."

Aredel turned away, squeezing his eyes shut. If only he'd known sooner that Jinji was his elder brother. If only he'd tried harder to convince the storyteller not to push his frail body past its limits.

If only...

So many regrets.

"I will leave you to your thoughts," whispered Thrissa.

Aredel opened his mouth. Words settled on his tongue, but he choked them back as the grass whispered in the fae's wake. He couldn't warn her of his charge. He couldn't risk Artassa, Anadin, and young Rille.

I must see this through.

Yet, for the first time in his life, Aredel doubted his ability to kill.

He dreamt of Jinji.

The shepherd sat upon the hillock near his cottage in Shing, sheep bleating around him. Jinji looked up from the crook he carved with a knife, and a warm smile brightened his turquoise eyes. He looked healthy; color brightened his face; his frame was slim but solid, not papery as it had been during the last years of his life.

"Hello, my brother." Jinji's smile dimmed. "Your troubles weigh you down so."

Aredel's steps quickened until he reached the storyteller's side. He slumped to his knees and caught Jinji's shoulder. "You're alive?"

Jinji's smile strained a little. "I'm afraid you are dreaming, Aredel. But while I do not breathe upon the fields and fens of Nakania, life does not end after death. All things go on."

Searching those crystalline eyes, Aredel swallowed against a burning sensation in his throat. "Just after we buried you, Jetekesh and I saw you walking beside Prince Sharo."

"And walk beside him I do," Jinji answered. "Though not as a living person. My current realm lies between worlds, between space and time. I await the True King's call. When Shinac and Nakania reunite, I will be allowed to come and go at his command."

Aredel's grip on the storyteller's shoulder tightened. "Will he call you? Will you always be out of my reach?"

Lines appeared around Jinji's eyes and his smile gentled further. "Ah, my dear Aredel. I will never abandon you." He caught Aredel's arm, his fingers strong like they hadn't been in years. "I've come to you to ask you to forfend your actions. The *Unsielie* have asked a cruel thing of you, but you are not without allies. Please, Aredel. Sharo must live. He is more important than you know."

"I'm aware of his significance as the last heir of your king."

"He is more than that to so many." Jinji tipped his head to one side. "Protect him, Aredel. Please."

"You ask the impossible of me, Jinji. Two hostages will die if I spare him, and our brother will be made utterly mad."

Jinji's brow pinched. "You must find a way to save them all."

The Blood King jerked back, freeing himself from Jinji's grip. "And will you guide me to this solution?" He dragged fingers through his long black hair. "I know nothing of Shinac—of any allies who might help. Of how closely I am watched by those who threaten my family. What am I to do?" He slapped his hand against his thigh.

Jinji caught his wrist. "Aredel, your instinct is well-honed. Trust it. Speak with Thrissa."

"That cold fae?"

"That cold fae is an elven queen. She is ancient and wise. Tell her."

Squeezing his eyes shut, Aredel let his frustrations bleed away. "I don't trust myself, Jinji. I feel lost now that I've given up all I conquered. What is left of me? I'm a mere relic from a dying age."

"Feeling lost is the first step on the path to finding your truest self." Jinji set his half-carved crook aside and knelt squarely before the Blood King. "Heed me in this, Aredel: You have uprooted your past actions. You have turned your back on the rotted principles of your father and your tyrant forebears. Leave all that behind—as frightening as it is. Seek a higher road. Follow in the steps of those who have inspired this change in your heart. You will not become them. But you may become *like* them. Above all, remember this: You are not beyond change or redemption. No one is."

Aredel bowed his head to hide the mist in his eyes. He wasn't in the habit of crying. He'd never taken time for it before. He hated to start now—yet his heart throbbed, and his soul thrummed. "I miss you, my brother." His voice was the barest whisper.

"No need for that," said Jinji in soft tones. "I'm always nearby."

Aredel woke with tears tracking down his face.

He sat up and stared at the closed tent flap. Through the fabric, the faint light of dawn glowed orange. The soft breaths of Anadin and Rille carried on, unruffled by his stirring.

He wiped his eyes, stood up, and slipped into his billowing sleeveless shirt. Strapped his sword on. Tiptoed out into the crisp morning air.

He didn't trust himself—but he trusted Jinji.

Aredel would find Thrissa.

CHAPTER 13
TURNING SOUTH

Later than he'd wanted, Yeshton reached Kyon Taro with the Amantieran contingent in tow. Shevek and Ledonn followed like restless devils from the two hells. Why the Blood Knights didn't go ahead without him, Yeshton couldn't guess.

At the Amantier-Shing border, Yeshton had presented King Jetekesh's seal and orders and received an escort of Shingese knights to accompany the Amantieran soldiers. The Shingese captain was a man named Kita, who spoke the trade language fluently—and eagerly. The combined company followed a wide stream until they reached a branch of the Tindo River, and from there they moved among the bustling traders going to and from the imperial city.

Outside the city walls, Yeshton left his armed men at a designated area near the camped Shingese forces. He entered the red gates of Kyon Taro, riding behind Captain Kita, with the Blood Knights flanking him like his personal protectors. The rest of the Shingese knights rode at the rear of their train.

Yeshton spared a few moments to admire the ornate craftsmanship of curving rooftops and ornamental gardens with bamboo trees, flowing fountains, fierce statues, and intricate designs drawn through sand.

Merchants and peddlers parted in the streets to let the contingent of Lotus-crested soldiers by. Dark eyes tracked Yeshton and the two KryTeeran Blood Knights, while whispers dogged their trail up the cobbled road leading toward the grand Lotus Palace atop a hill.

Yeshton led his mount up the gradual incline, and soon, yellow-roofed markets gave way to spacious, red-roofed mansions. The gardens along the high echelons put the small flower boxes in the yards below to shame. These were massive, with pillars, gazebos, and blossoming trees whose fragrances tickled Yeshton's nose.

As the small contingent passed through several imposing gates into the palace proper, incense invaded the floral perfume. Horns blared, likely announcing their arrival.

A courtyard full of dignitaries met them.

Captain Kita reined in before a cluster of silk-robed men, and Yeshton halted his mount to examine the welcoming party. Most were bearded and middle-aged, with a few younger fellows at their backs. A single woman stood amidst the group, clad in simpler raiment than the rest. She was in her twenties with long black hair and keen eyes that speared Yeshton as her lips pressed tight. She was the most beautiful woman he'd ever seen.

Captain Kita swung from his horse and bowed, pressing his palms together. "Venerable ministers, I bring the ambassador of Amantier, as well as two allies from KryTeer. We left their force of arms at the camp of the Dragon Waters. This is Sir Yeshton of Sage Province. And these are the Blood Knights, Shevek and Ledonn."

Fear rippled through most of the ministers as they studied the two KryTeeran warriors. Little wonder. Ledonn and Shevek were

Aredel's best knights—they'd helped him conquer most of the known world. Most in Shing knew their reputations.

"Welcome to Kyon Taro," said a minister who'd found his voice. "I am Prince Jung Tep."

Yeshton knew the name. He clicked his heels together and bowed. "An honor, Your Highness. King Jetekesh sends his condolences on the passing of Emperor Majinglee. He's also gratified that peace has been maintained between our lands despite recent disturbances." He rose. "I bring a promise from King Jetekesh to the incumbent emperor, Prince Hyeun. Your people will not face the southern threat alone. Beyond the force of one hundred men that I've brought to Shing, we pledge an army of fifteen thousand to stand at your side as in the days of High King Cavalin the Third."

Prince Jung Tep's somber face lifted in a smile that touched his eyes. "Your words bring us great relief. Your king is a most honorable man, as is his son."

Yeshton blinked at that. One year ago, he'd never have believed anyone would call Prince Jetekesh anything other than spoiled and petty. But he'd joined the prince on a perilous quest to find the Arch into Shinac through the Drifting Sands, and he'd seen Jetekesh's growth since then. "That they are. I thank you."

The woman stepped from the cluster of ministers. "Sir Yeshton, I am Song, Lady of Crimson Lilies. I had the privilege of traveling recently with Prince Jetekesh and learned a little about your journey with Jinji of Shing."

Her words sent a slew of emotions through Yeshton's frame. This was the legendary Song? She spoke of Jinji with fondness cradled in her tones. Her keen eyes gentled as she spoke.

"Lady Song," he said, inclining his head. "I trust the prince was well last you saw him?"

"He was. And he's in good company."

Yeshton smiled. "Lord Emerin is a legend, much like you are, my lady."

"It seems your prince is destined to know legends," she said. "Speaking of which, I had the spirits' good fortune to meet Jinji once." Her smile softened. "He changed my life."

Those words. How many times had Yeshton heard similar phrases spoken by commoners and gentry alike over the past few months? He and Rille had worked hard to restore Sage Province, spending hours among the coastal villages, then traveling inland. It seemed wherever they stopped, people knew Jinji, or they knew of him. His stories stayed with them. Children in the streets pretended to be Prince Sharo, the fairy Ashea, and the dragon Taregan.

Jinji had impacted so many.

A lump formed in Yeshton's throat, but he choked it down. "He changed my life as well."

Song smiled. "How long will you be in Shing, Sir Knight?"

"Now that I've brought the advance force from Amantier, I must try to catch the prince's company and find the Arch leading into Shinac. My duty leads me there."

"I understand, Sir Yeshton." Her black eyes settled on Ledonn and Shevek. "In that case, I have a boon to ask of you, Blood Knights—unless you're set on accompanying this knight."

"We intend to catch up with Prince Jetekesh's company, as well," Ledonn said. "Our goals align with his. We only came here to speak with the Norvian girl who crossed over the mountain pass."

"The girl is gone," said Song. "We suspect she joined Prince Jetekesh's company against his wishes. I will understand if that makes you want to chase them down even more—but with your auspicious arrival, I had hoped to employ your expertise."

Shevek lifted a brow. "Killing people?"

"No, my lord. Spying on the enemy." She turned south to the

snow-capped mountains. "I intend to cross into the secret country of Norva unseen. I need strong and stealthy companions. I can think of none more skilled than you." Her attention returned to the Blood Knights. "What say you? Will you reconsider?"

The KryTeerans exchanged a long look.

Yeshton glanced between them, nerves taut. He needed them in order to navigate the wilds of the Clanslands. He wasn't foolhardy enough to think he could survive those jungles on his own.

The Blood Knights stepped away from the assembled officials and conversed in low tones. As they gestured and shifted their stances their armor glinted under the sunlight. At last, Ledonn nodded, and Shevek gave a sigh.

Ledonn returned to the group. "Very well, Lady Song. Our holy Blood King would deem this action wise. We will accompany you."

Yeshton rubbed a hand against his neck. "Very well, then. I—"

"We know this leaves you in a lurch, Sir Knight," Shevek said. "But our king's goals outweigh our personal desires—even in his absence—and frankly, we need to go where we're most useful. King Aredel can care for himself far better than we, though it pains me to admit it. He'll protect Lady Rille well enough, too. Why not join us, Yesh? We could use your blade—and I suspect Rille would want it this way."

Yeshton snapped his mouth shut, wrestling against the man's logic with every fiber of his loyalty, but the blasted knight made sense. He turned away, armor rattling. His eyes landed on the nearest cherry blossom tree, vibrant pink under the cloudless blue sky.

Rille would want me to spy on Norva. She knows I'm more useful gathering information for our allies than riding off into strange lands to try to find her. That's plain enough.

He pinched the bridge of his nose, then exhaled. He turned to face the others, his gaze settling on Song. "It seems I have few sensible choices. I'll join you as well."

Her shoulders eased. "Thank you, Sir Knight. Please know that I appreciate your sacrifice. The four of us will leave at first light."

"Why not now?" asked Ledonn.

Shevek snorted.

Yeshton eyed them dryly. "I, for one, would like a bath and some warm food."

"Yes, Ledonn," Shevek said. "The mortals need rest."

"I suppose it can't be helped."

Yeshton and the Blood Knights followed Prince Jung Tep, Lady Song, and the rest of the ministers into the palace.

After a long soak, a five-course meal, and a full night's rest, Yeshton felt more himself than he had in weeks. Still, his stomach tightened when thoughts of Rille flittered through his head. He knew she wasn't alone. In company with Aredel and Anadin, she couldn't be safer, yet Yeshton worried.

Rille's parents were dead, just as Yeshton's were. Despite Rille being connected to King Jetekesh and his son, distance separated them. In the ruins of Keep Lunorr, Rille and Yeshton had no one else but each other in an ocean of servants and guards. They'd become a sort of family.

She was like a little sister to him.

Her absence left him hollow.

After dressing, Yeshton strapped his sword belt on, slung his satchel over his shoulder, and stepped from his borrowed bedchamber. Song and the Blood Knights stood in the corridor. The latter two wore common KryTeeran apparel, their armor strapped in packs behind them.

"Good morning," Song said, dipping her head.

"Good morning. Sorry to keep you," Yeshton said, straightening his tunic. He'd left his armor in the chamber, deciding it would be conspicuous and impractical in the snowbound passes. Instead, he wore layers beneath his tunic for padding, and he would add more layers before they reached the high snows. Eyeing the Blood Knights' packed armor, he hesitated—but he had no desire to lug his heavy things up the mountains.

Song looked him over, then she nodded approval. "Let's be off. Prince Jung Tep sends his best wishes with us. The incumbent emperor would wish the same, I'm certain, though he's too busy to send word just now."

Ledonn snorted. "What good are wishes? We need the strength of the gods."

"Luckily, we provide that." Shevek shifted the curved sword at his hip. "Ready when you are."

Song ignored their banter and led the way outside the eastern side of the palace to the stables. Fresh horses were already saddled and waiting, nickering as they shuffled their hooves, impatient to be off.

A young Shingese boy near Rille's age stood beside the horses with a quiver of arrows on his back. He wore a plain Shingese-style tunic and calf-length pants, and his expression was unnaturally somber for someone of his years.

Song halted and her eyes narrowed into slits. "No, Yin."

He turned his grim gaze on her and spoke in rapid Shingese.

The woman shook her head and replied in clipped words.

"Is he wanting to join us?" asked Yeshton.

Song didn't break eye contact with the boy as she nodded. "He's my little brother."

"Ah." Yeshton studied the youth's determined expression. "Can you speak the trade tongue, Yin?"

The boy blinked, then nodded. "Yes."

Yeshton offered a smile. “Then heed me in this: It’s noble to prove your bravery and skill in a far-off battle, but it’s nobler still to stay behind and protect those who cannot fight. Obey your sister’s will in this. Your time to fight *will* come—and too soon, I’d wager.”

Yin stared at him, then his shoulders slumped. He slid the quiver strap off his shoulder and stepped away from the horses.

Song spoke to him in Shingese, and the boy padded past the company, back into the palace.

As the doors clicked shut, Yeshton turned to Song. “Forgive my interference.”

“Nothing to forgive. Sometimes a boy needs what no woman can give him: a man’s wisdom. Your counsel is good.”

“’Tisn’t mine. A wiser man than I told me the same thing long ago.”

Song’s eyes brightened. “Jinji?”

“No, a knight called Sir Palan.” Yeshton’s chest tightened. “He taught me that and much more.”

Song strode to one of the horses and strapped her pack behind the saddle. “I’ve heard of Sir Palan. He is a legend even here in Shing. Honor flowed through his blood, my grandfather said.”

“So it did.” Yeshton tied his satchel to the back of his chosen mount, then swung up into the saddle. Stroking his horse’s neck, his eyes drifted southward, where the orange streaks of dawn painted the snowcaps.

The creak of leather drew his attention back to his companions, and he adjusted his grip on the reins. Ledonn was the last to mount after checking the pack horse carrying their food and bedrolls. Judging by how little the pack horse carried, Yeshton was glad he’d brought layers for under his tunic and trousers. Climbing over the southern passes would be frigid, and shelter would be had only when they found a cave or overhang.

The four horses trotted out through a narrow gate and down a wide street along the sleepy paths of Kyon Taro. Hooves clopped over the paving stones, loud in the gloomy silence. The streets flew by in a blur as Yeshton guided his mount toward their faraway destination.

Norva. A country hidden in the Snow Wastes.

An army grew there, led by someone with enough power to break a demon free from Prince Sharo's magical chains.

Yeshton clutched his reins tight. The odds weren't favorable for Song's little company, but then, he was used to that.

CHAPTER 14
FAR FROM HOME

As Kajsa sank into the natural hot spring, the hot water swallowed her, easing her aches and bruises. Steam rose around her, curling her usually straight platinum hair and kissing her cheeks until they flushed.

Nearby, Anenyasha leaned back against the slick rocks, her eyes closed, a rare smile edging her lips. She'd let her tiny braids down from a knot, and they floated on the water like dark snakes, bleeding pink chalk.

The men of the company remained at camp, a fair walk beyond the dense bamboo trees surrounding the spring, awaiting their turn in the near-scalding water. Thinking of the scrapes and bruises they wielded, guilt nibbled at Kajsa's insides. They needed this soak far more than she did.

Her fingers throbbed. Wincing, Kajsa flexed them. The water had softened the blisters where she'd held her bowstring taut again and again the past two evenings since the *vashalan* ambush. Jetekesh had been training her just as he'd promised.

Two days since the attack.

Lord Emerin was still feverish in the wagon bed following his stunt with the blazing wreaths of fire. He'd not woken up yet.

Kajsa had asked Jetekesh about Emerin's ability after the monstrous corpses had been burned. He'd shrugged and said, "He won't talk about it."

What had Kajsa expected? People didn't wield fire like that—not in Nakania. Yet Emerin had. Was he from Shinac like Kethalas was?

Her mind drifted to the memory of the man-dragon flying above the encampment, wings glittering like ice in sunlight, fire dancing around him.

So many strange and wondrous things are happening, Axel.

She ached to see her friend again. To share her fear and awe with someone who would feel the same way. But Axel was still in Norva, enamored by Navolleth's promises of conquering the known world.

Kajsa had hoped against hope for several years that Axel might one day reciprocate the feelings she secretly held for him, and it had seemed he might...before he discovered Navolleth in the snow. Now, the impending war was everything. Ambition and control had seduced him, and all Kajsa could do was flee and warn the people north of the Snowblinds. Children shouldn't suffer for the greed of adults.

Ripples on the water cascaded before her vision. Anenyasha was stirring her dark hand through the pool, staring into the depths with an intent gaze.

Kajsa opened her mouth to ask what was wrong but snapped it shut again. Anenyasha didn't speak the Old Tongue, and Kajsa had no prayer of learning the Clans Tongue quickly. The sounds were complex, beautiful, but beyond her tongue's limited dexterity. Despite that, she was glad of Anenyasha's company. Having another woman nearby was heartening—though she didn't mind the men so much anymore.

Even Emerin and Lafe were less frightening than they'd been in the beginning. Emerin was surprisingly kind to her. She cherished his gift of embroidery threads.

Kethalas and Dakarai were always gentle and full of laughter.

And she felt strangely comfortable around Jetekesh.

Her heart twisted. Poor Harn was dead, and he'd always been good to her too.

Don't focus on that. Best clean up and let the men have a turn.

Kajsa dunked herself under the water, letting it penetrate every inch of her skin and hair. She raked her fingers through her tresses, thorough in her quest to untangle and scrub every last strand. Her blistered fingers stung while she worked, but she didn't stop until she was satisfied that she was clean.

Straightening up, she swept back her waterlogged hair, wiped droplets from her eyes, then dragged herself from the pool. She and Anenyasha had brought blankets, and she wrapped one around her slim form, skin prickling with the evening's coolness, though she felt cooked through.

A bird fluttered in a nearby thicket. Jetekesh had mentioned that Northern Shing was unseasonably cold, yet it was warmer than Norva in late spring. So much greenery encircling her dazzled Kajsa. If only she could show Axel the variety beyond evergreens, ferns, and meager crops.

She frowned. *He would just want to steal these lands more.*

She dried herself off, then slipped into fresh clothes. The light fabric breathed over her skin, loose and wonderful. Kajsa fingered her sleeve cuff, then stepped into the slippers Jetekesh had purchased for her.

A splash in the pool informed Kajsa that Anenyasha was exiting, too. Rather than hover, Kajsa folded her damp blanket and started back for camp, relieved by how refreshed she felt. Axel had taken her and Ingrid to a warm spring once, years ago, but it was too far off to visit often, especially as Ingrid had grown frailer.

Kajsa's heart squeezed, remembering Ingrid slumped across her cottage floor, dead. Killed by *vashalan*.

Clutching the blanket closer, Kajsa drew a few steadying breaths.

A twig snapped just ahead.

She froze in place, lungs pinched.

"'Tis only me," said a soft voice.

Kajsa exhaled softly as Kethalas came into view along the path, his silvery eyes glistening in the growing gloom of twilight.

"You frightened me," she whispered.

Kethalas cast her an apologetic smile. "That wasn't my intent. I smelled your approach and thought to join you."

She tilted her head to one side. "Why?"

"Because I prefer that no one is alone in these strange woods." His eyes coasted over the bamboo trees.

"Anenyasha is still at the spring."

The dragon's fangs showed in a grin. "*That* one can take care of herself. She's better with a spear than Dakarai is."

He fell into step beside her. His tall, lean frame was a comfort among the thin shadows stretched over the forest floor. Glancing at his face in profile, a question clung to her tongue.

"What is it?" he asked without looking at her.

"Oh. Um." She flushed. "It's just...I thought dragons were evil."

Kethalas's step faltered, then he turned to stare at her. "Where did you hear such nonsense?"

Her cheeks burned. "F-from the elder of my village. And Ingrid. From all the folk back home. Everyone says dragons are bad."

"Ah." Kethalas rapped his knuckles against his chin. "We are fierce, that's true. And deadly. But we don't eat people—most of us don't. We're hunted by people more than we have ever hunted them. Some dragons are *dark*, mind you, but that's not the same as being evil." He stared past Kajsa's shoulder. "Some of us have been controlled, and that's where the myths come from, I suspect. Witches and warlocks enjoy enslaving young dragons. So do other fell beings. But we're quite content to leave humans alone, so long as they extend the same courtesy."

She nodded. "I—I didn't mean to offend."

"Oh, you haven't." He set a hand on her shoulder. Claws gleamed on the end of each finger, glittering as though touched by frost. "Rest assured. It is unlikely *you* could offend a dragon." His smile drifted toward a frown. "There are dragons who have gone mad—those are the truly tragic stories. King Cavalin the Great was bonded to a magnificent dragon. Upon the king's unfortunate death when he battled Tallat the Treacherous, 'tis said the dragon lost his mind and his heart broke in twain." Kethalas sighed and rubbed the scar on his cheek. "What truth there is in that tale, I couldn't say. Perhaps the Marked Prince can."

They'd reached the edge of camp, and Kajsa let her eyes drift to the campfire where Jetekesh stood in conference with Lafe and Dakarai. The prince clutched his sword, perhaps discussing his training. Judging by his mussed hair and wrinkled clothes, he'd just finished his evening lesson. A gleam brightened his eyes, and he wore an easy smile.

The lesson must have gone well.

Kajsa steadied her nerves and approached the cluster of men, Kethalas at her side.

The prince turned toward her, and brightened more. "Feel better? I always do after a hot bath."

She offered a timid smile. "It was very soothing."

"That's putting it mildly, I suspect." Jetekesh slid his blade back into its sheath. "Is Anenyasha returning soon? I'm eager to soothe my own throbbing bones."

Dakarai chuckled. "After that thrashing, I little doubt it, fair prince."

Jetekesh hefted his chin to look down his nose. "I did rather well this evening—if I say so myself." The flash of a grin betrayed his mirth.

Lafe set a hand on the prince's shoulder. "You are improving, Your Highness. But don't tell Lord Emerin I said as much. He'd have my head."

Dakarai and Jetekesh laughed, riding high on the heels of the sword bout.

Jetekesh's laughter faded, then he cast Kajsa a glance. "Your own training went well. How are your fingers?"

"Fine. Thank you." She ducked her head, cheeks burning. So much attention still baffled her. Somehow, she wasn't an outsider here, so far from the home where she always had been.

"Food should be done soon." The prince glanced at the roiling pot. "Rice again, I'm afraid. I'm craving that gingerbread."

Dakarai grunted. "I would take anything sweet. You may enjoy the treats of my country, Your Highness."

"I'll look forward to any change by the time we cross the inlet." Jetekesh rubbed a thumb over the jeweled pommel of his sword, the ruby winking in the fire's glow.

Kajsa glanced northward. "How big is the inlet?"

"It's a fairly large bay," Dakarai said. "It takes a few hours to cross, but it's much faster than traveling around it."

She drifted toward the fire. She'd never been on a boat before. Thinking about it tied her stomach in knots. Axel had told her once that he'd gotten seasick when he'd visited a distant canton across a big lake. She hated the idea of vomiting.

Dakarai stooped over the pot. "A few moments more." He straightened up. "Ah. Here comes my lovely one." He clicked a few rapid sounds as Anenyasha appeared in the growing darkness, then he turned his grin on Jetekesh. “The spring is free to use, Your Highness.”

The prince sighed and flopped onto his saddle, wincing slightly. “Food first. I’m famished.” He motioned Kajsa to sit beside him. “After I’m cleaned up, do you want to keep practicing archery?”

A full smile bloomed on her lips. “Yes, please.” She could think of nothing she wanted more.

CHAPTER 15
SILVER LIGHT

The midnight sky sparkled like a dragon's hoard.

Kethalas sprawled across the top of the wagon, content to absorb the song of crickets and owls in the wood. He resisted an urge to whistle an old fae lullaby so he didn't wake the company.

Convincing Lafe and Dakarai that he could handle the middle watch for the night had proved difficult, but once he'd sworn he would alert them at the first whiff of danger, they'd agreed. Thank the spirits. Kethalas couldn't handle another night stuffed inside the wagon, especially now that Emerin shared the cramped space with him.

The lord hadn't stirred since he'd wielded fire against the *vashalan*. Small wonder. That level of magic required tremendous mental fortitude and control over the spirits of fire. Without that control, a person could accidentally tap into one's own life force. From what Kethalas understood about Nakania—no longer tied to the magic of Shinac—the use of such power was nearly impossible. Even lethal.

He frowned. *That puts Jetekesh at risk as well.*

Kethalas sat up. Brushing back threads of pale blue hair, he stared below at the pulsing embers in the dying fire. A horse nickered, then stamped a hoof. Kethalas tensed. Was the animal nervous?

He stretched his senses, willing his pointed ears to identify any sound beyond the keen of crickets. Far off, a deer darted through a thicket. Kethalas's mouth watered, but he ignored the instinct to chase game.

He was in no shape to hunt. Nor should he abandon his post.

The horse grew silent. Kethalas inched to the edge of the wagon and peered down at the group of animals. One flicked its tail in sleep, standing upright among the rest. Otherwise, they didn't stir.

Kethalas settled back down, careful not to agitate the wound in his side and the hidden tear in his wing. He'd drawn both wings inside, where his dragon form slumbered until he needed to stretch into it.

Staring at the stars, he dredged up the lullaby and murmured the words to himself.

Soft in slumber, sweetly lie,
'Til your troubles pass you by.
Weightless, drift to far-off shores.
Dream on wings that let you soar.

Kethalas's nose twitched as the scent of smoke tickled his senses. He bolted upright, tugging on his wound. Hissing, he wrenched around to find the fire. Its embers glowed fainter than the stars.

A horse whinnied.

He sprang to his feet. Favoring his wounded side, he searched the bamboo trees.

No glint of orange light. No flicker of flame.

Yet the odor of smoke rose, growing stronger.

His eyes dropped to the wagon roof beneath his boots. Cursing, he leapt to the ground behind the wagon, whirled, and wrenched the wagon's back flap aside. Firelight spilled across the packed earth. Emerin was engulfed in flames. The man's face was contorted in pain, though the fire didn't consume his flesh. Flames climbed the walls of the wagon and several barrels and sacks blazed as the conflagration gorged on them.

"Lafe! Dakarai!" Kethalas shouted.

He jumped inside the wagon and knelt beside the fevered lord. Flames licked at the dragon's fingers, but he summoned enough ice to shield his skin as he stooped over Emerin. Any more than that would leach him of strength too fast. "My lord. Awake, my lord!"

Emerin's eyes cracked open, then fluttered shut. His mouth twisted in agony.

Biting out a curse, Kethalas wrenched the man from his bedroll. He slung Emerin over his shoulder with gritted teeth, and stumbled toward the hole where fire ate at the flap, forming a ring of gnawing heat. Emerin's body burned where it made contact. Melting ice dripped from Kethalas's encased skin, cooling him.

Lafe appeared in the ring, then Jetekesh. The prince's eyes were wide and bright in the raging firelight. He lurched forward, but Lafe caught his arm and shook his head.

Kethalas reached the opening and hefted Emerin from his shoulder, still holding him against his body. "Take him, Lafe."

The knight shot out his arms and caught the lord just as Kethalas wobbled. The dragon crashed to his knees. Ice melted into water, pouring down his back and limbs. He didn't have the energy to drag himself forward, let alone shield his body.

Jetekesh plunged through the ring and caught Kethalas's underarms. He tugged hard. "Come on."

Alarm spiked through Kethalas's head. He parted his lips to

protest—but sense caught up to him. He'd save precious seconds if he let Jetekesh help, and the prince would be less injured. Willing the last dregs of his power through his body, ice trickled from his fingertips, coating Jetekesh's skin in a flexible film.

Let it be enough to spare him deep burns.

Kethalas staggered upright, and Jetekesh wrapped the dragon's arm around his neck. Together, they ducked beneath the arch of fire. Dakarai's strong, dark fingers caught Kethalas's arm. The clansman was perched on the step hanging from the back of the wagon, clutching the sideboard with one hand.

"I have you," Dakarai said. "Step through."

Kethalas mustered the last of his strength and lifted his legs through the flames to step out into the fresh night air. Dakarai held him firm while he stepped down. Jetekesh sprang down after them, panting, his brow glistening with water. The prince wiped his forehead, brushing back damp hair. His shoulders trembled, likely more from shock than pain.

Still, Kethalas reached out a hand, letting Dakarai support him. "Your Highness?"

Jetekesh looked up to meet his gaze, but his eyes stuck on something behind the dragon. The prince's jaw slackened.

Kethalas craned his neck to glance over his shoulder. Emerin still blazed with fire where he lay on the road. Lafe stood nearby, helpless.

Dakarai clicked a foreign word, then eased Kethalas to the ground. "I'll get water."

"It will do no good," Kethalas said. "He must put out the fire himself or be consumed."

The clansman met his eye. "The wagon is still on fire. I can do something for that, at least." He bolted toward the feed bucket near the panicking horses and snatched it up. Then he ran off into the night, likely aiming for the stream running within the trees alongside the road.

"Why is Emerin burning?" asked Jetekesh. "What can we do?"

The dragon tore his gaze from Dakarai's retreating shape. Jetekesh's brows were pinched together, his eyes bright with fear.

"He's cursed, I'd guess," said Kethalas. "He wields fire at the cost of his soul, and he's used too much of the element. It's eating him up from the inside out."

Jetekesh wrenched his attention from the inferno to stare at Kethalas. "Can't we help?"

"Not while Emerin's fevered—not unless we can get through to him. He must shut it off."

The prince set his jaw. "I'll try, then." He sprinted toward the flaming lord, but Lafe stepped in the way. Jetekesh halted. "Move, Sir Knight."

"I'll not risk you. Nor would Lord Emerin."

Jetekesh rolled his shoulders back. "As your prince, I command you to let me pass." His voice softened. "Trust me."

The knight stiffened, a tick twitching in his jaw. Then he bowed his head and stepped to one side. "Please be wise, my prince."

Jetekesh trotted to the edge of the blaze, dropped to his knees, and reached out a hand. Flames curled over his fingers. Kethalas expected the prince to cry out or flinch back—*something*—but Jetekesh plunged his hand into the glutting fire.

Kethalas bent forward, leaning heavily on one trembling arm. The faintest tinge of light surrounded Jetekesh—a pale kind of silvery hue, like his aura bled through his frame to protect him. It grew as he moved, brightening into the beam of light Kethalas had seen from the Drifting Sands. The beacon that had called him to Nakania's one hope.

The Marked Prince.

Jetekesh caught Emerin's shoulder and spoke. His words were soft, barely a whisper, but Kethalas's sharp ears caught every syllable.

"Emerin, fight. Beat back the fire. We need you. You can win."

Simple words. Desperate. Yet heartfelt and ringed with authority that rippled through Kethalas like a clarion note from the high towers of Valliath.

The flames flashed from angry orange to bright silver, then they died down, down, down—until they snuffed out, smokeless, like a mere ghost. At the same moment, the flames engulfing the wagon died, leaving charred remains.

Jetekesh swayed, then collapsed across Emerin's broad chest.

Lafe dropped to his knees beside Jetekesh and checked the prince's pulse. Exhaling, his shoulders eased. He dragged his prince from the lord, and lifted Jetekesh into his arms.

Dakarai raced back into sight, panting, with a sloshing bucket in hand. Anenyasha appeared behind him, clutching a bucket of her own. Dakarai's eyes roved from the black bones of the wagon to Emerin slumbering across the ground to Jetekesh dangling from Lafe's arms.

"What happened?" asked the clansman.

Kethalas managed a weak shrug. "The Marked Prince quieted the curse." Movement snagged his attention. He glanced toward the forest, his nerves tight. It was Kajsa. He blew out a breath.

The girl clutched a sopping blanket, probably returning from the stream where she'd dunked the blanket to beat the flames down. Clever girl.

The dragon offered her a fanged smile. "All is well now."

"In a sense." Lafe shifted his grip on the unconscious prince. "We've lost our provisions—including our peat moss."

A hoarse voice spoke. "That *is* problematic."

Kethalas's heart jolted. He whipped his neck around so fast it popped. Emerin was sitting up. Even with his blond hair a tousled mess around his shoulders, and dark circles around his eyes, he looked otherwise hale. There were no singe marks on his clothes or skin.

Lafe let out an explosive breath. "You're—awake."

Emerin arched a brow. "That, or I'm a reanimated corpse. You can pick." Wavering, he got to his feet. Kethalas jerked forward to help him but stopped himself. Seated on the ground, weak as a newborn ice phoenix, how could Kethalas hope to aid the man?

The keep lord steadied himself before Dakarai reached him, but the clansman caught his elbow and held it without a word.

Emerin scanned the remains of the wagon, then turned to Jetekesh. "Better lay the prince inside the tent, Sir Lafe. We'll not move on until morning." He squinted at the sky. "How close are we to KriShen Bay?"

"Two days to the closest harbor," Dakarai said, watching Lafe's retreating form as the knight moved to the tent. "We can make it as we are if we hunt along the way. We lost none of the horses."

Emerin nodded. "We'll proceed that way. The wagon would've stayed at KriShen anyway." He grimaced. "Any food intact? I'm famished."

Kajsa dropped the wet blanket with a soft slap, then trotted forward. The lord and clansman hadn't been speaking in the Old Tongue, but many of the words were similar. Perhaps she'd understood.

She halted a few feet short of the keep lord. "Food. I will get it." Her accent was heavy, but the words were correct. Without awaiting Emerin's reply, she raced to the remnants of the campfire where the pot sat, half-full of rice, in preparation for an easy breakfast. Crouching down, she scooped the grains into a clay bowl, then returned, clutching a spoon as well.

"Thank you, Kajsa," Emerin said in the Old Tongue, accepting the bowl. He offered her a fond smile.

"Cold," Kajsa said, using the trade language despite the lord switching over. "But still food."

Emerin grunted, then scooped up a spoonful. He reverted to

the Trade Tongue. "I'm too hungry to care." He shoveled rice into his mouth, then gestured with his spoon. "Sleep." The word was thick through a mouthful of rice.

Kajsa nodded. "Goodnight." She bolted toward the tent, head ducked, nightgown flowing behind her. She slipped into the tent and closed the flap.

"Are you injured, Lord Dragon?" asked Emerin.

Kethalas turned a rueful grin on the keep lord. "Weak, more than anything. I agitated my wound, but I didn't reopen it, I think."

"That's good." Emerin's eyebrows lowered until a storm filled his face. "I apologize...for that occurrence. I...can't explain."

Dakarai spoke before Kethalas could. "You needn't. We each have stories we would rather not tell. Not unless it endangers our cause. And then, only what is most necessary."

Sucking in a breath, Emerin nodded. He scooped up another spoonful of rice and chewed as his eyes skimmed the treeline. After a moment, he swallowed. "The sooner we find the Arch, the better."

Dakarai turned to Kethalas. "I will escort Lord Emerin to the tent, then return for you."

The dragon waved him off. "I'll just sleep here. I won't get cold." He leaned back, settling against the packed dirt. The stars winked at him, distant, not as vibrant as they were in Shinac.

Despite his protest, Dakarai returned and sat beside him, taking up the last, long watch of the night.

Neither man said anything before dawn.

CHAPTER 16
THE GLADE

As Aredel approached the elven woman, he slowed his steps. Thrissa stood perched on one foot upon a palisade log, the other foot pinned against her booted ankle.

Long, silvery hair twined around her in the early morning breeze. Her pale eyes stared toward the ring of sunlight peeking over the southeastern mountains capped with snow. She'd shed her cloak and wore a tunic and breeches in shimmering colors that had no name which Aredel knew.

"My lady?"

She maintained her vigil over the dawn.

Aredel halted and set his hands behind his back, content to wait—even if he must wait for hours.

Moments stretched on. The encampment stirred, beginning as a faint hum, peaking with a high clamor of voices as the smithy's hammers rang out. Shouts and cheers burst from the training grounds.

At last, Thrissa lowered her foot and stood atop two upright logs that helped make up the palisade. She craned her head and eyed him with a long, quiet look. "Did you need me, Blood King?"

"Do you have time to speak?" He glanced at a cluster of soldiers laughing among themselves as they trod the path leading toward Aredel. They were proud of their morning matches, and eager to fight against King Darint's forces.

Aredel turned back to Thrissa. "Elsewhere."

She fell so still she might have passed for a statue. Then she nodded and sprang from the logs to land lightly. A puff of dust lifted around her boots. "This way." Her fingers danced in a broad westward direction, and they moved among the now-vacant tents until they reached a gate where sentries bowed to Thrissa, scraping hasty looks over Aredel. They let the two pass through the gate out into the field.

"A little farther," Thrissa said.

They strode to the border of trees where birdsong chorused as the fowls fed their squawking young. Thrissa slipped into the shadows of the foliage, and Aredel followed. The dimness thronged his eyes, then fell away. His heart stuttered.

Blue lights danced and sparkled among the stately trees, and the air shimmered with raw power. Aredel hesitated. This was ancient, untainted ground.

A glade lay not far ahead, and Thrissa headed for it.

Aredel plunged after her. The air rippled around him, almost sentient. The trees watched, alive somehow, aware of his intrusion. But they kept their peace.

He had forgotten—had been too preoccupied in recent days to notice—that somehow, in the lands of Shinac, a new sense stirred within him. An awareness. A subtle knowing. He couldn't read minds, but he *saw* people as he never could, or had never tried, in Nakania.

The two reached the glade where grass swayed, rippling like

velvet. Trees hummed a faint song. Drafts of crisp, minty air sparked.

Thrissa turned to face him, her hands clasped at her back. "Speak your peace, Blood King. None will hear us."

He held her stern gaze without expression, weighing the litheness of her body, the strength of her mien, the thin blade at her hip, the gleam in her eyes. He squared his shoulders and held his arms at his sides, indicating this wasn't a fight.

"My companions and I were enticed into Shinac by *Unsielie*."

Thrissa's eyelashes fluttered. "How?"

"They crossed into Nakania using an Arch hidden in Northern KryTeer." He shrugged. "The *Unsielie* appeared while we sought the Arch on behalf of Prince Jetekesh and a dragon who had come through what is now a shattered Arch within the Drifting Sands."

Thrissa's brows flew up. "A dragon crossed into Nakania—and the Jade Arch was shattered?"

"Indeed. But the dragon didn't cross alone—he came through while wrestling a dark entity, by Lady Rille's report. Nakania is in grave danger."

The elf frowned. "Prince Sharo must be made aware. Thank you for telling me."

"That's not all." At last, he had come to it. Setting his feet wide apart, he braced for her reaction. "The *Unsielie* lured me here using my first wife, and they hold her now in a dark fortress within a swamp filled with Dusk Pixies, east and south of here. They have threatened her life—and others—unless I kill Prince Sharo."

Thrissa fell still as a statue once again. No, not quite. Her eyes darted between his, probing. A soft breath plumed from her mouth, sparking blue as though the air was charged with lightning. "Why have you told me this?"

"Because I would prefer not to kill him. I need your aid."

"You place your wife at great risk." Thrissa's tones were soft, cautious.

He inclined his head. "She is already at great risk, and I have little confidence the *Unsielie* will keep their word even should I follow through on their request. They have also threatened my brother and young Rille. I would prefer to save all parties involved. Give me hope, and I will wield it as a sword."

The elf set her hand against her chin and probed his face again with a deep look. "The *Unsielie* would keep their word—once made, they cannot break a pact without inviting the direst of consequences. But even so, I'm glad you've revealed their hand. They have no personal grudge against Sharo. That they do this means they are employed by another."

"Ah." Aredel recalled Jinji saying the same thing once the dark overlord Peresen had been killed and left to the desert wastes in Nakania. "Then he has an enemy elsewhere."

"Sharo has many enemies, just as he has many allies." She turned aside to stare into the ancient trees. "But one enemy, most of all, would have the means and disposition to employ the *Unsielie* for such an underhanded deed."

"The prince's father, yes?" Aredel relaxed his stance. The elven woman was too sensible to blame the Blood King for his problem—just as Jinji had implied.

Thrissa rapped a knuckle against her chin. "King Darint has no love for his son—especially since many humans in Shard are now rallying under the prince's banner against the tyrant. Darint's only recourse is to silence Sharo before the war truly begins. Without Sharo, our cause fails. He alone can keep the clans and factions united."

Aredel pursed his lips, weighing the ramifications of killing Sharo. "Peresen wasn't alone in his plan to breach the barrier of our worlds and conquer Nakania, was he?"

"Doubtful," said Thrissa. "Since time immemorial, tyrants

have strived to swallow up all they see—and then reach farther still. Greed is a parasite, ever hungry."

"Do you think the creature that attacked the dragon and broke the gate has the same goal?"

Thrissa frowned. "That, I couldn't guess. It is possible, but many dark souls in Shinac would escape for other reasons. Some lofty and ambitious. Others small and personal."

He nodded absently, his mind returning to the major issue. "Will you help me save the hostages used against me, or will we be enemies, Lady Thrissa?"

Those eyes, ancient, blue-tinged in the dim light, coasted over his face again. Her lips twisted into a deeper frown. "You've risked much to tell me what you have. I thank you for that, Blood King. Let us do what we can to protect the innocent souls entangled in all this." She took a step toward him. "Swear to me you will not harm Sharo, and I will protect your brother and Rille."

"And my wife?" he asked, Artassa's face flashing through his mind. "What can we do to protect her?"

"I will speak with Sharo upon his return." Thrissa rubbed a thumb over her chin. "He will know the best means of saving her. No one knows the *Unsielie* as he does."

Aredel arched his brow. "Not even the *Unsielie*?"

A fluttering smile brushed her lips, then vanished. "Least of all them. Fae do not understand themselves—they merely are."

"Yourself as well?" asked Aredel.

"Most assuredly." She rested her hands on her hips, the shimmery material of her tunic glinting in the sparking air. "Shall we return, Blood King? Sharo will not arrive today, so we must wait. If you're amenable and wish to avoid boredom, your skills may be useful upon the training field. Many new recruits need a proper breaking in."

He revealed his teeth in a grin. "Gladly."

THREE DAYS PASSED before Prince Sharo rode into the encampment on the back of his white stallion, Amaranth. Cheers rose as the horse galloped through the wide eastern gates, a stream of fae warriors in armor at his back. Golden pennants with the stamp of a strange fiery bird snapped above the intricate gleaming helms. Under the midmorning sun, Aredel studied the rows of seasoned warriors with their long hair of pastel hues; delicate plates of armor; and lithe, lean frames.

King Aredel and Rille stood beside Thrissa, watching Sharo's approach, while Anadin wrestled with a pack of hunting hounds close by. The KryTeeran prince had spent the past several days behaving like a child—full of life, wonder, enthusiasm.

In contrast, Aredel was weighed down by nervous energy, and he took it out daily on the new recruits. He held back, of course, but impatience marked his sword strokes. He hated waiting. He hated to think of Artassa, alone and frightened in the *Unsielie* fortress.

He hated feeling helpless.

It was reminiscent of when he'd been betrayed and beaten by his own men in Shing, then tossed into the river to drown. Jinji had found him, aided him, healed him—and lost everything in the process.

What I touch is always ruined.

Jinji, dead. Half of Bahadronn, capital of KryTeer, burned to the ground. Thousands of soldiers killed upon numerous battlefields in the name of Emperor Gyath. Always, Aredel's hands were stained with blood.

I am not fated for peace.

Amaranth cantered close, and Prince Sharo's pale blue eyes lit up. His mouth curled toward a broad smile. His silver armor gleamed, bright, oiled, and his boots and gauntlets looked new—a far cry from the shabby apparel he'd worn when last Aredel had seen him. The fae prince wore an ornate silver circlet on his brow, delicate and bright, twinkling with tiny sapphires.

Sharo lifted a hand to wave. His snowy hair, bound in a high tail atop his head, streamed in the breeze behind him. "Hail, Blood King! A pleasant morning to you."

Aredel tensed. Sharo's use of his current title was unexpected. Ashea hadn't known he'd become king until Anadin had mentioned it.

Jetekesh said he'd seen Jinji striding with Sharo as the seabells chimed in the Drifting Sands.

Could Sharo commune with the storyteller? Had Jinji explained Aredel's decree, transforming KryTeer from an over-reaching empire into a kingdom engaged in equal trade with the known world? Prince Sharo had appeared in Nakania at Jinji's summons, banished *Erisyrdrel,* and slain Emperor Gyath on his throne. But he would have assumed Aredel would inherit the title of emperor.

Sharo reined Amaranth up. He dropped the tethers, swung from the stallion's saddle, then clasped Aredel's shoulders. He searched the Blood King's face. "You looked better when last we met, my friend."

Aredel scoffed. "The pressures of ruling, I'm afraid." He looked Sharo up and down. "You, on the other hand, have moved up in the world."

The fae prince grunted. "My mother's folk will not let me say no to their gifts." His eyes twinkled. "I think they believe compensation is due for past years when I lived so far from them."

"You live with them now?" asked Aredel.

"No. They live with *me*. For now, at least." He swiped a hand at the troop of elven soldiers still mounted on horses behind him. "Meet my kin."

Aredel skimmed the impressive number, and his eyes up traveled the banner staffs to study the fiery bird in a field of gold. "What is the fowl called?"

"A phoenix." Sharo tracked his gaze. "My mother is of the phoenix folk, elves of the west—though, in truth, they were once of the far eastern realm under Valliath's eye."

Aredel nodded. "The phoenix is a bird who dies and is reborn, isn't it?"

Sharo nodded. "Yes. To my fae folk, it is also the symbol of the True King's return one day, and of Shinac's rebirth when he does." The prince's gaze flicked to Aredel's side. "And who is this?"

Rille stepped forward and curtsied before Aredel could speak. "I'm Lady Rille of Sage Province, daughter of Lunorr, once duke of Amantier."

"Ah." Sharo clicked his heels together and bowed at the waist, his silk cape rippling behind him. His ponytail slithered down his shoulder. "An honor to meet you, my lady. Jinji has spoken highly of your gift—and, more importantly, of your soul." He rose and offered his hand. "I am Prince Sharo."

She accepted his hand, her cheeks coloring. "The honor is mine, Your Highness. Jinji also spoke highly of you."

Sharo grinned, then kissed the air above her knuckles. Straightening, he whipped his ponytail over his shoulder and switched his gaze to Anadin seated on the ground, surrounded by contented hounds. "And this last stranger?"

"My brother," Aredel said. "Prince Anadin elvar Rann d'ara KessRa."

"Hello," Anadin said, then giggled as a hound nosed his cheek. "I hope you'll let me take your fine dogs hunting."

The fae prince chuckled. "Certainly. They would enjoy that. I'm honored to meet you, Prince Anadin of KryTeer." He swiveled back to Aredel. "I trust you've all been made comfortable in my absence?"

"Yes. Thank you." Aredel glanced at Thrissa. "The hospitality of your camp is excellent."

"Glad to hear it." Sharo traced Aredel's look, and his expression softened. Stepping forward, he set a fist to his heart, then inclined his head to Thrissa. "Most of all, I hope you've been well, my mother."

A jolt blasted through Aredel's veins. He jerked around to face Thrissa and his brows shot up.

She pointedly ignored him as she glided forward, took Sharo's wrists, and stood on tiptoes to kiss her son's cheeks. She lowered herself to level ground, then cast a look at Aredel. "You seem surprised."

"I am," he said. "I had assumed..." He paused, then shrugged. "I had assumed you were lovers."

Thrissa and Sharo blinked in unison, then Thrissa frowned. Sharo set a hand on her shoulder and tipped his head back, letting his mirth roll out in gales of laughter.

"It isn't that amusing," Thrissa said.

Sharo straightened, still chuckling. "No, and it's an entirely understandable mistake." He winked at his mother. "It's because you're so sullen. People always assume my mother would carry my disposition."

Aredel grunted. "That's true. Sages say that opposing personalities are drawn to one another in romance. Such was my assumption." His brow arched again. "Yet that leaves the question: From where does your disposition stem?"

Sharo chuckled again. "A fair question. The answer may surprise you. My father is to blame for my affability."

Aredel fell still, trying to reconcile that with the images Jinji had painted of the tyrant King Darint. He'd envisioned a sour man prone to mood swings. But then, that was all Aredel had known in his own father. Looking back on the actual stories unfurling in his mind's eye, Darint hadn't been an obese man refusing to acknowledge his own mortality, forcing others to serve him. Darint had been a tall, strong, independent force. Aredel recalled the vision of a quick smile on Darint's face in the days when Sharo had been indulged as a child.

"My father has a red-hot temper when he's displeased," said Sharo, breaking into Aredel's memories. "But otherwise, he's the sort of fellow you wish to please—not out of fear, but out of a desire for friendship. It's how he's kept his throne so long, placating ambassadors and overseers with grand gestures and ready laughter. He also pays his minions well, and they're pleased to turn a blind eye to his..." Sharo hesitated "...his sins. That's what they are."

"Darint can be charming," Thrissa said. "The snake hides his coils well in honeyed words and velvet shadows."

Aredel tried to read Thrissa's face. He knew she'd been captured by Darint, forced to marry him, and bear an heir for Shard Kingdom. Eventually, she'd left alongside Sharo when the prince was banished by King Darint. The marriage contract between the tyrant king and the fae woman had since been dissolved. Aredel had seen all of this unfold under Jinji's power—though he'd heard the stories long enough ago, he'd forgotten the details of Thrissa's appearance.

Aredel folded his arms. "I could ask a hundred questions, but I think we shouldn't stray from what's most important."

"Agreed," said Thrissa. "My son, I need to speak with you on an urgent matter. Come with me to the Glade."

"Gladly, Mother." Sharo dipped into a bow, then smiled at Aredel and Rille. "I shall return soon. I long to catch up on matters in Nakania—and learn why and how you've come to Shinac this time." He turned and followed Thrissa toward the eastside gate, passing his new elven recruits with a quick word of dismissal.

The elves dismounted and led their horses toward the corrals.

Rille stepped up beside Aredel. “I expected you to run him through.”

“That would hardly be subtle.”

She shrugged. “You’ve been far less so before.”

“Not by choice, only by necessity.”

Rille’s amber eyes pressed into him. “Are you questioning your resolve?”

He shook his head. “I’ve already made my choice.” He started to walk away, unwilling to discuss the matter further. He hadn’t dared explain his conversation with Thrissa to Anadin or Rille. He couldn’t guess who might be listening outside the Glade.

He wouldn’t take any chances.

CHAPTER 17
RABBIT

The southern mountains were steeped in snow that piled thigh-high in places. Yeshton kept his pace slow and measured, as did the other three members of the company. Song took the lead, more familiar with the terrain than Yeshton or the two KryTeeran knights.

They'd left their horses at a farm near the roots of the mountains, before traversing the pass toward Norva. Yeshton carried two packs slung over his back, and Shevek and Ledonn did likewise, along with their bloodred armor. Song carried a bow and kept her eyes peeled for any hint of what she called *vashalan*.

Yeshton had heard the canine beasts howling, but he hadn't yet seen any.

He prayed to the saints that would remain the case.

Shevek and Ledonn spent the hours taking bets on what animal might scamper across the path next or what color the sunset would be. If they tired from trudging through snow so heavily burdened, they never complained.

Three days up the mountain pass, just as the sun sank toward the western horizon, they found a cave.

"That looks like a promising campsite," Ledonn said.

"I'll investigate." Song crept toward the dark maw of the cave, her steps soft.

Yeshton watched her back until shadows swallowed her up, then he waited, ears straining for any hint of growls or a human cry. Nothing sounded in the pitch-black hole. Time dragged by.

Shevek scratched his chin, then grunted. "I'm going in after her."

"Wait a moment more," said Yeshton. "She might shoot you if you startle her."

Ledonn snorted. "True that. Remember, she's the Lady of Crimson Lilies."

"Like we would forget." Shevek grinned. "She's strong enough, she'd almost make a convincing KryTeeran woman."

"You may be right." Ledonn leaned against a scraggly cedar tree that had grown up bent from constant mountain winds. He folded his arms. "Exactly the sort of woman Father favors."

Shevek nodded. "I believe she's yet unmarried."

Yeshton's glance moved between the two Blood Knights. "I hadn't realized you were brothers."

"Half," Shevek said. "Our mothers are both part of our father's harem. Ledonn is from Father's first wife. I, from his second. We're only a month apart in our age."

Studying their faces, Yeshton read pride and affection as they eyed each other. He scratched his stubbled jaw. "I'll never understand harems."

"Of course not," Ledonn said, a gleam in his dark eye. "Amantieran men are barely strong enough to handle the temperament of *one* wife, let alone many."

Yeshton's mind flitted to Kyella, soon to marry Prince Anadin. Did the young woman accept her fate as the first of many wives and concubines—or had she not thought that through?

She's a smart girl. She wouldn't agree to something she didn't approve of.

He shook his head. "I think weakness has little to do with my preference. If ever I wed, I'll do it solely for love. Not convenience or prestige."

"Ah," grunted Ledonn. "A romantic. We have those in KryTeer, too—like our beloved prince, Anadin. But *then* you take on other wives for the times when you and your beloved have a disagreement. You see?"

"No." Yeshton shook his head. "I mean no offense, but that feels like cheapening a marriage promise—like what Queen Bareene did."

Ledonn and Shevek grinned like tigers.

"No offense taken, Sir Knight." Shevek batted the air with one hand. He and his half-brother had exchanged the curl-toed shoes of KryTeer for proper boots and winter attire, and Yeshton wondered how both men handled the weight of what they wore on top of their belongings.

"Agreed," said Ledonn. "We understand that our traditions seem strange to you. We view yours similarly. One god. One wife. One sword." He patted the two blades strapped to his hips. "To us, more is always better."

Yeshton rubbed his gloves together. "Well, to each their own. I *am* glad we can disagree in a civil manner."

Shevek's grin turned lopsided. "While not as interesting as disagreeing in an aggressive manner, it's certainly more likely to guarantee—"

Pebbles crunched within the cave.

Song appeared, bow slung over one shoulder, her arrows tucked into their quiver. She offered the three men a tight smile. "Looks like the cave goes on for miles. I turned around when I reached a crossroads. If anything lives in there, I can't tell. I think we should risk camping here just the same."

"I agree," said Yeshton. "If we press on any further, we may not find decent shelter for the night."

Shevek grunted and strode into the cave. "I've always liked exploring these. The even temperature is welcome as well." He dropped his bags inside the wide interior. "Should we light a fire?"

Ledonn traipsed after his half-brother. "If we can find proper kindling, yes." He set his bags down. "We should enjoy the perks of a fire's warmth while we can. Get too near the pass's summit, and we'll need to forgo any such luxuries. I'm going out to find wood." He prowled back outside.

Song caught Yeshton's eye. "Thank the good spirits of the earth, I'm in company with intelligent people."

He offered up a grim smile. "A rare boon indeed these days." Stepping into the shelter of the deep cavern, Yeshton discarded his bags, his crossbow, and broadsword, then blew hot breath over his covered fingers. "I'll help Ledonn find some wood. If I see any game, I'll bring it back."

"An excellent notion," said Shevek, digging through a food satchel.

Song hoisted her bow. "Take this to hunt with."

Yeshton glanced at his crossbow propped beside his bags. It would be heavy, and his muscles were tired. "Thank you." He accepted the bow and her quiver of arrows, slung the latter over his shoulder, and set off into the white wastes.

Evergreens stood tall around him, and the shorter cedars looked small and hapless beneath their stately shadows. The sky burned a brilliant orange, catching the clouds on fire as Yeshton trudged along a rabbit trail carved into the snow. Birds sang overhead, calling to their mates.

A fallen tree cradled a snowdrift. Yeshton set aside the bow and peeled off his gloves to dig out his boot knife. He hacked at a few limbs, ignoring the pine needles biting into his hands.

The birdsong died.

Yeshton paused his harvesting of the trunk. He lifted his eyes to the dense trees. The air held its breath. No stray breeze wafted across the frigid path. No hint of pine spice teased his senses. The clouds hung suspended like a woolen blanket overhead.

Red eyes flashed among the pines.

Yeshton eased his hand toward the discarded bow. His fingers slipped around the smooth wood. He should've brought his crossbow, no matter how heavy.

Or my sword, at the least.

Grimacing, he eased an arrow from the quiver, keeping his stare trained on the trees.

He tensed. Did a second pair of inhuman eyes stare back at him?

His heightened senses vibrated through his body, and his heartbeat thudded in his ears. After all his years of soldiering under Duke Lunorr, he couldn't fathom *why* this moment hammered into him like a novice just before his first battle.

Yeshton nocked his arrow. Raised his bow. Tightened the string.

Aimed.

Silence hummed over the snow.

He licked his lips. Sweat trickled down the back of his neck. His leg itched, but he resisted an urge to scratch it.

Twigs snapped.

Something growled. Darted away.

Yeshton pulled the string further back.

A howl sailed over the trees, long, mournful. Yeshton's skin crawled as a dozen more howls rose in a chorus, echoing the sentiment. His muscles tensed more.

The refrain died. Wind lifted to snatch at strands of the knight's dark blond hair. Silence resumed its reign. He squinted in the shadows and waited. Minutes passed. He maintained his vigil, even as his arm ached and the itch on his leg bit deeper into his flesh.

Something crashed from the underbrush. A rabbit darted into view and froze, nose twitching, ears perked up. Its black eyes stared at Yeshton like he was a living nightmare.

A large canine creature sprang out of the trees and snapped its jaws around the rabbit. As the rabbit screamed, the canine lifted its head and peered at Yeshton with fierce eyes. Red. Gleaming. Matted fur tufted around impossibly exposed ribs.

Just as Song had described them. *Vashalan*.

Yeshton swallowed and steadied his bow.

A spear shot past him and skewered the beast's skull. The canine staggered and dropped, and the rabbit writhed and screamed between its teeth.

Yeshton jerked around and found Ledonn ambling toward him. Bloodlust flickered in the warrior's eyes.

"Appreciate the help," Yeshton said.

Ledonn grinned. "Sorry to rob your sport. My hand reacted reflexively."

Yeshton shrugged and inched toward the still creature. He nudged the matted fur with one boot. The canine didn't twitch. Stooping, Yeshton reached for the jaws where the rabbit still writhed.

"Careful," said Ledonn. "Song suspects that the teeth carry venom. I wouldn't eat that rabbit for anything."

Yeshton grunted and wrenched the *vashalan*'s jaw open. The rabbit staggered free, then loped toward the trees. Yeshton straightened and watched the furry creature's retreat. "After that, I couldn't bring myself to eat the poor thing anyway."

Ledonn padded to Yeshton's side and grimaced. "It will die if it was poisoned."

"The One God will see to His province." Yeshton glanced at the Blood Knight. "Any luck finding firewood?"

"Some," said Ledonn. "I dropped it back there." He jerked a thumb over his shoulder. "Help me collect it, and we'll see about hunting down another rabbit."

They retraced their steps to a scattered bundle of twigs and branches. Yeshton stacked the load in Ledonn's arms, then nocked another arrow and kept an eye out for rabbits or other animals along the trail. His thoughts veered back to the encounter near the stand of trees.

"Why do you think the *vashalan* didn't attack me? Why go after the rabbit instead?"

Ledonn shook his head. "I couldn't say. I agree it was peculiar."

Yeshton's mind turned over the breathless moments before the rabbit appeared. The snapping twig. The sorrowful cry followed by a chorus of howls.

Had that single note told the nightmarish *vashalan* to back down?

I suppose musing over it will accomplish nothing. Either Yeshton would learn the truth, or he wouldn't.

Something scurried near a cedar tree. He lifted his bow and arrow. Took aim.

A rabbit scurried from the snow.

He let his arrow fly.

Best to focus on what he could control.

CHAPTER 18
ICE FOLK

Every muscle throbbed.

Jetekesh rolled over, groaning. Sunlight slapped his eyelids, and he flinched, nestling deeper into his bedding. Somewhere, a bird sang, and Jetekesh wanted to throttle it into silence.

But that would require movement.

And the bird couldn't help its nature any more than Jetekesh could help his soreness.

Why do I feel so terrible?

He shifted, startled by a sharp point digging into his thigh. Why by all the blessed saints was something sharp in his bed?

He inched away from the offending object, ignoring his muscles' protests. His hand flopped over the edge of his bed, striking the cold ground.

Jetekesh wrenched upright with a splutter. Reality crashed into his head. The shattered Arch; the *vashalan*; the fight against *Erisyrdrel*; Harn's death; Emerin's flames. Every event since Jetekesh had left Kavacos flooded through him until his stomach knotted and bile climbed his throat.

Running a hand over his face, Jetekesh swallowed down the acidic taste, then gulped deep breaths, easing his stomach into quiescence. He ran his fingers over his scalp until tangles snagged them.

His vision misted. He'd tried hard not to think about Harn since the man had been disemboweled by those hellish creatures. A quick burial far from his home was all the honor the wagoner received—and that thought ate at Jetekesh's conscience. He leaned forward and buried his face in his hands.

So many deaths. So little reason for them.

If Jetekesh had only seen the truth of the attacking canines sooner, he could've saved Harn and spared Emerin from needing to summon fire again.

If I could only be strong enough, no one would have to die.

Jetekesh let his hands slip to his lap. He inhaled a long, rattling breath, then pushed to his feet. The sounds of the birds rose above the faint murmur of voices and the crackle of flames. Likely, breakfast was underway. He'd overslept.

After running a comb through his hair, he dressed as swiftly as he could. Jetekesh stepped from the tent, the fragrance of smoke curling up from his smudged clothes. Outside, he came face to face with Sir Lafe. The knight's glower could have curdled milk.

"Good morning, Sir Knight," Jetekesh muttered, wrenching his gaze away.

"Highness," was the man's clipped reply.

Jetekesh tried to sidestep Lafe, but the knight anticipated him and mirrored his step.

Pulling a face, Jetekesh hoisted his head to meet those blazing eyes. "Do you have something to say?"

"Is this going to be a habit, Your Highness?" The man hefted one heavy eyebrow.

"Be specific. What habit?"

"You, risking your life to spare a lesser man?"

Jetekesh's lungs pinched. His lips lifted in a snarl. "If by lesser you mean Emerin, then yes. And Dakarai, and Kethalas, and you. I won't stand idly by and let *anyone* else be skewered or burned to a crisp. I'll count no one here as less than myself."

"I'm supposed to heed your commands," Lafe said. "But I *will* disregard them to save you if I must—and since that's the precedent you yourself have set, I trust you won't argue the point."

Jetekesh frowned. Annoyance flamed over his chest. "No, I'll not argue. Nor will I stop doing what I think is right." He stabbed a finger against Lafe's chest, ignoring the throb that followed the impact of skin on plate armor. "Mark me well, Sir Knight. I'll never repeat what happened in Emperor Gyath's court. That's final."

Lafe's brows dropped low, darkening his eyes. "Did you stop to consider, Your Highness, that your rash actions of now are more likely to harm others than any inaction in your past? Whether nobly or selfishly meant, you're continuing the same pattern of behavior that got Palan and Tifen killed. Your running pell-mell into danger forces others to follow. It's what gets them killed."

Fingers of ice raked through Jetekesh. He stared up into Lafe's eyes. The man's words echoed through his head, drumming into his skull, hammering at his resolve.

He's right. I've learned nothing.

Jetekesh's shoulders drooped. The world dimmed in his periphery. He stared at a spot on the ground, the odor of smoke teasing his senses, while that incessant bird still chirped in the trees. Chipper. Useless. Like Jetekesh.

He pivoted away from Lafe and marched toward the fire, keeping his head down.

I haven't grown at all, have I?

The realization chained his heart. He slumped onto his saddle, recalling the empty stares of Palan and Tifen in the KryTeeran court, sacrificed after Jetekesh had let his mouth run.

"Good morning, Prince Jetekesh," said Dakarai in tones to match the cheery song in the trees.

Jetekesh didn't look up. He said nothing. The crushing weight of his failures bled into every facet of his soul. Harn, Palan, Tifen, Jinji, Sir Blayse—the lost knight of Shinac—and even Mother.

All dead.

Because of me.

Why was he such a fool? Why did he think exchanging thoughtless words for thoughtless actions would prove him changed?

In the end, I'm still a pathetic, whiny child.

His mouth felt as parched as the desert wastes. He longed to lose himself in a bottle of wine. He'd resisted the pull of intoxication for so long.

That won't solve this. Don't give in now.

He glanced toward the wagon, and his chest squeezed tighter. Destroyed. Blackened. Even if he chose to give in to his craving, he doubted any wine had survived the conflagration.

A hand settled on his shoulder.

Jetekesh wrenched his head up and met Emerin's bright green gaze. The lord wore an easy, almost gentle smile.

"I heard what you did for me last night," Emerin said. "Sir Lafe's lecture aside, I must thank you for risking yourself for me. I wasn't quite ready to die."

As Jetekesh recalled his impulse of last night, a chill rushed through him. He'd been filled with a desire to calm the demonic charge rushing through Emerin's body, and the knowledge of how to do so.

He held Emerin's gaze. "You're cursed."

The lord jerked his hand from Jetekesh's shoulder like he'd been stung. He heaved out a sigh that weighed a thousand pounds. “Yes, Your Highness. I’m cursed.” He sought the sky. Rays of golden light blanched his irises, turning them the palest shade of green. “It happened when I was taken to Shinac.”

The camp fell silent. Even the birds muted their song.

Jetekesh studied the lines of pain etched on Emerin’s face, making the man appear older than he was. He knew Emerin had disappeared long ago. He’d only returned in recent years, just in time to inherit the Keep of the Falls on his father’s passing. Some thought Emerin had caused his father’s death, but Father didn’t believe it.

“Taken?” asked Jetekesh in a faint voice.

Emerin didn’t lower his gaze from the heavens. He grunted. “Taken.”

“By what?” asked Kethalas, limping from the far side of the fire where the last of their peat moss—the bundle that hadn’t been in the wagon—burned. His silver eyes were riveted on the keep lord, probing his face like Emerin held the secrets of the world.

“I’d been out hunting,” Emerin said. “It was a trip that took my party high above Bard Pass, north, where the snows never melt even in high summer.” A dry smile curled the corners of his mouth. “My good friend, Sir Beninn, believed that a skulk of ice foxes lived among the tallest peaks, and he was determined to make a cloak from their pelts for his wife as a Nocturne gift.”

Jetekesh knew of the legends of ice foxes—white creatures with blue ears and twin tails to match. Some called them a bad omen. Few believed they were real.

“Did you find them?” asked Jetekesh.

“Oh, yes. We found them.” His voice rumbled. “They lived near the Arch.”

A thrill raced through Jetekesh, part excitement, part dread. “Is this the Arch you say is no more?”

“Yes.” Emerin’s voice pitched low, scraping over his throat.

"Beninn couldn't see it. He only saw the ice foxes which, I presume, guarded the entrance. On impulse, I shouted at him to not loose his arrow, but he did just the same. When he struck his target, the other foxes responded. Hundreds of them descended on us."

Emerin closed his eyes and a shudder claimed his body. "They dragged us through the Arch. All of us, save one man who died in the struggle. Even the horses were taken through the portal."

Jetekesh inhaled so fast, he choked on smoke and started to cough. Going through the Arch without a proper invitation meant never returning to Nakania. Breathing deeply through his nose, Jetekesh conquered his coughing fit. "How did you return?"

Emerin fell so still, he seemed not to breathe. His eyes fluttered open. "That's hardly important. I did return, after all."

"What did the Ice Folk do to Sir Beninn?" asked Kethalas, fear curling around his tones.

Ice Folk. Then, the foxes weren't really foxes. Jetekesh glanced between the man-dragon and the keep lord, dread heightening to a hum in his ears.

"They killed him. Slowly." Emerin's eyes hardened into a dagger's edge. "The Ice Folk are as cold as their namesake. As heartless as rime."

Kethalas took a step closer. "How did you escape them? No one I know ever has."

Emerin stood in silence, his fingers balling into fists.

Jetekesh's insides writhed. "What are they?"

"Fae," Kethalas said. "The kind that is neither good nor bad. More wild than not. Ice Folk dwell in the highest peaks and within the deepest holes. They like the cold and not much else. They keep to themselves. Unless provoked."

Emerin's brows pinched together. "Yes. Except for that."

Rubbing the leather of his saddle, Jetekesh weighed the implications of a fae race that could seemingly transport between

Shinac and Nakania without any cost. His gaze strayed past Emerin to stare vaguely into the bamboo forest. "What happened?" he found himself asking.

"I escaped—but I slew several of the Ice Folk in my efforts. They...didn't take kindly to that." He shifted, drawing Jetekesh's attention back to him. "I found myself in a strange, magical country I'd assumed to be mere myth. Survival was difficult." He dragged a hand down the side of his face. "I tried to find another Arch to come home but never succeeded. At last, I accepted my fate. I had to remain in Shinac."

His eyes found Jetekesh's. "Then the Ice Folk found me and gave me to... Well, let's just say he was a thing crafted from nightmares. He placed a curse on me: fire magic. Under the conditions of the curse, I must wield flames every-so-often or die. Yet each use siphons my life away, drop by drop."

"A cruel curse, indeed," Dakarai said. The clansman stood near the fire, stirring the contents of the pot. What food had been rescued from the wagon, Jetekesh couldn't tell.

Emerin grunted, then lifted his gaze to the sky again. "The dread *creature* sent me back. One last act of cruelty. Here, I can't find the means of breaking this curse. Day by day, I'm dying. Strong. As able-bodied as ever. Yet dying, bit by bit."

"That's why you're fighting to get back to Shinac," Jetekesh said. "To break the curse."

"Not just that." A muscle in Emerin's jaw ticked. "I lost something..." He breathed in until his lungs hitched.

"Something," said Kethalas, "or some*one*?"

Emerin's eyes squeezed shut. "That question has no bearing if we don't find another Arch."

"And so," Dakarai said in cautious tones, "the Arch near the Keep of the Falls, where the ice foxes were, it is no more?"

The lines around Emerin's eyes deepened. "I searched a thousand times or more. All I found, in the end, were fragments of the Arch—and one human skeleton."

The man-dragon rubbed his chin. "Did some other creature get through that way, I wonder. This happened long before this recent breach when I reached Nakania, yes?"

"Yes. Years." Emerin's haunted expression vanished and he pivoted toward the fire. "How is breakfast coming along?"

"It's been ready for several minutes. Kethalas, will you fetch the women from the hot spring?" Dakarai held up a ladle. "Best eat quickly. We're losing the day."

After shoving down plain rice, Jetekesh and the rest of the company dragged the burned-out wagon off to the roadside, then mounted their horses. With the team of horses free, there were enough mounts for everyone to ride alone. Kethalas didn't mind riding without a saddle. Kajsa, though, politely rejected that idea and rode behind Anenyasha as before.

Jetekesh suspected the girl had little experience with horses.

As the company trotted along the road, Jetekesh's mind wandered northward, toward the Clanslands. He'd heard stories of the dark jungles all his life. Lord Father had once planned a trip to hunt there, but Mother wouldn't hear of it. That must've been long before she'd decided to poison her husband—when she might have even cared about his well-being.

Jetekesh's heart twisted in his chest. Once, he'd deluded himself into thinking he led a happy life in Rose Palace—doted on by Mother, loved by Father—content to spend his life in the lap of luxury.

Now...

Now, his entire world had upended, and he marched toward a

strange jungle to face untold dangers, with companions he'd once have looked down on.

Jetekesh wrung his reins. *You can't fail them, Kesh.*

Somehow, he needed to strike a balance between letting others protect him and reckless action.

The day grew sweltering. Sweat stuck strands of hair to the prince's neck and he wrestled against a desire to hunch in his saddle. The company stopped now and then to drink from the trickling stream and stretch their legs, but no one was eager to waste time.

The bay was nearby.

The Clanslands were just on the other side of that.

Jetekesh set his sights on Dakarai's homeland with growing impatience. Every second counted. Even if Navolleth couldn't march his army across the mountains before the next summer, Emerin was dying. Kethalas was far from home and wounded. *Vashalan* plagued the roads, fields, and towns of Shing—and maybe even Amantier now.

And Rille had rushed off to KryTeer to aid King Aredel in answer to a vision. What obstacles did they face?

He urged Hickory into a gallop.

The company kept up.

CHAPTER 19
ACROSS THE BAY

KriShen Bay glistened like the sapphires on one of Mother's favorite diadems.

Jetekesh adjusted his black cloak and squinted in the broad midday light. Nearby, Emerin bartered with the harbor-master for passage across the wide inlet. Apparently, hiring a boat was pricey, since few souls dared to brave the dark jungles.

Poppycock. Jetekesh suspected that was the story the harbor-master told every traveler. And judging by Emerin's tones and gestures, the keep lord agreed the cost was outrageous.

Until now, the only dark-skinned people Jetekesh had ever seen were Dakarai and Anenyasha. KryTeerans were olive-complected, true, but even they appeared pale next to the deep hues of clansfolk. In the tradetown of KriShen, dozens of folk from the jungles had set up stalls bursting with colorful wares. Their dark eyes sparkled as they called out to Jetekesh and Lafe, but Dakarai batted the merchants off with a wide grin.

"Ignore them," said Dakarai in low tones. "Anything on this side of the bay is overpriced."

Anenyasha approached a nearby stall where jewelry made

from shells and beads draped from hooks. She eyed the goods, then grimaced and twisted away in an obvious act of disdain.

Jetekesh held back a laugh.

Kajsa stood near the horses, content to keep out of everyone's way. Pitying her discomfort in a sea of people, Jetekesh made his way to her side.

"Hungry?" he asked, switching to the Old Tongue.

Kajsa managed a faint nod.

"Once Emerin's finished with the harbormaster, we'll know how much money we have left for food and supplies." Jetekesh's gaze drifted across the sparkling water to the dark landmass on the far side. "We'll want to stock up. I don't know what clan food is like." He turned a conspiratorial grin toward Kajsa. "I would never recommend KryTeeran fare."

She shyly smiled. "Why not?"

"Spice. There's no flavor, just spice."

"No need to worry about that," Dakarai said, striding closer, a twinkle in his eye. "The food of my country is far superior to that of KryTeer or, indeed, Shing and Amantier."

Jetekesh huffed. "Doubtful on that last point."

Dakarai set his hands akimbo. "Oh, yes, Your Highness? Yet all I experienced in Amantier was a variety of poorly seasoned meats, tasteless vegetables like potatoes and turnips, and cheese too fresh for proper consumption."

"Too fresh?" scoffed Jetekesh. "I presume you prefer yours blue and fuzzy?"

"Certainly!" Dakarai jutted out his chin. "In the Clanslands, we believe in *flavor*."

Kajsa stared between them, eyes widening with every retort.

Jetekesh folded his arms and took a step forward. "At the high cost of an early death. Anything moldy shouldn't be eaten."

"Anything not yet ripened hurts the stomach," Dakarai said.

"Overripe is hardly better, sir."

Kethalas's voice sliced through the debate like a blade through grass. "I prefer raw myself." He stood beside Hickory, hidden in his cloak, a brush in his clawed fingers.

Jetekesh and Dakarai whirled on him.

"That's disgusting," said Jetekesh.

"Keep out of this civilized discussion, you barn animal," Dakarai said at the same time.

Kethalas blinked at them, then his fangs glinted as he laughed. "Barn animal, am I?"

Kajsa caught Jetekesh's sleeve. "Is this in jest?"

Jetekesh winced. They'd switched from the Old Tongue in their debate, leaving her out of the context. He took her wrist. "Yes, sorry. We're only playing around."

"Which is a sight I've sorely missed," Emerin said, strolling over, the money pouch in his hand still fat. The keep lord's eyes caught fire under the sun. "Let's try to keep this mirth up as we press ahead. But first"—his eyes cut to several busy stalls down the street—"a delectable aroma is tempting me from *that* direction. Shall we?"

As the company followed Emerin with sounds of assent, Jetekesh let the day's warmth and the fragrance of food and sea wash over him. They'd stopped just before KriShen to bathe at the nearby Shingese bathhouse, and despite Dakarai's insistence that a natural hot spring was always better, he hadn't complained about the accommodations and seemed taken with the soft drying cloths.

Now, safe, clean, and heading for food, Jetekesh let the last vestiges of tension bleed from his muscles. Soon, they would cross over into unknown regions with Dakarai as their guide. For the moment, the prince could relax.

Emerin purchased piping hot loaves of bread, pesto, strawberries, wedges of aged cheese—not yet blue—and several skewers of lamb meat and smoked fish. KriShen seemed to accommodate the palates of Amantier, Shing, and the Clanslands alike. To indulge Dakarai and Anenyasha, he allowed the clansman to buy a sort of pancake topped with spicy vegetables, meats, and herbs. A single sniff was enough to wrinkle Jetekesh's nose, and he passed on eating the Clanslands fare, despite Dakarai's persistence.

"I hate spicy food," he declared with finality when they'd settled in the grass near the shore.

Kajsa, on the other hand, explored every dish and seemed to favor Dakarai's contribution. She laughed at her prickling tongue, then ate on.

"The boat leaves at sundown," Emerin said through a mouthful of bread. He swallowed and passed a handful of strawberries to Kajsa with a fond smile. "We'll need to restock our supplies before then." He glanced at Dakarai. "Will our horses be all right traveling through that jungle of yours, or should I find the harbor's stablemaster?"

Dakarai selected a chunk of cheese. "We're better off bringing them. It's a long road to my clan."

"Are we going there first?" asked Jetekesh.

Dakarai nodded. "I think we should. The watchwoman may provide the best path to finding the Arch."

Jetekesh sucked on a strawberry, letting his gaze coast over the bay. Large ships rocked in the water. Flags snapped in a rising breeze that cooled the prince's brow. Fishing boats unloaded their catches from early in the morning, while coins passed between the fishermen and the merchants.

Squinting, Jetekesh could see the mouth of the bay where the open ocean gleamed, broad and wild despite its current calm. He'd only been on a boat a handful of times, most recently traveling to and from KryTeer. His stomach had rebelled on the passage home a few short months back. He didn't savor the idea of crossing this large bay, especially on the heels of a big meal.

Oh well. Since when have I ever found travel comfortable?

Still, the thought of seasickness ruined his appetite. He discarded his last morsels. Lying back in the grass, he closed his eyes and listened to the din of the harbor. A bell chimed somewhere, and his heart clenched with the memory of KryTeer's seabells.

Jinji, what's the point of my gift if it only endangers me and others?

The thought curled over his soul, hovering, mocking.

Jetekesh pried his eyes open and stared up into the heavens. Mere wisps of clouds scudded near the sun; otherwise, the sky was the purest shade of blue he'd ever seen.

Heaven is up there somewhere. So claimed the priests of Amantier. So he'd always believed.

Is Harn up there too?

He rolled onto his side and stared at the blades of grass before his face. The hot sun, the cooling breeze, and the lulling noises around him dragged his mind toward sleep, and he let himself succumb.

NIGHTFALL QUIETED the merchants but not the ships preparing to sail out to sea. Voices on the docks called out commands while workers loaded the hulls.

Emerin had already seen to the supplies the company required, and most of the horses were loaded onto the barge hired to take them to the far shore. The extra horses had been sold for coin.

Jetekesh stood on the dock, wind tugging at his hair beneath the hood of his cloak, his feet planted on the solid boards while water slopped beneath them. His stomach already churned at the prospect of boarding.

Kajsa stood next to him, frozen, her lips pressed thin. Pale hair floated around her, catching threads of moonlight until she glowed like platinum. With a jolt, Jetekesh realized how pretty she was. He'd been so preoccupied with his quest, his strange new gift, and the safety of his company, he hadn't noticed.

"Ready, Your Highness." Emerin used the Old Tongue to call down the gangplank, and Jetekesh suspected that was to prevent anyone on the harbor from hearing the prince's formal title.

Squaring his shoulders, Jetekesh strode up the ramp, Kajsa right behind him. The others were already onboard—making certain the vessel was secure—all but Lafe, who had positioned himself behind Jetekesh all day in dead silence. Jetekesh and the knight hadn't spoken to each other since their exchange on the road two days prior. As far as the prince was concerned, there was nothing left to say. Lafe had made his position plain.

As Jetekesh stepped onto the barge's main deck, his stomach clenched.

Please don't get seasick...

A quick survey of the lantern-lit vessel showed it was tidy; even King Aredel would approve, and he'd been an utter tyrant about order and cleanliness en route to KryTeer across the western channel.

The prince's lips twitched toward a smile at that twist of nostalgia. So much had changed since that fateful, heartbreaking journey.

A crewman shouted the cast-off and others flung ropes to the docks. Two Shingese men shot Jetekesh a suspicious glare, then moved off to see to their duties. The barge was underway. Jetekesh turned to face the Clanslands ahead. Somewhere in that dark, brooding jungle, he must find an Arch into Shinac.

Toward midnight, the barge slid into the Zindwéan harbor among other boats. No lanterns bobbed to light up their decks.

Jetekesh leaned over the barge's railing to watch Emerin disembark and approach a hut where a single lantern hung. A figure lad in bright colors stepped from the hut interior. He spoke with Emerin in tones lost to the crash of the waves beyond the harbor.

Losing interest, Jetekesh turned to eye the black line of dense trees that made up the border of the Clanslands' jungles.

Voices rose from the shore. Jetekesh wrenched around to eye Emerin and the presumed harbormaster. Their hands jerked around them like they were arguing.

Dakarai moved up next to Jetekesh. "I think I should go down there."

"Good idea."

Dakarai trotted down the gangplank and across the sandy beach to stand beside Emerin. The voices calmed until the waves took over as the predominant power, then Emerin whipped around and stalked toward the barge, Dakarai right behind him.

The harbormaster hollered after them, then charged toward Emerin. Moonlight glinted off a dagger blade. Emerin whirled, catching the blade with his sword. The dagger flew across the beach, flashing, before it buried itself in sand.

"Looks like we're in for some trouble," said Kethalas, slinking from the barge's shadows to stand near Jetekesh. He still wore his black cloak.

None of the company had entered the cabin. They were too eager to watch the approach of the jungle even under the semi-darkness of the waxing moon. Kajsa and Anenyasha held back, hands on their weapons.

The voices lifted again above the crashing tides.

"We should help." Jetekesh started toward the ramp.

"Wait," Kethalas said. "I'm confident that Emerin and Dakarai can handle themselves."

Jetekesh slowed. That was true.

The Shingese barge captain slipped ahead of Jetekesh. "I don't want trouble," he said in a thick accent, jabbing a finger at the argument below. "Take your things. Disembark promptly."

"And if we're not welcome down there?" asked Kethalas.

"I'm not staying." The captain hefted his chin. "I leave at the next chime."

Jetekesh marched forward to halt before the short man. "We're here under the protection of the House of Lotus—as you know full well. Will you betray your new emperor?"

The captain's eyes narrowed. "I would die for my emperor—but I'll not die for Amantieran swine." His dark eyes flicked to Anenyasha. "Nor for jungle folk. Get off my barge."

A clatter to the side of the barge, a splash, and a resounding cry spun Jetekesh around. Several sailors flung more baggage over the side. Kajsa played tug-of-war with her satchel, trying to wrest it back from a stocky man.

"Stop," growled Kethalas, wrenching back his cowl. His fangs bared in a snarl. "We'll leave your infernal boat, but if you damage any more of our belongings, I'll take your innards with me." His claws flexed and the ship captain lurched back a step.

"Begone, demon," the captain breathed.

Jetekesh had forgotten how superstitious sailors were, even those aboard a measly bay barge. Throwing back his shoulders, Jetekesh glowered on the captain. "I'll remember this slight. It will be reported to the House of Lotus."

"Get off," the captain choked out, easing back another step.

Jetekesh marched down the gangplank, Lafe right behind him. Kethalas remained behind—presumably to make certain the women weren't manhandled.

When Jetekesh hit the beach, his boots sank into the sand. He trudged around the harbor to discover which bags had been flung into the sea. Several floated near the dock. Most were foodstuffs.

He turned a glower toward the shadow of the barge, fury scoring his veins. "What about our horses?"

"Kethalas will see them safely unloaded," Lafe said.

Anenyasha and Kajsa trotted toward them. The clanswoman hurried across the dock, then leaned over to start fishing the supplies out of the black water.

"Sir Lafe, help her, please." Jetekesh stepped to one side to let the knight slip past. Kajsa also moved forward to help.

Jetekesh turned to find Emerin and Dakarai still farther up the beach. He'd expected the two men to have a handle on the situation—but the single stranger had been joined by a dozen others. Jetekesh's heart sank. Emerin's hands were held high above his head. His sword lay in the sand several feet away.

Dakarai had been forced to his knees by one clansman wielding a jagged spear, which was set against the clansman's throat.

The barge captain called for his men to set sail. No sign of Kethalas or the horses.

"Lafe," Jetekesh called. "Hold fast. We have bigger problems than our food just now."

No answer. He turned to seek out his protector, but something solid rammed against his skull, and he sank to his knees—stunned. The world wavered, then bled into black.

CHAPTER 20
OATHS OF MAGIC

When Prince Sharo returned to the encampment in the afternoon, Aredel recognized the weight pressing down on the fae man's shoulders.

The Blood King dropped from the palisade where he'd kept a watch. He reclaimed his seat at a bench within the camp where he'd been oiling his sword, daggers, and a spear he'd commandeered for training earlier that morning. Where Rille and Anadin had wandered off to, Aredel didn't know. He assumed they'd be fine, so long as Rille guided their steps.

Sharo approached him with a tense smile, his blue eyes grim.

"Might we share a word or two, Blood King?" he asked.

"Certainly." Aredel rose from the bench.

Sharo led him to the largest tent where several flags flapped in the midday breeze. Clouds had wrapped their arms around the sun, dimming the usual sparkle of the well-ordered camp. The two men entered the command tent, and Sharo moved to a table strewn with unlit candles, feather quills, ink, parchment, and sealing wax. He plucked up a golden feather quill, then turned to

Aredel. His face held grim lines. The quill twisted between his fingers.

"Thrissa told me of your plight."

Aredel stiffened. "Should we discuss this here?"

"This tent is secure for now." Sharo's pale eyes flicked up to the peaked canvas roof, then back to Aredel. Their intensity pinned Aredel in place. "There are reasons why the *Unsielie* do not attempt to end my life directly. One of those is that they cannot locate me." He lifted his arms to either side of his body in a wide shrug. "Observe." He put his hands behind his back.

Nothing changed beyond a cloud passing over the sun, shading Aredel's vision more in the gloomy tent.

No, not that. Sharo hadn't darkened. He'd faded. And as Aredel watched, the Shinacian prince faded more until the Blood King could see straight through him to the feather quill still spinning between his fingers behind his back. The feather was solid, while Sharo—body, armor, sword—faded to the dimmest outline. Then the prince smiled and sprang back into focus.

"It's not foolproof," Sharo said. "And I cannot maintain the façade indefinitely—but if I perceive an enemy, I can slip away. And if I tap into only a bit of that gift, I'm undetectable at a distance." He tossed the quill onto the table. "An extension of my ability lends me the power to cloak intimate conversations such as this. My limit is half a chime. Any longer and I lose consciousness."

Aredel grunted. "That's a special gift indeed."

"So it is." Sharo flashed him a grin. "I'll have to tell you the story of how I acquired it another time, but as I said, there is a time limit to our secrecy." He cupped his hands behind his back again. "Thrissa assures me you have no intention of following through on harming me—so long as we can save the lives of Rille, Anadin, and your wife."

"Just so," said Aredel.

“Well, then. By all means, let us tackle the root.” Sharo stooped over the table to write on a blank parchment. “I must make arrangements in my absence, but Thrissa is a fine commander without me.”

Aredel arched his brows. “Where are you going?”

The scratch of the quill halted. Sharo looked up from his missive. “Why, with you, naturally. It’s only right. You aided me against Peresen, and now I will return the favor. Let us storm the Hold of Tarradarryn where they have your wife, hm?” His eyes sparkled. “I’ll not let those close to you suffer any harm for my sake.”

“Ridiculous.” Aredel folded his arms. “You’ll be going into the very cobra’s nest. It serves the same end as me killing you myself.”

“Perhaps.” Sharo returned to scribbling instructions. “But this is a far less certain death than facing you head-on. Besides, I’ve wanted to take down that fortress for years, and you know its location. This makes things much simpler.” He dipped his quill, then wrote on, tongue appearing at the corner of his mouth. Finished, he tossed the quill aside and powdered the parchment, then blew it clean. Sharo straightened up. “I’ve always preferred simplicity.”

Tilting his head to one side, Aredel let his brow lift higher. “Is your *mother* going to be fine with this?”

“She hates the idea, which is why she is not present for this conversation.” He shrugged. “Fortunately, I outrank her in such matters.”

The Blood King didn’t know Thrissa well, but he was confident that angering the fae woman was a terrible idea. Sharo was indeed a brave soul—one step short of foolish.

“I think we should leave this very night,” Sharo went on, slicing through Aredel’s contemplation. The prince rolled up his parchment and strode toward the tent flap, armor clinking. “I’ll order the groomsmen to have horses ready for us—and all the supplies we need." He paused at the doorway and glanced over his shoulder. "I don't suppose young Rille will be joining us. What about your brother?"

Aredel's mind sprinted through the prince's words, then he lifted a hand as he caught the present thread. "A moment, Your Highness."

"*Sharo*, please. What is it?"

"I appreciate your zeal—Sharo. But there's more at stake here than this matter alone. Did Lady Thrissa tell you of the shattered Arch and the fell creature that reached Nakania? Did she mention the dragon called Kethalas?"

"She did. And that is a grave matter indeed. But not one we can deal with at present. Far more pressing is your wife's circumstance. We must address these matters in their turn." He blew out a breath. "Besides, Ashea informed me that several nobleborn maidens have recently disappeared from the southlands. It seems something very foul is stirring, requiring potent sacrifices. We cannot ignore the movements of the *Unsielie*. The Hold of Tarradarryn may provide answers."

"Very well." Aredel grimaced. "Despite what you say, I hesitate to leave Rille behind. She's a target. If the *Unsielie* should discover my treachery—"

"Then she will die," Sharo cut in. "Here or there. At once. But she's safer here from any other threat. Thrissa will guard her well."

Aredel's mind raced over the idea of infiltrating the keep he'd seen in the swamp. "Anadin would be an asset to us. He's quick with a blade, and cunning when serious."

"Excellent. Then, by all means bring him along." Sharo flashed a smile, then turned and drew the flap aside. "Meet me at the corrals at dusk. Bring all your weapons."

Streaks of violet stained the darkening sky. Aredel swung into the saddle of his borrowed, black-spotted gelding. Beside him, Anadin mounted a chestnut mare. The prince adjusted his grip on the reins.

Sharo appeared in the growing gloom, dressed in a plain tunic, breeches, and cloak. Gone was any sign of the princely figure beyond his regal bearing and the pointed tips of his ears. Whether snowy white hair was common or not in Shinac, Aredel didn't know.

The disguised elven prince tied his pack to his horse, then leapt into his saddle with the grace of a dancer.

Rille hadn't been happy when Aredel had taken her to the Glade and explained Prince Sharo's plan. She'd gone so far as to beg to come along, but the Blood King didn't relent. An *Unsielie* fortress was unsuitable for a child no matter how clever and resourceful. When she'd backed off a little too quickly, Aredel went straight to Thrissa and shared his concern that the young seer would follow them. Thrissa had given her word that she would watch the girl.

Anadin had been eager to come along, and he'd spent most of the afternoon packing, unpacking, and repacking his satchel with useless odds and ends while he hummed a sea ditty to himself.

Now, as the sun's last rays dipped beyond the trees, Aredel caught Sharo's eyes. The prince nodded to him, and the three of them cantered from the encampment.

Aredel had spent the day resting. He couldn't sleep—his mind was too full for that—but he did lay still and keep his eyes closed. Meditation was nearly as good as slumber.

It had worked, judging by how alert his senses were as the horses traveled south. They approached the bridge Thrissa had brought Aredel across mere days ago and conquered it in single file. Plunging into the dense forest, Aredel risked a glance back. The encampment had vanished.

Setting his sights ahead, he rode with his companions through the night.

As dawn wove golden threads through the trees, Sharo slowed Amaranth's gait. The two other horses matched the white stallion's pace.

A whispery warning breathed over Aredel's senses.

The birds sang like nothing was amiss, but Aredel's gelding flicked its ears and whickered.

Sharo sat straighter in his saddle. His head canted like he listened for something Aredel couldn't detect.

Anadin urged his mare forward until it matched Aredel's steps. The KryTeeran prince caught his brother's eye and mouthed, "What's wrong?"

Aredel shook his head, his fingers curling over the hilt of his sword. Nothing smelled, looked, or sounded dangerous. Yet his instinct assured him that the horses and the fae prince weren't overreacting.

He searched the trees. An insect buzzed near his ear.

The fragrance of dew tickled his nose, mingling with the perfume of sap and loam.

There. A flurry of feathers.

Aredel drew his sword with a hum of metal. He caught the talons of a large bird—much bigger than an eagle—against his curved blade.

A gryphon?

No. A woman with red eyes hissed, baring fangs. Blue feathers beat the air. She retreated into the branches of an old bent tree—the talons at the end of her wings writhing—and three more figures swooped down.

"What are *these*?" Anadin yelped, slashing with his blade. He forced one winged woman back.

"Harpies," Sharo answered, wheeling Amaranth around to fend off his own assailant.

Aredel flung himself from his saddle, too unfamiliar with his horse to risk it in combat. He trusted his own feet better. The third harpy shrieked as she lunged toward him.

Aredel threw a dagger at her wing. It caught, and she lurched back with an ear-splitting scream. Pressing his advantage, Aredel swung his broadsword, shaving feathers from one wing before the harpy twisted away and staggered into a thorny shrub.

Wings beat the air behind him.

Aredel spun to face his opponent, throwing a second dagger. The harpy dodged, but he sprang up and wrapped an arm around her wing while she was distracted.

The Blood King thrust his sword through her side, piercing her chest, lungs, heart, before the sword punctured the other side.

They tumbled to the ground together.

Blood slipped from her mouth. Her final breaths rasped.

Aredel recovered, wrenched his sword free, then turned to face the remaining harpies just as Sharo lopped off one's head. It rolled through the brush, disappearing.

Anadin had tackled his opponent from behind. He clung to her wings, while she tossed her head and growled. She backed up against a tree trunk to try to dislodge him. He held on tighter.

Aredel charged the harpy, adjusting his blade for a proper strike.

"Keep her alive," Sharo called.

Aredel angled his sword. He reached the flailing creature and plunged his blade through the flesh of her upper arm. She yowled and tore at the air with her one good arm, eyes squeezed shut.

Anadin took the opportunity to sink his dagger into her wings.

Sharo darted over. "Who sent you?"

She tossed her head and bared yellow fangs.

Aredel twisted his blade at the same moment Anadin twisted his dagger. The harpy sank to her knees, and a tear leaked down her cheek.

"Who sent you?" asked Sharo again.

The harpy's red eyes snapped open, slitted pupils narrowed into needles. "Your father sends his greetings, spawn of light." She spat the last words out.

Sharo's eyes burned like rime. "So, my father *is* behind these attempts." He sighed and the hard edge left his face. "I hate to kill any creature—but we can't let you live to report back." He glanced at Aredel, a silent question hanging on his lips.

Aredel nodded, wrenched the sword from the harpy's arm, then stabbed her through the heart. Anadin ripped his dagger from the feathered wings, and pulled back, letting the harpy slump against the tree.

"Thank you." Sharo's hands curled into fists. "Forgive me. The ending of any life is like a physical wound."

"No need for apologies," Aredel said. "Keep your conscience. Otherwise, you will end up like me."

"Or me," said Anadin. The KryTeeran prince had shed the look of an innocent. In its stead, a being of shadows stood before the harpy's corpse, blood smeared on his cheek, his chest, and dagger. The kin of Gyath Bloodyhand had long ago lost their souls to darkness.

Sharo looked between them, perhaps pondering that fact. Then his kindly smile spread across his lips. "We must go on. It seems my father is desperate enough not to leave my fate to any one faction. *Unsielie* and harpies are likely not the last dark creatures hired for the task."

"What else do you have in these woods?" asked Anadin, wiping his dagger clean on his handkerchief.

Sharo caught Amaranth's reins and stroked the stallion's neck. "Shadow pixies, ogres, goblins, dark dragons—any who might heed the blood cry of a tyrant." He swung into his saddle. "Keep your eyes peeled."

"We will," said Aredel. He caught the reins of his borrowed gelding, impressed that none of the horses had bolted. "When we reach the fortress, have you a plan?"

"The start of one," was all Sharo said.

Aredel frowned at the trees. "How did the harpies find you?"

"Ah, as to that..." Sharo glanced at him with a sheepish smile. "I once encountered a harpy en route to rescue a dragon hatchling. Since then, my gift hasn't fooled them. A harpy's blood essence is impossible to scrub away entirely."

Aredel glanced at the flecks of blood staining his shirt front. "That's troublesome." He mounted his horse.

"Very." Sharo clicked his tongue and Amaranth trotted southwest. "Luckily only another harpy can track that essence. It's useless to other dark fae folk." He cleared his throat. "Enough gloom for now. Tell me about Nakania—good things only."

Aredel's gelding and Anadin's mare followed the white stallion. "You already know I'm the Blood King, rather than emperor. Perhaps you know more than I."

The fae prince chuckled. "Only what Jinji has told me. He cannot come often enough to keep me up to date on all matters."

The Blood King's heart tripped. "Then you do see Jinji from time to time."

"Yes." Sharo turned a smile on him. "He has been given a rare gift indeed. He can transcend worlds."

Aredel swallowed hard to battle a burning sensation in his throat. "I dreamt of him recently."

"You did?" asked Anadin. "You didn't tell me that."

Aredel avoided glancing at his brother. "I couldn't find words until now."

"Grief is a tremendous weight," said Sharo, eyes fixed ahead. "Jinji is well. He is free of his illness, and dwells now with Shinac's True King."

A frown touched Aredel's lips. "Why is it that the True King hasn't returned to Shinac yet? He's not lost anymore. Does he no longer care about your country?"

"He cares," Sharo said. "But he wages a war against the dark force that stole him away. If he were to return now, Shinac would be caught up in the turmoil. He doesn't want that. This land has enough troubles all on its own."

Aredel's frown deepened. "Even so, it seems as though he's abandoned you. Doesn't he have tremendous power? Can he not send someone or something to aid you while he's away?"

Sharo glanced over his shoulder. "In ages past, Shinac broke faith with the oaths of magic. We must prove ourselves now before we can be saved by any such force. I intend to do just that: Prove Shinac is worthy to be saved."

The steady rhythm of the horses' hooves filled the silence that followed Sharo's words. Aredel's heart panged. They sounded so much like something Jinji would say.

"How did a mass of land break faith with magic?" asked Anadin after a while.

Evidently, he'd been weighing the same words on a different scale.

Sharo's knuckles whitened against his reins. "Alas, my father's line broke faith first. It is through the actions of people—not the land—that Shinac suffers. But the land always bears the consequences of its denizens' choices." His jaw tightened. "You know of the True King's heartbreaking childhood, do you not?"

"I do," said Aredel.

At the same time, Anadin said, "No."

Sharo relaxed his fingers. "I'm no storyteller. I'll try to make this succinct. Long, long ago, the rightful heir of Shinac spent a beautiful childhood in the Veils of Valliath, loved by his noble parents. But his father was killed...and his fae mother remarried to keep the kingdom stable. Alas, her new human husband was as evil as he was comely, and the lady queen and her son endured great cruelty at that tyrant's hands."

Anadin sighed. "Why are good people always subjected to such hardship?"

"Evil will always pray on light," said Sharo. "Alas, the kindly queen died very young, and the young crown prince finally had enough. Whether by the will of the good spirits or through some act of treachery, the tyrant king was struck down by illness. A single rare herb would heal him—and he commanded his stepson to obtain it. Prince Ehrikai—that is the True King's name—did indeed bring the herb to the tyrant's bedside, and he held it above the dying man's bed. He made the tyrant beg for the herb—and he still wouldn't administer it. The tyrant died reaching for the cure."

Sharo's lips twisted down. "Poetic justice in its way. More than not, I feel a great deal of sympathy for Prince Ehrikai. He was too young to face such a choice, yet life deals us hard blows."

"I'd call that moment cathartic," Anadin said. "I've dreamt often of doing such a thing to my own father."

Aredel said nothing, though he'd indulged in such fantasies as well over the years.

Sharo spoke on like he hadn't heard the KryTeeran prince's comment. "All this I explain so you understand that this is where the crack started. That same night, a dark force captured Ehrikai and left Shinac far behind. Humans led assaults against Shinac's borders, demanding justice for the death of the human king. Valliath, seat of power, closed its borders. The blood fountain—a significant landmark—likewise disappeared.

"Much else that happened, you already know. Shinac vanished from the world of Nakania and now resides in a sphere outside tangible sight or touch. Only those humans with noble hearts were allowed to remain in this fae land—granted such on the passing of High King Cavalin in honor of his death upon the field.

"Alas, the humans remaining within Shinac were quick to be corrupted. My father's line wished to rule." Sharo's eyes stormed. "My human ancestors weren't content with the lands granted to them by the heirs of Ehrikai."

"The True King produced heirs?" asked Aredel.

"No, he was very young when he was taken," Sharo said. "His nearest heirs are cousins." He drew a breath. "Thrissa was his mother's younger sister."

A jolt spiked through Aredel. "Then you are indeed a direct cousin."

Sharo nodded. "True. Yet my line is also connected—through my father—to that same tyrant king who abused Prince Ehrikai. It is a strange heritage." He waved that off. "All this to say that the humans who remained in Shinac swore to uphold the oaths of magic which keep Shinac in balance." He pointed at a tree as he passed it. "The roots of these trees drink from a reservoir of magic. The air we breathe is permeated with it. To act in a way that counters the flow of magic will bring destruction to the land.

"Yet humans have risen to attempt to claim Shinac. They are jealous of magic, just as their forebears were. They have enlisted the aid of dark fae—those bound by contract to act—to upset the balance of magic. They enslave magic in order to destroy it." The fae prince studied the canvas of leaves overhead. "They would rather ruin Shinac for *all* than live as subjects to its laws. Such is their blind greed."

"Foolish," said Aredel, but he wasn't surprised. Most people were fools from all he'd observed. Jinji had always argued to the contrary, but so far Aredel had witnessed no proof that most humans were good or noble. Only the rare ones, like Jinji, like Rille —and like Prince Jetekesh.

His thoughts stalled on that. *Jetekesh is changing from a spoiled coward into a courageous leader. It's as Jinji said, then, is it? People are bad in their ignorance, and noble in the truth.*

Could humanity be saved from itself?

Can I be saved?

"So," said Anadin, "that's why you march to war. To wipe out the humans and return balance to Shinac. That's sensible."

"Nay," said Sharo gently. "Not to wipe out humans. To free them. My father and his kind are the rare few who stifle humanity's goodness. I do not reject my human heritage. I mean to redeem it."

The Blood King's heart hitched at that. He stared at Sharo's profile, drinking in the hope this fae prince laid before him with a few simple words.

Don't reject yourself. Redeem yourself.

How? Aredel didn't know. But perhaps watching Prince Sharo would provide the answer he sought.

Jinji, guide me.

CHAPTER 21
FIGHT OR FLIGHT

The summit of what Song called Bird Haven sparkled with fresh snow.

Yeshton stared down the southern slopes, one gloved hand pressed against his numb nose. Beside him, Song's breath appeared in a plume before her ruddy face, while her black eyes coasted over the tree-littered peaks around them.

Ledonn and Shevek reached the summit behind them, wheezing for breath in the thin air of the heights.

"Oh, good," said Shevek. "I've always preferred a downhill slog to the uphill variety."

Ledonn stomped down the snow around him. "This had better prove to be a worthwhile expedition, Lady Song. I do not know if I have toes in my boots any longer."

Ah. There were the complaints they'd been holding back.

"Knowledge is worth the cost of a few appendages," said the Lady of Crimson Lilies. "Especially any spawned in KryTeer." She flashed Yeshton a secret smile, then trudged down the slope, heading for the southern Snow Wastes.

Norva. Where an army amassed.

Yeshton followed Song down the mountain, keeping his pace quick to stay warm. He hugged himself, tucking his hands into his armpits, while he picked his way along the slippery trail. Wind buffeted him, snatching at his cloak and hair. His muscles seemed to creak in the cold, and his feet stuttered. Their supplies were low, and game was rare. He'd been lucky enough to trap a few snowbirds the night before, but the meat had been meager. It wouldn't sustain them for long.

"Did the Norvian girl give any indication of how far her village was from the summit?" he called over the shrieking wind.

"No," Song called back. "I meant to ask her, but she ran off before I could."

Yeshton grimaced but kept on walking. What else could he do?

Since the incident with the *vashalan* and the rabbit, the little company had twice more seen the demonic beasts lurking close but never attacking. Last time, Shevek had started to chase after them, but Ledonn had tackled his half-brother and pinned him to the ground until Shevek agreed not to be so reckless.

Slogging down the southern side of the pass, Yeshton's eyes darted between icy crags, narrow canyons, and snowy banks. He couldn't imagine that the *vashalan* would hold back much longer, nor did he fool himself into believing the company entered Norva undetected.

From the little that Song had learned from the Norvian girl, the man who raised an army in the Snow Wastes wasn't human. Prince Jetekesh had suspected Navolleth was the one who had unleashed *Erisyrdrel*. Some inner madness within Yeshton conjured up images of the *vashalan* reporting to their master: a cold, serene figure, who stroked the matted fur and preached patience.

He shook the vision off like a dog shaking off water. He didn't need to tense up, not if he wanted to be ready for a potential battle. His nerves were raw enough without an overactive imagination making things worse.

THEY TRAVELED three days down the slopes, tripping and lumbering through high, crusty drifts. At last, the drifts gave way to dense pine trees that bordered the trail, offering a reprieve from the biting wind. Yeshton was grateful.

There they stopped and Ledonn climbed a tree to set his sharp eyes on the far valley below. He reported several war camps. Song jotted down his notes in a little book she kept in her pocket. By the Blood Knight's calculations, the enemy had mustered a bigger force than they'd expected from a people bound in a snowy land for centuries. Thousands strong.

Tucking her book away, Song stood up from the rock beneath Ledonn's tree.

The KryTeeran knight jumped from the lowest branch. He straightened up, scowling. "It's unnerving how prepared they already look."

"Agreed." Song tensed.

Nerves humming, Yeshton scanned the forest, expecting glowing eyes to peer back at him.

A howl sliced over the pines.

Shevek cursed in KryTeeran. He and Ledonn unsheathed their curved blades in unison.

Song nocked an arrow and trained it on the trees to the left. Yeshton shifted to face right, drawing his sword while he searched every shadow under the needled boughs. The temperature dropped several degrees. Chills marched up his spine.

From the corner of his eye, Yeshton saw something down the path. He twisted to face it. A tall figure cloaked in deep blue velvet stood unmoving amidst a swirl of snow caught in a breeze.

Navolleth.

Yeshton's heart stammered.

The other three in the company moved at the same moment to face the unnerving sight.

"Welcome to Norva," said the voice in soft, sorrowful tones. "You've come a long way."

Faint rumbles filled the air. Dozens of *vashalan* crept from the trees. Their rank breath appeared like puffs of cloud before their snouts, and their bloodred eyes gleamed.

"Abandon your weapons. Come quietly." Navolleth's tones carried across the frigid air despite how soft they were.

"And if we don't?" snarled Shevek. He lifted his sword.

The figure drew back his cowl, revealing a fair face, molten gold eyes, and long pale hair. "I should think the answer to that query quite obvious. Die here or come quietly. Choose."

"Why not kill us now?" asked Song.

"You may yet be useful to me." Navolleth shrugged. "Or perhaps not. *Choose*." The last word rumbled with power, despite the calm way he said it.

Song cast a glance at Yeshton, and he frowned. Dying here would accomplish nothing. He needed answers; he must find a way to rescue Rille. Slowly, torturously, he lowered his blade.

One of the KryTeerans at his back hissed out a protest, but Song spoke over it.

"We surrender," she said. "Better to live another day."

Navolleth dipped his head. "A wise choice, Lady of Crimson Lilies." He motioned with one hand and several *vashalan* moved up to flank the company. "Walk with me."

Shevek let out a growl. "I protest, Lady Song. This is unacceptable. Blood Knights never surrender."

She glanced over her shoulder, her black eyes flashing. "Then stay here and let the *vashalan* eat you. Yeshton and I will proceed to the village."

The KryTeerans eyed the surrounding canine monsters, likely weighing the odds with so many at their heels.

Shevek ground his teeth.

Ledonn sighed and sheathed his sword. "We must live for our king, Shevek. Pride can't blind us this day."

With a huff, Shevek slammed his blade into its sheath. "Very well. I will dishonor myself for our Blood King. May the gods forgive my cowardice."

They unbuckled their weapons and left them on the trail.

Navolleth glided down the path, his long cloak raking the snow behind him. Yeshton and Song started forward, and the KryTeeran knights followed, their faces dark with anger. Yeshton sympathized, but his pride wasn't so wounded as theirs must be. He didn't live under the rule of merciless gods; he lived to protect Rille, and he would face any indignity to reach her.

THE NORVIAN VILLAGE was built against the forested foothills above a greening valley. Most of the residential structures were built from wood, with ornate swirls carved into the lintels and window frames. Turf served as roofs. Below the pass, spring had set in. The road was thick with muddy slush and dappled with puddles.

At the village border, the *vashalan* had halted, then slinked into the trees. Navolleth alone led his procession of prisoners onward. The cloaked man drifted by the villagers along the muddy road. Every onlooker bowed their head until he passed. Surreptitious stares followed Yeshton and his companions, and whispers were tossed on the eddying breezes.

Near the village center stood a lodge whose solid yet intricate structure was foreign to Yeshton. Smoke plumed from the stone chimney, scenting the world with the fragrance of pine sap. Navolleth strode onto the wooden porch, then slipped inside between doors featuring carvings of antlered animals. He turned around to encourage his prisoners to follow.

Yeshton entered a wide chamber boasting an enormous hearth where a blazing fire danced and crackled. Warmth caressed his beard, then seeped into his clothes. The odor of pipe smoke and ale curled over his nostrils, and his throat stuck, parched.

Near the hearth stood a man of middle years, a woman with a tight platinum bun, and a bowed-over elderly fellow with gray hair haloing his head. Not far off stood a much younger man, barely grown, draped in fine embroidered clothes, hair cut short but for a long lock adorned with beads. The young man eyed the newcomers with narrowed eyes of pale green. He frowned.

"What are these, my lord?" asked the man of middle years in the Old Tongue.

Yeshton lifted his head. He hadn't expected to understand Norvians, but if they spoke the Old Tongue, he'd be fine. Palan had taught him some of it on their travels, and Duke Lunorr had insisted his militiamen learn it. Once, the Old Tongue had been the trade language of Nakania. If a man couldn't understand a foreign language or the common trade tongue, he could lean on the old ways to get by.

"They are spies from three of our enemy nations," answered Navolleth. "The woman is Shingese, the blond man is from Amantier, and the other two are KryTeeran devils."

Yeshton didn't glance over his shoulder, but he imagined Shevek and Ledonn exchanging proud grins.

"So," said the woman wearing the bun, "Kajsa truly did betray us."

The young man with the beaded lock stepped closer to the rest of the Norvians. His pale eyes shone in the firelight. "She did so out of fear. She's too naïve to understand what we're trying to do. Let me go after her. I'll bring her back to our cause—I'll make her understand."

"I cannot spare you, Axel," said Navolleth in his smooth voice. "Not even for her."

Emotions passed over the young man's face, pride mingled with guilt among them.

"True," said the middle-aged man. "We must carry on. If our enemies know of our coming assault, all the more reason to remain here until we're ready to march. Any more of our people crossing the Snowblinds will give them information. The Archon wants us here. And you, Axel, most of all."

"As my superiors command, so shall I do." A smug smile flittered over Axel's lips, then he tucked it away.

Ambitious youth. Yeshton recognized the signs. A boy determined to prove himself a man might easily sell his honor for the prize, tarnished though that prize would be.

Navolleth lifted a hand. "Axel, will you deliver our prisoners to their accommodations? See that they're made comfortable. They speak our tongue, so communication will not be difficult."

Axel inclined his head again. "As you please, my lord." He slid a dagger from his belt. "This way."

Song followed him, forcing the others to adhere to the boy's command. Axel led them from the audience chamber and down a corridor at the back of the lodge, where the smells of roasting meat and baking bread made Yeshton's stomach grumble. He set his jaw and willed himself past an open door to a large kitchen where several women milled about, wisps of hair falling loose from their tight, pale braids due to the heat from the ovens.

A back door led outside to a garden where leafy plants peeked up along tidy rows of soil, promising a harvest. The ringing hammer of a smithy nearby beat at the air. Tree sap and smoke curled their strong scents around Yeshton, and the mountain air cooled his cheeks. He'd been inside just long enough to thaw, and his fingertips tingled.

A path wended into the trees. Axel took it, leading his procession away from the village.

"How is Kajsa?" asked the young man, glancing over his shoulder.

Song answered at once, perhaps anticipating the youth's question. "She reached Kyon Taro hungry and cold but otherwise well."

"Did you imprison her?" An edge caught Axel's voice.

"No," said Song. "She never gave us a reason to."

He grunted at that. "And the wolf with her?"

Song's step stammered. "Kajsa said he died protecting her."

Axel froze, then whirled around. "You *killed* Raum?" His dagger flashed in a white-knuckled hand.

Yeshton stepped up beside Song, but the woman lifted a hand to stop him from engaging. She met Axel's glower with calm eyes.

"No," she said. "According to Kajsa, her wolf companion was killed upon the mountain pass by the venom of the *vashalan*."

"The what?" asked Axel.

"The demonic wolves that have been plaguing your lands and ours," Song said.

Understanding dawned in the youth's eyes. "Those horrors?" He seemed to wrestle against his rage, then swallowed hard, and spun around. "This way."

Song glanced at Yeshton and switched to the trade tongue. "He doesn't appear to know that the *vashalan* belong to his leader."

Yeshton nodded. "Noted that, too. Should we tell him?"

"Speak so I can understand you," barked Axel.

"Pleasant fellow," Yeshton murmured in the trade tongue.

Song sniffed a quiet agreement. "Let us hold that knowledge in reserve for now."

"Stop talking," Axel barked.

The company maintained its silence after that. They rounded a bend in the path and a clearing opened before them. A round, two-story building rose above a stone wall topped with sharpened wooden spikes. Sentries stood before a single gate, armed with spears.

Axel strode over to the sentries. One guard pushed open the weighted gate to let the prisoners through. Within the muddy prison yard, Axel turned to face the prisoners. The gate shut behind them. Another guard approached, dressed in leather armor, a plain sword strapped to his back. He wore a braided beard, his hair the same pale blond as everyone else's.

The guard looked each companion up and down, then spat at the ground and spoke in a dialect of the Old Tongue so thick that Yeshton caught only snatches of his words. Something about foreign filth, unsurprisingly.

Axel replied in clearer tones. "No, Navolleth wants them alive. The perspective of our enemy could be a great boon to our plans. They'll remain unharmed for now." He waved his arm toward the circular prison. "This way."

With the guard's glare hot against his back, Yeshton trudged through the swirls of murky water to the front door. Axel entered first, then Song and Yeshton stepped inside next. The Blood Knights came last. The circular chamber was bare, except for a single table and chairs at the center. Barred windows let in strips of light, and dust motes sailed in lazy loops where the sun painted the wooden floorboards. In the darkest corner, Yeshton glimpsed a chamber pot and washstand.

Axel pointed to a set of stairs near the far wall. The stairs climbed up through a square hole.

"Sleeping quarters are above," the young man said. "Food is delivered twice a day. Waste is removed at the end of each day."

He turned toward them. “If you try to escape, you’ll be shot. Our archers are very competent. Don’t test them.”

“We didn’t surrender to Navolleth only to die now,” Song said.

Shevek made a noise like a snort.

The Norvian’s eyes skimmed over the company. “I’m glad you’re sensible.” He brushed past them and marched back to the door without another word. The barrier closed after him, and the heavy scuff of a bar sliding over the door grated through Yeshton’s ears.

Imprisoned again. How many times would that occur in his life?

Ledonn let out a sigh. “As fun as this has been, how much longer must we endure this imprisonment, Crimson Lady?”

“As long as necessary.” Song strode toward the stairs. “Depending on how comfortable the beds are.” She started up the wooden steps.

Shevek definitely snorted this time. “I hope they’re hard as the flame rocks of Driodere’s two hells, so we can wreak havoc soon. I’m starting to itch.”

“Shevek always itches when he can’t fight,” Ledonn said. “He’s allergic to peace and quiet.”

Song, who had paused on the steps, rolled her eyes, then vanished above.

Yeshton trod over to stand beneath the steep steps and peered up through the opening. “Is it worth the view?” he called.

The ceiling creaked where Song walked out of sight. “It’s nothing grand, but the beds are more than just rolls.”

Shevek let out a foreign curse.

Ignoring the KryTeerans, Yeshton climbed the steps until he poked his head through the opening. Sturdy bunk beds lined the center of the chamber, eight beds in total, with intricate quilts spread over them. Down pillows finished them off, promising a full night’s sleep.

Yeshton glanced down the steps. "Looks like we're staying here for a while."

Another curse answered that.

The Amantieran knight climbed the last few stairs and came to stand beside Song. "There isn't much space for privacy."

She offered him a slanted smile. "I didn't have any on the trail either."

"True. But we can shift things around if you'd like to amend that." He padded to the nearest bunk and set his hands on a smooth wood post. "What say you, my lady?"

Footsteps thumped up the stairs and Ledonn appeared, followed closely by Shevek. The KryTeeran knights eyed the room with obvious displeasure.

"We're avoiding mayhem for *this*?" asked Shevek.

Ledonn set a hand on his half-brother's shoulder. "Easy now. Resting up for proper mayhem is in keeping with the Blood King's wishes."

Shevek shook his head. "I'm still feeling itchy."

Yeshton suppressed a chuckle, then turned back to Song. "My lady?"

She cut off a second eyeroll, and her lips quivered toward an unbidden smile. "I suppose for chivalry's sake, I'll accept your offer, Sir Knight."

"What offer?" asked Ledonn, lowering his arm to his side.

Yeshton slapped the bedpost. "Help me move this. We're turning it into a wall for the lady's privacy."

The KryTeerans obliged and soon the beds had all been arranged—with one for Song's use, another as the wall, and the two remaining bunks for the three knights. The Shingese woman shed a quilt from the middle bunk and tucked it into the upper mattress of the same bunk as a dividing screen.

Yeshton wandered over to the nearest of four barred windows and peeked out at the forest. The trees were tall enough that he couldn't spot anything beyond the prison yard below. He prowled along the circular wall, pausing at each window, but the view was the same. Muddy yard, pacing sentries, and trees.

With a sigh, he stalked to one of the beds and sprawled across it widthwise, letting his legs hang off.

"No." Shevek's voice struck him like lightning.

Yeshton scowled and cracked one eye open. "No, what?"

"I want the bottom bunk."

Yeshton closed his eye. "Fight over the other one. This one's mine."

"It's fine," said Ledonn. "I prefer the higher bed."

Shevek sighed. "You only say that to keep me from picking a fight."

"Yes," Ledonn agreed.

Yeshton cracked a smile as the brothers bantered, but he didn't sit up to watch them. His muscles wouldn't budge. After days of hiking the snowy ridges between Shing and Norva, nothing short of food would entice him to twitch.

—Until Song's voice drifted from a nearby window. "Looks like Navolleth isn't done with us. He's coming this way."

Yeshton sat up. His chest tightened and his fingers ached for a sword. "Alone?"

"No, that Axel boy is with him. They've reached the gate."

"With or without food?" asked Ledonn, like he could read Yeshton's mind.

"Without," Song said. "It seems you'll starve."

Ledonn muttered a KryTeeran curse.

Yeshton rose from the bed and moved to the window beside Song. He glimpsed Navolleth's deep blue cloak just as the man and Axel moved across the yard and out of sight. The creak of the front door followed.

"Shall we greet them downstairs?" asked Shevek.

Song was already striding toward the stairs. "Yes."

Yeshton stayed on her heels, nerves prickling with curiosity. Had Navolleth returned to taunt them, prod them for information, or for some other reason? Thunking down the steps, Yeshton ducked to view the room below before he reached the floor. Navolleth stood in the relative gloom alone. Axel must be waiting outside.

The man eyed the four prisoners with the calm he'd unceasingly wielded since encountering them.

"Thank you for coming down to meet me," the man said. "I wish to discuss what I hope will be a matter of mutual benefit to each of us—except perhaps for Lady Song." His eyes rested on each of them in turn before he continued. "I know what three of you have come here to discover. Join my cause, and I will help you gain access to Shinac."

CHAPTER 22
A SPECK OF GOLD

Jetekesh jerked awake. The world was pitch black.

His head pounded against him like a smith's hammer, and his skin burned like he'd been dragged several leagues.

The attack on the beach.

Jolting upright, his body protested the sudden movement. His hands scuffed against grit. He shifted his weight in the darkness, and his back struck a cold, damp surface. His boots and stockings had been taken, though the rest of his clothes remained on his frame. That was something.

Twisting, he patted around in the dark.

His fingers met a stone wall.

I'm in a prison.

Jetekesh drew his knees to his chest and shivered. "Hello?" he asked the darkness.

No answer. No sound beyond the occasional drip of water somewhere to his left. He huddled into himself, trying to draw out warmth and fight off the mist collecting in his eyes.

You're not a child anymore, Kesh. Be strong.

Pulling in deep breaths of stale air, he weighed his next steps.

He could accomplish nothing by moping in the dark. Setting his teeth, he wobbled to his feet. The pounding hammer against his skull intensified, and he leaned hard against the wall behind him until a bout of dizziness subsided.

Jetekesh inched forward, careful not to stub his toes against a stray stone. His hands stretched out before him, groping over the air to avoid colliding with a hard surface in his search for a door. He padded ten paces before his fingertips struck rough stone. Easing himself closer, his feet found sand. Shallow, wet, horrible between his toes.

He grimaced but tried to ignore the unpleasant sensation while his hands explored the wall. He followed it sideways until his pinky caught a corner. Exploring further, he traced the new wall for another ten paces and found yet another corner. The confines of the room were small, and as he set about tracing the last spare section of wall, he determined there was no door.

It must be above. I'm in a pit.

The thought tied his stomach in knots. His grimace deepened and he shoved back his loose, tangled tresses. His fingers brushed against the goose egg where he'd been struck and he flinched. Dried blood matted his hair.

The hollow emptiness of this forsaken pit sent shudders up his spine. He hugged himself and rubbed warmth into his arms through his grimy shirt.

Hungry. Cold. Alone. Where were the others?

Panic swept through him, chilling his bones. He whirled to face perpetual darkness. "Hello? Kajsa, Emerin, Dakarai—anyone?"

Nothing. Just the drip of water.

"Be brave, Jetekesh," he whispered, tasting salt as a tear reached his lips. He swiped it away, annoyed with his own cowardice. What would Aredel or Yeshton think? Or far worse, Palan and Jinji, who had both died bravely to save others.

His nose ran, and he wiped at it with his sleeve. He could use a glass of wine right now—just one glass, to warm him up and steady his nerves.

A laugh answered the thought. *His* laugh. It startled him, but his lips quirked in a dry smile. "That's right, Jetekesh. You're on your own this time. No one and nothing to save you or offer escape. So, what will you do? Snivel in a corner, or endure this trial like a proper man?"

He shoved his hair back again, tugged his shirt straight, and paced out what he assumed was the center of the room. Stooping, he groped until he found pebbles among the grit and sand littering the stone floor.

Taking aim, he tossed the pebbles upward, each time striking the same solid sound of stone on stone—until the eighth throw. It struck a hollow, wooden note, then clattered to the floor somewhere to Jetekesh's right.

He let himself grin. He'd been right. A trapdoor leading in—and out.

He threw more rocks until he judged that the door stood about ten feet above him and a little to the left. He couldn't jump that distance, he knew that, but he still tried. He stretched his arm as high as he could, sprang up, and groped air before he crashed back to the hard ground. Pain slammed into his skull and sunbursts exploded across his vision. He sucked in air and sank to his knees.

As the pain subsided, Jetekesh considered his options. He couldn't just sit here, hoping against hope that he'd be rescued. If the others were in similar cells, then the odds were against him. He couldn't account for Kethalas, but the dragon was still injured, and he might've been caught or killed.

Gritting his teeth, Jetekesh unfolded himself and stood upright. His head thudded dully, and his balance wavered. Ignoring that, he stepped through the darkness until the pads of his fingers brushed the cold wall, and he traced it again around the circumference of the cell while he used one foot to probe the ground for a stick, a bone—anything that might help him reach that trapdoor.

Nothing.

He lowered himself to his knees and crisscrossed the room, over and over, narrowing his search inch by inch, until he was certain nothing but grit and pebbles resided with him in the dank space.

Frustration built up, closing his throat. He flung himself against the wall and groaned as his head bloomed with fresh pain. Ducking forward, he pressed his palms to his eyes and let out a quiet scream.

He shrank into himself, letting the pain and panic wrap around him, slipping into a well of misery.

Only for a minute. Then you must get back up.

Yet what good would pacing the cell do him? He'd run out of options. He couldn't do anything but wait.

He couldn't see in the darkness. By the saints, he couldn't even hear out of one ear.

What good am I? On this whole quest, what have I done?

His mind tumbled back to the battle against *Erisyrdrel*. He'd invoked the True King's name to banish the water demon from Nakania, hadn't he? Yes, with Jinji's guidance, but it was something to Jetekesh's credit.

He straightened his back and stared into the black space.

Can I see if I look?

Not this reality, perhaps, but something *beyond*?

He'd glimpsed dragons and fairies before.

He'd been straining his eyes to see through the shadows, but what if he stopped straining? Propping his head back against the wall, Jetekesh drew deep breaths, easing the tension in his body. He let his gaze drift across the blackness.

Nothing changed. The thick void remained before his eyes. His breath quickened and frustration tightened his chest.

Stop. Relax. What else do you have do? Give it time, you stupid, spoiled prince.

He set his jaw and studied the encompassing obscurity. His mind glided and he let his tension bleed away. If all he accomplished in this exercise was sleep, so be it. That would pass the time, at least.

Something sparked before his eyes. Or had he started to drift off?

Jetekesh jerked forward, but the darkness remained.

With a sigh, he slumped back and returned to his study of the void.

The spark happened again. He tensed but didn't straighten.

Like a tiny golden mote, the sparking something meandered through the air, and as he watched, its shape seemed to expand until it formed a tiny person. Memories of Ashea, the lady of the willow—Sharo's fairy companion—snapped into Jetekesh's mind.

His eyes widened. The glowing form veered toward him. It wasn't clear enough to make out anything but the faintest outline. But it was real enough.

"Fair prince of Amantier," said a familiar voice in bell-like tones. Ashea's voice. "You call from the other side, and I must answer—yet I cannot come to your aid myself. Hold fast. I shall seek help from your side."

She winked out of view, pulling the dark curtain back over the cell.

Jetekesh swallowed down a lump, torn between satisfaction and anxiety. Ashea had heard him. Somehow, he'd called for aid. But what could she do from Shinac?

How did she communicate with me at all?

He wet his lips and set his head against the wall again. The bump on his skull throbbed. He angled his head to reduce the pressure on his wound and closed his eyes. Nothing left to do but sleep, he supposed.

A smile touched his lips. *I did something though. Hopefully, it will be enough.*

CHAPTER 23
RESCUE

"Kethalas."

The dragon's wings missed a beat. Kethalas glanced around for the source of the clarion voice in the predawn gloom. He still wore his human form—apart from the wings he'd drawn out—too weak yet to take on his proper shape for more than a few moments. Hovering in place, suspended far above the Clansland jungles, he let his wings bear his weight.

"Who calls me?" he asked.

"I, Ashea of the Willow," came the voice.

His eyes widened. "How does my lady reach me here in Nakania?"

"He who wields the Mark of Valliath has weakened the barrier between our worlds," she said in a ringing voice.

Kethalas's heartbeat quickened. "So then, he *can* find the Arch we seek."

"Heed me," Ashea said. "My presence in Nakania wanes. Prince Jetekesh requires your aid."

"I know. I'm seeking him." Kethalas gestured to the trees.

"The wild scents of this place make it impossible to track my companions."

"Come," said Ashea. "I will guide you true."

The faintest wisp of golden light flashed over the air, then streaked across the heavens like a falling star.

Kethalas shot after her, beating his wings over the cool gray air. He'd spent most of the previous night and the following day searching for his companions, following his skirmish aboard the Shingese boat. He'd managed to toss off the occupants and secure the sails, then calm the horses below deck—but by the time he'd returned to shore, everyone else was gone.

He knew clansfolk had taken them. He'd seen that much while he'd battled the Shingese sailors. But the tracks had vanished a few yards inside the jungle, and he'd found no clues to their general direction.

Soaring above the trees, Kethalas trained his gaze on the speck before him, pushing himself to keep up. His wounded side throbbed as he pressed on, fighting the currents of wind that tried to steer him off course. His injured wing ached but held him aloft.

A quarter chime later, the fairy dove into the trees. Kethalas swooped after her.

There.

The faintest hint of a scent: humans. He twisted around a tree, dodged a second, and landed on the branch of a third. Ashea lighted upon the same tree. Kethalas tucked his wings and peered through the dense foliage while a cacophony of night sounds filled his pointed ears.

Ahead, a single-story stone structure stretched east to west. Men with spears surrounded the building, grim and menacing with their color-streaked black hair caught in beads. A single wide door promised entry, but a cluster of clansmen stood before it, speaking in low, clicking tones.

Kethalas grimaced. He couldn't fight so many, not in his current condition.

I had better just slow them down.

He reached inside his core and tapped the cold center where his ice sub-element resided. He drew it forth. His side throbbed more. Ice crackled, sliding down the tree trunk. It crossed the hard-packed earth, coating ferns and trunks as it stretched toward the structure. Kethalas closed his eyes and willed the ice to travel faster. It expanded past the trees, popping and cracking, and skimmed over the open ground in a rapid advance.

A clansman snapped his head up and exclaimed a warning, jabbing his spear toward the ice. It reached him seconds later, encasing his bare feet. The man shrieked. Other guards whirled to escape the ice. It caught them, nonetheless.

Kethalas sprang from the tree branch and landed on the ice without slipping. He flashed a fanged grin, spreading his wings.

The clansfolks' eyes bulged, and they shouted, stabbing fingers at him. Kethalas knew he looked like a demon in Nakania—he couldn't blame anyone for reacting to his pale blue leathery wings, his strange hair and eyes, and his ice magic. Nor did he mind much. In a land without magic, he couldn't avoid the temptation of intimidating the mundane folk just a little bit.

He strode past them, keeping his feet on the ice as well as any Ice Folk would. Reaching the front door, he willed ice to crackle up the wood until it reached the lock. The cold shattered the mechanism. Kethalas pushed the door inward and stepped into the gloom.

His dragon sight engaged, and he gazed around the confines as ice traveled past his legs to coat the inner chamber. The interior was plain, unfurnished but for several torches and a half dozen colorful flags hanging from the walls, denoting one of the hundreds of clans within the jungle country. The heraldry depicted crossing spears.

The clansmen inside looked up from some sort of dice game they crouched over. Ice pushed them from their feet to skid several yards. Kethalas strode past the yelping men, searching until he spotted a door flanked by torches. He took it and entered a wider space, dark and cool. His acute vision unveiled small square doors set into the floor at intervals across the wide expanse.

He prowled forward, scenting the air. Mingled with dust, mildew, and grime, he caught the unique fragrances of his companions dotted across the chamber. So, he just needed to check every trapdoor. He approached the first, paused to sniff, then grimaced and moved on. That prison lay empty.

Shouts rose from the front chamber. He willed a thick wall of ice to encrust the doorway, blocking entry. Grinning to himself despite his trembling limbs, Kethalas paused at the next trapdoor.

Keep going. Push past your limits.

He scented the air. The distinct cedar scent of Lord Emerin answered.

He knelt, flinching as his side pulled, then tapped his knuckles against the wooden barrier. "Stand back, my lord." His voice cracked as he raised it, and he stifled a scowl. Human voices were just so...weak.

He counted to five, then unsheathed his claws and tapped into a sliver of his dragon strength. A single slash split the door asunder, and splinters crashed into the pit. Kethalas bent over and poked his head through the opening.

Emerin had pressed himself up against a stone wall below. He wore a dry smile. "You're late."

"Sorry," Kethalas said. "Blame the fairy."

The lord of the keep lifted a brow but didn't ask. "Did you bring a rope?"

"No." Kethalas scratched his smooth jaw with one claw, careful not to nick himself. "I can come down and..." Dizziness robbed his vision, and he gritted his teeth until the wave passed.

"You're in no state to leap hither and thither." Emerin strode forward and halted beneath the opening. "Have you found Prince Jetekesh?"

"No, you were the closest." Kethalas twitched his nose. "But I can smell him close by. This chamber is full of trapdoors."

Emerin nodded. "We need rope. You can't fish us all out of these pits unaided."

Kethalas straightened up and scoured the vast room. Torture implements lined the far wall, some discolored. He grimaced, dragging his eyes further along the wall until—there. A rope.

"Found one." He rose to his feet and jogged around the rows of trapdoors. Something smashed against the wall of ice he'd erected, but it didn't break. Still, Kethalas paused to send a fresh coat of ice crackling up the wall, fortifying the barrier. He picked up his pace, reached the coil of rope hanging from a hook, and snatched it.

He wheeled and started back across the chamber, then faltered as he passed the trapdoor where Jetekesh's scent was strongest.

Get Emerin first. You need help to protect the prince.

The dragon reached Emerin's prison. He tossed down one end of the rope, then darted to the closest wall where hooks allowed him to secure the other end of the rope. "Okay, climb out," he called before he reached the opening. He dropped to his knees to offer a hand to Emerin when the lord neared the top of the pit.

Emerin accepted his hand and dragged himself through the opening with Kethalas's aid. The keep lord rolled over to sit beside the dragon and ran a hand through his disheveled hair. "Let's find the prince."

"I can smell him." Kethalas pointed toward the far wall. "Back there."

"Smell him, huh?" Emerin snorted. "Well, that's useful." He grunted, rising to his feet, the metallic odor of blood wafting from him.

"Are you injured?" asked Kethalas.

"Just minor abrasions. They weren't gentle casting me in there." Emerin tossed a glower at the pit. "Let's go."

Kethalas took care as he stood, but his side still panged. He first unhooked the rope, and coiled it, then led the way toward the trapdoor where he'd scented the Amantieran prince. His gaze strayed to other trapdoors as his nose located the remaining prisoners, most familiar. A few scents, he didn't know.

Best leave them be. We don't need to start an interclan war.

He reached the trapdoor where Jetekesh's lavender scent hovered. "Here."

Emerin took the rope from Kethalas and stepped back to let the dragon work.

"Your Highness," Kethalas called. "Best stand back."

CHAPTER 24
FIGHTING FREE

Jetekesh jerked out of sleep. The dragon's words reverberated through his sluggish mind. He pulled himself to his feet and leaned heavily on the wall. Blood rushed through his deadened legs.

A heartbeat later, the trapdoor shattered, and wood chips rained down. Several splinters clattered across Jetekesh's bare feet, and one brushed his cheek. He flung an arm over his face until the crash settled into silence, then he lowered his limb to stare up into the dim box of light above.

"Are you well, Your Highness?" asked Emerin in his deep timbre.

Relief flooded through him. "Y—yes, I'm fine."

A rope dropped through the opening and slithered to the floor. Jetekesh rushed across the gritty ground and snagged it, his heart pounding against his ribs. He'd thought he'd be stuck in this hole for days, maybe even weeks. He tugged the rope once and, after assuring himself that it was secure, hauled himself upward.

Seconds into his climb, his arms ached. Ascending the rope

was harder than it looked. He set his teeth and dragged himself up, arm over arm, ankles hugging the rope as it swayed under his advance.

What felt like an eternity later, a hand reached for him, close enough to touch. He grasped those strong fingers, and Emerin pulled him from the prison. Jetekesh sprawled across the cool floor, gasping for breath. His limbs shook with excursion and his skull pounded. He'd thought himself fit until this moment.

I must work harder.

A hand rested on his shoulder. He managed to crane his neck until his eyes met Kethalas's. Those liquid depths regarded him with concern.

"Are you badly hurt?" asked the Shinacian.

Jetekesh tacked on a grim smile. "Apart from a goose egg, I'm well enough off. Although I'm famished."

"A goose egg?" asked Kethalas.

Jetekesh sat up, and gently patted the back of his head. "A bad bump."

"Ah." Kethalas frowned. "We'll need to treat that soon." His eyes cut to something behind Jetekesh. "Best we leave this place first."

"Agreed," said Emerin. He'd climbed to his feet and now extended his hand to Jetekesh again. "Can you stand, Your Highness?"

The prince nodded. "Yes. I think so." He let the keep lord haul him upright and gave himself a moment for his headache to subside before he followed the other two men toward another trapdoor.

"I'd thought you might use your fire against your captors," Kethalas said, glancing at Emerin.

The lord grunted. "I nearly did—but thought better of it. Afterward, I'd only have been a burden during our escape. I knew you would be seeking us and thought patience might serve me better than impulse."

"Wise." Kethalas veered right. "Here." He halted before a trapdoor several yards from Jetekesh's prison. "I believe both Anenyasha and Kajsa are in this one."

After a shouted warning from Kethalas, the dragon burst open the trapdoor and soon Kajsa climbed free of the pit. Jetekesh guided her away from the opening. He was impressed; she didn't seem exhausted from her climb. The girl smiled at him, saying nothing.

Anenyasha poked her head through the hole moments later, then hoisted herself to solid ground with Emerin's help. The clanswoman straightened to her full height, and her black eyes swept over the assembled company, settling last on Jetekesh. Her expression never changed.

Kethalas lifted his chin and scented the air, nostrils flaring. "This way."

They followed him in a short train, and the dragon called out a warning before he blasted the next trapdoor into oblivion. Below, Lafe peered up at them.

"About time, dragon," he growled.

Kethalas bore his fangs in a smile. "Next time, I'll leave you there to rot."

Lafe chuckled—actually chuckled.

Minutes later, he climbed up through the opening, and his gaze locked on Jetekesh like a homing pigeon. His broad shoulders relaxed, and he approached.

Jetekesh offered him a weary smile. "Glad you're well, Sir Knight."

"And I, you, Your Highness," Lafe said. "Are you wounded?" He leaned to one side, peering hard at Jetekesh's head. "They gifted you with quite a crack on your skull."

The prince winced at the memory. "It hurts, but I'll recover."

Lafe grunted, and the train moved to another trapdoor farther away from the cluster housing the rest of them. Kethalas called out his usual warning, then smashed in the trapdoor. Jetekesh craned his neck to peek down the hole.

Below, Dakarai lay unmoving among the wood debris.

Anenyasha let out a cry as Emerin cursed.

The keep lord tossed down the rope after securing it to the closest hook. "I'm going down." He lowered himself into the pit, each movement deliberate. His muscles bulged through his grimy tunic shirt as he descended into the shadows.

He released the rope and dropped the last two feet, then stooped to check Dakarai's pulse.

"Alive. He's been tortured."

Relief poured over Jetekesh, even as fire rose in his chest. *How dare they torture him.* He knelt before the opening. "How badly is he injured?"

"It's not terrible. Looks like they've been breaking him slowly." Emerin patted Dakarai's cheek. "Heigh-ho, Dakarai. Can you hear me?"

The clansman groaned, then shot upright, ramming a fist into Emerin's diaphragm. The keep lord doubled over with an audible whoosh of breath.

"Apologies," Dakarai gasped out, retracting the fist buried in Emerin's middle. "I—I thought..."

Emerin lifted his head, brows pinched together, teeth gritted. "S'fine. Can't blame a man for sharp reflexes." He pressed a hand to his ribs. "I'll survive."

They supported each other as they rose to their feet. At the keep lord's insistence, Dakarai climbed the rope first, and Kethalas and Lafe helped to haul him from the pit. Blood speckled his torn clothes and smeared one cheek. He tried to smile, though it was obviously painful.

"Glad to see you well," the clansman said, inclining his head toward Jetekesh. "This delay was unfortunate, but it seems it has been cut shorter than I'd feared." His eyes strayed to the far door coated in ice. "Having a dragon on one's side is certainly a blessing."

"So I'm not a barn animal anymore, hm?" Kethalas said with a glinting grin.

Anenyasha nudged past Lafe to get to her fiancé's side, and she whispered in Dakarai's ear.

He flashed her a smile and clicked something back that softened her expression into what Jetekesh couldn't mistake for anything other than adoration. Dakarai took her hand, and their fingers entwined.

Jetekesh's cheeks flushed and he turned away. He felt like an intruder barging in on their private affections. His gaze collided with Kajsa's as she, too, twisted away from the tender moment, her cheeks pink.

Jetekesh froze as she did, then they cracked a simultaneous smile.

Emerin cleared the trapdoor, straightened to his full height, and brushed grit from his pants. "Is there any chance you could sniff out our boots, lord dragon?"

"Unfortunately, I think not," Kethalas said.

"Too bad." Emerin scanned the vicinity. "I'd prefer not to leave them." His gaze settled on the nearest stretch of wall. "Fortunately, we have weapons of a sort." He strode to the display of torture tools and caught up a whip. "Arm yourselves. Let's seek an exit as we search out our belongings."

Jetekesh's hand strayed to his waist where his sword belt usually hung. "Good idea."

The company moved toward the back of the chamber, away from the icy barrier separating them from their enemies. Emerin took the lead, and Jetekesh pushed his way up to his side. Lafe caught up and planted himself on the prince's heels.

At the far side of the chamber, they located a second door. Emerin kicked it open. Beyond lay a cluttered storeroom where they found their boots, stockings, cloaks, several satchels—but none of their weapons.

Emerin issued a low growl. "They probably divvied them out amongst themselves. I liked that sword, too."

Jetekesh's fingers throbbed at the memory of holding his own blade; a gift from his father upon his return to Kavacos after Jinji's funeral. He'd become accustomed to its weight and balance, and the loss dug deeper into his heart than he'd thought possible. He'd also lost the ruby dagger King Aredel had once gifted him. Between that and the spare dagger the *vashalan* had destroyed, he was down to nothing.

Scowling, Jetekesh jammed his feet into his boots.

Dakarai sighed. "My spear was a family heirloom. It is unfortunate, indeed." His eyes sparked with anger. "The Tavahac clan has been at times aggressive but never this much. They are looters, it's true—but I did not expect them to guard the boundary into my country so openly."

"Why were they torturing you?" asked Emerin, lowering his voice.

Dakarai's frown deepened. "I think they wanted to understand Prince Jetekesh's beacon light. Perhaps it frightened them. They asked me many questions, but I answered nothing."

Jetekesh's chest tightened. *I drew the looters to the beach.*

"Figures," Emerin said. "The sigil seems to attract trouble." His gaze cut to Kethalas. "Any luck obtaining our horses and baggage?"

"Yes. Both are safe, excepting some of our food supply," Kethalas said.

"Good enough." Emerin stepped from the storeroom and scanned the walls. "I see no other option than fighting our way free."

"Agreed," said Lafe.

Emerin caught Jetekesh's gaze. "Any protests?"

"None," said the prince, though his insides writhed. Without his sword, he wasn't certain how well he could fight. "The sooner we distance ourselves from these ruffians the better."

"Well then." Emerin held up his whip. "Choose your weapons wisely."

Jetekesh stepped to the wall and examined the metal bars, pins, and other blunt-force instruments. A long set of pincers caught his eye, and he hefted it. Heavy, but hardly worse than his lost broadsword. He swung it, compensating for the change in weight.

Acceptable. He turned to find the others armed. Anenyasha and Dakarai had each selected wooden poles. Lafe had chosen a heavy steel rod. Emerin had secured another rod to go along with his whip. Kajsa had grabbed several long, thin pins.

"Careful not to touch the tips," Dakarai warned the Norvian girl. "They are poisoned."

Kajsa's eyes widened, and she held the pins further from her chest.

"Shall we?" asked Emerin, a gleam brightening his eyes. He prowled toward the ice-blocked door on the far side of the chamber.

The prince hurried to catch up, the rest following. As they neared the door, ice popped and crackled.

Jetekesh glanced at Kethalas. "That's a very handy trick."

The dragon's grin widened. "Thank you kindly, Your Highness. I rather like it." His eyes darted to the door and narrowed. A bead of sweat trickled down his face. With a shriek, the door burst apart. Shards of frozen wood flew across the air in every direction.

Shielding his face, Jetekesh peeked between his fingers and

glimpsed clansfolk scattering on the other side of the doorway, arms covering their heads.

Emerin charged through the opening, makeshift weapons lifted. Did Jetekesh imagine flames licking up the lord's metal rod?

He'd better not push himself too far again.

Jetekesh darted forward, heart in his throat. He'd trained hard over the past year, determined not to be a burden anymore, but he'd rarely crossed uncovered blades—or any weapon—with fellow human beings. Killing *vashalan* was one thing. Taking a human life was something else.

He reached the doorway, but Lafe pressed ahead of him into the adjoining foyer, rod swinging. It met a sword—Emerin's. The emerald gems sparkled on its hilt where a clansman's dark fingers gripped it.

Lafe forced the clansman back with a series of ringing blows against the stolen sword.

"Easy there," Emerin called out, blocking an opponent's strike. "Don't blunt the blade. I want that back!"

"Apologies," Lafe said through gritted teeth. He drove his assailant further into the foyer. "I'll do my best."

Jetekesh missed Emerin's reply as he spun to fend off yet another sword. A grin blossomed over the prince's lips. He lunged across the puddled floor. This clansman wielded *his* sword.

"That's mine," Jetekesh said, striking the sword with his pincers. His bones rattled on contact. He swung again. "Give it back."

He hacked and blocked his way across the dim foyer, out into the trees. Patches of ice littered the jungle floor where puddles hadn't yet formed. As Jetekesh forced his opponent back, he risked a glance behind him. The others were all engaged in combat. Even Kajsa had stabbed a clansman with one pin and was withdrawing from a second man.

Jetekesh staggered backward, letting his assailant pummel his pincers. He guided his feet toward the Norvian girl. Dakarai stayed on her other side, beating down any who approached, despite his oozing injuries. Several unconscious clansmen spread before him on the slick ice. Anenyasha was doing most of work defending her fiancé and Kajsa. Her pole strokes were too fast to follow, and she wore an open grin that broadened with every strike.

Jetekesh's boot caught a patch of ice, and he slipped, smacking into the ground with a whoosh of breath. He stared skyward through the tangle of trees. Pain exploded through his skull. Bile climbed his throat.

Emerin appeared in his line of sight, chasing back the man who wielded the prince's sword.

Jetekesh tried to inform him that he needed that sword, but breath wouldn't come.

Idiot, letting the ice take you down.

He gritted his teeth and sat upright. His elbow stung, and his lungs burned as he coughed. The ringing in his good ear quieted, and he lurched to his feet and collected his pincers.

Emerin fell back to stand at his side. "All right, Highness?"

"I will be," Jetekesh muttered, whipping back tangles of hair. His bump throbbed. "Remind me to kick Kethalas later for his ice."

The keep lord grunted, catching a blade with his weapon. "Your sword, right?"

"Yes." Jetekesh set his jaw. "My favorite, too."

Flames licked over Emerin's rod. "Then allow me to win it back for you, my prince." He charged forward, fire tracing the air behind him.

Jetekesh choked down a command. He wanted to win his own sword back—but try telling that to Emerin when the lord was in a battle frenzy. Twisting around, the prince found Lafe still dueling against the clansman who had claimed Emerin's sword.

A smirk slipped over Jetekesh's lips, and he charged the clansman, pincers at the ready. Kethalas swooped low overhead, tackling another clansman who tried to jump Jetekesh from behind.

Jetekesh hefted his pincers and swung hard as he neared the man with Emerin's sword. The clansman caught sight of the prince in his periphery and stumbled aside, allowing Lafe to take a step forward and knock the blade from the enemy's hand. Jetekesh didn't slow down. He swung his weapon again, and the clansman stumbled deeper into the jungle.

A new opponent stepped inside Jetekesh's view and let loose a crossbow bolt with a crack. The bolt slammed into Jetekesh's upper left arm, digging deep, spinning him around. The ground caught him, hard and damp. He lay stunned. Cold seeped in where the sharp pain pulsed through his bones.

Lafe's answering bellow tore through the air. The clash of metal on metal resounded through Jetekesh, jarring the prince's insides. He realized his mouth was open, and he snapped it shut.

Get up. Don't just lay here, you pathetic hunk of meat.

He shifted, dragging his good arm under him. As he pushed himself up onto his elbow, twigs and grit bit into his skin.

A little more.

He twisted, flopping his legs around. Why were they useless? They'd not been hit.

His left arm was on fire, despite the chill creeping across his body. Adrenaline still pounded through him, and his bad ear throbbed. He shoved hair from his face, catching the scent of mildew on his sleeve.

Dragging his eyes across the clearing before the prison, he witnessed Lafe lop the clansman's head off with Emerin's sword.

Cringing, Jetekesh looked away. Kethalas chased another

clansman into the trees, pale blue wings spread wide, ice crusting the ground around him.

Jetekesh probed his wounded arm with ginger fingers. The area around the bolt was growing colder. Shock must have set in. He clutched his arm close and searched for the rest of his companions. Kajsa remained with Dakarai and Anenyasha. Emerin was missing, but smoke billowed out from the jungle. He must be fighting within the dense foliage.

No clansfolk, apart from Dakarai and Anenyasha, remained in the clearing. No one alive, at least.

Lafe ran to Jetekesh's side and knelt, panting. Blood flecked the knight's face, and his hands were slick with it. He still clutched Emerin's sword.

"Your Highness, how bad is it?"

Jetekesh shook his head. "The pain is less than it was. I didn't dare remove the bolt." He ground his teeth. He'd meant to win Emerin's blade back—not injure himself. Not become a burden.

Idiot. Will you ever learn?

Lafe probed the puckered flesh around the bolt. "You might be poisoned."

Alarm flared in Jetekesh's mind, but it dimmed fast. Perhaps too fast. "Get it out."

"I will," Lafe said.

Feet thudded close, and Jetekesh craned his head to find Kajsa approaching, a small satchel in her hands. "Herbs," she said in the Old Tongue, patting the embroidered bag. She must've wrested it back from that sailor on the barge. That was fortunate.

Lafe motioned her over with a jerk of his head, his fingers pressing the skin close to the bolt.

Jetekesh let out a hiss as fire scored his arm. "Be careful, man."

"Apologies," Lafe whispered but probed on with the same firmness.

"We can't stay here," Jetekesh said. "More of the clan may appear."

Dakarai and Anenyasha approached, the former leaning on the clanswoman.

"Agreed," said Dakarai. "More *will* come. We should treat him, but not here."

"It's likely poisoned," Lafe offered up.

Footfalls hammered over the ground, and Jetekesh didn't have to look behind him to know Emerin had returned. Thank the saints the man hadn't passed out from using too much of his fire.

"How is he?" Emerin came into view. His clothes were torn, his hair tousled, but otherwise, he looked whole.

"Can't tell yet," Lafe said. "Dakarai insists we leave before we treat him."

Emerin's gaze swept up and down Jetekesh. "Then we'd best hurry. Where's Kethalas?"

"Here." The dragon sauntered from the trees. His flesh was pale as a cloud, but he stood upright, and the blood smearing his hands was doubtless someone else's. He took one glimpse at Jetekesh, and his step quickened. "Let's go. Our belongings are stashed not too far from here."

Lafe hefted Jetekesh to his feet. "Steady, my prince."

Jetekesh's mind pitched sideways, and the world slanted into darkness. He resisted, but to no avail.

CHAPTER 25
ON THE RUN

The orange blur of a campfire danced in Jetekesh's vision. The song of the jungle filled his good ear like a banshee's cry.

He sat up in his bedroll. Memories slammed into his head. Dizziness claimed his sight. Jetekesh leaned forward, groaning. His upper arm crawled with needling pain, and he grabbed the bandages wrapped around the wound.

"Easy there." Emerin's deep, soothing voice. "Don't want to flare up any residue of poison, hm?"

So, I was *poisoned.*

He scowled. He was such a foolish, headstrong idiot. How many times must he learn not to charge headlong into a fight? Lafe hadn't needed him. And because Jetekesh had been so bent on winning Emerin's sword, he'd missed the real threat.

A hand settled on his shoulder, firm and strong.

"How do you feel?"

He hoisted his head to meet Dakarai's kind, dark eyes. "Nauseated."

The clansman grunted. "And you will for a while. You have a

slight concussion, and that poison is a nasty one. You're very lucky. Kajsa's skill with herbs is all that saved you."

Jetekesh broke from the man's gaze to search those around the fire. Kajsa wasn't among them. "Where is—?"

"She's asleep, after spending all day tending you. Kethalas stands watch nearby."

Dakarai's words sent niggling guilt through the prince. He must thank the girl later.

"Hungry?" asked Emerin.

Jetekesh's stomach churned at the idea. "Not just now."

The keep lord shrugged, then set aside a bowl of what Jetekesh guessed was rice. Emerin stood from his grounded saddle and approached. Kneeling before the bedroll, the keep lord patted something on the ground beside Jetekesh.

"Got these back for you."

Jetekesh's eyes fell on his sword, polished and sheathed. Beside it lay the ruby dagger Aredel had given to him. A lump swelled in his throat. "Thank you...my lord."

"Why so glum?" Emerin's eyes flashed with humor. "We won the day, didn't we?"

Jetekesh dragged his stare down to the lord's hip and the emerald-studded blade hanging there in its sheath. "So you did."

Silence hung between them. "Ah." Emerin's hand lightly smacked Jetekesh's leg. "In a campaign, the victory of the whole is the victory of the one." He rose. "Best rest a little longer, Your Highness. We should leave at first light."

Jetekesh let himself nod. He didn't feel the least bit appeased by the keep lord's words, but he wouldn't argue the point. He lay back against his bedroll and stared up into the dense canopy hiding the heavens. His breaths came even, and the pain in his arm was dull. Likely, Kajsa had given him something to keep him comfortable through the night.

Yet, something had woken him.

His mind drifted toward sleep, and the alien sounds around him began to lull him deeper—until something sparkled before his eyes. He pried them open.

The sliver of golden light had returned.

"No time to rest, Your Highness," chimed the voice of Ashea. "You are pursued."

Jetekesh sat up. "Emerin, someone's coming. We need to move."

The keep lord spun to face him across the fire.

"You're certain?" asked Emerin.

"Yes."

Emerin cursed under his breath. "Pack up. Let's go!"

THEY PLUNGED through the dense foliage on foot. Every step pounded through Jetekesh's bones, flaring up every injury despite the herb concoction Kajsa dosed him with en route. Still, he kept up, leading Hickory by the reins.

This part of the jungle was too dense to safely ride through according to Dakarai. Instead, they trudged at a haphazard pace through the tangles of ferns and across marshy ground. Insects swarmed them. While the horses flicked their tails with infinite patience, Jetekesh ground his teeth and thought up as many foul curses as possible.

No one spoke over the cacophony in the trees. Strange animals swooped down to observe the company's struggle, and Jetekesh's jaw ached as he ground his teeth harder. A root caught his toe, and he stumbled but caught himself before Lafe's hand shot out. Batting the knight off, Jetekesh tugged Hickory on. The stallion obeyed.

The cry of the *vashalan* sliced over the jungle music.

A shiver snaked up Jetekesh's spine. *Even here?*

His muscles tightened. Of course, here. Hadn't Dakarai said his village was overrun by these vile things? That was why they suspected an Arch dwelt in the Clanslands in the first place.

How had Jetekesh thought himself safe from Navolleth's reach?

No one spoke, but the company's pace picked up. Twice, as the night crawled on, Jetekesh glimpsed the golden glow of Ashea, though the fairy said nothing. The sight of her heartened him a little; they must be going the right way.

After what felt like an eternity, the trees gave way to a long clearing, offering the company room to breathe. Even Hickory nickered approval. Moonlight bathed the jungle floor from a rare crack in the canopy of leaves, revealing rivulets of brackish water running between wide-spanning ferns.

Emerin paused to glance back. "All right?" he called.

"All right," Dakarai answered. "Keep on."

Emerin nodded and pressed ahead. Jetekesh longed to exercise his royal rights and demand a respite, but a chorus of *vashalan* song changed his mind.

Too soon, the canopy of ferns closed back in, snuffing out the moon's glow. The company trudged onward.

Morning eventually dawned, pale and humid. The day promised to be hot.

Jetekesh's reins slipped from his sweaty palms. He stooped down to catch them, and his legs caved beneath him. Mud seeped into his hosen. He couldn't bring himself to care. Heat clashed with cold. His body trembled.

"Your Highness." Lafe crouched beside him. "You're ill again."

Jetekesh shook his head. He couldn't be ill. He didn't have that luxury.

What does that even mean? He nearly laughed at his jumbled thoughts.

Lafe hooked a hand under the prince's arm and hefted him to his feet. "On the horse, Your Highness."

Jetekesh allowed the knight to haul him onto Hickory's back. He slumped against the stallion's neck. Its coarse mane made for a strange pillow.

"Just hold on." Lafe's voice came from afar off.

As Hickory swayed beneath Jetekesh's feverish frame, he found himself chuckling.

"What's funny, my prince?" asked Lafe.

"I don't really know." Jetekesh stared at the sideways jungle passing him by. "Perhaps everything. I remember...traveling with Jinji...I wanted to ride more than anything. I hated walking."

"And now, it's different?" asked Lafe.

Jetekesh managed to nod, scratching his cheek against Hickory's bristly hair. "Now, I want to walk—so I have to ride. I don't get anything I want anymore." He laughed again.

"Life's like that most times," Lafe said. "That's best, you know."

"Is it?" Jetekesh spied a colorful bird perched on a twisting tree branch. It stared back, then craned its neck to groom its plumage.

"Yes, my prince," said Lafe. "We learn little except in the lean times. When you were comfortable in your palace, with your toys and trinkets, with your grand food and wine—did you want for anything?"

"No..." Jetekesh grimaced. "Well, yes. I wanted friends." Mother had never let him associate with the young men and women at court.

The knight was silent for a long time. "There. You see? They were lean years, after all. And you learned that you were lonely. We only learn when we want for something."

Jetekesh turned that over in his mind. "I don't know, Sir Knight. Do we ever *not* want for something? Especially greedy men. Yet is theirs a lesson I wish to learn? They don't seem to improve much from their experiences, except to be more covetous."

"Right or wrong, we learn," Lafe said. "More important is relearning if we learned wrong the first time."

How well Jetekesh knew that. Mother had taught him so many wrong lessons. He chewed his lip, then sighed. "Before we relearn, we must unlearn. That's the hardest of all, I think."

A bird cried out overhead.

Lafe let out a breath. "You're right. I think we spend a great deal of our lives unlearning."

"Do we?" Jetekesh's heart sank in his chest. "Well then, I may be doomed."

"No," Lafe replied without hesitation. "You're doing well, Your Highness. Very well. Keep on."

Keep on. Jetekesh's eyes drooped shut. "I'll try..."

"Jetekesh, look out!"

He tore his eyes open just as a *vashalan* sprang from the trees, its eyes scorching, its jaws open wide. It slammed into Hickory, claws sinking into Jetekesh's flesh. The beast dragged him from the horse.

He crashed into the ground, staring up into a monstrous face.

So this is how I die.

CHAPTER 26
LAST CHANCES

Aredel reined in his horse and studied the dense trees to the left of the wide road. Even from this distance, the odor of the swamp settled in his nostrils, stagnant and fetid.

Sharo halted his stallion beside the Blood King, his blue eyes skimming the swamp stretching to his left. "This is it?"

"Yes."

Sharo rubbed his chin. "I've searched this realm from one side to the other and never found this fortress. It must be well cloaked from my eyes."

Aredel shifted in his saddle. "Let us hope Anadin and I can still see it."

"I never saw anything," Anadin piped up, reaching forward to pat his mare's neck. "Only a lake and that frightening *Unsielie*. Oh, and dusk pixies."

Aredel frowned over his shoulder at his brother. "Perhaps I alone could see it, as I struck a deal with the creature." He turned his gaze on Sharo.

The fae prince tipped his shoulders up in a shrug. "We shall soon discover all or nothing at all." His gentle smile flashed like gold across his face, then he nudged Amaranth off the road and toward the swamp. "Stay close. Dusk pixies are among the only kindly souls within the Cragen Swamplands."

"Is that so?" asked Anadin. "We were never molested—except by the bloodsuckers."

Sharo's hand settled on his sword pommel. "Further evidence of your elder brother's theory. He may be under the protection of fell souls until his dark deed is accomplished. Either way, be on your guard."

"I always am," Anadin said, then whistled a merry tune.

Aredel nearly cracked a smile. His brother had always been a free spirit, but never so much as now, unfettered from Gyath's bloody grasp and happily in love with Kyella. The Blood King prayed Anadin's joy would continue—that they would return to Nakania and Anadin could marry the farmer's daughter, while Aredel and Artassa worked to repair Bahadronn.

As the three horses neared the swamp, the scents grew stronger, and the noises within filled Aredel's ears until a headache lodged between his temples. He ignored it, accustomed to discomfort. His hand fell to his blade. His eyes probed the shadows for any hint of a threat, while Anadin's whistling faded into silence.

Sharo plunged into the wetland first, guiding Amaranth along. The steadfast stallion didn't so much as flick his tail, and the other two horses followed with the same boldness. Within the gray swamp, Sharo gave Amaranth the reins, and the horse picked his way along the spongy ground, wending around pits and rivulets.

The familiar trees, covered in moss and chain-like vines, creaked and groaned under the power of an odorous breeze. Insects hummed close but never near enough to sample the riders' blood. Aredel studied Sharo's back. Was the fae prince the reason the insects steered clear?

A song rose in the treetops among the vines. The words were foreign, but the music weaved a sound that prickled Aredel's instincts as effectively as a battle horn's cry.

Sharo's shoulders rolled back. He craned his head to glance behind him until his bright eyes met Aredel's. "I think we're on the right track. Dusk pixies always issue a warning when a fae approaches danger."

The Blood King lifted an eyebrow. That could be good, or it could have nothing to do with the *Unsielie* fortress. His fingers slid around his hilt, loose, ready.

The wind died. Frog song rose, joining the harmony of dusk pixie music. The company plunged deeper into the swamp. A long-necked bird sat within a pool of scummy water, its oversized bill clamped over a strand of vine. The gray bird's beady eyes tracked the horses passing by, never stirring—until a frog bounded into the pool, casting ripples across the green water. The bird spread its great wings—flashing gold feathers—and flung itself into the air. It headed for a stand of trees where a nest draped across several sagging branches. There, it hunkered down in the shadows.

Anadin laughed. "What is that great old thing?"

"A crown crane." Sharo's voice was tight. "They're a bad omen."

Aredel's senses whispered confirmation. Something was amiss. He drew his blade, unwilling to lose even a moment should an enemy strike. Sharo and Anadin mirrored him, their blades sliding free in unison.

In the silence that followed, a howl rose over the swamp. More followed, lifting in a chorus that chilled Aredel to his core.

Not wolves.

Something else.

Something evil.

Sharo caught up Amaranth's reins. "Steady, my friend." He risked a glance at Aredel. "Stand firm. We face the *vashalan*. They're to be feared in any realm—but most of all, within the dark vales and marshes of *Unsielie* lands. Here, their power is at its greatest height."

The howls pitched higher, drawing closer.

"Can they be killed?" asked Anadin.

"Yes, but—"

A canine beast sprang from the undergrowth, startling Amaranth. The horse reared, and Sharo tumbled from his back, snatching at air. His sword slipped from his gloved fingers and plunged into a stagnant puddle.

Aredel had no time to assist the fae prince. Two more creatures shot from the shadows, yellow fangs bared, mangy fur jutting up to reveal bleached ribs. They lunged at him, paws glinting with sharp black claws. Aredel wheeled his horse around to meet them, sword flashing. The blade bit into the first creature's throat, and Aredel flung himself from his steed, throwing all his weight into the attack.

The *vashalan* whimpered as the Blood King ground his boots into its reeking flesh. Wrenching the sword loose, he spun to cut down the second creature, but it dodged aside and drew back several paces. Feral red eyes pierced Aredel to his soul. This *thing* was devil-spawn. Something in its expression could've been human; it *hated* him.

If Aredel were a superstitious fool, he'd fear the canine was possessed by his late father Gyath—but that was ludicrous.

And even if it were possible on the ancient soil of Shinac, I am not afraid. I am stronger than my father by far.

A bright, high, mournful tone pealed over the air. "*Destroy the Nakanians*." The voice sailed across the air, disembodied, coming from everywhere and nowhere. "*Destroy them both.*"

Aredel spun, seeking the source of the voice—until his gaze landed on Anadin. The KryTeeran prince held his own against the *vashalan*, just as Sharo did nearby, sword reclaimed. Yet Anadin's eyes glowed with fear, the grin on his lips plastered like a lie to hide his feelings.

The Blood King hefted his blade and charged the canines encircling Anadin. He plunged the sword into the first creature, scraping bone as he pierced the place the heart should be. The creature fell, writhing.

Aredel moved on.

"*It isn't enough,*" said a voice that wasn't his own. "*You will be overrun, Nakanian king.*"

Aredel cut down another beast, ignoring the intangible voice. Nothing would prevent him from saving his brother.

Nothing.

"*You serve the* Unsielie. *You must be stopped.*"

As he sliced his blade across a *vashalan*'s throat, blood sprayed Aredel's face. The creature collapsed, gurgling.

Anadin twisted to fend off another monster, and Aredel reached him, then spun to fight off the comers behind the KryTeeran prince. Back-to-back, they stood firm.

"*And what of your queen? Will you sacrifice her to spare Prince Sharo, or will you destroy Shinac's heart to spare a few insignificant lives? How tainted is your soul, Bloody-handed king?*"

Aredel's fingers clenched tighter over his curved blade's hilt, his jaw snapping shut. He sliced through the maw of an attacking canine. What dark force was this? Certainly, the voice wasn't aligned with the *Unsielie*, yet it wasn't a wholesome power.

"*Hold fast, my pets.*"

At the voiceless command, the *vashalan* drew back, baring their terrible teeth.

The Blood King's eyes skimmed the foliage, seeking Sharo. The prince had vanished, perhaps under his own power.

As though on a silent command, the *vashalan* fell back to circle the two brothers.

"*What say you, Blood King? Do you know the state of your soul? Do you not understand what goal they have through you, or do you not care?*"

Aredel clenched his fists and stared into the trees. "Enough of these riddling statements. What is your purpose here?"

"*To make you think. What master do you serve, Nakanian puppet? Does Gyath reach his hand beyond the grave to achieve his ends through you, even still?*"

Anadin pressed against Aredel's back. "Are you arguing with the *Unsielie?*" he whispered.

"No." Aredel scanned the higher boughs drenched in chain-like moss. "This is something else." He hefted his chin. "What would *you* have me do, specter?"

Silence breathed through the wetlands, carrying the odors of death and decay. Then the voice returned, wretched in its heartache: "*Stand aside. Accept your losses, and do not approach the Hold of Tarradarryn. It is a fell place and brings only misfortune. Do not interfere.*"

"I can't do that." The Blood King sought Sharo among the foliage around the gnarled trunks but found no sign. "I will not lose any more of what is precious to me. I will not surrender to *any* will."

Pressure built on the air, stifling the hum of insects, closing in around the KessRa brothers like a great smothering hand. "*If you interfere, you will lose more than you know. Do not seek the fortress. Turn aside. Do not be a fool.*"

"No." Aredel's voice rumbled, and white smoke curled from his sword.

The breath fluttered through the trees again, resigned. "*Let the cost be upon your head, puppet.*"

The pressure lifted. Aredel's ears popped as though he'd come down from a high mountain. He grimaced and searched the ground for any remnant of the *vashalan*. They'd vanished.

He spotted Amaranth and the other two horses standing near a viny tree, calm as a breezeless day. Sharo was nowhere in sight.

Anadin slinked over to his mare and dug out a waterskin from his saddlebag. "Need a drink?"

"No, thank you." Aredel wiped his blade clean, then sheathed it, nerves still taut. "Did you see where Prince Sharo went? Did the voice claim him?"

"I don't think so." Anadin uncorked his waterskin and took a long swig, then lowered it with a smack of his lips. "Did he chase off after one of those horrors, perhaps?"

"Not likely." Aredel approached the horses and studied Amaranth. The white stallion stood in perfect stillness but for the swish of its cream tail. He caught up the reins and patted the stallion's neck. "Easy there. Where is Sharo, hm? Do you know?"

The horse's ears flicked, but otherwise the stallion remained stationary.

Aredel stroked its neck, murmuring as he searched the branches of the tree. The crown crane had moved there, its white and gold wings shimmering in the light and shadow dancing through the branches. Beside the crane sat a dove with bright blue eyes. It stared straight back at him.

The Blood King allowed himself a faint smile. Relief flowed through him. No foul force had taken the fae prince. "Well," he said, turning back to Anadin. "We must assume he was taken by the *vashalan* or some other unsavory beast in this cesspit."

"What do we do?"

"Track him." Aredel turned to his horse, then swung up into the saddle, still clutching Amaranth's reins. "I have a job to complete."

"I don't like it," said Anadin, though he too swung into his saddle. He took up his reins and clicked his tongue at his mare.

"There must be some way to extract yourself from this agreement, without hurting Artassa, Rille, and me."

"If an answer comes to you, please let me know, *shaqel.*"

The KryTeeran prince sighed. "I'm not nearly clever enough—and I know nothing of magic."

The two brothers continued into the swamp. The faint beat of wings tickled Aredel's ears. He didn't glance toward Amaranth, though he caught motion in his periphery. Likely, the dove had landed on the stallion's saddle horn.

You failed to mention this *gift, Prince Sharo.*

Still, Aredel was grateful. He spent the afternoon pretending to track Sharo as he directed the horses toward where he believed the dark fortress stood. It seemed, whatever Sharo's reasons for transforming when the dread voice had fallen on them, the elven prince agreed they must still seek out the Hold of Tarradarryn.

The sun arced down, casting long shadows before the mired path. Aredel kept his pace steady.

Once, as he halted to survey a stream barring their way, his eyes passed over Amaranth. The little dove remained perched on the saddle horn. Stifling a smile, Aredel guided the horses across a shallow crossing in the sluggish water.

Soon dusk drew a shroud over the marshland.

"I'm hungry," Anadin said. "If we don't eat soon, my stomach's roaring will surely draw the attention of every foul beast dwelling in this forsaken realm."

Aredel grunted. "We'll stop soon."

The prince sighed. "And then what? Meat will take another hour to cook, or longer, if we can first hunt some."

"Eat an apple to tide yourself over." Aredel tracked a shadow moving between two gnarled trees. The fine hairs on his arms stuck up. He stretched his hand to Sharo's saddle and caught up the bow attached to its side. Stealing an arrow from the quiver hanging beside it, he nocked an arrow into the weapon, aimed, and let loose.

The arrow struck the shadow, and a baleful scream answered.

A great bearlike creature barreled from trees, its mouth wide open and boasting bloody fangs.

Not a bear.

The ogre clothed in matted furs and chainmail lurched toward Aredel despite the arrow jutting from its chest.

Aredel took careful aim and lodged the second arrow through the ogre's left eye. The looming green-gray monster reeled back and slammed against the earth with a deafening cry—then fell still.

In the following quiet, Aredel nocked a third arrow and lifted it toward the dense trees. "Come forth and surrender or abandon your hunt. I'll kill each one of you before I break into a sweat."

Anadin pulled his sword free. "How many?" His tones were low and soft.

"More than a dozen," Aredel whispered, tracking the subtle movements in the treeline. "Don't waste my time," he said in a louder voice. "I'm here under *Unsielie* orders." The words dried his tongue, and his mind whispered the accusation of the disembodied voice: *Nakanian puppet.*

Voices lifted in muffled tones at that pronouncement, harsh, guttural.

Did they understand him? He wasn't certain ogres had much intelligence.

Moments stretched out as the voices argued, then one lifted above the rest, speaking in a weighty brogue. "Be on your way, servant of darkness. Pass while we can abide to let you."

Aredel risked a glance at Anadin while keeping his bow aimed at the trees. "Move."

Keeping his sword unsheathed, Anadin nudged his mare on.

The brothers trotted southeast, passing close to the stench of rotting breath and unwashed bodies.

Aredel didn't lower his bow until the prickling along his arms and spine ceased. He let out a slow breath. "All right, *shaqel*?"

"No," said Anadin. "But I'm not hungry anymore. Who could eat after that stench?" He batted a hand over his nose. "Haven't they heard of soap?"

"Perhaps if they scrubbed too hard, they'd wash themselves away." Aredel hooked the bow back on Amaranth's saddle, and his gaze met the dove's. The bird offered a single nod, perhaps approval.

Aredel set his jaw and drew his sword. He'd not rest properly until they were long gone from this awful place.

The disembodied voice whispered in his ear. "*You are a fool, Blood King.*"

CHAPTER 27
SWITCHING SIDES

A way into Shinac. Could Navolleth really deliver such a promise?

"What will you do?"

Yeshton looked up from his sparse dinner of turnips and pheasant meat. He offered Song a wan smile in the gloom of their prison's ground level. He didn't need to ask her for clarification. Every member of their party wrestled with the same question. How would they respond to Navolleth's offer?

Song alone had no choice to make—that was clear enough. She needed nothing from Shinac. At least, nothing Navolleth would let her obtain.

But Yeshton couldn't dismiss the temptation entirely, as ludicrous as siding with Navolleth would be. He could *pretend* to help the man just long enough to enter Shinac and rescue Rille. After all, Kyella had charged him to bring the young seer back—as well as her beloved. Could he dishonor himself to accomplish that task?

Am I a fool for entertaining the idea?

The Shingese woman sat beside him on the pinewood floor

and drew her knees toward her chest. “I’d struggle, too,” she said, “if Yin were trapped in Shinac.”

Yeshton’s mind flitted to the memory of the boy who’d begged Song to let him come along. Her little brother, near Rille’s age.

“What wouldn’t we do to protect the young,” he said into the quiet.

She nodded. “There isn’t much I wouldn’t compromise on.”

He hadn’t said anything about the depths of his feelings for Rille, his unflinching loyalty, the almost paternal instinct to defend her, but perhaps he didn’t need to. Song must feel the same about her orphaned brother—that strange blend of parent and sibling.

“More to the point,” said Yeshton. “Ledonn and Shevek have less to lose by joining the Norvian cause.”

“True.” Song wrapped her arms around her knees. “I wouldn’t put it past them.”

“No.” Yeshton set his plate aside and sought the nearest window with his eyes. Red-tinged strands of daylight seeped into the room between the trees outside; a last burst of fire before darkness snuffed out the sun. “Nor would I blame them. Their loyalty lies with their Blood King and no other.”

Song said nothing.

He rubbed a hand over his chin, the scratch of his beard loud in his ears. “The answer isn’t as complicated as I’m making it.”

She shifted her chin against her knees. “Isn’t it?”

“No.” A chuckle climbed his throat, nearly escaping. “Rille would *never* forgive me if I sacrificed Nakania and my principles for her sake. And, believe me, that child’s wrath is nothing to scoff at.” He shoved back thoughts of Kyella’s disappointment.

Song cracked a smile. “That’s relieving to hear, Sir Yeshton. An honorable answer.”

“A simplistic one,” said Ledonn. He descended the steep steps from the second story, then jumped the last few feet. Shevek climbed down behind him. "Which is exactly what I'd expect of an Amantieran knight," Ledonn continued. "Your people always settle for the idealistic vision of tomorrow rather than the practical reality of today."

Yeshton folded his arms. "The ideals of tomorrow craft my decisions today."

Ledonn paused, then dipped his head in a nod. "A fair answer, Sir Yeshton—but it doesn't quite unravel our resolve."

A grimace folded Yeshton's lips into a frown. "I can't say I'm surprised, only sorry."

The half-brothers shrugged in unison.

"It can't be helped," said Shevek. "Without our king, KryTeer will fall. Sitting idly in this prison won't serve him or our country. The best hope we have is to rescue King Aredel—and *he* can deal with Navolleth. It's a win-win scenario."

Reason flavored their argument, yet Yeshton couldn't betray Nakania even for any hope the Blood King might offer. And Rille would still never forgive him. He shook his head. "Do what you must. If you should see Rille in Shinac, please let her know my fate here."

The KryTeeran knights exchanged a look.

"You could come with us," Ledonn said. "It amounts to the same thing. *We're* the ones betraying Nakania."

"Sorry," said Yeshton. "I can't. It goes against my code as a knight."

"Fine." Ledonn tugged on his tunic. "We can deliver a letter if you want. To Rille, that is."

Yeshton shrugged. "I'm still learning my letters. I can't write a message. Better just to ask you to watch over Lady Rille if you should find her." His eyes cut to the door. "Assuming Navolleth keeps his word and quickly."

"True." Shevek scratched the bridge of his nose. He glanced at

Ledonn who nodded, and the Blood Knights both marched to the prison door. Shevek rapped his knuckles over the wood. "Guard." He rapped again. "Guard, we need to talk to you."

The door bar lifted, then the barrier swung inward, revealing Axel rather than some nameless guard on duty.

"You've made a decision?" asked the young man, clutching a drawn sword that gleamed red in the sunset.

"We have." Shevek straightened his shoulders. "Please inform Lord Navolleth that Ledonn and I are willing to join your cause—with a few provisions. We'll discuss those with him directly at his earliest convenience."

Axel dipped his head. "I'll tell him at once." He hoisted his chin and skewered Yeshton with a look. "And you?"

Yeshton shook his head. "My honor won't permit it."

Axel's lips pulled tight, then he grabbed the door and swung it shut. The bar fell back into place and footsteps splashed across the muddy prison yard, growing softer.

"Well, that's that." Ledonn turned back to face Song and Yeshton. "Now we wait and try to prevent Shevek from shriveling in his boredom."

Shevek glowered. "I can wait. I'm not that undisciplined."

"What if it's all night before Navolleth returns?" asked Ledonn.

A tick started in Shevek's jaw, then he groaned. "It had better not be that long."

Ledonn chuckled and shook his head, clapping a hand to his half-brother's shoulder. "Rest. *Sleep.* Tomorrow will come faster that way, and I won't complain of a real bed for one more night."

Shevek lowered his arms to his sides and rolled his eyes. "Fine. But you know I hate sleeping in prisons."

"Does that happen often?" asked Song.

The Blood Knights grinned.

"Five times, now," said Ledonn.

"Six," Shevek said.

"Six?" Ledonn lifted his hand to count off the places. "Bahadronn, that night after the festival." He winked at Yeshton. "We were young and drunk. Might've disturbed the peace a little."

"Shocking," Yeshton said.

Ledonn curled another finger down. "Then there were the dungeons at Neminar."

"Twice," said Shevek.

"Twice?" Ledonn's eyes brightened. "Ah, yes. Forgot about that fiasco. So, yes, that makes six." His fingers curled in quick succession. "Bahadronn, Neminar twice, then the Clanslands, that misunderstanding in Lormenway—and now here." He scratched his neck. "We need to get out more. Amantier and Shing haven't yet had the privilege of hosting us in their dungeons."

"Nor Vylam and Tivalt," Shevek added.

"Is this something you'd *wish* to expand on?" asked Song. "Even though Shevek can't sleep in prisons?"

The Blood Knights grinned.

"Makes for interesting stories afterward," Shevek said. "Losing a little sleep won't kill me."

Yeshton shook his head. "I've heard all my life that the Blood Knights of KryTeer are as deranged as the House of KessRa—but I suspect you may be more so even than your Blood King."

Shevek laughed, but Ledonn's smile slipped away.

"Don't go underestimating our Blood King just because he's given up so much conquered land," Ledonn said. "He's no fool, no slouch, and no Amantieran saint."

"This we know," said Song.

"True," Yeshton said. "My words weren't meant disrespectfully. I've seen enough of both Aredel and Anadin to mark their strength and prowess. But they seem more stable than you."

Shevek snorted. “Then you know them little after all, Sir Yeshton. We’re far tamer than they.”

Yeshton’s mind flitted to his first encounter with Prince Anadin. He’d glimpsed the prince’s darkness buried under a pleasant persona, and he knew well the reputation of the KessRa line. “I don’t belittle them,” he said again. “I merely suggest that as impressive as they are, you both remind me of wolves.”

“Wolves, are we?” Ledonn rubbed his chin. “Perhaps. But our princes—they are tigers, far fiercer, far stronger, and far, far less tame.” He stretched his arms over his head. “I’m off to bed, as there’s nothing else to do. Wake me if Navolleth comes soon.”

Shevek followed his brother to the stairs, and they ascended in a few long, easy steps.

Floorboards creaked as they moved across the upper room, and voices drifted down, speaking in flowing KryTeeran.

Song shook her head. “Why do they have to be so likable and irritating all at once?” She sighed.

Yeshton cracked a smile. “I think it’s part of KryTeeran culture.”

“Probably.” She propped her chin against her knees. “What happens now, I wonder? With two Blood Knights on the side of the Norvians, Navolleth will learn a great deal more about Nakania. Shing’s weaknesses. Amantier’s. Unless Prince Jetekesh succeeds in locating that Arch, we will have little chance of winning.”

“Not necessarily,” said Yeshton. “The reason KryTeer methodically conquered each country was because we didn’t unite against Bloody-handed Gyath. This time, Shing and Amantier are allied. And if the Clanslands also unite to fend off the Norvian forces—and perhaps even KryTeer, once the Blood King returns—then Navolleth won’t have a real chance.”

“That’s a lot of ifs,” said Song, turning to study his eyes in the growing shadows. The remains of sunset faded to a whisper, painting crimson over her black irises. Her beauty struck Yeshton, and he stiffened, turning away from her intent gaze.

Rarely had he conversed with a woman one on one, beyond Kyella, who was more like a sister. He was always too busy training and protecting his charge to think much about romance. The few maids he'd known in Duke Lunorr's keep had already been married or were far too young to consider in that way.

Best not to consider it now.

They were prisoners in a foreign land, and she was nearly a stranger—not to mention her being the Lady of Crimson Lilies, highly capable and a little intimidating. He pulled his thoughts away from impractical impressions, and back to their conversation. The impending war. Jetekesh's quest. Navolleth.

Sucking in a breath, Yeshton thumbed the hem of his tunic. "We still outnumber the Norvians."

"Perhaps," she said. "We would know that if we'd gotten farther in our surveillance. Unfortunately, there's an equal chance we're the ones outnumbered. If Norva hasn't suffered much from in-fighting, they've been left more or less unmolested by foreign powers."

"True. But this country is cold. Sickness would cull them faster than war."

She nodded, drawing his eye again. "Shing and Amantier *are* allies, but our truce is tentative at best. If I were Navolleth, I would use that to my advantage."

"He likely will. Especially if he was allied with *Erisyrdrel* and knows the politics of Shing from Emperor Majinglee's perspective." Yeshton rubbed at his beard as frustration bubbled up, but his mind snared on the memory of Jetekesh, determined, stubborn, and softened by Jinji's careful ministrations. "But Prince Jetekesh will succeed," he said aloud. "Mark me: he will."

"You sound very certain." Song straightened up and flipped her black hair over her shoulder. "I understand your faith. I watched him most carefully as we traveled toward the Clanslands from Amantier, and then against *Erisyrdrel* in Shing. He's strong where it counts, and he blazes like a beacon lit by the very spirits of flame."

A grin stretched across Yeshton's face. "So he does. It started in KryTeer." Memories of that bittersweet event when Gyath was killed by Prince Sharo of Shinac—bursting into the grand throne room like a bolt of lightning—filled Yeshton's mind. Sir Palan and Tifen had died there, far from their Amantieran soil. Jinji had also collapsed and never woken again. Their losses, though devastating, had done something for the spoiled prince of Amantier. Their sacrifices had broken through the years of damage Queen Bareene had inflicted on her son to make him dour and mean.

As Jinji had died, it seemed, Jetekesh had awakened. One man's autumn became the other's spring. No one had noticed the light at first. Yeshton, too, had dismissed it as a brightened disposition. Oh, certainly, Jetekesh still had fits of temper. He was so used to getting his way, he sometimes demanded the impossible—but he'd turned that inward, for the most part, and instead demanded too much of himself.

His inner light grew. Each day, it stretched beyond the confines of the mortal prince.

The last time Yeshton had seen Prince Jetekesh, within Rose Palace in Kavacos, the prince had radiated such light the knight was almost blinded. Hearing about the prince's victory over *Erisyrdrel* in Shing, knowing what he did of Jetekesh, Yeshton could only imagine how brightly the heir of Amantier glowed now.

Dragons and demons sought him.

What will he become, I wonder?

Yeshton stood and padded to the nearest window. He stared out into the shadowed woods beyond the high prison wall. "He'll find the Arch." His voice came out low and soft. "Jinji will guide him."

Song reached his side and stared outside. "I believe you. Jinji would never forsake Nakania in our time of need."

Nodding, Yeshton set his hand against the windowsill. Clouds crept over the sky, shrouding the cold, distant moon. "No, he never would."

CHAPTER 28
BY THE RIVERBANK

Fangs snapped at Jetekesh's face. Claws dug into his shoulders.

He squeezed his eyes closed and threw out a single word: "Jinji!"

Light burst before his eyelids, and he flinched, blinded even with his eyes shut. A scream and a whimper slammed into his good ear. The *vashalan*'s weight tumbled off him. He rolled away from the creature, cracking one eye open to find the source of the light.

Me. I'm glowing.

Silver flames curled over his muddy fingers, heat nibbling but not burning him. The light softened until he could stare at it without scorching his retinas. He wrenched his gaze up. His brilliance illuminated the strange trees and his company—all of them, along with their horses. No sign of the *vashalan* remained. Emerin's sword was drawn. Dakarai and Anenyasha each wielded their spears. Kajsa had an arrow nocked in her bow.

We must've gotten all *our weapons back. That's a relief.*

His hair stirred around his shoulders, caught in a breeze that didn't seem to affect the others.

After a heartbeat, Kethalas approached, his silver eyes reflecting the flames dancing across Jetekesh's body. The man-dragon offered him a fanged grin and he held out one hand.

"How fare thee, Your Highness?"

Jetekesh's lips wobbled toward a smile. He lifted his hand to grasp Kethalas's but hesitated. *Will it burn him?*

Perhaps reading his expression Kethalas hefted his hand higher, and a coating of ice crackled across his palm and fingers. "You'll not harm me, Prince."

Grasping the dragon's hand, Jetekesh allowed Kethalas to lift him to his feet. Dizziness sparkled across his vision, and he caught Kethalas's forearm with his free hand, determined not to fall.

Emerin approached. "That's quite the display, Your Highness." He tipped his head toward the silvery flames. "Evidently, I'm not the only one who can conjure up a light show." He flashed a grin, though lines creased his brow.

Jetekesh glanced at himself again. "If only I knew how to turn it off. If I was a beacon before, what am I now?" He managed a nervous laugh.

"Try pulling it inward," Kethalas said, his gaze one of fondness mingled with pride. "Just that. Pull it inward like you might draw in a breath."

That seemed sensible. Jetekesh shut his eyes and inhaled, imagining the silver flames slithering down into his pores. The light quivering before his eyelids dimmed, and he cracked one eye open. Darkness had swallowed his surroundings.

"It worked."

"Too well," said Emerin. "Now we can't see anything."

Odd. Dawn had been nearing, hadn't it?

"We've reached the Deep Jungle," Dakarai said. "Here, no light penetrates from beyond the trees. That's good news for us, in a way. Though we've overshot my land because of our capture, we have crossed into the lands of allies. Here, we might sue for rest."

"I'd feel better about that," rumbled Emerin, "if I could *see*."

Light flared up as though to answer the keep lord. Near the horses, Kajsa stood with a torch in hand and a shy smile twinkling in her pale eyes.

"Well done, Ky," said Kethalas. "Ever the resourceful one, aren't you?"

She shook her head, but her smile bloomed brighter.

Jetekesh started forward, but his knees gave out, and he sank into the mud. His vision wavered, the torch sputtering before his eyes. "I think...I'm too weak to move yet."

Emerin crouched beside him. "Between poison, a concussion, and the magic you managed to conjure up just now, I'm not surprised. Let me bring your horse to you."

"I don't know if I can ride on my own," Jetekesh whispered.

Emerin shrugged. "Then ride with me. Hickory can follow."

Jetekesh lowered his gaze. Shame heated his cheeks. "Thank you, my lord."

"Don't stew on it," said Emerin, rising. "I've been incapacitated more than once on this venture. Who stands in greater disgrace?" He winked, then strode over to catch his stallion's reins.

The torchlight bobbed near, and Jetekesh looked up to meet Kajsa's gaze. She offered him a sunshine smile, then knelt before him.

"The weakness will pass," she said. "The poison ran deep, but if you're careful now, it won't cause lasting harm."

"I think I told you that my father nearly died of poison. Small doses of *traveria*, over time."

Kajsa blinked. "*Traveria*? That is a legend in Norva. How did he survive it?"

"Apparently, it kills non-magic folk—unless you add magical blood into the mix. The Blood King of KryTeer saved him, though what blood he used he never said. I understand *traveria* is actually beneficial for fae-kind."

Kajsa ran a hand over her lips. "That's amazing. If only Ingrid..." The sparkle in her eyes dimmed and she whispered words too soft to catch.

This girl has been through so much...

She started to rise, but he caught her wrist. She froze, tense as a fawn before a hunter.

"Thank you, Kajsa. For warning us. For everything. It must have been so frightful."

Her eyes searched his face, and the twinkle rekindled in their depths. "Thank you for believing me," she whispered.

When the prince released her wrist, she stood up and went back to the horses.

As he watched her go, he realized his heart was beating fast in his chest. He didn't know why his cheeks were still warm. Fever, perhaps.

Yes. That must be it.

As Jetekesh rode behind Emerin, clinging to the man like an unsteady toddler, muggy air agitated the prince's throat. The leagues of jungle stretched on in endless torment, from incessant bloodsuckers to chattering monkeys, screaming birds, singing frogs—and worst of all, colorful snakes.

Dakarai told the party to avoid that last one at any cost.

Why wasn't Jetekesh surprised when one fell before Emerin's horse, causing it to rear? For a second time, the prince tumbled from a stallion, landing hard against the fern-filled floor. Lights flashed before his eyes, and he lay stunned for several long seconds before breath found his lungs again.

He wasn't the only one thrown. Lafe landed in the dense undergrowth nearby, and a string of curses followed as he hacked his way free with his broadsword. The knight reached Jetekesh's side, hauled him into a sitting position, and pressed a flask of water to the prince's lips.

Jetekesh drank greedily, but immediately regretted it, vomiting up bile.

Unfortunately, Lafe's horse had been bitten. Emerin killed the poor animal to spare it an agonized end.

"Ride Hickory," Jetekesh commanded his protector before he eased himself back onto Emerin's mount, stomach still churning. Every muscle flared, and his head pounded with a headache that nearly crossed his eyes.

Lafe didn't protest. The company pressed on, leaving the dead horse behind on the trail. They didn't have tools or time to bury it.

Ages later, Dakarai called a halt, clutching the guiding torch in his hand. "We will not reach a village tonight. Best to set up camp and have two stand guard at any given time until morning."

"Agreed." Emerin swung his leg over the saddle horn, dismounted, then offered a hand to Jetekesh. "I think the prince has taken enough of a beating for one day."

Jetekesh couldn't even conjure up a denial. The sooner he lay in a bedroll, the sooner his nerves might quiet down. Every alien sound, every beat of a wing, every scuff of hooves on stone, had his fists bunched and his jaw clenched.

Emerin leaned close. "You look feverish again, my prince." He tugged off a glove and rested his wrist against Jetekesh's forehead. "Kajsa, he needs your care."

The girl reappeared like a ghost in the darkness, and she gently steered Jetekesh to a wide rock near Hickory. Lafe stationed himself beside the rock, sword at the ready, eyes flicking between ground and trees.

"Water," Kajsa said, pressing a flask into the prince's hands.

He took short, careful swallows while Kajsa read his pulse, checked his eyes, then rested a wet cloth against his neck. A charge of cold raced through him and he shivered.

"Stay still," she said in tones like honey blossoms. "I'll return with herbs soon."

Anenyasha built a fire while the rest of the company worked to set up the large tent. Jetekesh didn't know how they'd brought all their supplies along, and most of their things had been aboard the barge before their capture.

His eyes strayed from the tent, and he blinked at two mules.

So, Kethalas had improvised.

Did the mules belong to someone on the boat?

Nausea swept over Jetekesh, and he leaned forward, retching.

"Kajsa!" Lafe's voice sliced over the air like a ringing blade.

The girl returned, knelt beside Jetekesh, and ran her hand in circles up and down his back. "It may be his concussion or remnants of the poison." She chewed her lip. "We cannot move until he's better. Too much jarring could kill him."

Lafe sighed. "Tell Emerin. Please."

She started off.

"Wait." Jetekesh lifted his head and wiped vomit from his chin, unable to banish an image of Mother's disapproving face. "We can't stay here. That would be a much more certain death. At dawn, we ride on."

Lafe shook his head. "I won't risk you."

"And I won't risk my company." A burning sensation climbed Jetekesh's throat as his stomach heaved. He turned away and vomited again. "I-isn't this a good sign?" Cold seeped through his body. "The poison needs to come out, d-doesn't it?"

"Yes," said Kajsa in muted tones. "It does."

He nodded and retched again, the acidic flavor blazing on his tongue. Was this really injury or poison, or had Jetekesh used too much of his new gift? It had killed Jinji by degrees.

Panic clutched his heart, and he swallowed hard. Darkness closed around him. He tried to twist to avoid collapsing in his own vomit but lost consciousness before he knew if he succeeded.

The storyteller sat at a lazy riverbank beneath a drooping willow tree, eyeing Jetekesh with open fondness. "You look terrible, my friend." He shifted his bare feet beneath the flowing water.

"Jinji!" Jetekesh raced to the bank. "Is this real?" A stab of panic caught in his lungs. "Am I dead?" He stared around the unfamiliar woods, and his gaze snagged on a cluster of fingernail-sized fairies flitting in the twilight sky.

"Those are dusk pixies," Jinji said, as though he could read Jetekesh's mind. "And no, you are not dead. Nor are you dying because of your magic. Rest easy in that knowledge. Your death will come another way, as it comes for all. But not this day. Not from this ailment." He patted the grass beside him. "Sit, my friend. We should talk awhile."

Jetekesh flopped down beside the storyteller, disregarding his dignity. His heart swelled. "Is this a dream, then?"

"Akin to one," said Jinji. His turquoise eyes roamed the trees on the opposing shore, and Jetekesh tracked his gaze. Shadows clung to the ancient, mossy trees, and more dusk pixies flitted between the boughs like tiny hummingbirds.

Silence wrapped its fingers around the two friends, and Jetekesh reveled in the comfortable quiet. His nerves were still, his mind didn't race, and his heart was soothed in proximity to his lost friend.

After several moments, Jinji stirred. “You fear death. That is natural, I think.”

“Did you fear it?” asked Jetekesh, turning to study Jinji’s profile.

“Yes, in a way.”

“In what way?”

The storyteller folded his hands in his lap. “I feared a life with no purpose.”

The words seized Jetekesh’s heart in a vise. *That’s it. That’s my fear.*

Jinji’s sympathetic smile told him that the man understood. “In that fear, I failed to understand something vital, Your Highness.”

Jetekesh’s heart squeezed tighter. “Don’t call me that. There are no titles between us.”

The storyteller’s smile gentled even more, and he rested a hand on Jetekesh’s shoulder. “As you wish, Jetekesh. Now, heed me if you can. No life is without purpose. The humble farmer grows food. The lofty king governs. We are like ripples in a lake, affecting change with every breath. Every step gives your life meaning. Do not shackle yourself to someone else’s ideals. Discover your own ideals, weigh them against your conscience, and let the fruits of your actions bear witness to your purpose.”

“But how?” asked Jetekesh. “Everything I try comes to nothing. I’m useless on the very quest I command.”

“Useless?” asked Jinji, canting his head. He let his hand drop from the prince’s shoulder. “How so?”

“I can’t fight like the others!” Each word spewed from his mouth like acid. “I’m not a healer. I’m barely leading them at all. Emerin’s so much better at it. People *like* him. How can anyone like me at all? I’m frail, I whine all the time—and I keep trying to change, but I keep failing miserably!” His fingers curled against his legs, bunching the fabric of his hosen.

A breeze stirred his hair and brushed his burning cheek like a gentle kiss. The faint scent of moss floated with it, stirring sensations from an early childhood trip Jetekesh barely recalled.

The storyteller withdrew his gaze to consider the languid river. "We fail every single day."

The words pattered over Jetekesh's soul like raindrops. He let them seep into every crack of his mind, turning them over. How could such an admission feel so soothing?

Jinji twisted to face Jetekesh. "That won't stop, not while we're still mortal. Perhaps when our souls slip beyond the fetters, the travails, the frailties of this sphere, that will change. But not so now. Don't despair, my friend. Rejoice. Each failure offers a lesson if we'll only seek it."

A bitter laugh escaped Jetekesh's lips. "How can I? I hate half the lessons—the *travails*—I must endure. I can't rejoice in them."

"Not in the pain, no," said Jinji. "But in surviving it, yes. Do you not see how precious, how very wondrous that is? Each time we stand after we've fallen is a victory following failure."

Jetekesh stilled at that. "Even so..." His voice cracked. He licked his lips and tried again. "Even so, I'm not very useful in those little victories."

"Aren't you? Is standing after you've been hit not inspiring to others?"

"Perhaps those weaker than myself. But the others in my company are stronger than I."

"Ah. There you are wrong, my friend. On what scale do you weigh your strength against others?" Jinji shook his head. "You've learned so much—and have much yet to learn. That is well. The moment you cease to learn is the moment you truly fail."

Jetekesh bowed his head. "Then I've failed already. I spent years not learning anything."

"And yet," said Jinji, "you're trying again. You see? No failure is permanent. Not unless we give in forever."

Mist drifted across Jetekesh's eyes. He blinked it back until his vision cleared. "Forgive me for despairing, Jinji. You brought me here to discuss something, I believe."

"Yes," said Jinji. "I wished to let you know how proud I am of you, and how much meaning your life has. Take heart, dear friend." The storyteller's words echoed in the fog settling across the riverbank, hampering the prince's view of Jinji. "Be brave. Fight on."

LIGHT LEAKED between Jetekesh's eyelids. He pried them open and a tear rolled from the corner of one eye to splash against his pillow.

"I'll try, Jinji. I promise."

CHAPTER 29
FLAMES

A village rose before the company. Jetekesh peeked around Emerin's shoulder to catch his first glimpse of how the clansfolk lived. Circular huts lined a wide, hard-packed road. Somewhere within one structure, an infant cried. Clouds covered the afternoon sun, casting everything in gray hues.

The village green was wide and lush, with a single well where a handful of spear-wielding clansfolk stood observing the approaching horses. Dakarai advanced toward the well after cautioning the company to halt and stay quiet.

The clansfolk conversed, their soft clicks lulling Jetekesh toward sleep.

Shaking himself awake, Jetekesh turned to study the thatched mud huts set against the tall, dark trees surrounding them. How anyone could live in such a place, he didn't know. The cry of animals, the poison serpents and foliage, the absence of proper drinking water except out of this one well... It made his skin prickle. Yet Dakarai seemed proud of his homeland. Proud of its strangeness, and even its dangers.

Did Jetekesh, too, take aspects of Amantier for granted that others found strange or even horrible?

I suppose living in a land out to kill you could help hone your skills.

Even with that grudging thought, he struggled to find any beauty in this saints-forsaken realm.

Jinji would find something.

That thought still didn't motivate Jetekesh to look any closer.

The clicking voices rose in volume. A clansman with orange-tipped braids trotted toward Dakarai. The two men grinned at each other, then embraced like long-lost brothers. The voices lowered, then ceased, and Dakarai returned to the horses, beaming. "We're welcome to stay as long as we need. My friend relocated here after the *vashalan* attack in our own territory. He has great sway over the village elders—as he has since married their chieftain's daughter. They are all strong warriors. They do not fear the *vashalan*."

Jetekesh eyed the clansfolk standing near the well. "Maybe they should."

Dakarai padded to his side and extended a hand. "Allow me to assist you, Your Highness."

Jetekesh accepted the offer. If he tried to slide off Emerin's mount alone, he'd probably teeter and fall. He'd already endured too many humiliations on this venture.

On solid ground, Jetekesh followed Dakarai to a nearby hut. The hut was empty but for a row of grass-stuffed cots, a low table, and several lanterns. Two windows, framed with colorful curtains, let in extra light.

"The village cooks will bring sustenance soon," said Dakarai. He left Jetekesh alone in the hut and went back out to help the others tie off the horses and haul in supplies.

The prince wandered to the nearest cot and eased himself onto it. His fingers curled around his dagger hilt. He'd been glad to get it back, along with his sword. Slowly, he let himself relax.

The cot was solid, and the grass was surprisingly comfortable. *This is certainly better than a bedroll on hard ground.*

He stretched out across the cot, tucked his arms under his head, and stared at the thatched ceiling. His stomach rumbled above the noise of the company outside. But he couldn't think of eating yet. Not with the taste of bile still fresh on his tongue.

Rolling over, he stared at the mud wall and traced the fine cracks running up its length.

They'd reached the depths of the Clanslands. Now what? Dakarai wanted to return to the remnants of his village and converse with the watchwoman there—but that would require backtracking. And what would it accomplish? She had sent both Dakarai and Anenyasha to Amantier in order to bring Jetekesh back—because somehow, he was meant to find the Arch hidden within this deadly country.

How, Jinji? What do I need to do?

He'd dreamt of the storyteller, yet he'd never asked Jinji the truly vital question.

Frustration rolled through him like a flash of heat, and he sat up with a growl. At the door, Kajsa froze, clutching an armful of packs.

They stared at each other.

Jetekesh pulled a hand through his hair with a sigh. "Sorry. I didn't mean to startle you."

She shook her head and inched into the one-room hut. She placed the packs beside the far cot, then turned to face him. "How do you feel?"

His shoulders slumped. "Exhausted, as we all are, I suspect."

Kajsa nodded and approached, rubbing her palms across her tunic top. "Let me see." She rested a hand over his forehead, the coolness of her skin welcome in the humid heat. He sank into her touch, closing his eyes.

"You should rest." Kajsa drew her hand back.

He pried his eyes open and nodded. “I know I should...if only my mind would keep quiet.”

Her ice-blue eyes darted across his face, studying him. “You doubt yourself.”

“Am I so easy to read?”

She shook her head. “No. Only to someone who understands, I think.” She caught a strand of platinum hair and stroked it in turns, one hand, then the other, dragging down in a nervous tick. “I’ve never been very confident.”

He nearly snorted at that. *An understatement if I’ve ever heard one.*

Schooling his expression, he offered a sympathetic smile. “I’m afraid until recently I had confidence in abundance. Misplaced, mind you. But I never lacked it.” He lowered his head and stared at his palms resting on his lap. His smile weakened. “A trait from my mother, I suspect.”

The Norvian girl knelt before his cot and rested her soft hands over his. “Don’t think of her.” Kajsa’s whisper curled over him like a caress.

Somehow, her voice did banish the image of that wretched woman. He lifted his head and tipped it to one side. “What are you? A fairy?”

She blinked, then laughed. “Me, a fairy? I’m not mischievous.”

He shrugged. “So you say. But you can’t be human. You’re not like other...” His voice faded. *I’m a fool. Not all women are like Mother. She’s the broken one.* Jetekesh shook his head and swallowed. “Forgive me. I’ve just never met anyone like you.”

“I’m surprised,” said Kajsa, slipping her hands from his to rest against her thighs. “Growing up, you must have seen many varieties of people in your castle.”

“Actually, no. My mother was...careful...with any influences in my life.”

Mother had always been afraid he might catch some plague or other that would mar his face or cripple his body. Only on rare occasions, when Father had plucked him up for an outing without Mother, could Jetekesh relish the wonders of childhood—the cool relief of a swimming hole, the clammy feel of a frog, the wonder of a night sky far beyond the pollution of city lights.

But he'd rarely encountered people outside his circle of influence.

Not until he met Jinji.

"You remind me of him." The words escaped Jetekesh's lips. His cheeks warmed, but he'd already blundered. He could only mend his declaration. "Not in everything, of course. He wasn't shy like you, or female. Or a hundred other things, I'm sure. But you're both gentle."

Kajsa blinked at him. "I remind you of whom?"

Blast. His attempts to mend things had only confused her and made him look more of a fool.

Jetekesh scratched the side of his neck. "Like Jinji. The—the storyteller."

Her lips parted in a silent O. Light caught her eyes and sparkled. "Thank you."

He ducked his head, strangely sheepish, and his stomach writhed.

Emerin took that moment to enter the hut, carrying a bedroll across one shoulder. "Feeling any better, Your Highness?" His gaze flicking between them with a diplomatically blank face.

Jetekesh blew out a breath. "A little. My legs still feel weak." He rubbed a hand against his knee. "I wish we didn't have to stop so soon. We need to find that Arch."

"Yes, but we can't if you keel over." Emerin slung the bedroll onto one cot, then untied it and peeled layers of blanket apart. "It's hot enough, I doubt we'll need more than one of these apiece

—but Dakarai assures me we need something to cover our feet. The rats here are huge."

Disgust churned in Jetekesh's stomach. "Lovely."

Emerin tossed a lightweight blanket to him. "Catch."

Jetekesh snatched it from the air. "I might sleep with my boots on."

The keep lord winked. "Clever. That's my plan too." He marched back outside where his rich tones entwined with the quieter voices of Kethalas and Dakarai.

"Sleep," said Kajsa. She rose and moved toward the door, her steps soft, nearly gliding.

Jetekesh lay back down and hugged the blanket with his good arm, unwilling to crawl under it in the heat. He turned back to the wall and tried to ignore his belly's fresh rumbles. A grimace touched his lips, but he shut his eyes.

This might be the last respite you get for a long time. Don't waste it.

He let himself fall into dreams.

Smoke clung to his nostrils and crept down his throat. Jetekesh wrenched upright, coughing. His lungs burned. The crackle of fire filled the hut. Heat licked at his skin. He sprang from the cot and searched the beds for Emerin—but every cot stood empty.

Flames climbed up the mud walls and blazed across the thatching above. The door was barred by fire. The windows, too.

He spun in a full circle, seeking an exit. Coughs tore from his throat.

Think, Kesh. Think!

A figure appeared before him, draped in a midnight blue cloak. Golden eyes peered out from under the deep cowl.

Jetekesh's heart skipped. "You!" His voice caught and a fit of coughs took him.

"I will spare you," said Navolleth, "if you only surrender to me."

Jetekesh wiped tears from his burning eyes and straightened up. The roar of flames crackled in his ears, and he raised his voice above the conflagration. "Why? What do you want from me this time? Is my death no longer required?" Each word charged Jetekesh's blood until his fear faded away. He took a step toward the cloaked figure. "You won't win, Navolleth. We'll beat your army and send you back to Shinac to answer to Prince Sharo."

The cloaked figure listed his head, then he drew back his cowl. "Will you then, boy?" Navolleth's lips twisted in disdain, but the sorrow remained in those gold eyes. "Your company will not find what you seek. It is gone. Destroyed. The dragon will perish in this wilderness of humanity. Each of your companions will suffer a similar end."

"Why?" asked Jetekesh, hands curling into tight fists. "What do you have against Nakania?"

Navolleth's eyes narrowed. "I will not waste words on your *ilk.*" He spat out the last word. "Die, child of Amantier. Know that they will mourn you. Regret with your last breath."

He vanished in the smoke.

Jetekesh's vision muddied, and he staggered to one side. Where were the others? Where was Lafe, always so vigilant?

Will I really die here?

He'd summoned light to swallow Emerin's fire before. Could he do it again now?

Jetekesh shook his head to clear it, then made his way across the room, circling the worst of the rolling flames. Each breath seared his lungs. He aimed for the closest window where the flames sparked and chattered, consuming the last of the curtain. Jetekesh halted, eyeing the fire.

Don't waste more time.

He could live with burns if he must. Just escape!

Drawing a deep breath, Jetekesh threw his arms over his head and plunged through the fire. It felt strangely cool against his clothes, like a breath of wind on a sweltering summer day. His knees collided with the wall, and he stretched one hand out to grope for the window.

There. His fingers caught the square window frame and the rough surface of dried mud. He blew out his breath, gripped the window well, and hefted himself through the tight space.

Hands seized him, pulling him through faster.

Night air curled around his face, cold after the blazing heat.

Jetekesh dropped to the hard-packed earth, gasping, trembling.

"Roll," said a commanding voice. "You're still on fire."

A hand guided Jetekesh to the ground, while someone beat a cloth against his arm. He obediently rolled, feeling nothing beyond the adrenaline pounding through his body. He hacked out cough after cough, but the sound was far away against the memory of roaring flames.

"Enough." The voice softened. "That's enough."

Jetekesh fell motionless and realized his eyes were still shut. He cracked one open and found the night sky sparkling before him, cradled in a circle of black trees.

Emerin appeared in his vision. A deep cut bled down his face. "Keep breathing."

The prince tried to suck in air, and his coughs returned, tearing up his throat.

"Wh-what happened? Where w-were you?" he gasped out between his rasping coughs.

"We left you to rest. Lafe stayed outside the hut while we joined the villagers for dinner. Kajsa intended to bring you back some food." Emerin twisted away, then back, clutching a water-skin. "Drink this, Your Highness." He placed his hand against Jetekesh's spine and helped the prince to sit up.

Jetekesh sipped the water, glad of the cool relief trickling down his raw throat.

Emerin spoke on, keeping a supportive hand against Jetekesh's back. "The *vashalan* attacked. Started tearing through the villagers like wheat before a sickle. Several in the pack drew Lafe away. He's badly wounded but still alive." The keep lord ran a hand over his face. "We didn't see the fire right away. I came as quickly as I could."

Jetekesh swallowed a long draught of water. Lafe. His heart pinched. "And the *vashalan*?"

"Gone. They retreated abruptly. I don't know why."

Another soothing swallow trickled down Jetekesh's throat. He licked his parched lips. "How is everyone else?"

"Scratches. Bruises." Emerin thumbed a cut on his cheek. "The only one I'm worried about is Lafe. He took a bad fall. I don't know if the *vashalan* bit him. Soon Kajsa can tell us more." His eyes darted up and down Jetekesh's torso. "How bad is the pain?"

"I...don't know." Jetekesh shifted, trying to assess the state of his body. He still felt detached from it somehow. "I can't feel much beyond my raw throat."

Emerin grunted, then reached out his hand and brushed Jetekesh's left shoulder. "That might scar. You need to get some kind of poultice on it."

Jetekesh craned his neck to find the injury. A burn, blistering, ugly, trailed down his arm where his sleeve had burned away. It didn't hurt at all. Staring at the red stripe, he swallowed hard. Shivers tracked up his spine. "Will...will this impair my fighting?"

"It could tighten the skin." Emerin rose, then hooked a hand under Jetekesh's uninjured arm and hauled him to his feet. "Let's get Kajsa to look at it."

As Jetekesh started forward, blood rushed into his pulsing head. He staggered, but Emerin steadied him.

"Am I badly damaged?" His voice cracked.

"No," said Emerin, tugging. "Let's go."

Jetekesh couldn't tell if the man was lying. Had his body been marred? He was walking. Had his gait changed at all? He glanced down at his clothes—what he could see as Emerin urged him onward—and found several singed places. Was his skin exposed on his left thigh? Was that black mark charred flesh?

The idea made him feel faint, but he set his jaw and walked on. Flames danced at his back, lighting the path to the other huts.

His left arm tingled. *Will it start to hurt soon?*

He sagged to his knees and stared at the shadows flickering before him on the ground.

Emerin hauled him back to his feet. "Almost there, my prince."

Jetekesh nodded, though the man's words were hard to make out against the growing hum in his head. He sought the sky above the trees. The fire at his back painted colors across the jungle silhouette. Finally, he found the stars. Golden light stretched fingers into that celestial framework, causing the stars to catch fire, too.

"It's beautiful," he said. "Like the Drifting Sands."

Emerin pushed him a little faster. "What's beautiful, Your Highness?" His tone was distracted. He was obviously trying to keep Jetekesh talking.

"The golden light. I've never seen fire do that before." The prince nodded heavenward. "Rille would love to see it."

"Yes, my prince." Emerin stepped up to a hut and guided Jetekesh inside.

The bright light of the interior slapped the prince's face. He was taken to a cot and commanded to sit.

"How is Lafe?" asked Emerin, moving off.

Jetekesh sat in silence, shivering. The voices around him were far away and unimportant. His arm began to prickle, sharp, deep.

He found the open door where village children peeked inside, their eyes wide.

The villagers were attacked too. How many lived?

Jetekesh shuddered. He stood up. His feet carried him outside, past the children who slinked back. He stared across the village at the burning hut. It was mere rubble now, consumed by the angry flames. Their packs were gone too.

Where's my sword and dagger?

Jetekesh turned, his concern bleeding away. He lifted his chin and stared up at the dancing heavens lit by gold.

"Your Highness?" The voice broke into his mind, ripping it from a place beyond pain.

Gasping, he shrank into himself. His arm *burned.*

Strong hands caught his good shoulder. "Come inside, Jetekesh. Come along." That was Dakarai's voice.

Jetekesh obeyed. Heat ravaged his arm and the left side of his neck. He sat on the cot again, and Kajsa appeared, a dripping rag in one hand. She set it against his arm. Jetekesh hissed out a breath. Tears gathered in his eyes.

"Sorry," she whispered, dabbing. "We must get the heat out." She rattled off instructions. The words slid off Jetekesh's mind like rain on a feather. Pain bloomed in his head and across his body. A dozen burns or more.

What's left of me?

Someone eased him down across the cot. Cool water touched his lips. It tasted bitter. He drank it anyway.

"Emerin." The words left his lips unbidden. "The golden light."

"Shhh," said the keep lord. "Don't talk just now. Rest. It's your best defense against the pain."

Jetekesh tossed his head. "The golden light. In...the sky. It's... what we seek. Northeast. Emer...in. Heed me..."

"Yes, Your Highness. Northeast. To the light."

A cool cloth covered Jetekesh's eyes. A faint coating of thin ice tingled down his arm. He sighed with relief. His head spun, dragging him into cool darkness, away from the fire. Away from Navolleth.

Away.

CHAPTER 30
GUIDANCE

Kajsa sat at Jetekesh's bedside, deftly preparing the herbs and roots she needed for a proper poultice. She'd used almost everything she had between Lafe's wounds and the prince's burns.

As she crushed her concoction using her pestle, her vision blurred. Lafe wouldn't last much longer. Her remedies were useless against the poison. Inhaling, she blinked back her tears. One escaped to slide down her cheek. It was like Raum all over again.

Jetekesh lay unmoving. His burns were many. Only three were severe. The one running from his neck, down his left shoulder and arm was the worst. Another on his thigh was small but menacing. The last was across his left calf.

Kajsa didn't know what to do for such deep burns. The one on his calf oozed. She had to frequently change the bandages. And his fever had returned. For now, he was quiet. She'd administered as much feverfew as she dared to keep him calm.

But it's not enough, Ingrid. What should I do?

The sounds of deep breathing filled the hut around her. Dawn approached, but it was dark yet, and a single lantern illuminated Kajsa's herbs. All the company slept in the hut except for Dakarai and Anenyasha, who had volunteered to seek out the herbs Kajsa was missing for her poultice. Apparently, Anenyasha knew some herblore—enough to identify what Kajsa needed.

At first, Emerin had been too restless, too agitated, to sleep. He'd kept watch, but that was pointless. Most of the village was awake and alert, many mourning their dead.

Kajsa had feared retaliation from the villagers after the *vashalan* attack, but Jetekesh had spared the company any such response. As Emerin had brought him from the burning hut, those in the village who had survived had witnessed the Marked Prince. His glow had reached the heavens.

They'd taken to calling him by a title. Dakarai said it translated to *He Who Guides*. Apparently, the title came from a Zindwéan legend from three hundred years ago—around the same time as Cavalin the Great.

"They will guard his rest," Dakarai had said before he left to gather herbs. "To the last child, they will fight to defend him. All is well."

In the cot, Jetekesh groaned. Kajsa set aside her pestle and leaned over him to turn over the wet cloth on his forehead. His eyes fluttered open, then closed again. His lips parted, and he murmured something unintelligible.

Kajsa dipped another cloth into a basin of clean water and dabbed at his lips to moisten them. When he settled into silence, she rose from her chair and padded to Lafe's cot.

The man was deathly pale. His breathing was shallow and rasping. The gash across his abdomen was heavily bandaged, but blood stained the outer layer. She couldn't seem to stem the flow.

Dragging her hair over her shoulder, Kajsa looped it into a knot, then leaned forward to apply more bandages.

"What's wrong?" asked Emerin.

Kajsa whirled. Clutching at her chest, she stared up into the powerful man's concerned gaze.

"Sorry," he said. "I forget how much like a rabbit you are."

She shook her head. "I—I'm fine." Too quiet. She swallowed and tried again. "He's not well. We're losing him. The wound... It should be cauterized. But the poison is still there."

Emerin scowled. "And we have no cure." His exhale stirred his hair. "How long does he have left?"

Kajsa turned back to the cot. "Hours, perhaps. A day at most."

A growl welled up in Emerin's throat, and Kajsa stiffened as chills spidered up her back. She didn't dare turn to face him.

A sigh followed his low growl. "Sorry, Kajsa. Do what you can."

She nodded, keeping her back to him. "Sir Lafe is fighting." Her voice trembled.

The lord's hand settled on her shoulder, nearly startling her out of her skin. "Really, I'm sorry. I don't mean to frighten people."

She bobbed a hasty nod. "I—I know."

"Yet I keep frightening you more." Emerin's hand retreated. "I'll be outside. Call me if you need help for any reason at all."

"I will." Her voice was a faint squeak. Shame burned her cheeks.

The man's footfalls faded toward the door. It swung open, then shut with a gentle snick.

Kajsa breathed out, muscles easing. Sometimes, Emerin's presence was too much for her. His intensity was just so—powerful. "Don't be such a coward, Ky." She shook her head, then continued adding bandages to Lafe's wound. "Ingrid, guide me. What can I do to save him?"

A cot behind her groaned. Kajsa glanced over her shoulder and found Jetekesh sitting upright, his eyes glazed over and staring before him, the cloth fallen from his forehead to cover his fingers.

"*Traveria*."

Kajsa blinked. "What?"

His head turned toward her, his eyes still unfocused. "*Traveria*. Ingrid says..." He shuddered. "Quickly, or he'll die."

Kajsa shook her head. "That's a poison, Jetekesh. Remember? It nearly killed..." But the *vashalan* were magical creatures, not mundane. Was Jetekesh onto something?

Ingrid says...

A glimmer danced in Kajsa's periphery. She shifted and gasped. Standing on the hut floor, glowing with iridescent light, was a black and silver wolf.

"Raum!" Tears gathered in her eyes. It *was* Raum, translucent, ghost-like, but still her faithful friend. He eyed her. Kajsa stood up. "Guide me."

Raum yipped, then slipped through the wall.

Kajsa grabbed up her herb satchel, darted to the door, wrenched it open, and raced to Emerin near the hut. He clutched his sword, eyes glinting like a wild animal. She couldn't let that daunt her just now.

"Emerin, I must find *traveria*. Guard the hut and care for Lafe and Jetekesh. I'll be fine." She tracked Raum hovering near the jungle's edge, waiting.

Light and reason returned to Emerin's eyes. He nodded and strode into the hut.

Kajsa hesitated, wringing her hands. She lifted a prayer to the mountain gods, though she was so far from home. Would they listen to her after she'd betrayed her people?

Gods, saints, spirits—whoever may listen—please protect me and guide Raum true.

With that, she chased after the ghostly wolf and plunged into the dark jungle.

CHAPTER 31
BLOOD KNIGHTS

Despite Shevek and Ledonn's choice to join the Norvians, Navolleth didn't visit the prison for three days. The two Blood Knights were like caged tigers. They lost their good humor within the first twenty-four hours, and only grew more feral with each passing moment.

At dawn on the third day, the prison door opened, tearing Yeshton and Song from their sparring match. Their weapons had been abandoned on the trail, but on the second day, Shevek had disassembled one of the bunks to make wooden implements. The four took turns training against each other.

Lowering his makeshift club, Yeshton turned toward the door. Sweat trickled down his spine and he caught his breath.

Navolleth stood in the doorway, Axel at his side. The swirling fragrance of spring danced around their legs.

Shevek and Ledonn rose from the floor in unison, both scowling like demons.

"About time," Shevek growled.

"Apologies," said Navolleth. "I was unavoidably detained

elsewhere." He stepped inside the prison. "I am pleased that two of you have chosen to side with me in my conquest of Nakania." His golden eyes fixed on Yeshton. "Why do you hesitate, Sir Knight?"

Yeshton lifted his chin. "My honor allows nothing else."

The man's solemn smile stretched into a quiet sneer, while his pupils constricted until they looked like slits. "Ah, yes. *Honor*. That most noble excuse for cowardice."

Chills raced up Yeshton's arms. Did Navolleth truly believe that?

"No matter," said Navolleth, turning his back on the room. "Come, my new allies. Let us leave the honorable prisoners to themselves."

"Hold on." Yeshton stepped forward.

Beside Navolleth, Axel rested a hand on the sword at his hip. Despite his quick response, Yeshton read an awkwardness in the gesture. The young man wasn't accustomed to a sword there.

"What happens to Song and me now?" Yeshton asked.

The enemy leader held still for several heartbeats. His shoulders relaxed and he breathed out, then he turned his neck enough to view Yeshton from the corner of his eye. "Nothing yet. You are my prisoners. You will remain so. If it becomes necessary to negotiate with the northern powers, I'm pleased to house two rather special guests for the purpose. Do not fear, honorable knight—I have no reason to torture or maim either of you. You have no information that I need. All I must do is prevent *you* from carrying back information to my foes." He faced the muddy yard through the open doorway. "A pleasant day to you both."

With that, the man strode from the prison, Axel on his heels.

The Blood Knights glanced at Yeshton, and Shevek offered what might be the KryTeeran equivalent of an apologetic smile. Or perhaps it was amusement. Difficult to gauge with them. Ledonn led the way outside, Shevek right behind him.

A guard stepped up and swung the door shut, then the bar clattered back into place. Footfalls pattered away. Somewhere outside, a bird trilled in the silence that followed.

"Well," said Song. "That's that." She threw her hands up, then huffed out a low breath. "This journey was ill-advised, and I can only blame myself."

"None of that." He rested a hand on her shoulder. "It was well conceived. We did our best. It doesn't always produce the results we desire, but that can't stop people from trying."

She stared at the ground, black eyes narrowing. "Those bloody-handed traitors."

Yeshton's gaze strayed to the barred door. "They aren't traitors. They were never more than temporary allies. They must go their own way, the way their conscience dictates."

Song snorted and pulled away to face him. "Weren't they your friends?"

He hesitated, weighing that against his soul. "Yes," he said. "I believe they still are."

"Pah." Her cynical laugh punched the air. "Friends don't abandon their friends in prison to join the opposing side."

"They do if they want a real chance to escape."

"Do you really believe that was all a ruse?"

"No." His answer was firm. "I believe KryTeerans will play all sides and work unimaginable devilry to achieve their ends. They meant it when they agreed to help Navolleth. *For now.* They will do anything and everything to serve their king. I've said that before. But I think they'll help us too, in their way, when they can. Watch. You'll see."

"They can't have it both ways. Eventually, they'll have to choose."

"No doubt." His eyes drifted to the window where a bird trilled again. Morning sunlight flooded the floor, gathering dust motes. "And they won't hesitate then either. Say what you will about the KryTeeran Empire, but they're always ready to make the hard decision, no matter the cost."

CHAPTER 32
GATHERING FLOWERS

Wild screams filled the trees.

In company with so many strong warriors, Kajsa hadn't been as afraid as she'd thought she would be —and now, following behind Raum's spirit, she was even less afraid. Purpose drove her on, keeping her feet steady.

With Raum here, nothing will harm me.

The girl and her wolf guide plunged deeper and deeper into the dense jungle. Vines snatched at Kajsa's hands, and colorful ferns tickled her legs. Raum lit the way, casting warm, silvery-blue light across the darkest shadows.

Ahead in the path, a massive spotted snake slithered down from the high branches of a twisting tree with broad prickly leaves. The serpent's tongue darted out. It hissed, eyeing her with ravenous desire.

Kajsa halted. Ice bled into her bones.

Raum growled at the snake, and the reptile flinched back. Another growl drove the snake into the dense foliage. The ghostly wolf turned to eye Kajsa, then tipped his head to encourage her to follow again.

She drew closer, then ducked as she passed under the branches where the snake had hung. Her nerves remained taut, humming in her ears like a drove of insects.

Still, they pressed on. The humid heat grew, though Kajsa couldn't tell the time of day under the thick jungle canopy. She tried to keep pace with the wolf, ignoring the branches lashing at her face.

A root caught her foot, and she struck the ground hard. Kajsa lay stunned, the cacophony around her muted to a dull, distant thrum as she wrestled to breathe. Panic coiled around her frame until she felt like a prisoner locked inside her mortal shell.

I can't do this.

Light curled close, warm. She lifted her head.

Raum eyed her, his wolfish eyes bright and concerned. Under the influence of that translucent yellow gaze, her lungs eased. The panic subsided, bleeding away in the wake of Raum's luminescence.

"Thank you, my dear friend." She shifted to her knees. Bruises throbbed across her arms and legs, but she was otherwise hale.

Raum barked, then turned, showing his tail to her.

Kajsa reached for it, expecting her hand to pass through the transparent appendage—but her fingers met soft fur. She clutched it, tears springing to her eyes. She stood and followed Raum, keeping hold of his tail.

As he trotted deeper into the darkness, she wouldn't let go for anything.

Mountain gods preserve and protect me.

Panic oozed back into her body, tensing her muscles, tightening her heartstrings. She wished she'd brought a real weapon, but the bow Jetekesh had given her had burned inside the hut.

My herb knife will have to do.

Raum leapt over a broken tree limb, and Kajsa scrambled over it, still clasping his tail tight. The trees thinned gradually, and she glanced around. Strange pink flowers hung in vines, covering the trees like thick cobwebs. A vague image of spiders large enough to weave those webs nearly sent Kajsa's heartbeat into a frenzy, but Raum's innate light chased off the shadows and calmed her fears.

No, it's more than just Raum. That's daylight.

The trees gave way to a sunlit clearing where a pool glimmered. Glancing skyward, Kajsa judged that it was nearly noon. Heat shimmered in the air before her, and the flowers circling the pool dripped as though they wept.

Raum padded to a flower and nosed it.

Oh. Kajsa trotted to the wolf's side and tugged her slender knife from a pocket in her tunic. She unfolded the knife, stooped, and studied the flower without touching it. *Traveria.* A poison to anyone without magic.

Powder covered the dewy petals, pink on pink, despite the droplets of dew. The petals themselves were broad; the flower was as wide as Kajsa's hand. Its center was gold and seemed to glow even in the shade at the edge of the clearing.

Kajsa sniffed the floral fragrance. Sweeter than honey with undertones not unlike the jasmine she'd encountered in Shing.

A frightful poison indeed if it tasted as good as it smelled.

She pulled a handkerchief from her pocket, pinched a petal with the cloth between her skin and the flower, and twisted it around to examine the stem system. It was like a chain, connected on the same vine to a host of other blossoms. Frowning, Kajsa tried to recall what little she knew of the legendary poison.

It killed if ingested. It maimed if touched directly. She could guess the powder contributed to both.

Which means I must preserve the powder without touching it. Tricky.

She traced the vine to its root.

Best bring the whole thing.

Kajsa used her knife to dig around the root at the trunk of a broad-leafed tree, then she carefully tugged the roots from the rich soil. They came easily. She slowly coiled the vine and its dozens of flowers together.

It's too big for my satchel.

She could improvise. Unfastening her tunic top, she pulled it off, leaving her in a satin undershirt and her cotton pants. She wrapped the coil of flowers in her tunic, folded it with care, then straightened up.

"We can go back, Raum," she said, eyeing the specter.

He huffed a reply and started back the way they'd come. Kajsa clutched her satchel and tunic close, praying that Lafe was still alive.

THE JUNGLE GAVE way to the village.

Kajsa's strength had flagged over the past half hour, but seeing the huts ahead, new life surged through her. She loped alongside Raum across the barren ground, legs pumping until she couldn't feel them.

"Emerin!" she called as she neared the hut.

The door swung open, and the keep lord darted outside, his hair bright under the broad sun. "Did you succeed?"

The hope in his voice sent a thrill through her. She wasn't too late. "Yes!" She held up the tunic so fast, it nearly slipped from her fingers. She hugged the tunic close to her chest and slowed her legs just before she careened into Emerin.

Dakarai and Anenyasha stepped out from the hut behind him.

"Welcome back," said the clansman. "We brought your herbs. Anenyasha administered a few."

Kajsa beamed at him, then slipped past them to enter the hut. Raum stayed at her side. She paused until her eyes adjusted to the gloom and she could make out the shapes of her sleeping patients.

Dakarai stepped up beside her. “Sir Lafe is a fighter.”

She nodded and moved to the knight’s cot, then knelt before it, and unwrapped her tunic. “I got the *traveria*, but I’m uncertain how to use it for this.”

While Dakarai bent over the tunic to eye its contents, Raum canted his head and whined.

“Very dangerous, that,” the clansman said. “Be cautious of the powder.”

Kajsa nodded, using a fresh handkerchief to uncoil the vine. “What part should I use? The root or the petals?”

“Both are deadly,” said Dakarai. “The root is deadly at a single taste. The petals—so long as the powder is intact—is a slower, and crueler end.”

She bit her lip. *Trust your instinct.* Too much potency could affect Lafe negatively. She would try the flower first. Just one. Pinching the stem of one pristine bloom, with cloth between her and its flesh, she plucked the flower.

“Please hand me my pestle and mortar,” she said.

Dakarai complied, and Kajsa took them with a fleeting smile. She remained kneeling and pressed liquid from the flower. As the flower bled, the sweet fragrance perfumed the air. The powder mingled in the mortar, thickening the paste. When every hint of the petals had been blended into the mixture, she sat back on her heels and exhaled.

“That should do.”

Now, to administer the poison. Should she rub it directly on the bite mark?

Yes, her instinct said. *That’s where the magic is.*

She stood up, praying to any gods or spirits who might be listening. If Jetekesh was wrong, if he’d spoken in a fevered fit, this would finish Lafe.

But he's dying anyway. This is my only option.

It made sense. If *traveria* killed those without magic, Lafe's magical wound would spare him that end. By the same token, Jetekesh had suspected that *traveria* was healthful for those who wielded magic. In Lafe's case, it might negate the *vashalan* venom and give him a chance to heal.

With deft fingers, Kajsa unbound the bandages around Lafe's abdomen, layer after layer, until she revealed the gaping wound. The sharp odor of the venom choked her, but as she tipped the mortar over the gash and used her pestle to scoop it over the wound, the honeyed fragrance washed away the smell.

Lafe's breathing changed from a shallow, hitching rasp, quickening. His chest convulsed. He screamed, thrashing under the blankets, until Dakarai caught his shoulders and held him still.

Kajsa flinched back. Had she chosen wrong? Was she killing him?

Raum huffed, catching her eye. She stared into the wolf's yellow eyes and found comfort there. It slid over her like the warmth from a fire on a winter's night.

Let the flower do its work.

In mere seconds, Lafe's writhing eased, and he fell back into a deep slumber. His breathing steadied. Kajsa mustered her courage and bent over the wound. It *looked* cleaner, somehow, despite the tint of the *traveria* ointment.

Should she dab the flower concoction away or leave it alone? Would it poison Lafe once the magical venom was purged?

Kajsa resisted wringing her hands. Instead, she washed her hands, tightened the knot holding her hair back, and set to work cleansing the wound. If he needed more doses of the flower, she had enough.

It will work. I'll save him.

CHAPTER 33
THE CROSSROADS

Dawn slapped Jetekesh's eyes.

Flinching, he tried to roll away from the pervasive light, but as he moved his arm raged with pain. Crying out, he fell still and gulped breaths.

"Shh, there now," said Kethalas in his smooth tones. "The pain will ease." A hand rested over Jetekesh's blazing flesh, and coolness spread. The fire eased, bit by bit.

Jetekesh cracked his eyes open and found the dragon's slitted silver gaze. Kethalas smiled down at him from his place on the edge of the next cot. Mud walls and a thatched roof surrounded Jetekesh. His throat closed. Smoke clogged his nostrils.

Fire! Burning! He tried to sit up.

"None of that," said Kethalas. "Relax. You're in no danger here. Let the memories pass."

The prince took deep breaths. "Wh—"

"Questions later," said Kethalas. "Rest in the knowledge that no one in our company has succumbed to death."

That was something. Jetekesh relaxed against his pillow. "The *v-vashalan*?"

"None have returned."

As his arm flared with greater pain, Jetekesh squeezed his eyes shut. Perhaps reading his face, Kethalas rested fingers over the limb again, and cold rolled through the burns.

"H-how bad?" asked Jetekesh between clenched teeth.

"Bad," said Kethalas. "You need a Shinacian healer. Anything less and you'll have permanent damage."

First his ear, now his arm—and possibly his leg. The fire flared there, too, though it was more distant.

Am I some mangled horror now?

Jetekesh let out a curse, vehement, searing his tongue as sharply as any fire.

Kethalas's cool fingers found his shoulder. "It's fine. Be angry. You have the right. But don't let it consume you."

Jetekesh jerked away from him, flinching. "Leave me alone. Just stop." He choked back tears.

Silence met his request, then Kethalas's voice drifted across the air. "As you wish, Your Highness."

The cot creaked, cloth rustled, then footfalls padded across the hut, crunching grit. A ring of voices rose from that quarter, too quiet to understand. Jetekesh hardly cared.

Mother always tried to protect me. Now I'm hideous.

The soft pad of feet approached. "Prince Jetekesh?" Kajsa's tones were tentative, and higher pitched than normal, probably from nerves.

A little of Jetekesh's anger dissolved. He peeled his eyes open and found her hovering above him, her hair like a luminous halo in the sunlight.

"What is it?" The tremor in his voice shamed him. He wouldn't cry, not in front of her.

Kajsa inched closer. "I thought..." Her voice cracked, and she dipped her head. "I thought I should tell you..." She licked her lips. "Your injuries. You should know..."

"I can feel them." The harshness in his voice surprised him, like a stranger spoke with his mouth.

The girl recoiled, and Jetekesh expected her to run, but she froze, then pursed her lips. Her hands curled into fists, and she inhaled a breath. "The pain is worse than the wounds." Her voice quavered, but Kajsa pressed on, tones gaining strength. "Please listen. Your arm, hand, and leg are bad, but while you will have scarring, most of the damage can be hidden beneath your wardrobe. Your face and one hand will mend."

How had she known? Was he so easy to read? Jetekesh's lips curled in a humorless smile. "Well, I suppose my vanity can assuage me each time I try to lift a sword."

"If that's what you want," came Emerin's droll tones.

Jetekesh found the open doorway where the keep lord stood like a paper cutout in the brilliant light. Emerin strolled inside, green eyes bright with a wild light.

The man approached, then halted at the foot of the cot to stare down Jetekesh. "Or," Emerin said, "we can find that blasted Arch and seek a Shinacian healer like Kethalas suggests."

Jetekesh grimaced. "I can't walk like this."

Emerin's eyes flicked to his feet. "Are they stubs now, no more flesh or bone upon which to stand?"

The prince flushed. "No, but—"

"Come now," said Emerin, meeting his eyes with a fervor that stung Jetekesh's soul. "I've seen warriors come home from the battlefield with no legs at all, and they still stood higher than you do right now." The words were meant to cut. Jetekesh knew that. Lord Emerin had precise aim.

Folding his arms, the keep lord sighed. "You have my full sympathy, my prince. Should we fail to find a healer, you will never wield a broadsword again. But that's not the only weapon you can master. Many require one hand, not two. I can train you. I know them all." He leaned forward, set one foot on the cot, and propped his elbow against his thigh. "What say you, Prince Jetekesh? You've reached a bitter crossroads, and only you can choose the way forward—or to stop altogether. Will you lie here defeated, the victim of your mother's will, or will you rise from near death as your father did, and walk bravely on, no matter how maimed?"

Fire rolled through Jetekesh, far deeper than his flesh wounds, blazing through him like a cleansing draught. He'd already made his choice long ago when a humble storyteller from Shing showed him the way into Shinac and a noble-hearted fae prince invited him into the realm of magic.

Jetekesh sat up, ignoring the agony that vaulted up his limbs. His gaze settled on Emerin, as steadfast as his resolve. "I'll stand, Emerin. I'll walk. And we'll find the Arch into Shinac."

Emerin's lips split in a broad grin. "And so we shall." He slapped a hand on his leg. "By the spirits, we're close. You saw it, Your Highness. In your fever, you saw the light of the Arch. You can see it again. Guide us, Marked Prince."

Hope winged through Jetekesh, dampening his pain. "When do we leave?" He scanned the hut, and his gaze stumbled on the transparent wolf standing near a cot. The animal thumped its tail against the ground. Jetekesh had seen the wolf once before in the Lotus throne room in Shing.

His gaze flicked to Kajsa. "Is that Raum?"

She glanced behind her, then whipped her head back around. "You see him too?"

"I do."

"The rest of us do not," said Dakarai. "But we did not doubt the fair lady's word, nor do we doubt your eyes." The clansman moved from the wall between cots, coming nearer. "We can leave almost at once, upon one condition."

Jetekesh lifted a brow. "And that is?"

"If you agree to leave Lafe here." Dakarai stepped aside, giving

Jetekesh a full view of the hut. At the far side, near Kethalas, lay Lafe. His complexion was ashen, and a heap of blankets covered him.

A lump formed in Jetekesh's throat. "Is he..."

"He will recover," said Dakarai. "Kajsa's ministrations have been excellent, and you did much to help her in your slumber. But he cannot be moved. It may be weeks before he recovers enough strength to sit up, let alone stand."

The clansman's words sent Jetekesh's brow higher, but he could ask questions en route. "Very well." He settled his expression into grim determination. "We leave tomorrow."

Emerin grunted. "Sensible. I'd suspected you'd have us leave immediately."

Jetekesh shook his head. "I don't want to remain here and risk the villagers any longer than necessary, but I think one more day of rest will do us all a great deal of good. Besides, from what I can recall of the light I saw, it was nighttime. I want to try finding the same glow tonight, so we're sure to head in the right direction."

"Sensible, indeed." Emerin removed his leg from the cot. "I'll see to preparations for our departure. Dakarai and Anenyasha will assist since they speak the clan tongue and I don't."

"What should I do?" asked Kajsa.

"Watch over our prince," Emerin said. "And keep Lafe comfortable. *And* try to rest a little yourself, eh?" He flashed a grin, then marched for the door.

"And I?" asked Kethalas, stepping away from the far wall.

"Help Kajsa. Make sure she actually rests. Keep a good watch, but don't strain yourself. Do you understand?" Emerin strode outside, Dakarai following. Anenyasha peeled herself from the wall outside the open door where she'd presumably been guarding.

Jetekesh shifted, discomfort pinching his chest. "Kethalas..."

The dragon lifted a hand. "No need to apologize, Prince. Your emotions are warranted." He tapped the scar on his face. "My own wounds have caused me no small measure of shame and grief."

"Yet I doubt you lashed out at others over them," Jetekesh murmured.

"Oh, but I did." Kethalas grimaced and rubbed the back of his neck. "An ice dragon like myself rarely loses his temper, but when we do..." His expression turned sheepish. "Fortunately, Taregan put me in my place."

Jetekesh didn't think he wanted to know what a dragon elder looked like when he disciplined a raging ice dragon. The only dragon he'd seen in its true form was Kethalas, and he didn't doubt Taregan—so much older—would be an even more astounding sight to behold.

Kethalas flashed the prince a grin, then turned and scooped up a bundle of stained bandages. "I'll see these get washed." The dragon left in a few fleet steps.

Kajsa offered a weak approximation of a smile. "I should apologize as well, Your Highness."

"It's Jetekesh," he said. "And no, you shouldn't. You've done nothing to deserve any such thing."

"I—I took a harsh tone with you," she said. "I tried to...to supplant your will. That was wrong of me."

He tipped his head to one side, eyeing this strange, humble creature. So much like Jinji, yet so timid. He wrestled down a chuckle. "If that's your idea of supplanting authority, you'll never conquer the smallest of islands. Rest assured, Lady Kajsa. I'm not offended or displeased."

Quite the contrary, he thought. *She's strangely enchanting.*

He let his gaze drift to the empty cots. "However, since you're so keen to promote my goodwill, do me the service of heeding me in one thing."

"What is that?" she asked, tones earnest.

"*Rest*, just as Emerin ordered. No arguments. Kethalas will return shortly, and he can see to my needs. I'm also confident he'll wake you if Lafe requires anything."

She hesitated, twisting the fabric of her undershirt. Then she moved to a close cot and sat down. Raum trotted to her side and seated himself nearby.

"Why is he still here?" asked Jetekesh.

"I don't know. I expected him to leave once he helped me gather *traveria*."

Jetekesh blinked. "*Traveria*?"

"Yes." Kajsa offered up a short version of events, starting with Jetekesh telling her to seek the plant in the jungle. As she spoke, Jetekesh's brow wrinkled.

The Sigil of Truth, hm? Jetekesh had seen what must be done to save Lafe's life, and Kajsa—saints bless her—had heeded him.

Die young or old, it doesn't matter. If my gift can save lives, I'll take whatever I must in return.

Jinji had been right. Dakarai, Kethalas, Emerin, Lafe, and Kajsa—they'd all been right, too. He wasn't useless, not as long as he sought to help others.

CHAPTER 34
THE GLASS BRIDGE

The wooded swamp was full of frog song, just as before. But this time, no fortress stood on the far side of the black lake. Only water birches and cypresses bearing the strange chain-like vines lined the distant bank.

Aredel stood on the shore for a long time, noting every detail, from the bobbing glow of the dusk pixies to the leaf mold covering the ground. Everything was just the same. He'd positioned himself exactly where he'd seen the far shore before.

But there was no fortress.

The blue-eyed dove settled on his shoulder to survey the sight.

"It's here," Aredel said. "We just can't see it."

The dove cooed and its wings fluttered.

Anadin prowled from down the bank near where the horses were tethered. He eyed the murky lake. "I think there's something dangerous lurking under the water, *shaqin*. I saw it move."

Hair rose on the back of Aredel's neck. His eyes skated over the water and adrenaline spiked. Since the fight against the *vashalan*, the swamp had offered up no further threats—and Aredel balked against his growing restlessness.

He would welcome any challenge.

The water held its breath, except for the insects skipping across its surface, leaving a trail of ripples behind.

His sword hand found his hilt. "We need to cross."

"How?" asked Anadin. "I don't want to swim with sharks."

Aredel wrestled down a smile. "I doubt a shark resides in this lake."

"You know what I mean." Anadin flapped a hand over the air dismissively. "Alligators are just as unwelcome."

"Whatever may reside within these waters," said Aredel, "is more likely magical than not."

His brother bared his teeth in a grimace. "I do *not* want to face an alligator with wings."

The imagery stilled Aredel, but he shook it off. Leave it to his brother to dream up such a ridiculous and terrifying predator and spout about it in a serious tone.

The Blood King neared the water's edge and stared out. The fog thickened as evening shrouded the world. Tapping knuckles to his chin, he studied every surface. "Unless we can construct a raft, I see no alternative to swimming."

"Raft it is then." Anadin's steps drifted off. "I'll find some poles. You gather the vines to lash them together."

Aredel turned to watch his brother's retreat, then shook his head. "We don't have time for that, *shaqel*." His voice was met with silence.

The dove cooed, then winged from Aredel's shoulder to land on the ground before him.

In a flash of light, Sharo appeared. "I can summon a fae bridge. It may be brittle in this vile realm, but it should last until we reach the far side." His hand grasped his sword. "Call your brother back and be prepared."

Aredel offered up a grin that showed all his teeth. "I am always prepared for battle, Your Highness." He angled away from the dark lake. "*Shaqel,* come back!"

Anadin's footfalls pattered among the dense trees. The KryTeeran prince reappeared, clutching a thin trunk covered in leafy branches. "I found our first pole." His dark eyes strayed to Sharo. "Oh, you're not a bird anymore. Hello again."

Sharo dipped his head. "Forgive me, Prince Anadin. We will be traveling my way to save time." He drew his sword. "Though it will give them warning."

"We probably can't help that at this point." Aredel positioned himself beside the elven prince. "I don't mind a loud entrance as long as we act swiftly."

Sharo's grim smile twisted into something almost wicked. "Agreed." Hefting his sword aloft, the fae prince set his legs apart. The blade hummed, then burst into silvery flames. Sharo set his jaw and his eyes burned with the same glow. He swung the blade before him in a vertical swipe that chimed across the air.

The silver flames danced forward, taking shape to craft a bridge glistening like delicate glass. It sparkled and winked. Dusk pixies weaved closer to examine it.

"I cannot long maintain it," said Sharo between labored breaths. "Leave the horses. Go!"

Aredel stepped onto the narrow, railless bridge. Despite its thin, delicate design, it held his weight like stone. He drew his curved sword and started across. "Come, Anadin."

Footsteps sounded behind him. A mere scuff on the glass surface.

Aredel raced along the bridge, willing himself to find the dark fortress. Nearly across, the bridge cracked under his foot. He glanced at the spidered glass, increasing his speed as much as he dared. Beneath the fragile surface, something large stirred the water.

Two yards from shore, the glass cracked again.

"Run!" cried Sharo. "I can't hold it!"

Aredel tore over the last few feet and flung himself from the bridge. Glass cracked. Shards plunked into water. He landed hard against the muddy ground and slid a few inches, twisting to catch sight of Anadin throwing himself from the collapsing structure. On his heels, Sharo and his blazing sword followed.

As Sharo leaped, the bridge failed entirely. Sparkling glass rained down on the water. Droplets sprayed the air, painting rainbows. The silvery flames twined through the growing fog. Sharo landed in the shallows, sword plunged into the ground, head bowed like a knight before a throne. The elven prince's breaths shuddered.

Did he spend all his strength to get us across?

Aredel frowned, then turned to survey his surroundings. Dense foliage, dusk pixies, and no sign of a fortress. *But it* was *here.*

"Watch out!" cried Anadin.

Aredel whirled, lifting his blade. But his brother wasn't warning *him.*

Tentacles had slithered from the dark waters, and two wrapped themselves around Sharo's ankles before the prince could move. Sharo wrenched his sword from the wet sand and swiped at one tentacle—but the other jerked him aside, and he missed his target. A second jerk sent Sharo crashing to the ground, his shoulder slamming into a mossy rock. The prince flinched but didn't relinquish his hold on his weapon.

Aredel splashed into the shallows and stabbed his blade through one sleek, black tentacle. It writhed, trying to free itself. Aredel sank his blade in deeper.

"Anadin, cover me!"

The command was needless. Anadin had already taken up a

position at his back. The KryTeeran prince staved off two more tentacles and pivoted to meet a third.

The Blood King wrenched his sword free, then chopped through the wounded tentacle, severing a large chunk of flesh. The appendage retreated toward the water.

Aredel spun and charged toward Sharo, who had managed to fend off one tentacle before the second had lifted him into the air. Sharo dangled upside-down and swung around, trying to slice at the monster.

Launching himself at the tentacle, Aredel swiped his blade. It bit deep into the leathery flesh, and the tentacle bucked, tossing Sharo. The fae prince flashed with light, forming into the dove again, but a second flash revealed his human form and he crashed against a cluster of rocks.

Aredel dragged the tentacle toward the ground, sword still embedded in it. He jerked his weapon free. The tentacle slithered back into the water. Plumes of black clouded the lake.

Spinning, Aredel raced to Sharo's side. The prince lay sprawled against the stones.

The Blood King caught his shoulder. "How badly are you wounded?"

"My magic is weakening. Some dark force hovers near." Sharo sat up, cringing. "I'm battered but unbroken, I think."

Aredel craned his head to watch Anadin fend off the remaining tentacles, his sword winking and flashing in the dim light. "What is that creature?"

Sharo shifted to his knees. "I think it's bespelled underwater foliage, not a creature at all. The tentacles are too many and too strong."

The Blood King nodded. "We should move away from the water."

"Agreed." Sharo struggled to his feet. "My ankle is twisted but I can still walk. Let's keep on."

"Anadin," called Aredel. "Fall back once we're out of range."

The KryTeeran prince twisted to fend off a new tentacle assault. "Get going then!"

Aredel caught Sharo's arm and helped him limp inland. The ground sloped up, and Sharo slipped once on several mossy rocks, but he scrambled up the crest with inhuman agility after that. Aredel kept pace. They stepped into the treeline, and Aredel turned around.

"We're away, *shaqel*."

The sounds of the skirmish faded, then Anadin's feet scuffed over stones and twigs and he clambered up after them. His long black hair was a tangled net around his face. His lips were set in a wild grin. "Where is yon fortress, my king? I shall destroy it for you all alone!" Anadin declared, fervor blazing in his eyes.

Aredel set his hand on his brother's shoulder. "Easy, *shaqel*. We go together." He turned to face the trees. "*If* we find the nest of vipers."

"We're on the right track," said Sharo. "Else that underwater bespellment wouldn't be there."

That, Aredel already knew. He wasn't wrong about the fortress's placement. But what if they never found it?

Sharo straightened his shoulders and gently pulled free of Aredel's support. "Keep walking. We may be guided yet again by the very snares they've set."

Aredel pulled ahead, flexing his fingers against his hilt. Sweat slickened his grip. His long hair clung to his neck, and his clothes were crusted in silt and grime. The silence on this side of the lake set his nerves taut as a bowstring. Surely, the *Unsielie* had seen Sharo's sword shining like a beacon. They must know by now that Aredel had betrayed them.

Is Artassa still alive? Have I failed her as I failed my people?

The thought rang through his soul, bitter, harrowing.

His fist tightened on the drawn sword swinging at his side.

If she is dead, they will pay to the last man.

His sword tip struck the air as though it were stone. Jerking his eyes upward, he stared at the trees. The chainlike vines hung before him, and a thin track led ahead. Eyes narrowing, he flicked his sword. The blade struck stone yet again.

An illusion?

"Sharo."

"Yes," said the fae prince, coming up beside him. "Our eyes are deceived." He lifted his sword. "By the blood of the True King, I command thee to reveal thyself." His blade swung down until it struck a hard, unseen surface, and the flames rippled out, cascading across the air, painting a black stone wall. High above that, beyond the wall, rose the dark towering fortress beneath a stormy sky.

Sharo grinned. "Praise the spirits. We've found it."

Aredel's blood warmed at the prospect of combat. Now, at last, he could face his enemies and make them suffer.

"Let's find the entrance." Anadin traced his hands over the stones as he moved to the left.

Aredel and Sharo followed.

A large, shadowed figure materialized before Anadin and unleashed a bolt from a crossbow. It struck, and Anadin jerked back, then fell, the bolt lodged in his throat.

"*Shaqel!*"

CHAPTER 35
UNDER THE LAKE

Spending one last night in the Zindwéan village hadn't been a waste. Braving the open air with Dakarai's support, Jetekesh had searched the sky, and a beam of golden light had answered like a beacon calling to him.

The clansfolk had gathered to watch him, a reverent hush enveloping the village. When he'd declared that he saw the light again, they'd cheered and offered up a celebration feast. The food had been peculiar, but not all bad.

The following afternoon, after a last long rest, the company packed what gear remained, along with most of their weapons. Luckily the steel armaments hadn't been damaged in the fire. They left the village while the inhabitants sang a song. The clansfolk music brought a fresh vision of fairies.

Shinac is nearer than we think. The thought comforted Jetekesh.

The company—including the ghostly wolf Raum—traveled through the night, then set up camp at a stream within the dense jungle as dawn approached. Dakarai had bargained for traps made of herbs and a kind of malodorous tar which kept most predators away, and he and Anenyasha set them while the others prepared a light meal and fed their horses.

They'd agreed to travel at night going forward to maintain their proper heading. With Raum in their company, glowing brighter than a string of torches, there was little danger of losing their way in the darkest stretches of jungle. No one except Jetekesh and Kajsa could see the wolf's shape, but somehow, the ghost's light was visible to all once true night fell.

After Jetekesh ate a little rice and some steamed vegetables, he settled down to rest. Kajsa had given him a draught to dull his pain. It did its work well. He didn't wake until Emerin shook him.

"Time to go," the keep lord said.

They traveled on, maintaining a steady pace despite the jostling that ripped over Jetekesh's bandaged burns. He batted off anyone who tried to coddle him. He could take this. He must. To save Amantier, Shing, KryTeer, the Clanslands, and even Norva, Jetekesh must enter Shinac and beg for Sharo's aid. He didn't doubt the fae prince would answer if he could.

Insects swarmed Jetekesh in the humid night air. His clothes were crusty with sweat. He longed for a cool bath, but nothing approaching that could be found in the wild Clanslands.

"How do you abide living here, Dakarai?" asked Jetekesh, swatting away a relentless bloodsucker.

The clansman chuckled. "This is the Deep Jungle. The villages that exist so far away from civilization are few. Most of us cluster toward ground more suitable for agriculture and fresh water. But we allow the illusion of the Clanslands' ferocity to endure, so that no one attempts to invade and steal what is ours."

That made a great deal of sense.

Jetekesh slapped his leg, purging Nakania of one less treacherous insect. "Even so, the heat is unbearable."

"Only if you're unaccustomed to it," replied Dakarai. "I, for one, find your southern realm a tad too cool."

Kajsa spoke up somewhere behind Jetekesh. “Then you would detest Norva.”

Dakarai grinned. “That I little doubt. Snow, and sleet, and ice, and I—we are best left as acquaintances only.”

Emerin laughed at the head of the procession. “Amantier and Shing are blessed with four seasons. Just as we weary of one, another comes. It’s better than always too hot or always too cold.”

Dakarai shrugged. “So say the faint of body and mind.”

Emerin snorted. “If you wished to spar with me tonight, you need only have asked.”

Jetekesh glanced between the two men, amused by their banter, grateful for the distraction. Lancing burns aside, the fire of the insect bites was enough to drive a man to drink.

Kajsa had wrapped his burns in layers of cloth lathered in cooling ointments, and she changed them whenever the company stopped to rest, but the burns had begun to itch even through the salve. His damaged arm hung in a makeshift sling to avoid too much jostling. Jetekesh’s good hand twitched each time the itching grew worse, but he refrained from giving in to his impulse to scratch.

Emerin reined in his horse and twisted in his saddle to eye the company. “Looks like water ahead. Let’s halt and rest while Dakarai and I scout.”

The two men dismounted, lit a torch, and moved ahead. Raum padded to Kajsa’s side, while Jetekesh gingerly slid from Hickory’s back. He reached solid ground with a hiss.

“All right?” asked Kajsa.

“I will be.” He rotated his free arm, stretching the muscles. “Anything to eat?”

“Let me see what I can find.” She moved to the pack horses where Anenyasha was already rummaging.

Kethalas came up next to Jetekesh and offered up a waterskin.

"You're enduring all this very well."

Jetekesh smiled, then drank his fill of water. Lowering the skin, he wiped his mouth. "How are your wounds?"

The dragon shrugged. "Not better, not worse." His silver eyes drifted to the path ahead. "How far to the Arch, I wonder."

An image of the golden Arch, with pillars of twining sand, flitted through Jetekesh's mind. A thrum climbed his bones. "It's close. Very." Something like music called out to him, and he turned to face the path. The waterskin slipped from his fingers and struck the ground with a slosh.

"Prince?"

Kethalas's voice was far away. Unimportant.

The music grew, caressing Jetekesh's ear. He moved toward it, passing Hickory, passing Emerin's mount. The jungle noises fell away and the music soared higher, higher.

"I'm coming," he whispered.

Hurry, called a voice. Ashea's, perhaps?

"I'm trying." He stumbled over a root, and his burns flared, but he pressed on. Footsteps followed. He didn't glance back. Ahead, Emerin and Dakarai came into view. They stood at the edge of a large lake whose waters shimmered with golden light.

Here. It's here.

Jetekesh's pace quickened. *I've found the Arch.*

"What's wrong?" asked Emerin, stepping toward him.

Jetekesh dodged the man and reached the lake's edge. The moon was reflected on its surface—but more than that. He stared into the depths where pillars of sand twined up themselves in an animated cycle, leading to an Arch hanging upside-down in the water.

"There." His heartbeat hammered in his good ear. "We've found it."

Strong fingers gripped his shoulder. "Where?" asked Emerin, his voice low and eager.

Jetekesh lifted a trembling hand to point. "In the water."

"I don't see any—"

The keep lord cut off when Jetekesh stepped into the lake. At his touch, golden light exploded above the surface. The prince stepped further into the water. The waves parted, giving him passage. Stairs formed in the mud, hardening into black stone that glistened with gilt veins.

"Jetekesh," said Emerin in desperate tones.

"Come on." Jetekesh glanced over his shoulder, smiling at the company hesitating on the shore, which now included Raum and the horses. "We'll enter Shinac."

"But without an invitation..." Emerin shook his head.

That was true. Jetekesh paused. *Was Ashea's voice enough?* Possibly not. What if only those of the true Shinacian line could issue a proper summons?

Jetekesh turned back to the light. "Sharo." His voice rang down the path between the many twining pillars, ending at the Arch whose golden light eddied. The music came from there, beckoning.

He stepped forward again and lifted his voice. "Sharo, call me!"

The music struck a higher swell of notes, and the eddying light in the Arch pulsed, then swirled the other way. "Jetekesh, friend of my heart, come!" Sharo's voice was like a clarion note.

"Call my companions as well," Jetekesh called back through the Arch.

"All with you are welcome. Hurry to my side. I need your aid!"

With that, Jetekesh raced along the lake bottom, his steps wide, oblivious to his burns. He was returning to Shinac! In a moment, he would meet Sharo again.

He asked for our aid. Be prepared for a fight.

Jetekesh faltered before the Arch. *I'm too wounded for combat. What can I do?* His body shook with a swell of frustration.

"Jetekesh," said Kethalas. "We're right behind you. Go in."

The prince's fingers curled into a fist. *Haven't you already decided to stand? This is what you came here for. The others can fight, even if you can't. Keep on, Kesh.*

He squared his shoulders, flinching at the pain that climbed up his ruined arm, then he strode into the golden light. The music filled both of his ears. The pain of his burns died.

Shinac, at last.

CHAPTER 36
LAST STRAW

Anadin's breath gurgled. His eyes dimmed like he stared into an abyss. He clutched Aredel's hand in his red-stained fingers. "I—I don't want..." Blood seeped from his mouth as he struggled for air. "Can't..."

The sounds of Sharo's blade against the looming figure's sword rang through Aredel's ears, distant, inconsequential.

"Stay," Aredel whispered. "Please, *shaqel.*" His heart cracked. His little brother tightened his hold. "Don't leave me, Anadin."

His brother tried to speak, but blood filled his mouth. His body convulsed. His eyes rolled back in his head.

"No, Anadin." A sob escaped Aredel's lips. The sound was foreign in his ears, unlike anything he'd made before. *First Jinji, now Anadin.* The Blood King curled over his brother's body, seeking the faintest heartbeat. The smallest hope.

Nothing answered.

Rage climbed Aredel's throat, escaping as a scream more animal than human. He laid Anadin's corpse upon the ground, claimed his curved sword from where he'd dropped it, and straightened to face his enemy.

The looming creature—glinting in obsidian armor—hammered his greatsword against Sharo, driving the fae prince back.

Aredel charged. Fury poured through his frame, boiling like magma, guiding his steps. He vaulted over a flat boulder, hefted his blade, and leapt at the armored creature near the fortress wall. The man knocked Sharo off his feet and into a thicket, then whirled to face Aredel head-on.

Their swords met like thunder. White smoke spiraled up Aredel's blade, brightening the sky. He was smaller than this insect—but that didn't matter. Aredel launched himself backward. He stepped to one side. Crouched, then pivoted. Swung his sword. His enemy blocked the slash with his weapon.

Disengaging, Aredel backed up, drawing on his newfound power. Because of the hostages, he hadn't been able to use it freely in Shinac.

Now, nothing would stop him.

Anadin.

The Blood King of KryTeer lunged, throwing his full weight into his attack, forcing power into his blade. It burst with light, pulsing like a storm. The armored man stumbled back under its radiance.

Anadin.

Aredel pressed his advantage, hacking, hacking, hacking.

His foe's sword clattered from a gauntleted hand.

The man tripped and landed hard.

Aredel didn't hesitate. He didn't think.

Anadin.

The Blood King plunged his sword through the weak spot between helm and gorget, piercing armor and flesh just where Anadin's throat had been struck.

The man didn't scream, nor did he fall back. His armor rattled, then black smoke burst from the cage, taking to the open air with the hiss of sand. The armor collapsed to the ground. Empty. Utterly empty.

Sand coiled upward, rising far out of reach.

Hatred seared Aredel. All that, all for naught. He'd avenged nothing at all.

Sharo rose from the thicket, speaking seemingly to himself, his back to Aredel. The Blood King couldn't hear him over the blood pumping in his ears. So much of what he loved, those things most precious to his heart, all gone.

He slumped to his knees, bowing his head. The hiss of sand assaulted his ears. His sword crashed beside him.

It's not enough.

Fury lanced his heart. He jerked his head back, eyeing the retreating essence of darkness—the fell magic that had struck Anadin down—and he unleashed the full power within him. He didn't think. He didn't have to. Emotion guided him like it never had before.

White smoke and lightning burst from his body, coiling up to meet the sand.

At the same moment, a clarion note flooded the air. Golden light split the sky above the pillar of black sand.

Stairs formed. At the top of those stairs, Prince Jetekesh of Amantier appeared, crowned with light. He was flanked by warriors wielding swords, as well as a wolf, and a girl with platinum hair leading several horses.

Aredel ripped his eyes from the sight to find the sand. Between his power and the Arch in the sky, the black pillar fizzled, dying with a faint shriek.

A tear tracked Aredel's cheek. *That's for you, Anadin, brother of my blood.*

He bowed his head and sat in the silence of his broken heart.

CHAPTER 37
STORMING THE CASTLE

Jetekesh reached the bottom steps, absorbing the scene before him.

Dusk crept into true night. Blood King Aredel knelt in an attitude of defeat among the reeds and hanging moss. Prince Sharo limped toward the stairs from beside a stone wall that circled a dark fortress. Behind the fae prince, Prince Anadin of KryTeer lay unmoving upon the puddled ground, a bolt lodged in his throat.

Swallowing a lump, Jetekesh turned from the sight to meet Sharo's piercing blue eyes. For a few precious seconds, caught between two worlds, Jetekesh hadn't experienced any pain. His body had been whole. But now every burn, every bite, every bruise, pulsed across his skin. His damaged ear ached.

But none of that could matter right now.

"Welcome back to Shinac," Sharo said. "I wish we were well met, but things are most dire here."

Jetekesh glanced at Aredel. "What we saw just now...?"

"Aredel defeated our current foe, but more foul things reside within the *Unsielie* fortress." Sharo gestured toward the stronghold. "Queen Artassa of KryTeer is held captive within."

How Aredel and his kin had found their way to Shinac was a question for another time. Perhaps they'd located the Arch within KryTeer.

Jetekesh rested a hand on Sharo's arm. "We'll help you storm the fortress." He slipped past the fae prince to approach Aredel.

The Blood King stared at the ground, eyes unfocused, shoulders slumped. Never would Jetekesh have believed such a sight possible. Aredel elvar Gilioth d'ara KessRa had won every campaign he'd ever started. His one known defeat had been in Shing at the hands of his own men—the occasion where he'd first met Jinji.

The Blood King looked shattered.

Jetekesh knelt before him. Aredel was highlighted in golden light from the portal steps. Jetekesh reached out his good hand, tentative, and brushed his fingers against Aredel's forearm. The Blood King tensed, hand flexing like he meant to reach for his sword—but the KryTeeran froze, then curled himself toward the ground.

"Aredel." Jetekesh's voice was a whisper. "You must get back up." He wrapped his fingers around the Blood King's wrist. "We're not done fighting yet."

The man jerked away. "Leave me be."

Anger stabbed Jetekesh's insides, but he shoved the feeling down. "I won't. What about your queen? She needs you."

"She's already dead." The words scraped from Aredel's lips.

"Do you know that, or do you assume it?" Jetekesh snatched the king's wrist again and rose, tugging hard. "Stand up. You're not beaten yet."

"Leave me alone!" Aredel wrenched free.

The words, so much like Jetekesh's not long ago, cut the prince to his core. He stared down at the Blood King. "If you stay down, Anadin died for nothing." He dropped back to his knees. "Look at me, Aredel. Look at me."

Aredel hunched forward more. "Stop. I've lost everything."

"Jinji." The word slipped from Jetekesh's lips unbidden.

Aredel tensed.

"What would he do?" asked Jetekesh. His heart panged.

"Shut up." Aredel's voice was a low growl.

"I *won't*. Stand up, Aredel. Rise as Jinji would want you to. As Anadin would. Don't allow their deaths to be in vain." The words reminded Jetekesh of a day over a year ago when he'd spurred Jinji into action—urged him to fight on. That was when the storyteller had given his life to defeat *Erisyrdrel* the first time.

Am I doing the right thing, Jinji? Will Aredel die today because I made him stand?

Jetekesh had never dared tell anyone his part to play Jinji's death. He hadn't wanted his condemnation confirmed.

How many nights had he wished he'd said one kind word to ease the blows he'd delivered?

It's not too late this time.

His expression softened. A smile trembled on his lips. "All right, Aredel. If you've spent your strength, then stay still. We'll rescue Artassa. You've done enough."

Before, he'd encouraged Jinji to save the company and defeat Gyath and *Erisyrdrel*. This time, Jetekesh would march at the head of the fray. He wouldn't use anyone else as a shield.

This is my purpose. This is my truth.

He turned from the Blood King and strode to Sharo's side. The light from the Arch and the stairway flashed and then vanished in a wink, closing the bridge between Shinac and Nakania. His heart clenched. Would he live to see Nakania again?

"I'm taking the fortress," he said. "All are welcome to join me, but none are required." He adjusted the sling holding his arm and turned to Sharo. "Will you come?"

"Of course, my friend." Sharo unslung a bow from his shoulder. "Does anyone need this?"

"Kajsa does." Jetekesh nodded to the Norvian girl. "She's proven herself efficient with one—and I know for a fact she'll not stay behind."

Kajsa's smile held an edge. She met his gaze steadily.

Sharo passed his bow off to her, along with a quiver of arrows. She accepted it, murmuring a thank you.

Jetekesh turned from the company to eye the stronghold. Instinct pulled him eastward. He let it lead his feet. The others followed behind him. All of them.

"Leave the horses," said Emerin.

As they moved, Sharo's soft voice drifted to Jetekesh's ear from a place at his back.

"How fare you, Kethalas?"

"Well enough for now, Your Highness," answered the dragon.

"He's lying," Dakarai interjected. "He's badly wounded and unable to use his dragon shape without harming himself more."

"I'm very sorry to hear that." Sharo's voice was full of sympathy. "Should we escape this mission alive, come to my war camp. Lady Thrissa may be able to heal you."

"I'm grateful," said Kethalas.

Feet scuffed closer, and Sharo came up beside Jetekesh as they neared the edge of the wall. "She may be able to help you as well, my friend," the fae prince said.

"I'm counting on it." Jetekesh unsheathed his dagger and peeked around the corner. Several dozen *Unsielie* draped in black lace robes guarded two looming gates. He pulled back and faced Sharo. "Why did they not engage you if they heard that skirmish?"

"Our foe was a powerful sand golem. Perhaps they didn't feel the need to interfere." Sharo frowned. "Although the opening of the Arch should have sent them running this way."

"Perhaps they could not see it," whispered Dakarai.

"'Tis possible." Sharo rubbed his smooth chin. "Let me fend off this force, Jetekesh. My blade should be enough. I'll lead out, then you follow in the path I carve for you. Enter the fortress, with or without me."

"Very well." Jetekesh glanced toward Emerin. "We can handle whatever awaits within, right?"

The keep lord's grin was strangely subdued. "Of course."

"I shall help," Aredel said.

The company parted until Jetekesh could meet the man's brown eyes. The Blood King's countenance was sharp as steel, dark as shadow, and sorrowful as rainfall.

"I welcome it," Jetekesh said. Wheeling, he nodded to Sharo. "Ready when you are."

The fae prince flashed him a grim smile, brandished his elegant broadsword, then turned the corner and charged at the guards.

Jetekesh drew a breath, then raced after him. A glimmer in his periphery turned his head, and he found Ashea winging at his side.

"Welcome back to Shinac, young prince," the fairy said in singsong tones. "I am glad you found the path."

"Thanks in no small part to you."

The clamor of engagement drew his focus to the fight ahead. Sharo and his bright blade pitched through the ranks, slashing and hacking. Dark lace wings fluttered and rippled around him. The hum of the fight reached Jetekesh's ears like a mad song, and his heart matched the rhythm.

He entered the fray.

His dagger sank into an *Unsielie* wing, and the fae creature shrieked, then whirled, tearing its appendage to escape the blade. It met Jetekesh's eyes; its angular face was androgynous, stunningly beautiful, strangely calm despite the fever pitch of battle.

The *Unsielie* lifted its thin blade. A diamond winked on the pommel, casting rainbows. The creature moved to strike, then its dark eyes widened. It stared hungrily at Jetekesh's face before staggering back and dropping its blade.

Jetekesh spun to parry another blow, confused by the fae's reaction, but unwilling to hesitate. He fought his way forward, his burned arm blazing. Every stab of his dagger jarred his wounds.

Emerin and Kethalas stayed close, the former's sword singing as he cut down foe after foe. Kethalas's claws flashed, swiping at all comers, his movements agile and swift despite his injuries. Where Dakarai, Anenyasha, Kajsa, and Aredel were in the melee, Jetekesh couldn't tell. Nor could he risk pausing to find out.

A thin blade swiped at his head, and Jetekesh dodged. Emerin plowed into the enemy, ramming his sword through the *Unsielie*'s chest. Several of the fae creatures had taken to the air, their wings humming. Gritting his teeth, Kethalas drew forth his pale, leathery wings, and shot into the sky to meet them.

Jetekesh dropped his eyes and met a sword with his dagger. The impact reverberated through him.

"This way." Emerin swung his sword, loping off the assailant's head. He spun and paved a path of blood for Jetekesh to follow. They escaped the thick of battle and ducked out to find themselves near the gates.

"Kethalas!" Emerin shouted.

The dragon, still in human form above, wheeled toward them, then veered as he read Emerin's hand gestures. The dragon landed on the wall and vanished on the far side.

Three *Unsielie* broke away from the melee and charged at Emerin and Jetekesh. The prince danced around his opponent with adrenaline-fueled agility. He saw each stroke before it fell, and his dagger lifted to answer.

Sidestepping, Jetekesh crouched and rammed the dagger into the fae's leg. He ripped it loose, sprang up, and jammed it through the *Unsielie*'s neck. Emerin cut down the second of his own assailants. As the corpses hit the ground, the gates rumbled.

The skirmish slowed. Heads turned toward the noise.

The gates swung outward slowly.

Kethalas had succeeded.

Emerin caught Jetekesh's shoulder, his fingers digging in enough to bruise flesh. "Go! Run! I'm right behind you."

As the thick wooden gate cracked open wide enough for a man to squeeze through, Jetekesh sprinted toward it.

A humming chorus rose from the *Unsielie* force.

"Faster!" Emerin cried.

Jetekesh pushed his way through the gates. Brilliant silver light seared the heavens. Sharo and his blade, most likely. Or perhaps Aredel. Jetekesh didn't dare turn around to find out. He sprinted across the bailey.

Several bodies littered the cobblestone ground—probably Kethalas's work—but not nearly the contingent he'd expected. Wings swooped overhead where stars sparkled in the sky. Jetekesh whirled to meet the threat, then relaxed. Kethalas touched down before him. Beyond the dragon, Emerin and Dakarai entered the bailey, followed by Kajsa, then Anenyasha in the rear. Torches illuminated their faces. Their weapons glistened with fresh blood. Crimson droplets stained their faces and clothes. Kajsa clutched her bow, half her arrows gone. Raum padded through the gates behind them.

Jetekesh started toward his companions. Where were Sharo and Aredel?

"Your Highness," said Emerin, "we need to keep moving. They'll be fine."

He was right. Jetekesh faced the looming fortress and raced toward it. Every movement agitated his arm and leg, but he didn't slow his pace. The fortress gleamed like obsidian stone. The style was not unlike Peresen's abode: tall, lithe, imposing like the

Unsielie who guarded it. Peresen had been a dread lord intent on invading Nakania, but his scheme had been thwarted by the efforts of Jinji, Sharo, and Aredel.

We'll thwart this plan as well.

A narrow doorway stood open at the top of a dozen steps. Torches guttered to either side of the entrance. Jetekesh braced his arm and took the steps two at a time. Near the top, he could peer inside the vestibule beyond. Still no guards.

He crossed the shallow landing and stepped into the fortress itself. Emerin stayed near, and the others arrived seconds later. Footfalls echoed across the expansive, circular entryway. A domed glass ceiling hung far, far overhead, and level after level of floors rose to meet it.

Closer, torches blazed in sconces set along the walls at intervals, casting orange light on the black stones.

"Where do we go from here?" Jetekesh asked, then winced as his voice echoed off the walls.

"What do your instincts say?" asked Kethalas in a much quieter voice. The sound still carried like he'd shouted.

Anenyasha spoke up. "Something is wrong."

Jetekesh stopped and whirled toward her, too stunned to reply. Could she speak the Old Tongue all along?

Dakarai nodded. "She says something is wrong, and I agree. This is too easy. The fortress is surely not abandoned."

"Y-yes." Jetekesh met the clansman's eyes. "I *heard* her."

Dakarai blinked. "You understood her words?"

The Amantieran prince bobbed a hasty nod. "Was she speaking in your native tongue?"

"Yes," said Dakarai.

"I understand all of you, too," said Anenyasha. "I have since we stepped through the Arch."

Emerin shifted his boots. "It must be a gift granted by Shinac. But we've no time for this just now, Your Highness."

Jetekesh pried his eyes from Anenyasha. "Right. Of course." He shook himself.

"Let's stay to the main level," said Emerin. "I don't want to get trapped above where escape is harder."

Jetekesh nodded and studied the walls. Doors were set around the vestibule. Five in total. He picked the middle one, at dead-center before him, and marched toward it. His fingers tightened around his dagger.

Emerin circled him to reach the door and swung it inward, revealing a wide corridor lined with more torches. The company traveled down it, Jetekesh and Emerin striding side by side at the head. They neared the far end, where an ornate obsidian door carved with runes stood before them. Jetekesh's flesh prickled.

This is a trap.

Yet what could he do besides spring it? They must rescue Artassa or learn her fate if liberation was too late. He owed Aredel that.

The prince swallowed, straightened his shoulders, and nodded to Emerin. "Open the door."

The keep lord obeyed, and the door swung aside to admit the company into a lavish chamber swathed in black lace. Massive onyx scales covered every inch of the walls. A grand chair carved from obsidian sat in the center of the rectangular chamber. Beside it, an *Unsielie* stood wrapped in black fur and white feathers. Threads of raven hair tumbled down the fae being's back, and eyes like deep pits eyed the company.

"Welcome, Marked Prince. I have waited many long years for thee." The *Unsielie*'s voice was like music.

Lifting a slender hand, the fae flicked one long finger, and the door slammed shut behind the company. Raum issued a low growl.

"Please," said the *Unsielie*, "be comfortable. Thee and thy companions shall not leave this fortress alive."

CHAPTER 38
UNSEALED

Jetekesh clutched his dagger tighter. "That's a bold statement." He hefted his chin. "What do you want with me? My blood? My soul?"

The *Unsielie* glided from its place beside the stone chair. "Answers in due course." At the faintest motion of its head, hidden doors sprang open around the room and dozens of *Unsielie* poured in, glaives gleaming in the torch glow. Despite the flow of so many feet, quiet hummed throughout the chamber, like the *Unsielie* hardly touched the ground with their boots. They circled the interior, blocking any hope of escape.

Their leader kept its gaze pinned on Jetekesh, and its lips curled into the tiniest of smiles. "This moment is a dream come true for me, O prince. Long have I awaited its fulfillment."

Jetekesh lifted an eyebrow. "You mean that you foresaw all this?"

"Not I, but a soothsayer did." The *Unsielie* drifted nearer. The feathers in its cloak fluttered.

Jetekesh stamped down on every instinct to run. Trying

would be suicide. "And now what happens?" He canted his head, hoping he looked nonchalant.

"Now," whispered the *Unsielie*, "we thank the mastermind behind your arrival." The fae's eyes drifted past Jetekesh.

The words sank in slowly like a chill breeze spelling autumn's advent.

"Thou hast done well, Lord Emerin."

The chill bit deeper.

The keep lord strode past the prince and folded his arms, eyeing the *Unsielie* with open contempt. "Throw me under the wagon if need be. I don't really care. It's time to fulfill your end of our agreement, Tavassed."

Every word Emerin spoke was like an arrow in Jetekesh's chest. He stared at the keep lord's back, disbelieving.

This is a mistake.

"In good time," said the *Unsielie*. "I must first see to my remaining guests." The fae's fingers twitched, and five guards peeled themselves from the walls. "Keep the Marked Prince and Lord Emerin here. Escort the others to their execution. After that, bring Prince Sharo and King Aredel before me. I hath need of our three royals."

With a roar, Kethalas transformed into his dragon form, filling the chamber with his mass. His magnificent scales sparkled as he lowered his great head to snap his maw over Tavassed, but the *Unsielie* merely lifted its gaze.

The dragon faltered, then shrank back into his human form and staggered to his knees, gasping.

Kajsa darted to his side, but a guard caught her arms and yanked her away. The clash of spears against glaives rang through the chamber.

Jetekesh squeezed his dagger hilt, then marched toward Tavassed and Emerin. The *Unsielie* eyed him, unmoving.

"Enough," Jetekesh growled. "We won't stand down and accept this."

"Ah, but you will." Tavassed slid a look toward Emerin. "My lord?"

The keep lord's face pinched, but he turned to face his companions. Flames burst from his hands and sprang up from the ground around him. "Enough!" His voice cracked like a catapult.

All fighting faltered. The flames blazed higher.

"Lay down your arms," Emerin said, his eyes flicking between each member of the company. "I will kill you *now* if you don't."

A surge of fury rolled through Jetekesh, but he held it back. *Think. Emerin is an honorable man. He must have a good reason for betraying us.* Hadn't Jinji likewise looked guilty at Keep Falcon when Aredel revealed himself and captured them?

I won't make assumptions without proof. Not anymore.

Jetekesh speared the keep lord with a searching look. "What hold does Tavassed have on you, my lord? Is this *thing* the cause of your curse?"

Emerin's lips twitched up. "Whether he is or isn't hardly matters now. Your lives are forfeit."

The prince of Amantier shook his head. "No. As long as I'm still breathing, I'll not give up. Never again."

Emerin's smile bloomed, gentle. "Ah. You've destroyed all of Bareene's shackles now. I would have been proud to call you my prince."

"Then do," said Jetekesh, "and help us defeat this slug."

Tavassed's brow lifted. Finally, a crack in the armor of his face. "Slug, am I?"

"Indeed." Jetekesh hoisted his chin. "I don't know all that you hold against Emerin, but I recognize that you've cheated and coerced him. I'll not believe for a moment that he would betray me otherwise. So"—he took a step forward—"I'll ask you just once to break whatever chains you've forged around him, and return my liegeman to me. If you don't, I will answer you with every speck of magic I possess."

Emerin stirred, opening his mouth, his brow pinched. Tavassed hissed out a warning, and the keep lord fell still.

The *Unsielie* shrugged, and the motion was strangely alien. "Thou wouldst fight to the last breath for thy liegeman? I believe it not. Defend thyself—and him—at thy peril."

Light suffused Jetekesh's frame, curling off him. Particles of light floated around him like tiny fairies swirling in a lazy draft. "I call upon the True King of Shinac for aid." The words chimed with power, striking against the darkness of the *Unsielie* fortress.

Emerin stepped forward. "Don't, Jetekesh."

The prince smiled. "I'll free you if I can, my lord. I'll free you and rescue Artassa."

The power grew, stretching over his head and spreading across the chamber. The *Unsielie* shrank back, all but Tavassed, who gazed at Jetekesh in open challenge.

"King Ehrikai," said Jetekesh, "I invoke thy name and harness thy power."

"Jet—" Emerin's protest cut short.

The beam of light shone like a beacon, crushing every shadow. The *Unsielie* shrank against it, writhing.

All but Tavassed.

"*No, Jetekesh!*" Sharo's voice, afar off. Desperate. "*Pull it back in! Do not unleash that power!*"

Tavassed's lips stretched in a grin that revealed needle-sharp teeth. "Too late! Thou art too late, O Prince of the Wood! 'Tis done!"

The floor cracked beneath Jetekesh. Raw power flowed through him, easing his burns, opening his damaged ear—and tumbling the stones of the fortress around him. Aredel's energy poured into him. Than Sharo's.

The earth trembled. Quaked. Roared.

The company fell at Jetekesh's feet. He couldn't stop the flow of magic. It overwhelmed him, pounded his body like waves against the breakers, drowning his senses.

What's happening, Jinji? What have I done?

The power answered, pouring knowledge into his mind like water through a sieve.

Then all fell into darkness. The power died, cut off, and Jetekesh slumped to his hands and knees. Breaths came out ragged and sweat dripped from his brow.

No. No, no, no. What have I done?

He dragged his head up and stared into the rubble that had once been the fortress beneath a starlit sky.

Not a fortress.

He settled back against his heels and stared at the bodies around him. The *Unsielie* were all dead, scorched to death by the True King's radiance, mere husks in a circle, except those crushed by the boulders. Tavassed was gone—perhaps crushed, perhaps vanished.

Jetekesh's company lay in a heap, too—though not charred or broken. All but Sharo, Emerin, and Aredel, who stood in a circle around the Amantieran prince, their auras visible. He'd tapped their energy and added it to his own. Ashea's fairy aura circled the group, protecting them from the worst of the rubble. Raum stood nearby, radiant though subdued.

"What happened?" asked Aredel, eyeing his glowing hand. "What was that?"

"That," said Sharo in shattered tones, "was the breaking of a seal, far, far too soon."

Jetekesh flinched. Heat scoured his insides. "I'm so sorry..."

"What does that mean?" asked the Blood King.

Emerin answered, his tones low and gruff. "It means Shinac has re-entered Nakania. All of it. All at once. The *Unsielie* have been working for a century to destroy the seals. This was the last."

He ran a hand over his face. "And I am responsible for it all." He dropped to one knee before Jetekesh. "Forgive me, my prince."

Jetekesh shook his head. "I'm the one who let Tavassed goad me. I—I'm responsible for this."

"Why is Shinac's return bad?" asked Aredel. "Isn't the resurgence of magic desirable?" He skewered Jetekesh with a narrow look. "Explain."

"Both worlds will be plunged into chaos," Sharo answered, "and now Navolleth will find himself with the option of two armies at his disposal, whether he was part of this plan or not. Man, fae, and dragon shall all be overrun before we can come to terms with magic and mundane and how to balance both. Shinac retreated for a reason, Your Majesty."

The elven prince turned his eyes skyward. "Now, those who desire to conquer—like my father—may do so at a mere gesture. Nakania, and those without magic, are doomed."

To be continued in...

The Blood Fountain

GLOSSARY

PEOPLE

Anadin [ANN-uh-din] — Prince of KryTeer and Aredel's younger brother.

Anenyasha [ON-enn-YAW-shuh] — A female warrior from the Clanslands.

Aredel [AIR-uh-dell] — Blood King of KryTeer.

Artassa [Ar-TASS-uh] — Queen of Kryteer. First Wife of Blood King Aredel.

Axel [axle] — A village hunter in Tuksa within Norva.

Bareene [buh-REEN] — Prince Jetekesh's mother and former queen of Amantier. Deceased.

Bennin [ben-inn] — A knight at the Keep of the Falls.

Cavalin [CAV-uh-linn] — Once High King of Nakania, he died defending his lands from a demon-possessed tyrant. He is the ancestor of Prince Jetekesh.

Dakarai [daw-kaw-rye] — A male warrior from the Clanslands.

Ehrikai [AIR-ihk-EYE] — The True King of Shinac.

Emerin [EM-er-inn] — The Lord of the Keep of the Falls of Moss Province in Amantier.

Erisyrdrel [eer-iss-SEER-drel] — A water demon who possessesed Emperor Gyath of KryTeer until she was banished by Prince Sharo.

Gyath [GYE-uth] — The deceased Emperor of KryTeer. Father of Aredel and Anadin.

Harn — A wagoner from Amantier.

Hyuen [hee-oon] - Incumbent emperor of Shing.

Hickory — Prince Jetekesh's buckskin stallion.

Ingrid — The wise woman of Tuksa Village within Norva.

Ivam [EYE-vam] — Prince Jetekesh's sword instructor.

Jetekesh [JET-eh-kesh] — The Crown Prince of Amantier.

Jetekesh the Fourth [JET-eh-kesh] — Reigning King of Amantier.

Jinji [JIN-jee] — A storyteller from Shing.

Jung Tep [joong tep] — Prince Liu's father in Shing.

Kajsa [k-EYE-suh] — A village healer-in-training in Tuksa Village within Norva.

Kayvar [kay-VAR] — The previous lord of the Keep of the Falls. Emerin's deceased father.

Kethalas [KETH-uh-LASS] — A dragon from Shinac.

Kita [keet-uh] — A Shingese knight.

Kyella [k-EYE-ell-uh] — A farmer's daughter from Amantier. Engaged to Prince Anadin of KryTeer.

Lafe [lay-f] — Prince Jetekesh's protector.

Liu [lee-YEW] — A prince of Shing.

Majinglee [mah-JING-lee] — Emperor of Shing. Deceased.

Navolleth [nuh-VOLL-eth] — A stranger who appears in Norva.

Norvik — A son of Cavalin the Great.

Palin [pal-inn] — A legendary knight in Amantier. Deceased.

Raum [r-ow-m] — Axel's tame wolf within Norva. Deceased.

Rille [rill] — Prince Jetekesh's cousin. She is a seer.

Sharo [SHAWR-oh] — A fae prince of Shinac.

Song — The Lady of Crimson Lilies from Shing.

Tallat [tuh-LOT] — A KryTeeran fisherman-turned-tyrant. He allowed Erisyrdrel to possess him in order to gain power. Ultimately he killed High King Cavalin in combat.

Tavassed [TAW-vuh-sed] — An Unsielie in Shinac.

Terinvala [teer-in-vah-luh] —A gryphon in Shinac.

Thrissa — A fae queen in Shinac.

Tifen [TEE-fin] — Prince Jetekesh's former protector. Deceased.

Vashi [VAH-shee] — An Amantieran saint and High King Cavalin's daughter.

Yeshton [YESH-tun] — A knight of Amantier. Rille's protector.

Yin — Song's younger brother. A competent bowman.

FAE RACES

Dusk Pixies — Tiny pixies that appear at twilight in Shinac.

Fae — A blanket term for magical races and magical abilities. Often refers specifically to the Sielie and Unsielie of Shinac.

Ice Folk – An elusive type of fae in Shinac. They can transform into two-tailed ice foxes.

Sielie — Light elven-like fae of Shinac.

Unsielie — Dark elven-like fae of Shinac.

Vashalan [vash-uh-lawn] — Wolf-like canines made from dark Shinacian magic. They carry a deadly venom in their teeth, and similar poison in their long claws.

PLACES

Alasiilay [alla-SEE-lay] — Sacred waters flowing through Shinac.

Amantier [ah-mawn-teer] — The country where Prince Jetekesh lives. Its people are the Amantierans.

Arch — A magical portal into Shinac.

Bahadronn [baw-hah-dron] — The capital city of KryTeer.

Bard Pass — A pass in the Flute Mountains leading from Moss Province in Amantier to the eastern realm of the country. It is one route to the Clanslands and Shing.

Clanslands — A jungle country with many tribes. Few outsiders venture there due to its many dangers. Also called Zindwéa.

Cragen Swamplands — A swamp within Shinac.

Flute Mountains — The northernmost mountains of Amantier.

Frostfire Canton — A city-state in Norva.

Karanki [kaw-ron-kee] — Dakarai's tribe in the Clanslands.

Kavacos [kav-uh-koh-ss] — The Rose City. Capital of Amantier.

Keep of the Falls — Lord Emerin's keep in Moss Province of Amantier.

KriShen Bay [kr-EYE shen] — A large bay between Shing and the Clanslands.

KryTeer [kr-EYE-teer] — An arid western country ruled by Blood King Aredel. Its people are the KryTeerans.

Kyon Taro [kee-on tar-oh] — The capital city of Shing.

Mahadri River [maw-HA-dree] — The oldest river in KryTeer. It runs north to south.

Moss Province — The northernmost province of Amantier. Lord Emerin's duchy.

Nagali River [nuh-GALL-ee] — It runs from the Clanslands, through the Flute Mountains, and into Amantier.

Nakania [nuh-KAWN-ee-uh] — The mundane world.

Norva [NOR-vuh] — A country hidden in the Snow Wastes south of Shing. Its people are the Norvians.

Purple River — A river running through Shing.

Rabahan Oasis [ruh-BAH-hawn] — An oasis north of Bahadronn in KryTeer.

Sage Province — A western province in Amantier. Lady Rille's duchy.

Shard Kingdom — The human realm within Shinac. Ruled by King Darint, Prince Sharo's father.

Shinac [shee-NOCK] — The realm of the fae and magical. To most, it's only a legend. Prince Jetekesh knows better.

Shing — An eastern country, considered the oldest known civilization outside of Shinac's borders. Jinji's homeland. Its people are called the Shingese.

Snowblinds — The mountains between Norva and Shing. Also called Bird Haven.

Snow Wastes — See *Norva.*

Tarradarryn, Hold of [taw-ruh-DAWR-uh] — The fortress in the swamplands of Shinac

Tild — The common name of the city-state proper of Frostfire Canton.

Tindo River [tin-doh] — A river running through Shing.

Tuksa [took-suh] — Kajsa's mountain village.

Valliath [VAL-ee-oth] — The Hold of Valliath is the realm within Shinac where the True King was born. Also called the Veils of Valliath. Also see *Ehrikai*.

Valliath, Light of — The brightest star in Shinac.

Zindwéa [zin-DWAY-uh] — The native name for the Clanslands.

TERMS

Archon [ark-on] — The ruler of each Canton within Norva.

Driodere [dree-OH-deer] — Grim Death itself. An Amantieran term, derived from the Old Tongue, for the spirit of death who guides the deceased to their final resting place.

Holy Nocturne — A festive Amantieran holiday that takes place at the Winter Solstice.

Sahala [suh-HALL-uh] — An old KryTeeran word meaning 'sparrow.' Anadin's term of affection for Rille.

Shaqel [shaw-KEL] — A KryTeeran term of affection meaning 'younger brother.'

Shaqin [shaw-KEEN] — A KryTeeran term of affection meaning 'older brother.'

Watchwoman — A seer within the Clanslands.

Wisewoman — The village healer in Norva. She is a seer.

Acknowledgments

This book was a mess. Middles usually are. It takes a village to polish a novel, and luckily, my team is the best of the best.

Special thanks to Heidi Wadsworth for alpha reading the trash heap that was the first draft. Your suggestions saved the day (or at least the pacing).

Another huge thank you to my beta team: Beba Andric, Laura A. Barton, R. K. Goff, and Mandi Oyster. Your tireless efforts pushed Jetekesh and company to new heights (they may not thank you, but I do).

Equally colossal thanks to my editors, E. L. McNicholas and Sarah B., for catching all my last errors (we hope) and giving me the strength to plow ahead in the mire of self-doubt.

As always, my family is my lifeline, and I'm deeply indebted to my parents, Duane and Deborah, and sisters Heidi and Tawnee, in particular for carrying my half-dead corpse until I could bring myself to come back from the dead. (Seriously, I appreciate the meals and encouragement during the darker moments!)

To the Kickstarter backers who believed in this trilogy enough to support Book One, this one is also for you.

To my Lost River community, you keep coming out to support me and it keeps blowing my mind. Thank you!

And to my Heavenly Father. You are my beacon.

—M. H. W.

SPECIAL ACKNOWLEDGMENTS

I must give special attention to my Kickstarter backers for believing in this series, for helping to bring this special edition into existence, and especially for keeping the fantasy genre alive and thriving!

Deep-felt gratitude to my fellow dragon-lovers:

Abigail, ALB, Amelia Anastasi, Andrew B, Andy99000, Angela Morse, Astridd, Barbara Meijsen, Christy, Danae, Dudley Pajela, Elizabeth Kiefer, Erynn M Flaherty, Francesco Tehrani, Gianna C., Greg Levick, Ian Brown, J Mills, Jacob Kirby, James R McGinnis Jr, Janice Muehle, Jayme Waltz, Jenny Trevor, K Hendrick, Karyne Norton, Katherine Leslie, Lea W Padgett, LJF, Mandi Oyster, Meredith Carstens, Mistril Merendras, Morgan G., OriginPlays, phoenix17, Robert Zangari, Ricardo E. Rubio, Rosa Thill, Sara, Sarah B, Seamus Sands, Sean Brady, Scott Casey, Silvia Morris, Stephanie Schwab, T Haykus, Travis Schirpke, W. Roongkham & Yael Levy.

About the Author

Writer of fantasy, magic weaver, dragon rider! Having spent the past two decades devotedly writing fantasy, it's safe to say M. H. Woodscourt is now more fae than human.

All of her fantasy worlds connect with each other in the Mithrinn Universe, forged with great love and no small measure of blood, sweat, and tears. When she's not writing, she's napping or reading a book with a mug of hot cocoa close at hand, while her quirky cat Wynter nibbles her nose.

Learn more at www.mhwoodscourt.com

facebook.com/mhwoodscourt

x.com/woodscourtbooks

instagram.com/woodscourtbooks

Also by M. H. Woodscourt

Mark of Valliath

High Fantasy/Young Adult

The Storyteller True

The Shattered Arch

The Marked Prince

The Blood Fountain

Record of the Sentinel Seer

Science-Fantasy/New Adult

Prince of the Fallen

Rule of the Night

Song of the Lost

Paths of the Broken

Heart of the Sentinel

Wintervale Duology

High Fantasy/Young Adult

The Crow King

The Winter King

PARADISE TRILOGY

Portal Fantasy/Humor/Young Adult

A Liar in Paradise

Key of Paradise

Beyond Paradise

www.ingramcontent.com/pod-product-compliance
Lightning Source LLC
Chambersburg PA
CBHW020306030826
48979CB00029B/2259/J
* 9 7 8 1 9 5 9 6 1 9 0 5 5 *